I0744876

Love Found: A Regency Romance Christmas Collection

Five Delightful Regency Christmas Stories
from

Arietta Richmond

Grace Austen

Isabella Thorne

Katherine Keats

Sophia Wilson

ARIETTA RICHMOND, GRACE AUSTEN, ISABELLA THORNE,
KATHERINE KEATS AND SOPHIA WILSON

Dreamstone Publishing © 2016

www.dreamstonepublishing.com

ISBN: 1925499421

ISBN-13: 978-1-925499-42-1

Disclaimer

These stories are works of fiction.

Names, characters, places and incidents are the product of the author's imagination and are used fictitiously. Any resemblance to events, locales or actual persons, living or dead, is entirely coincidental.

ARIETTA RICHMOND, GRACE AUSTEN, ISABELLA THORNE,
KATHERINE KEATS AND SOPHIA WILSON

Introduction

We hope you enjoy this Christmas Collection of Regency romance stories. As authors, we each have a different style, but we are brought together by our love for Regency Romance.

This collection presents some very different heroes and heroines, but the common theme is that they all find love, despite trials and tribulations along the way, at Christmas.

We have each also given you a bonus, with some previews of our other books. We hope that you love reading these stories as much as we enjoyed writing them, and that you will also go on to enjoy all of our other Regency books!

Thanks for reading 'Love Found: A Regency Romance Christmas Collection'!

Arietta Richmond

Grace Austen

Isabella Thorne

Katherine Keats

Sophia Wilson

ARIETTA RICHMOND, GRACE AUSTEN, ISABELLA THORNE,
KATHERINE KEATS AND SOPHIA WILSON

Table of Contents

Introduction..v

Lady Theodora's Christmas Wish.. 1

Dedication.. 3

Chapter One.. 5

Chapter Two.. 9

Chapter Three 13

Chapter Four 17

Chapter Five 23

Chapter Six 27

Chapter Seven 35

Chapter Eight 45

Chapter Nine 51

About the Author 54

Other Books in 'The Derbyshire Set' 56

Here is your preview of The Earls Unexpected Bride 58

Chapter One 59

Chapter Two 79

The Earl's Missing Christmas Heir 87

Dedication 89

Chapter One 91

Chapter Two 97

Chapter Three 107

Chapter Four 113

Chapter Five 121

Chapter Six 129

Chapter Seven 137

Chapter Eight 153

About the Author 164

Other Books from Grace Austen 166

Here is Your Preview of The Duke's Unwilling Bride 170

Here is Your Preview of Charming the Earl 176

Just One Christmas Kiss 189

Chapter One 191

Chapter Two 197

Chapter Three 207

Chapter Four 211

Chapter Five 227

Chapter Six 229

Chapter Seven 233

Chapter Eight 243

About the Author 248

Other Books By Isabella Thorne 250

Here is Your Preview of The Mad Heiress Meets the Duke .. 252

A Christmas Surprise 259

Chapter One 261

Chapter Two 267

Chapter Three 273

Chapter Four 279

Chapter Five 285

Chapter Six 289

Chapter Seven 295

Chapter Eight 303

Chapter Nine 307

Chapter Ten 313

Chapter Eleven 319

Chapter Twelve 329

Chapter Thirteen 335

Chapter Fourteen 339

Epilogue 343

About the Author 344

Other Books by Katherine Keats 345

Here is Your Preview of The Duke and the Dressmaker 346

Here is Your Preview of Rescuing the Earl 356

Chapter One 357

Chapter Two 363

The Duke's Christmas Blessing..375

Chapter One 377

Chapter Two 383

Chapter Three.. 387

Chapter Four... 393

Chapter Five... 397

Chapter Six.. 403

Chapter Seven 409

Chapter Eight 413

Chapter Nine.. 417

Chapter Ten 421

Chapter Eleven 427

Chapter Twelve.. 431

Chapter Thirteen 435

Chapter Fourteen 439

Chapter Fifteen.. 443

Chapter Sixteen 449

Epilogue 453

About the Author...................................... 456

Other Books by Sophia Wilson 458

Here is Your Preview of The Duke's Second Chance at Love 460

Chapter One... 461

Here is Your Preview of The Duke and the Earl's Daughter 468

Chapter 1 469

Other Books from Dreamstone Publishing 474

ARIETTA RICHMOND, GRACE AUSTEN, ISABELLA THORNE,
KATHERINE KEATS AND SOPHIA WILSON

The Derbyshire Set – Book 8.5

Regency Historical Romance

Lady Theodora's Christmas Wish

Arietta Richmond

Books by
Arietta Richmond

The Derbyshire Set

A Gift of Love (Prequel short story)

A Devil's Bargain (Prequel short story - coming soon)

The Earl's Unexpected Bride

The Captain's Compromised Heiress

The Viscount's Unsuitable Affair

The Count's Impetuous Seduction

The Rake's Unlikely Redemption

The Marquess' Scandalous Mistress

A Remembered Face (Bonus short story – coming soon)

The Marchioness' Second Chance (coming soon)

A Viscount's Reluctant Passion (coming soon)

Lady Theodora's Christmas Wish

The Duke's Improper Love (coming soon)

Other Books

The Scottish Governess (coming soon)

The Earl's Reluctant Fiancee (coming soon)

The Crew of the Seadragon's Soul Series, (coming soon
- a set of 10 linked novels)

Dedication

For everyone who had the grace to be patient while this book, and the ones before and after it, were coming into existence, who provided cups of tea, and food, when the writing would not let me go, and endured countless times being asked for opinions.

For the other writers in my Regency Romance mastermind group, who inspire me, and ask the kind of questions that make us all learn more about this fascinating period.

For the readers coming to know these characters well, and who inspire me to continue, by buying my books!

For my growing team of beta readers and advance reviewers – it's thanks to you that others can enjoy these books in the best presentation possible!

And for all the writers of Regency Historical Romance, whose books I read, who inspired me to write in this fascinating period.

ARIETTA RICHMOND, GRACE AUSTEN, ISABELLA THORNE,
KATHERINE KEATS AND SOPHIA WILSON

Chapter One

"Ouch!"

Lady Theodora's voice was sharp as she exclaimed at the sudden pain. She got no sympathy from Polly, her maid. Polly was used to her young mistress, and simply sighed.

"Miss, if you could just sit still while I finish putting up your hair, it wouldn't get pulled. I do declare, you're more fidgety than young Etta – but at least she has the excuse of being two years old!"

Polly had not yet adapted to calling Theodora 'my Lady' – for it was not all that long since the formal adoption papers had been signed.

Those papers had taken her from being simply 'Miss Theodora Rockingham', the Earl of Stanningfield's ward, to being 'Lady Theodora Rockingham', the Earl of Stanningfield's daughter.

Theodora herself was not yet used to it, although it was delightful to be able to call the Earl 'papa' after so long.

It had been, in a way, his present to her for her 17th birthday – the finalisation of the adoption process. And, that afternoon, she had been given yet more wonderful news – it had been a truly amazing few months!

For that afternoon she had been told that not only was there to be a Christmas Ball at Havisham Hall, but that she would be permitted to attend, as an adult!

It would be the first Christmas Ball held there since the old Earl's passing, some eight years or more ago.

Theodora wanted nothing so much as to rush down to dinner, so that she could sooner ask for more details of the Ball, but the sting of her pulled hair, and Polly's patient admonition, made her try very hard to stop fidgeting and wait – after all, if she was to be treated as an adult (finally!), it was best that she act like it – at least enough that Polly did not compare her to baby Etta!

Once she sat still, allowing her mind to drift off into fairy-tale imaginings of how the Ball might be, populated, of course, with handsome gentlemen who quite fell in love with her on the spot, Polly had her hair untangled and all pinned up in no time.

Once it was done Theodora stood, and looked at herself in the mirror. Her dress was new, for she had entirely grown out of all of her old clothes, so another part of her birthday delights had been the ordering of a whole new wardrobe.

And these clothes were definitely those of a fairly fashionable young Lady, not a child.

She was amazed at what Polly could do with her mass of rich dark brown hair, taming it into intricate, yet delicate coils, which almost glowed in the light, with glints of red and gold as the natural highlights shone through. The dress she wore was a pale rose gold colour – perfectly setting off her hair, without being too strong a colour for a young woman.

She almost didn't recognise herself!

The stillness did not last long though – she had never been one to sit quietly by – Theodora was more likely to be found in the stables, or running about in the grounds, given the chance, than sitting demurely with embroidery.

She whirled, the artful tendrils of her hair lifting, like the skirt of the dress, with the force of her movement, as the excitement took hold again, and, laughing in delight at the sensation, went down to dinner.

ARIETTA RICHMOND, GRACE AUSTEN, ISABELLA THORNE,
KATHERINE KEATS AND SOPHIA WILSON

Chapter Two

Etta ran around and around the nursery, pushing a wooden train, and making her best imitation of train noises – which was a little difficult, as trains were so new, that she, like most people, had never actually seen a real one. Such minor issues did not concern her. At 2 years old, Etta was secure in her world, and was quite able to deal with imagining the train to be real, no matter what.

Eddie, just one year old, did not have any concerns – he sat happily on the rug in front of Theodora, gurgling and laughing, simply because Etta was laughing, and Theodora was rolling a ball to him.

Theodora was having a hard time concentrating on playing with the children, even though she usually adored doing so. Her mind kept drifting away into thoughts of the coming Ball. In just a few weeks, the house would be full of guests, the Ballroom decorated and brilliantly lit, and she would be amongst it all!

"Tia, Tia!"

Eddie demanded her attention, holding out his little hands for the ball. Eddie had just begun to talk, and, like Theodora herself, at that age, could not manage to say 'Theodora' – so Tia it was. Hearing it still shook Theodora's composure - for she had not been called Tia for more than 4 years, since Gran died. To hear it in the child's voice was bittersweet – it brought back all the sad memories, even though the children were a delight.

And now, she thought with satisfaction, they were officially her brother and sister! She rolled the ball again, then obeyed Etta's command to watch her, and applaud the train's speed, but was soon lost in thoughts of the Ball again.

For surely there would be handsome gentlemen there. Gentlemen that she had not met.

Gentlemen who would dance with her, who would, she most intensely hoped, fall in love with her at first sight. Of course, it would also be delightful if she fell in love with one of them.....

She wanted romance, wanted love, wanted, oh so very much, all those things that her mother had not had. She pushed that part of the thought away, and went back to imagining herself swept away to dance with a handsome man, wooed, and even kissed. Whatever that might feel like – she was certain that it would be wonderful.

Eddie tugged at her hand, wanting her attention again, and Tia (for, inside, that was how she still thought of herself) turned to him, smiling. In that moment, it occurred to her that she would like to have children of her own one day.

Which would definitely require a handsome gentleman to fall in love with!

She silently vowed to herself that one day she would – and that she would make sure that their childhood was very different from hers (for whilst she had been loved, always, she had not had the circumstances or the money for much more than just love).

The desire to see her own children, and for them to be as happy and carefree as Eddie and Etta, was an ache of such intensity that it surprised her.

Her musings were interrupted when Etta, having become utterly over exuberant, tripped on the ball that Eddie had just rolled, and collapsed in a crying heap, tangled with the wooden train. Gathering her to her with calming words, Theodora resolved that she would think more, later, about what it might be like to have a child of her own.

ARIETTA RICHMOND, GRACE AUSTEN, ISABELLA THORNE,
KATHERINE KEATS AND SOPHIA WILSON

Chapter Three

Catherine, Countess of Stanningfield, looked up from the list that lay on her small writing desk in the informal parlour. She started out through the terrace doors across the winter gardens, letting the pen drop from her fingers to the side of the paper.

She was quite sure that she had forgotten someone who should be invited. She had not, before now, realised quite how difficult it would be to formulate a guest list for the grand occasion of the first Christmas Ball at Havisham House since Charles had become Earl. The matter of her own, somewhat lowly, origins made choosing guests even harder.

For she would wish her mother to attend, and, although her mother had become used to mingling with some of the nobility on occasion, she was still not entirely comfortable with many. Charles' wide circle of acquaintance, and complex tangle of family, meant that he would wish a large contingent to be invited. And then there were those of the ton who must be invited (even though many would not make the journey, as winter was making the roads less and less pleasant to travel).

But for Theodora's sake, they must be invited. If she was to be launched in the coming London season, she must meet as many people now, as possible, to ensure that she was accepted, and that no touch of scandal or question of her heritage might tarnish her opportunities in life.

As if the thought had summoned her, Theodora tapped on the door and entered, followed by Charles. Catherine smiled in genuine pleasure, delighted by how beautiful Theodora looked. Charles came to Catherine and bent to kiss her lightly. They had been married three years now, but were still as delighted in each other as they had been at the start.

Catherine sighed, looking up at Charles.

"This list is becoming huge, and yet I am still not sure that I have remembered everyone who should be invited! If they all choose to attend, I've no idea where we will put them all – the house will be overflowing, and so will the Inn in Harteston, and perhaps the Inn in Lavenham too!"

Charles laughed at her worried expression.

"My dear Catherine, I am certain that the innkeepers will be most pleased with us, if we bring them customers! And we will manage to squeeze many of those closest to us in here, never fear. For now, let's go through the list together, and make sure that all of 'the important people' are on it."

Theodora, who had been standing to one side, surreptitiously trying to read the list that lay in front of Catherine, could not contain her enthusiasm.

"Oh yes, please, can we do that? I want to know all about everyone who will be here!"

Charles and Catherine shared a smile at her reaction. Charles and Theodora sat, and Catherine passed the list to Charles. He sat quietly, reading through it, muttering as he did, much to Theodora's annoyance.

She forced herself to sit still, at least for the first few minutes.

She knew that well behaved young ladies did not leap up and lean over people's shoulders to read what they were reading. It was a very tempting idea, though….

After a few minutes, Charles and Catherine began to discuss names – some that Theodora recognised, like Viscount Bellham and his wife, the Marquess of Hemsbridge (whose marriage had caused quite a scandal), the Earl of Derbyshire, his daughters, and their husbands, and a number of others. Then they strayed into names that she had not heard before.

It would be quite an exalted company, from the sound of it, with so many titled and wealthy people. But…. Theodora still did not know which of the names that she was hearing were those of unmarried and eligible gentlemen…

"But papa," she asked "who are these people you are mentioning? Please, won't you tell me about them?"

"Well," Charles paused, looking at her with barely repressed amusement, "Am I correct in assuming that what you really want to know is which gentlemen attending might be young and handsome?"

Theodora blushed, but had the good grace to be honest and nod, acknowledging the truth of his words.

"There are at least 15 eligible gentlemen on this list, although a few of them are perhaps rather old from your point of view. The most eligible is Chase Harringdon, the Duke of Montford. He only recently came into the title, somewhat unexpectedly, when his uncle died without an heir. Mind you, I'm not at all sure that you should be looking at him, he has rather a rakish reputation, not to mention being, at nearly thirty, somewhat older than I might like for you. Everyone thought him unlikely to marry, with his brother his heir for the Marquessate, but, now that he is the Duke, and his brother the Marquess, he will need to marry, and get himself an heir."

Theodora said nothing, her mind already floating off into excited imaginings again. A Duke! And thirty was not so old, if he was handsome. She pushed aside any concern about the idea of a rakish reputation, finding it, in the manner common to fanciful young girls who were just out of the schoolroom, rather more exciting than not.

The Earl had continued speaking, naming another three gentlemen who might be of interest to a young lady, but Tia did not hear a word of it, she was so lost in her imaginings.

Over the next hour, after much discussion, the guest list was finalised, and the arduous task of writing out all those invitations begun. Tia was drawn out of her dreaming and recruited to help Catherine with the writing, for she had a fair hand. Crafting beautiful writing was, Catherine reflected, one of the few parts of her schooling that Theodora had actually enjoyed – for the most part, she had been more interested in playing with the kittens in the stables than in learning anything of use about the world.

Chapter Four

With the invitations all sent, and acceptances flowing in, the next few weeks became a whirlwind of preparation, with the staff continually calling on Catherine and Charles for decisions and instruction, as vast quantities of food were ordered, decorations arranged, an orchestra engaged, and the thousand and one small essential details involved in providing accommodation and food for a horde of house guests addressed. With decorations being progressively placed throughout the house, it was starting to feel like Christmas, Christmas as Tia had never seen it before, and her excitement increased every day, until she was living at fever pitch.

Somehow, between helping where she could, and spending time with the children (for, whilst their nurse, Mrs Millwood, was a truly wonderful woman, she did need to rest sometimes, and the children truly missed Tia if they did not see her, and spend time with her, every day), she still found time to dream, in a few quiet moments here and there.

Those dreams featured, usually, a handsome Duke, who swept her off her feet, danced with her, kissed her hand (or maybe more!), and singled her out for his attentions in a most satisfactory way.

Those dreams also, a little to her shame when she considered it, often featured the few female acquaintances of the nobility that Tia could claim – featured them watching her with envy. For, as the ward of the Earl of Stanningfield, she had been, always, neither one thing not the other – not really of the *ton*, like the other girls were, nor really of the lesser classes. Stuck in between, Tia had been tolerated, but not really accepted, not drawn into their close friendship. They had been all too ready to speak of her disparagingly, if only to make themselves feel more confident in their superiority.

Chide herself as she might, she could not but enjoy the thought of their discomfiture now.

If nothing else, even if she did not catch the attention of a handsome and eligible gentleman, with the formal adoption as Charles and Catherine's daughter, she was officially of their class, and it would be much harder for them to ignore her now. A few might even welcome her, which would be considerably more pleasant than dealing with the few who would still disregard her as much as they felt they could, without directly offending the Earl.

On her way to the nursery, Tia passed the ballroom doors, just as the footmen exited, after having put in place yet more decorations. She couldn't resist quickly taking a look. Slipping through the doors, she found the room empty, just for now.

The vast space was transformed by the elegant cloth drapes that had been hung all around, and the huge decorative urns and vases that stood all around, waiting to hold festive greenery and hothouse flowers on the night of the Ball.

The chandeliers shone, with every crystal having been polished, and she envisaged how wonderful the room would look, with all of the candles lit, and sparkling traces of light scattered across the rich drapes.

Imagining the orchestra in place, and the room full or swirling dancers, Tia could not resist – she closed her eyes, humming the music of a scandalous waltz softly, and danced around the room, imagining herself to be in the arms of a handsome Duke, who had eyes only for her. The trailing curls of her hair escaped, as always, from their pins, lifted with her movement, the light fabric of her favourite day dress swirled around her ankles and, for that few moments at least, her life was transformed.

An odd thump noise startled her out of the beautiful vision, and she stopped, wobbling inelegantly, as she spun towards the door, just in time to see the footmen hauling another large marble urn into the room.

"Our apologies Lady Theodora – there's no damage – it just slipped a bit, and Tom here thumped into the wall. But we've got it now."

She smiled, assuring them that she was not concerned, and went on her way to the nursery, happy that they had not seen her dancing about like a mad thing, all alone in the Ballroom.

But she didn't regret doing it. If the real Ball felt as wonderful as those few moments had……

Tia's obsession with the coming Ball only increased, as the days went by. She would tell herself not to be silly, that the Duke might be ugly, or look old and fat, or, having been a rake for some years, might be worn, cynical and uninterested in unsophisticated young ladies, but part of her was utterly stubborn, and would not let go of her dreams.

She danced about the house whenever she could, she danced the children around the nursery floor, much to their delight, she told them stories of princesses and heroes, and, all the while, she came, more and more, to realise how desperately she wanted to meet someone special.

For some time now, Tia had been feeling rather out of sorts, and had not really known why. But now she did – she was grown, yet she had not really been an adult. She was no longer a child, but had no life of her own as an adult.

She loved papa and Catherine very much, but…. They were still, only three years into their marriage, very caught up in each other, and their new children. It had left Tia feeling somehow excess. She wanted someone of her own – someone to feel about her, as papa so obviously felt about Catherine.

Someone that she could love like that too.

The more that she thought about it, the stronger it became, until, one day, yet again standing in the Ballroom, she closed her eyes, and made a wish, a Christmas wish. For this Christmas, she would like a very special gift.

She wished that, at the Ball, on the eve of Christmas, she would meet someone special, someone who could give her that life and love that she wanted, someone to marry, and have children with. She wished for a sign. She wished that, if she met the right person at the Ball, she would know – know because he would kiss her, she who had never been kissed....

The intensity of the wishing took her breath away, left her heart aching in her chest. It would happen – she was sure of it!

ARIETTA RICHMOND, GRACE AUSTEN, ISABELLA THORNE,
KATHERINE KEATS AND SOPHIA WILSON

Chapter Five

Theodora glared at the dress that Polly was holding up for her. The bed was covered with other dresses, as were the chairs in the room. And she wasn't happy with any of them. Choosing what to wear was so difficult!

It had to be just perfect, for this, her first Ball!

She took a deep breath, and valiantly resisted the urge to throw a foot stamping, screaming tantrum from frustration. She was an adult now. She had to remember that.

Closing her eyes, she imagined, again, that she was dancing with a handsome Duke.

In the imagined scene she cast her eyes down, trying to see what she wore. All she got was a faint impression of colour, but it was enough for her to know, instantly, which dress to choose.

Opening her eyes, she went to the bed, and carefully extracted one dress from the pile. It was a pale ivory dress, with an overlay of delicate golden tissue lace.

It almost glowed from the soft gold, and she knew that it made all of the highlights in her hair glow as well. It was decorated, tastefully, minimally, at the bodice and hem, with some tiny clusters of red rosebuds with intense green leaves, all made of silk. The red drew the eye, and the green made her brilliant green eyes seem even more so.

It was pale and demure enough to not offend those who thought that young ladies shouldn't wear anything of strong colour, but interesting enough to be different from all of those insipid white dresses she saw illustrated in the fashion journals (when any of those managed to reach them, all the way from London). It was also elegant in its simplicity – no massive flounces and frills for her.

It was exactly what she wanted. Polly nodded in approval of her choice, and patiently started putting all of the other dresses away.

It was immediately obvious what jewellery she should wear with that dress too – Papa (how wonderful it was to finally be able to call him that!) had given her a pearl set on her birthday – a necklace of pearls with tiny gold drops between them, two strings of pearls for twining in the hair, and a matching bracelet. They would suit the dress wonderfully.

Theodora sighed, utterly relieved, as Polly carefully took the dress away to make certain that it was clean and perfectly pressed, for the Ball was in two days' time, on Christmas Eve. She settled in the comfortable chair in front of the window, and stared out at the grounds, where a light dusting of snow decorated the evergreen hedges of the maze and the leafless branches of the trees stood out stark against the winter grey sky.

She had never liked winter much, but this year was different, for with winter had come her birthday, the Ball, and the chance to meet eligible gentlemen.

Remembering her wish, she allowed herself to dream again, picturing herself in the beautiful dress, dancing with a handsome man. He would be tall, strong, with dark hair and piercing eyes. She could not quite imagine his face, but everything else was quite clear. Relaxing, the daydream stayed with her, as she drifted into a doze in the chair

Polly found her there, sleeping, curled like a kitten against the cushions, with a smile on her face, when she came to help Theodora dress for dinner.

ARIETTA RICHMOND, GRACE AUSTEN, ISABELLA THORNE,
KATHERINE KEATS AND SOPHIA WILSON

Chapter Six

Theodora fidgeted on the stool, nervous and eager in equal measures, as Polly gave a long suffering sigh and tried her best to get Theodora's hair in place, without jabbing her with the pins as she wriggled.

At last, it was done, and Tia stood, looking at herself in the full length cheval mirror. It did not look like her. Where had this poised and polished looking lady come from? Polly was a miracle worker, as was the modiste who had crafted the dress.

Impulsively, she spun around and startled Polly by kissing her cheek, afraid to hug her in case she crushed the dress.

"Thank you! I have no idea how you make my hair stay in place like that!"

Taking a deep breath, Theodora left the room, and, feeling like a princess in a story, walked slowly down the stairs. Charles and Catherine, both in immaculate and beautiful evening wear, waited at the bottom, ready to greet the guests once they began to arrive.

Watching Tia descend, Charles barely suppressed a gasp. He was full of pride in his daughter, but, at that moment, she looked so like Monique that it was a bittersweet joy to see her so. Catherine watched him, then turned to watch Theodora, her heart full of love for both of them. This was a wonderful moment.

She reached the bottom of the stairs and smiled, a little shaky still, but full of excitement, which bid to break free at any moment. She was afraid to let it do so, for surely she would completely ruin the impression of an elegant and composed young lady if she spun wildly about the hall for the joy of it!

Catherine took her hand, the sparkle in her eyes hinting at the fact that she had guessed Tia's thoughts, and drew her forward.

Just as she did, there came the sound of carriage wheels on the gravel, and then a knock at the door.

"Come, it is time for us to greet our guests." The Earl placed Catherine's other hand on his arm, and led them both forward, as Wilton opened the door, and ushered the first guests inside.

~~~~~

Well over an hour later, the flow of arrivals finally slowed. Tia thought that every Inn for many miles would be full tonight and the next few nights, she had never seen so many people in the one place at the same time before!
~~~~~

Her feet hurt from standing in the one place, and her face ached from smiling at all of the guests as she had greeted each one. But most of all, her heart ached. For, whilst there were a few somewhat appealing gentlemen, most were married. Those who were not, were either old, rather ugly, or rather unpleasant – some in ways that she could not entirely define, but which made her not even want to allow them to take her hand in greeting.

Annoyingly, those who did not make her want to flinch away mostly seemed to barely notice her. As if, being now officially the Earl's daughter, and being seventeen, made no difference. She hated feeling invisible!

Most significantly of all, there was, as yet no Duke, handsome or otherwise. Tia could feel her dreams crumbling away inside. Perhaps her wish had been foolish, childish. Was this what being an adult was about? Having to be polite to boring people, whilst inside everything fell apart? It would seem that there was no chance of her wish coming true.

They were about to turn away and go into the ballroom to mingle with the guests, when the sound of one more carriage on the drive reached their ears. The Earl stopped, sighed, and patiently waited for the butler to show the late arrival in.

Tia shifted from foot to foot, wanting to move, to ease the ache in her feet – standing in the one spot on a marble floor was painful after a while.

The door opened, and Wilton announced, in his most pompous voice (which usually made Tia want to laugh) "His Grace, the Duke of Montford."

Tia's head snapped up, her eyes sought the newcomer, and, instantly, her evening was restored. For the man who was walking towards them was everything she had imagined, and more. Now, she thought, blushing, she had a face to put to the man in her dreams.

The Duke was looking at her, as he approached, and she was certain that he could see her blush – which realisation only made her blush more. His eyes caught hers, and she could not have looked away if she wanted to. They were deep brown eyes, with a faint gold light in them, like the touch of sunlight on the best German velvet. She quite fell into them, forgetting her surroundings for a moment.

She forced herself to look away, for staring was the height of rudeness. Her eyes slid from his, noting the angled planes of his cheeks, and the curve of a smile on his lips, the strong chin below them, before coming to rest on his hand, as it reached out to take hers.

He bowed over her hand, placing a kiss on it, a kiss which lasted just a little longer than was proper, before standing straight again, a full smile lighting his face at her confusion.

"Enchanted, my Lady."

His voice was as rich and dark as his eyes, so resonant that she felt it on her skin, as well as hearing it with her ears.

Most amazingly, she thought, it sounded as if he actually meant it, rather than simply delivering the expected words.

He was, she realised, a little older than she had expected, even given Papa's description of him, but the age sat well on him.

He had not run to fat from an excess of indulgence, as so often happened to those who led the life of a rake and libertine.

She realised that she was woolgathering again, and that he knew, and was amused. Blushing, she spoke, knowing that she had been silent too long.

"Welcome, Your Grace." She curtsied, elegant and practiced (and very, very glad of that practice now), and he released her hand, moving on to speak to Catherine.

∿∿∿∿∿

Chase was more shaken that he wanted to admit. He had quite forgotten, until it came time to greet the Countess, that he still had hold of the girl's hand. She was a pretty enough chit, and certainly more pleasant to look on that the silly girls that the matchmaking mamas of the *ton* kept thrusting at him. But that was no reason to forget himself – it wouldn't do to seem too interested in any girl, no matter how small his actions, or the gossip would be marrying him off. He most definitely wasn't ready for that!

Anyway, this one was barely out of the schoolroom – he had always liked his women rather more sophisticated and experienced than the average young Lady of the *ton*. He had to admit though, he could no longer hold to his determination not to marry. The Dukedom needed an heir. He pushed the though aside, finished his greetings, and turned, with his hosts, to go into the Ballroom.

~~~~~

Catherine had watched the interaction between Theodora and the Duke with some amusement – she suspected that Theodora was smitten.

Which may well be a good thing, so long as it did not go too far. Theodora was a dreamer, she was a girl made for romance, for activity and adventure, not for sitting quietly by and being bland in the way that was usually expected of the young ladies of the *ton*.

And Catherine was glad of it, where many mothers might not be. For her own mother had been scandalous in her time, and Catherine and Charles' marriage had also been rather dramatic and touched with scandal. They were none the worse for it, and she was quite sure that love was worth it. Let Theodora find her own way, so long as she was not trapped into anything she did not want. Catherine would watch, and protect, but she would never try to lock the girl away.

The Duke was a bit of a surprise. She had not seen him for a year or so, since the wedding of James Blackwood, who was now Viscount Weirton, (his great uncle having finally expired of his longstanding illness) when the Duke had still been the Marquess of Travers, and had stood up with Blackwood at the wedding.

Then, he had been a confirmed bachelor, with a history of dissolute and rakish behaviour to rival Blackwood's. It would seem that becoming the Duke had reformed him rather.
~~~~~

Or perhaps it was the effect of seeing Blackwood a changed man, and happy for it? Whatever the cause, he looked fitter, steadier, and more handsome as a result.

<div align="center">~~~~~</div>

Meanwhile Tia was finding herself, now that she had been released from the duty of receiving guests, rather overwhelmed by the flock of gentlemen who vied for her attention.

It seemed that her dance card would be full, but she was having some difficulty in arranging things to ensure that those she did **not** want to dance with were not deeply offended. It became easier when she realised that there were more gentlemen than dances.

But... he had not joined the throng – how could her dream happen, her wish come true, if he did not dance with her? She had no more time to consider, as the orchestra struck up with the tune for a well-known country dance, and the gentleman who had claimed her swept her away to the floor.

Three dances later, she was beginning to see that dancing so much could be exhausting, but that conversing with some of these gentlemen as she danced was even more so. She fanned herself vigorously, glad of the short break between dances, but beginning to be annoyed with the press of gentlemen.

Tia was, however, rather pleased to see that those young ladies who had most scorned her company in the past were looking most envious now, as the eligible men flocked to her.

At least that part of her dream had come true (however poor spirited of her it had been to wish it).

Glancing away, wishing something, anything to look at except Viscount Albemarle's spotty face, as he rambled on in an insipid attempt to flatter her, she looked past his shoulder, to discover the Duke watching her, from across the room. For a moment, again, their eyes locked, and Viscount Albemarle's rather grating voice faded away, and it seemed that there was nothing, and no-one, in the room, but her, and the Duke.

Chapter Seven

"Lady Theodora?" Viscount Albemarle's irritating voice brought her back to awareness. It seemed obvious that he had been attempting to get her attention for some time. "Are you quite well?"

She fanned herself even more vigorously before replying.

"Why yes my Lord, I was simply overcome by the warmth for a moment – it is such a crush! "

Albemarle seemed reassured, and Tia wondered briefly what he had been saying. But those thoughts were almost immediately interrupted, when an unexpected voice spoke.

"I believe you promised me this dance, Lady Theodora?"

It was him! The Duke of Montford stood before her, having somehow caused the crush of her admirers to step back a little. He extended his hand, waiting for her to react. As if in her dream, she took the offered hand, smiling.

"Why yes, Your Grace, I believe I did." Theodora spoke, knowing full well that she had done no such thing, but, in that moment, intensely grateful that she had been rescued from the crowd of annoying would-be suitors. And to be rescued in such a manner! It was beyond wonderful.

He placed her hand on his arm, and led her across the room, to the area cleared for dancing. She went, feeling as if she floated, aware, through her glove and his clothing, of the warmth of his arm beneath her fingers, and of the scent of him – a mixture of lemon, something exotic like sandalwood, and something else unidentifiable, yet completely masculine.

It was only as he turned her into his arms that she realised, with complete shock, that the music she heard was a waltz.

Instantly, she knew that all eyes would be on her. At barely seventeen, and not yet officially out, the rules of propriety indicated that she should, most definitely, not be dancing a waltz! The dance was still regarded as rather scandalous by the older and more conservative members of the *ton* - after all, it brought the lady and gentleman into very close contact, with their bodies almost touching.

Startled, Tia looked up at him, to find him watching her, those deep warm eyes filled with amusement, a slight, almost sardonic smile on his sculpted lips. She blushed, instantly. His smile widened.

"Shall we be scandalous, my Lady? Surely you will not be cruel enough to deny me the dance, now that you have escaped the attentions of that flock of young fops?"

There was laughter in his voice, and a challenge.

Tia had never been one to refuse a challenge. And, whilst she was, in many ways, wise beyond her years, at that moment she could not bring herself to care one whit about scandal. For this was her dream, only better.

Taking her silence for acquiescence, he began to move, sweeping her into the dance.

They swirled about the floor, and Tia felt even more dreamlike, floating, poised and balanced, safe and protected in his arms, as they moved effortlessly through the other dancers, almost as if they were alone. She was still looking deep into his eyes, but could not look away, no matter how terribly forward of her it was. They barely spoke, comfortable in their silence, trapped in each other's' gaze, happily ignoring everyone else.

When she had practiced dancing, learning the steps of the dance from Catherine, she had not realised that it could feel like this. This was completely different, and so much better than even her imagination could have conjured. Eventually, Tia became aware that the music had ceased, as they swirled to a halt at one side of the room.

The Duke released her, seeming (but perhaps she was imagining it?) reluctant to do so, and bowed over her hand again.

"Thank you, my Lady, that was delightful. Shall I escort you to your father?"

"Why yes, I think that would be best, Your Grace, I fear that my appetite for Viscount Albemarle's conversation is quite sated for now."

Her remark surprised a laugh from him, and another of those brilliant smiles.

When he smiled at her like that, everything else simply disappeared. As he led her across the room, to where Catherine and Charles stood, chatting with some friends, she noticed, again, how many envious eyes followed her, and how much whispering went on behind the fans of the cluster of young ladies near the terrace doors.

Perhaps they really had been scandalous. If so, she would treasure the fact, rather than flinch from it!

The Earl looked up as they approached, and watched them with interest, but made no comment until the Duke had again bowed over her hand, and taken his leave of her.

Then he spoke, quietly. "Was that wise, Theodora? For now you are most certainly going to be an object of scrutiny for all of the more conservative matrons."

Tia was not sure what to say and as she hesitated, Catherine spoke.

"My dear, I do not think that we can chide Theodora for being somewhat unconventional. After all, our wedding was not without scandal."

The Earl smiled at Catherine and took her hand.

"You are quite right my Lady – I am sure that we will all deal with the opinions of others as we must." He turned more to Tia again, and asked "Scandal aside, are you enjoying yourself, child?"

"Oh yes, Papa, it is wonderful! Well..... everything except Viscount Albemarle's conversation is wonderful."

Charles and Catherine exchanged another smile at her words – how typical of Theodora! They all stood talking for a short while, before the hopeful young men came to claim Tia for more dancing.

$$\sim\sim\sim\sim\sim$$

Chase was, despite his intentions, finding Lady Theodora interesting. Whilst she seemed, at first glance, simply another fresh young thing, it was obvious that more thought went on in her head than in most young ladies heads. That remark about Albemarle, for example, indicated a quite cutting wit.

He also had to admit that she was stunning.

The simple pale gold gown set her off to perfection – it was actually elegant, rather than a froth of frills like so many young ladies' fashions. The gold lights in her rich dark hair seemed to echo the colour of the dress, and for one insane moment, he had wanted to pull down all that careful coil of hair and pearls, to bury his hands in the silken softness of it. And her eyes – he had quite fallen into their intense green depths, depths where blue flecks drifted, like the colours of a tropical sea.

For a while, as they danced, he had seen nothing else. Well, nothing else but her lips, he admitted to himself. Lips which he had wanted to kiss. A thought which was overwhelmingly inappropriate in the circumstances. But still, it was tempting.

She had felt good in his arms. He had been quite unable to resist capturing her for that waltz, however scandalous it might have been.

And the fact that she chose to be scandalous, rather than cry off, made her all the more interesting. He shook his head – what was he doing, he, the confirmed bachelor, with a rake's reputation and habits, even passingly being interested in a girl barely out of the schoolroom?

Yet he could not get her out of his thoughts. He found himself following her with his eyes, watching her dance another country dance with an over-dandified fop, whose over fussy clothing looked even more so, when contrasted by her understated elegance.

Obviously, he needed to distract himself. He had always found the best distraction from a woman to be another woman, so, resolute, he turned from watching her, and sought out a girl to dance with. They were all watching him, he realised, as he scanned the room, suddenly making him feel as a mouse must, surrounded by cats.

Just for the devilment, he looked for the quietest wallflower there, and found a girl with mousy pale brown hair, in an ill-fitting grey dress, who appeared to be hiding behind some potted greenery near the doors. As he approached her, he was watching, from the corner of his eye, the expressions on the faces of the cluster of more fashionable girls.

It was almost enough to make him laugh out loud.

He bowed before the mousy girl, and led her, after she stuttered her shocked agreement, into the dance. As a distraction, he discovered, she was less than satisfactory.

She had no conversation, and, to make matters worse, she almost tripped over her own feet.

There was none of the delicious sense of floating effortlessly through the steps that he had felt with Lady Theodora, and, this not being a waltz, he could not even hold her close and support her when she stumbled.

His eyes followed Lady Theodora, no matter his intent not to look for her. Grimly determined, he proceeded to dance with each of the uninteresting girls in turn, until his teeth ached from gritting them together as he forced a socially acceptable smile. He wanted, more and more, to dance with Lady Theodora again. But that would be taking scandalous just a little too far, and he would not do that to her.

But still, he could not stop himself from watching her.

$$\sim\sim\sim\sim\sim$$

Tia danced. And danced. And danced. But none of it felt like that waltz with the Duke. By comparison, all other dances were ungainly and awkward.

The gentlemen were either ridiculous, trying to please her with extravagant flattery, or were so self-important that all they could speak of was themselves. Tia was, to her own surprise, bored by them. Unintentionally, her eyes sought out the Duke, she somehow could not help herself.

He danced, as was appropriate, with many different ladies, never singling anyone out for too much attention, providing no fodder for gossip, beyond their scandalous waltz. She hated seeing him dance with others, for each time, she was wishing that it was her in his arms, or touching his hand as they passed in the figures of a dance.

But she could not bring herself to look away. Her partners found her distracted, and after some time, she was overcome with the need to get away from them all. If she could not dance with him again, she found that she did not wish to dance at all.

That waltz had felt like her Christmas wish dreams come true, but to now have to watch him with all of the other girls, to have to dance with these other men was just too much to bear. It tarnished her wish and spoiled her dreams.

As the next dance ended, she excused herself from them all, and left the room. She would spend some time in the family parlour – her favourite room - and read, until she could face them all again. The supper would not be served until after midnight, and she could surely restore her spirits enough to return by then.

The parlour was blessedly quiet, and she sank into her favourite chair with relief, the latest novel in her hand. Annoyingly, she found that she could not settle to reading, her thoughts, instead, replaying, again and again, that waltz.

How it had felt, the look in his eyes, the scent of him, the feel of his arms holding her, the magical way in which they had seemed to float across the floor. It was wonderful…. But…. Her wish had gone further than the dance… and now, she thought, she wanted the rest. Oh so much, so much more even than when she had first wished it.

She ached for it, imagined what it might feel like, for him to hold her again, even closer than in the waltz, imagined what it might feel like to be kissed.

For she had never been kissed. The sensible part of her mind said that she was behaving like a wanton.

The part of her that believed in dreams and wishes shoved that thought aside. There was nothing wrong with wishing!

ARIETTA RICHMOND, GRACE AUSTEN, ISABELLA THORNE,
KATHERINE KEATS AND SOPHIA WILSON

Chapter Eight

Chase released his latest dance partner back to her hopeful looking Mama, and turned away with relief, intending to seek out a drink to fortify himself before selecting the next young lady to torture himself with. Automatically, he looked for Lady Theodora, and was surprised to see her slip from the room. Frowning, he wondered where she had gone.

A few minutes later, drink in hand, he casually scanned the room again. She wasn't there. It was, of course, none of his business where she was. Perhaps she needed the ladies' retiring room. Still, he found that he wanted to know.

Downing the drink, he deposited the glass with a passing footman and, before he could think too closely about his actions, left the room through the same door that Lady Theodora had used. The empty hallway led towards the back of the house, and whilst internally he argued with himself about what he was doing, his feet had no doubts – he proceeded down the hallway, looking for any sign of where she might be.

He felt a bit of a fool, wandering the corridors of a house he didn't know, on the off-chance of finding a girl he shouldn't be looking for, who might not want to see him even if he found her. But he kept walking.

Right at the end of the hallway, a partially ajar door released a strip of light onto the floor – perhaps she was there? Chase slowed as he reached it – what was he doing? But he kept walking, until he could see, through the partially open door, that it was, indeed, Lady Theodora in the room – alone.

His heart beat faster. He should turn and walk away. She sat in a large armchair, a book on her lap, staring into the fire. He wondered what she was thinking about.

She was beautiful, in a charming, unstudied way. The red gold light from the fire made the gold tissue lace of her dress glitter, and the red and gold tones in her hair echoed the flames. Again, he felt that urge to pull all of the pins from her hair and tangle his hands in it.

Without conscious though, he found himself moving. He stepped quietly through the door, and, just as quietly, shut it behind him. An internal voice screamed at him to get out – for to be found alone with her here would surely result in scandal and marriage. He ruthlessly silenced the voice, and stepped forward.

∿∿∿∿∿

Tia stared at the flames, unseeing. All she saw, instead, was his face, as he had looked at her when they danced.

46

She had no idea how long she had been sitting there, and she didn't care. This was infinitely more pleasant than dancing with fops and boors.

Then something broke through her dreaming. A sound?

Perhaps the quiet 'snick' of the door closing?

She turned, feeling still in the dream, and saw him walking across the room towards her. She did not consider the fact that he should not be there, or that she should not be alone with a gentleman. In the dream, it was entirely reasonable, nay utterly desirable, that he be there.

Tia stood, rising smoothly from the chair, the book falling, unnoticed, to the rug at her feet. She walked towards him, her eyes on his, her heart in her eyes. Somehow, she discovered, her hands were reaching for him, and he took them in his, bringing them to his lips. He turned each hand, and kissed her palms, taking her breath away with the sensation, as a heated tingling spread out from the point of each kiss.

He released her hands to fall naturally on his shoulders, and pulled her against him, one hand around her waist, and the other cradling the back of her neck. She went willingly into his embrace, her heart beating hard and her breath coming faster as she felt the hard planes of his body pressed against her softness. It was her dream – but this was real, at least she thought it was.

And then his head came down to hers, his lips brushed hers, softly at first, then harder, as he deepened the kiss. Tia stilled, unsure. Then, as if she had always known how, she began to kiss him in return.

His tongue traced the lines of her lips, and she gasped at the sensation, then melted against him as his tongue explored her mouth. Tentatively, she explored his in turn.

Heat rushed through her body, leaving her tingling in ways she had never felt before. It was then that she was certain that this was real, that she had not fallen asleep in the chair, and dreamed of his kiss, but that he was really here, in her arms, kissing her. For there was so much more to the kiss than she had ever imagined. It was beyond what she could have imagined, deliciously, intensely *more*.

His hands slid over her body, gentle caresses, which aroused her, and held her, making her feel wanted, needed, and utterly safe. That this was, in any way, contradictory, did not occur to her.

Eventually, after some unknown length of time, which was both forever, and not long enough, he pulled back from her with a groan. Tia heard a little moan of denial escape her own lips at the loss of his touch.

They stood, still close but no longer touching, simply looking at each other, both, it seemed, stunned by the intensity of their kiss. At almost the same moment, they both become conscious of the fact that they should not be here, alone. But Tia could not speak, she had no compass for a moment like this, and did not want to break the dreamlike state.

"Lady Theodora, it seems I must apologise. That was very wrong of me. But…. I cannot say that I am sorry it happened, however inappropriate it may have been."

His voice was warm, caressing, and the look in his eyes told her how much he had wanted it – as much as she had, or perhaps, even more.

"Your Grace, I am in agreement. I am not sorry either, although indeed tis most inappropriate." Tia's eyes sparkled with a sense of mischief he found enchanting, and the fact that she simply agreed with him, rather than instantly screaming 'compromise', and attempting to trap him into marriage, was more attractive than anything else she might have done.

His face lit with a smile and, after a moment, he laughed, causing Tia also to burst into laughter. It seemed so silly, that such a wonderful thing should be something to apologise for.

He reached for her hand again, and, bowing over it, as his touch sent waves of tingling warmth through her, kissed her hand slowly, then standing, reluctantly released it as he spoke.

"My Lady, to protect your honour, I will leave you now. But I will, of a certainty, seek your company in a more suitable way tomorrow." Bowing again, he turned and left the room. Tia thought that perhaps she should have spoken, then realised that it wasn't necessary – for, unquestionably, he knew how she felt. And that was a remarkable and wonderful thing, all of itself.

<div align="center">~~~~~</div>

Chase felt bemused, detached from reality, as if he had stepped into a strange dream. What had he just done? And why?

He had always made it a rule not to in any way corrupt innocents, or take advantage of young ladies, lest he end up married to them. Yet he had just voluntarily put himself in a position which could easily have resulted in them being discovered, and forced to marry.

How had he known that she would not reject him, that she would not cry 'compromise'? He had no idea, yet he had been certain. It had seemed dreamlike, completely right. She had just walked into his arms, as if she had been expecting him.

And the kiss had been remarkable, he could not quite define how or why – it had simply been more than any previous kiss in his life. In a situation where he might have been expected to run as fast as he could, congratulating himself on a close escape, he had, instead, truly meant it when he had said that he would seek out her company tomorrow, in a more appropriate manner.

Lady Theodora was an unexpected delight. Beautiful, willing to be unconventional, not, it appeared, interested in gossip or spite, with a sharp wit and an honest open manner. About as opposite from most of the young ladies he was acquainted with as was possible.

For the first time ever, Chase contemplated the idea that, perhaps, a female could be good to be around for more than just physical gratification. Perhaps, now he had the tiniest insight into the sort of relationship that some of his friends had found.

Chapter Nine

Tia sank back into the chair, leaving the book, still forgotten, lying at her feet. Her fingers drifted to her lips, feeling their slightly swollen tenderness, and she was aware of his taste still on her tongue, as she relived the memory of his arms about her, warming her through, as they drew her against his hard body.

Time passed, but Tia saw no point in moving. She wanted to treasure this moment as long as possible. She was still sitting there when the clock struck midnight, and Christmas Eve became Christmas.

Sighing, she rose, knowing that she should return to the Ball, for supper would be served soon, and her Papa would worry if she was not there.

Straightening her dress, she smiled – for her Christmas wish had come true, and his kiss was the best Christmas present she could ever receive.

And then there was his promise to seek her out again. Suddenly, her world seemed full of potential… wonderful things could happen.

Tia hummed happily to herself as she went back to the Ballroom, already starting to imagine what might happen tomorrow.

The End

Discover more about Lady Theodora in

'A Gift of Love' – a subscriber exclusive story, available free when you sign up for my newsletter at
www.ariettarichmond.com/newsletter-signup/

and in Book 1 of the Derbyshire Set –

'The Earl's Unexpected Bride'

And also in the forthcoming Book 9 in the series

'The Duke's Improper Love'.

About the Author

Arietta Richmond has been a compulsive reader and writer all her life. Whilst her reading has covered an enormous range of topics, history has always fascinated her, and historical novels been amongst her favourite reading.

She has written a wide range of work, from business articles and other non-fiction works (published under a pen name) but fiction has always been a major part of her life. Now, her Regency Historical Romance series is finally being released. The Derbyshire set is comprised of 6 shorter novels. She also has a standalone longer novel shortly to be released, and two longer series of novels in development.

She lives in Australia, and when not reading or writing, likes to travel, and to see in person the places where history happened.

To find out first when Arietta's next book is released, sign up for her newsletter at http://www.ariettarichmond.com

When you do, you will receive a free copy of the <u>subscriber exclusive</u> prequel novella **'A Gift of Love'** which ends on the day that 'The Earl's Unexpected Bride' begins

This story is not for sale anywhere – it is absolutely exclusive to newsletter subscribers!

Other Books in
'The Derbyshire Set'

The Derbyshire Set - Book 4
Regency Historical Romance
The Count's
Impetuous
Seduction
Bestselling Author
Arietta Richmond

The Derbyshire Set - Book 5
Regency Historical Romance
The Rake's
Unlikely
Redemption
Bestselling Author
Arietta Richmond

The Marquess'
Scandalous
Mistress
The Derbyshire Set - Book 6
Regency Historical Romance
Arietta Richmond
Number 1 Bestselling Author

The
Marchioness'
Second
Chance
The Derbyshire Set - Book 7
Regency Historical Romance
Number 1 Bestselling Author
Arietta Richmond

Here is your preview of

The Earls

Unexpected Bride

Book One of the

Derbyshire Set series

Chapter One

As the water closed over her head, the events of the last few minutes replayed themselves in Catherine's mind, with the intense clarity that sometimes comes in dreams. But this was all too horribly real.

The water was such a cold shock after the warm sun of the bright May morning, and part of her believed that she would drown, even while she flailed against it.

*

She had been walking along the road from Lavenham to Harteston, returning from a visit to her mother's friend, Mrs Brown, when she first heard the sound of a horse's hooves.

Not those of just any horse she might have heard, picking its steady way along the hard-packed earth of the road, but a powerful, fast horse, obviously in some considerable hurry, hooves pounding out the urgency of its pace. It stopped her right in her tracks for a moment, so out of place was that rush on this quiet road.

The thudding rhythm, the pounding of its progress - she heard it coming up ahead of her, on the other side of the bridge, although she could not yet see it, for the trees and the high bank on the side of the road quite obscured what might lie around the corner.

She was, for no sensible reason, filled with a sudden dread - not a horrible sense of fear, or a real worry for her safety, but a dread nonetheless, at what was approaching, at the source of that clamour, coming towards her from around the corner.

Then, taking her first few steps onto the bridge over the Shimpling stream, she saw him.

He came clattering onto the wooden slats of the bridge, apparently unconcerned by the prospect of any passer-by.

The first thing that struck her, in that first instant that she saw him, was the rider, his thighs, to be precise, inappropriate as that may be. He sat the horse with the confidence of long years riding, and controlled the stallion without apparent effort. His powerful thighs, flexing as they held him effortlessly in place, spoke eloquently of power and authority.

She was embarrassed by her thoughts, and a flush of colour came to her cheeks, but she could not drag her eyes away.

His breeches, creamy white and tight as skin, clung to him, giving definition to every muscle and sinew. His boots were almost as magnificent, well-worn black leather, the same colour as the horse's glistening hide. Everything about him spoke of wealth and power.

He sat atop his animal with an easy grace, casual almost in his manner, unencumbered by a glove or a hat.

From the other end of the bridge, she could take in all of his magnificence, the broad strong chest, the shoulders that seemed to span the entire width of the road, the chin that jutted forward. His face was strong, robust and masculine, with chiselled cheek-bones below dark eyes.

And on top of it all, above the square manliness of his face, and the rather wild look of his eyes, was a rich mane of dark hair, shot through with red and gold tones, that glinted in the sun, tousled, swept aside by the onrushing wind and lent buoyancy by an irrepressible energy that could be felt the moment you saw him. She suspected that hair was not easily controlled. So focussed was she on the sight in front of her, that she had simply stopped walking, unaware that she had done so.

The horse did not stop as it came towards her. Its rider seemed not to see the small and simply dressed young woman on the the bridge, who also had cause to cross the green expanse of the Shimpling stream, late this Thursday afternoon in May.

He spurred his mount on, charging over the rickety structure, as if he were master of all he surveyed.

She realised, with a gasp, that he was not going to stop for her, and, with a cry, threw herself to the side. Almost brushing the stallion's flank, she hurled herself against the side rail, but could not stop herself from toppling, tumbling over the rickety rail and into the stream.

With an almighty splash, and a roaring in her ears, she was in the water.

She could feel the slimy grasp of the reeds, feel the weight of all the water on top of her as she flailed about. She panicked.

She had never learned to swim. The mill pond at the back of her village school had always seemed too terrifying to enter, and she had never learned. The thoughts rushed through her mind, replaying, over and over, the last few minutes, as she desperately fought the water, all to no effect.

She grasped around for the bank, for something to cling onto, but nothing presented itself to her flailing hands. She could barely see in all the darkness of the stream, and could feel her dress and petticoats soaking up the water, weighing her down, pulling her to the rocky bed of the stream. Every moment she became more certain that she was about to drown.

But then she felt something, a firm hand, a grasp from above, a man's grip. She was dragged up until she broke the surface of the water, spluttering uncontrollably. Some heroic force hauled her onto the river bank, onto the dry grass just above the shore.

She was held in a standing position, only by the strength of her saviour's grip – he legs as yet refused to support her.

She looked up, still panting for breath. It was him. Of course it was him. Her assailant had become her saviour. He held her close, waiting to see if she could stand, if she would pull away.

Looking past his shoulder, she could see that the stallion was tied to a tree in the background, pawing at the grass, obviously wishing to be away and running again.

She looked up into those dark devilish eyes and could not help but smile, even though her teeth chattered from the chill of the water.

"Are you quite all right?" he asked, with an uncertainty to his voice that betrayed his concern.

"Yes, yes quite all right." Her voice was shaky, and she was still short of breath, nerves still jangling from her watery encounter. She suspected, strongly, that she sounded unconvincing. Her eyes met his and she drank him in – he was just as good to look upon close up, as he had been from a distance.

"I must thank you kind sir, by your hand I appear to have been rescued from a watery grave."

"It was only because of me that you found yourself in such a predicament to begin with" he said, without hesitation.

His tone was that of man used to making declarations, to ordering the world around him. She realised that he held her slight frame in his embrace still, and could not but feel a shiver at the sensation.

She knew that she should pull away, should put distance between them, that this was highly inappropriate, yet she did not want to.

It was pleasant, every once in a while to have a saviour this handsome.

She was not used to anyone else taking care of her, except her mother.

"I must apologise for my haste in crossing the bridge," he continued.

"It appears to have compromised your passage somewhat. I was, unfortunately, rather distracted – after a trying morning, I just wanted to ride, and ignore the world."

"Oh, not at all sir" she replied, (although it was patently obvious that he spoke the truth).

She was still shaky, and unable to find anything sensible to say - she had often struggled to maintain her composure around handsome gentlemen – in fact, she had very little experience with gentlemen at all.

Regardless of the fact that he had caused her fall into the stream, her gratitude to him for saving her was immense, for surely, without him, she would have drowned.

"Please!" he cried, cutting her off. "Do not deny it, the fault was entirely mine."

He released her, apparently having finally noticed that they were in a rather inappropriate proximity to each other, and stepped back cautiously, watching to make sure that she could stand on her own. His immaculately tailored coat of bottle green superfine clung to his shoulders, quite as beautifully tailored as those breeches, and showing of his devastatingly well-made body.

She was horrified to see that the fabric was marred by splashes of water, and that the pristine whiteness of his breeches had rather suffered from the muddiness of the stream. Yet she was shocked to realise that she felt a desire to be back in the embrace of those arms, it had made her feel safe, to be held so, and she could not but consider what might follow such an embrace.

Her breath hitched at the thought, and, as he looked at her, patiently waiting to see what she would do, his eyes still full of concern, she became conscious of her wetness, of how it must make her face red and shiny, of how her hair was clinging unflatteringly to the side of her head and of how her bodice was clinging rather revealingly to her body, the cloth made somewhat translucent by the water.

The light stays that she wore, and the somewhat old and thin state of the fabric of her gown, did little to conceal her figure, once totally soaked in the water of the stream. It brought a blush to her cheeks, but he did not look concerned.

"I must regretfully confess, I can often become rather distracted when I take my afternoon ride." As he spoke was looking over at the horse, gesturing.

She looked down, blushing, and ashamed of her state, and realised that he was wet up to his knees, his beautiful Hessians undoubtedly ruined.

He had waded into the stream to save her, compromised his own dignity for her safety - how remarkably unlike most of the noble gentlemen that she had met before (admittedly, there were not many). This, she allowed herself to think, was quite an unusual man.

That, she thought, following the line of his hand to the horse, was quite some animal. It would take a remarkable man to tame it.

She could not ride – a humble village girl had no chance or reason to learn – her feet, or the innkeepers cart, had always been enough for her.

Yet she knew a quality horse when she saw one.

"I recently acquired this splendid mount" he waved to the horse once more "at an auction at Tattersalls. I was informed by my dealer, Mr. Redgrave, that he was bred in the stables of the Maharajah of Nackulpande, renowned as the greatest horse breeder in all of His Majesty's colonies".

He fixed his gaze back on her. "His studs are renowned for their power and virility. Thaddeus here came at a not inconsiderable expense, but I believe such extravagance to have been worthwhile."

She nodded, unfamiliar with such matters – she could tell that the horse was quality, but of what type, or to what extent, she had no idea.

She had never once ridden a horse herself.

"He is as powerful as he is headstrong. I see plenty of my own self in him – that is probably why we suit."

He looked back, when she made no response. She could think of nothing to say, she was too caught up in watching him, in the obvious energy that he brought to everything he did. It was compelling, and exciting. He mistook her silence for disinterest.

"I pray I have not bored you with all of this discussion of the stallion. As an unmarried man, I am not often called upon to converse with ladies outside the confines of the drawing room and the ballroom. But where are my manners – here I am rambling on about my horse, and you are standing there, dripping wet and cold. Come, let me help you up the bank to the road."

He offered his hand. She clasped it, and felt a quaking in her breast, a quivering in the bottom of her stomach. He was unmarried! And so handsome and wealthy! How was it even possible? This chance encounter appeared to offer one of the great excitements of her life, and she could already feel her mind brimming with new passions, new hopes, new desires.

Village girls dreamed of things like this, of accidental meetings with handsome, wealthy noblemen, and, of course, those dreams always had a happy ending, with the couple falling in love. She shook herself, mentally – this was reality, no dream, and the chances of anything happening were remote, to say the least.

"I thank you sir" she said, a little shakily, as she reached the top of the bank, and stepped on to the edge of the road. "And I must say that it is not at all tiresome to hear so eloquent an insight, on a subject with which I was not previously familiar."

"You flatter me" he said, with an ironic smile. "But I know enough of young ladies to have some awareness that the subject of stallions and auction houses does not generally greatly excite their interest."

He smiled and she could not help herself but smile warmly back. He had revealed another side, the tiniest hint of softness, of charm.

"Tell me miss, what is your name?" he enquired, with a renewed gravity. His warmth was hidden again, tantalising her in the background. She examined her feet humbly before she could look him once more in the eyes.

"My name is Catherine Thornberry."

"A charming name. The sweetness in the wilderness. I have always had a fondness for it." She blushed at this spontaneously poetic response.

"Allow me to introduce myself; I am Charles Rockingham, Earl of Stanningfield. I must confess that I am surprised to have stumbled upon you. I had presumed myself to be familiar with every pretty young lady in the county, but it appears that at least one had slipped my notice - and barely a mile from my own estate. Amusing is it not, how these things can pass us by?"

"Oh yes sir, indeed it is!" she said, in a rush, excited by his flattery.

The Earl of Stanningfield, here on Shimpling bridge, plucking her, Miss Catherine Thornberry, from the stream as if it were the most natural thing on earth! Catherine had a horrible suspicion that she was gushing, that she was making a fool of herself, but this man had an odd effect on her - she found that she struggled to think sensibly in his presence.

She was awestruck. Having never seen the Earl before, but having heard, from her friends and from her mother, much of his exploits, she had not anticipated that he should be so young, so handsome, so gallant in his readiness to help a young lady in distress.

The tales she had heard painted him as a rake, as a man with a great deal of life experience. She had expected an older man, heavy of body from overindulgence, and jaded in his attitude to life. Nothing could be further from the man who stood before her.

She tried, as hard as she could, not to allow another red blush to flush her face, but it was all too much. It was all unreal, as if in a dream.

"Do not look so thunder-struck Miss Thornberry." He spoke forcefully - "You may have formed some idea of my reputation on the basis of idle parish gossip, but I must assure you that the overwhelming bulk of it is hearsay."

"I'm sure that it is sir, undoubtedly!" She was gushing again - it had always been a profound concern of hers that she came across as too enthusiastic in the presence of gentlemen. She checked herself.

"I have been at great pains to impress upon the county my courteous nature, but regrettably, I have an unfortunate past that seems to stalk me like a wolf."

She nodded gravely. She had heard some such stories, and always suspected that there might be some truth to them. Nevertheless, being of a kind and trusting nature, she had always wanted to believe that they were false, or at least, misrepresented. She found that she did not want to believe this man capable of terrible things.

"We shall speak no more of such unpleasantness. Please, allow me to escort you homeward. It would be the least kindness I could offer after our unfortunate interaction on the bridge."

"Oh sir, that will not be necessary. I am quite capable of completing my journey unaccompanied."

"I insist" he said, not as a politeness, but a declaration.

"You are shaking like a willow in a gale and as wet as a hunting dog, and all on my account. It would be most improper of me to abandon you here." His expression was serious as he spoke, and, again, she felt that the concern in his eyes was genuine.

"I will not have it said of me that I abandoned a fair and defenceless lady, drenched, on the side of the road. And besides" he added, with a glimmer in the corner of his rich brown eyes "what on earth would your neighbours say if I did?" they shared a chuckle at his little joke.

"Thaddeus awaits!" laughing, he took her hand, tugging her towards the horse.

"But sir!" Catherine exclaimed "I regret to confess, I have never ridden before, and I do not know how!"

"Good heavens above!" he seemed genuinely shocked "Not ridden a horse? Why it is one of life's greatest pleasures! I would not wish to deny the thrill of a good, vigorous ride to my worst enemy. Allow me..." before Catherine even had time to make an objection, he had scooped her up. She clasped his thick, muscular shoulders and found suddenly that her face was close to his, so close, in fact, that she could see every bristling hair, every tendon in his neck.

Close inspection did him justice. His scent came to her, an earthy mixture of horse, leather, and an undertone of some more exotic scent, some cologne of citrus and spices. It was like nothing she had smelled before.

She found it stimulating, and extremely pleasant.

"Time I think, for your first ride!" he chortled, before depositing her unceremoniously to sit sideways across Thaddeus' saddle.

She felt the animal shifting beneath her, full of vigorous life. She clung to the abundant mane that drifted back over her hands, holding on as if for dear life, anxious that the horse might suddenly take off without warning, or that it would deposit her once again into the stream.

It had a will of its own and a powerful body after all, but her saviour, the Earl, held firmly to its reins.

He gently stroked the horse's nose to calm it, putting it under his spell, before firmly commanding it to stand. Then in a single, graceful movement, he swung up into the saddle, lifting her to sit, still sideways, across his knees, his arms either side of her shaking body, and took charge of his stallion.

"Hold on tight" he declared, and she obeyed willingly. There was a moment where she hesitated, aware that her soaking clothes were already shedding even more water onto his attire, before a movement of the horse convinced her that she was quite happy to sacrifice his clothing for her safety. She wrapped her white arms, still cold and wet, about his splendid torso, as tightly as she dared, her head resting against his shoulder.

The shape and definition of his firm abdominal muscles could be made out beneath his coat and shirt. The sensation quite took her breath away.

"Now where would you like me to take you, Miss Thornberry?" he asked, after a moment.

"To Hawthorn Cottage in Harteston" she replied. "Do you know it?"

"I know Harteston, but not the exact location of Hawthorn Cottage" he said. "A fine village indeed - do you live there alone?" As he spoke, without warning her, he had shifted Thaddeus into motion, and already they were crossing the bridge at a gentle canter. She was, again, impressed at his gallantry, as he was now heading the opposite way to his own original route.

With the unfamiliar rocking motion of the horse, and the stress of its forward motion pressing her ever more tightly against the body of her saviour, she could feel something thrilling stirring within her. A new sensation, pleasurable, dangerous, was creeping up her inner thighs and into her bosom. She bit the back of her lip. It was entirely inappropriate for her to be thinking such thoughts about this man.

He was far above her, he was courteous enough to have saved her from drowning, and here she was thinking like a wanton. Well, she thought that's what it was – actually, she had no idea, no idea beyond the fact that her body was reacting to its proximity to his – and she was scandalously enjoying it.

"Or..." he continued with a roguish chuckle "have you a sweetheart in Harteston perhaps?" This time she was wise to him. This time she played the game.

"I am unmarried, my Lord. However..." she added, with a slight laugh of her own "I must confess that the innkeeper's son and I have developed something of a rapport in recent times. He is a most handsome young man."

"Oh undeniably" replied the Earl, rising to her challenge. "Indeed I have often thought to myself, on visiting that very fine inn, that he would make a most attractive catch for a young girl in the village. Nevertheless", He paused in his speech a moment, as if considering the right words to use.

Thaddeus was picking up speed. Her lower body was assailed with a new vigour, rocked against the Earl's thighs, and the front of his body, in a rather intimate fashion.

The warmth of his body was penetrating the chill of her wet clothes – it made her want to press herself even closer against him.

Having obviously chosen his words carefully, he continued "Are his manners and breeding not a little coarse, for a young lady of distinction, such as yourself?"

Catherine did not allow herself to laugh, but she was overwhelmed.

This man was clever. He knew the workings of the female heart.

Moreover, by asking this question, which she now, perforce, had to answer, he had coaxed a difficult admission out of her, concerning their relative status.

"I am but a humble schoolmistress, sir" she said reluctantly. "I have education and, I flatter myself, a little breeding – but certainly not any significant status in the world."

"Stuff! I could tell the moment that I saw you, that here is a lady who carries herself well, evident poverty notwithstanding."

"You are indeed, courteous, my Lord. Nevertheless, I could never make any claims to be a noble lady. My mother, with whom I share Hawthorn Cottage, has long maintained that we are descended from the de Quincy family, who came over with William the Conqueror no less, but I fear, from what little she is willing to tell me of the detail, that lineage may be rather obscure now, to say the least."

"The de Quincys?" he came back, not bothering to disguise how impressed he was. "Not bad at all. Tell me, how does a girl with such a fine pedigree find herself reciting the alphabet to ungrateful village brats?"

"I suppose some ancestor of ours must have fallen on hard times" she said, keeping her poise.

Thaddeus was going at quite a speed now, and it was necessary to raise her voice. She tried as hard as she dared to disguise the quaking in her body that the movement of the ride, and the sensation of his body against hers, was giving her.

"Mother has mentioned a gambler, in my great grandmother's generation, who may have lost us our estates. That is long ago, and of no relevance to our lives now. I am unused to luxury, and the life of a humble schoolmistress is easy enough to bear."

He had exposed a quiet sadness in her, a longing. For years she had ignored her mother's pining after their heritage, her obsession with the importance of ancestors on their family tree, but now, in the presence of a real gentleman, she was, for the first time, embarrassed by her circumstances.

She had no land, no money, no prospects of a higher match.

All she had ever hoped for was to make an honest living and to marry one of the boys in the village, but now, something else had stirred in her, passion, ambition, a reaching for something more. Thaddeus' movement seemed to fill her with a greater lust for more in life, as well as most interesting sensations in her body, with every galloping stride.

"I suppose someone's got to force some knowledge into 'em" he laughed, urging the horse along.

The countryside sped by. She took in long, drooping willows, plump cows chomping in the fields, water mills churning, as they had for hundreds of years. It was not such bad country, Suffolk, especially as it had such charming people in it. The speed at which the road went by amazed her, so used was she to the time it took to walk this distance.

"Still, it is a terrible shame for a great and noble family to have fallen on hard times. Alright, I suppose, if you're happy enough looking after other people's infants, and cavorting with innkeepers' sons, then I can think of worse fates."

"Why yes sir. I suppose I am happy enough." She knew, even as the words came out, that she was lying to him. Had someone asked her the question yesterday, then that answer would have been truthful, but today, she was alarmed to discover, something in her had changed.

She was no longer satisfied with what she had.

"Well, jolly good then." He appeared to focus his concentration on riding now, for the first time taking his attention away from her. She could not help but feel a small pang of disappointment.

Thaddeus thundered on, down a shallow hill, and then splashed across a ford. Before she knew it, having never ridden upon a horse or experienced just quite how fast these noble animals could move, she was in the village of Harteston, shaken by the journey, quivering and awake deep in her body, and intensely aware of his body where it pressed against her.

"Here we are" he declared confidently. "Harteston - where I suppose I shall leave you."

"Yes. I must thank you my Lord, your kindness has saved me much effort, and possibly even preserved my life. For surely, had I not drowned, by now I would have taken a terrible chill on the road home."

"No need to thank me Miss Catherine, I am sure that you would have done the same were our roles to be reversed."

"I suppose I would have. Thank you again."

She released her grip on his body, regretfully, and he lifted her gently, supporting her as she slid down the side of the horse to land on her feet.

She hesitated, unsure of what to do now, part of her not wishing this moment to end, but unable to see any reason for it to continue. Then, not wishing to betray the feelings that he had stirred in her, and holding her crumpled bonnet high upon her head, she dipped him a curtsey, and set off for home.

The Earl however, had never been the kind to let a pretty young lady get away from him, so coldly and suddenly. As she had silently, privately hoped, he swung out of his saddle and came straight after her, catching her in just a few steps.

Grasping her fragile waist, he turned her suddenly towards him. She gasped, her eyes wide open. He pulled her against him, and the heat of his body against hers felt like fire rushing through her veins.

"Not so fast" he whispered, close against her ear. "We haven't even said a proper goodbye" and then, just like that, he kissed her, fully, without apology, on the lips. He gripped her for a moment that felt like it should last forever, a moment deserving of a painting or a symphony to capture it and preserve it. She felt his strong tongue, his hot mouth and his firm lips. Their bodies pressed together, seeming moulded just for that, and she could sense the longing they shared could feel the hardness of his desire, tangible through their damp clothing. Her body throbbed, with the sensation of the kiss, and the vitality imparted by the ride.

Just as suddenly as he had captured her, he pulled back, looking a little shocked himself, at what he had just done. He mumbled goodbye, and swung back into the saddle, heading for home.

Catherine stood a moment, dazed, watching him go. She had never felt such a thrill in all of her twenty-four years on God's earth.

ARIETTA RICHMOND, GRACE AUSTEN, ISABELLA THORNE,
KATHERINE KEATS AND SOPHIA WILSON

Chapter Two

Charles Rockingham, Earl of Stanningfield, was bemused. He rather feared that he had just made a fool of himself, in front of a young lady.

Not something that he had ever been prone to doing. *That is,* an insidious thought reminded him, *except for the colossal fool he had made of himself, at 17, with Monique.*

He pushed the thought aside. That was old history, beyond being changed. Today, he should be focussing on his current problems. And what problems. He groaned as it all forced itself back to the surface of his mind, now that he no longer had a ready distraction to hand.

He chose to shove the thoughts away again, an act made easy by the fact that his clothes were uncomfortably damp, and his toes squished alarmingly in his boots, which were, he suspected, full of water.

They were certainly coated in mud.

The condition of his attire would draw the wrath of his valet, and he expected that Johnson would be effective at making his disapproval known, without ever saying a word.

Still, even if he had rather made a fool of himself, it was, he decided, worth it. He had been in such a temper when he had left the house. His morning, reading through applications for the role of Theodora's Governess, had been enough to drive anyone to despair.

They were, universally, terrible. The sort of women he would definitely never want in his house – the sort who would turn a bright, if sometimes difficult, girl into a prudish, boring society Miss, incapable of conversing on any topic except the weather.

He knew that the best solution to such a mood was a good hard ride, on a quality horse. And Thaddeus was quite the best horse that he had ever owned.

But it had been spectacularly unwise of him to ride, at that pace, along the road – over the fields would have been a far better choice.

Well too late to change anything now. And…. Would he want to?

The girl was beautiful – and, it seemed, completely unaware of that fact. He had not seen her, not until it was too late. He had been so wrapped in his thoughts that the world around him had been barely registering.

He might not have seen her, but the thump against his leg as he rode across the bridge, followed by the scream, and the huge splash, had certainly attracted his attention.

At that point he had no idea who or what he had just caused to fall into the Shimpling Stream, beyond the fact that it was almost certainly a person, as nothing else screamed quite like that. Unwilling to leave anyone floundering due to his inattention, he had hauled Thaddeus around (somewhat against the stallions wishes at the time!) and gone back to investigate.

What he dragged from the water was a delectable surprise.

A girl, or young woman rather, her shape thoroughly displayed by the unfortunate saturation of her gown, her piercing blue eyes shocking in her pale, water soaked face, her sodden hair seemingly a golden brown colour – although the mud made it hard to tell. She had blushed charmingly as he held her, waiting for her to be steady on her feet again.

She held herself well – there was obviously some breeding there, or at least some education, but the gown was, as far as he could tell after its dip in the stream, rather worn. It had been good quality once, but the hems showed signs of it having been turned, and the fabric was thin from wear. Thinness he deeply appreciated, as it ensured that the water had made it almost translucent. It had taken all his concentration to avoid staring at her breasts rather than her face.

Apart from the sodden gown, and its exposure of her attractions, there was something about her that took his breath away, in that first look. It took only a moment to realise what – her shape, the turn of her cheek, the fall of her hair, even sodden, brought to mind, just for a second, Monique.

He had pushed that recognition away, and focussed on her more mundane attractions.

He had been a rake for too many years not to appreciate a woman's body when he was given an unexpected viewing. But, it seemed he was rather out of practice.

The sight of her body had robbed him of sensible, coherent conversation, and he had made a complete ass of himself, prattling on at her about the horse, of all things. Women, in his experience, did not give a damn about horses, so long as they transported them where they wanted to go. He was depressingly sure that he could not have made a bigger fool of himself if he had tried.

And then, to top it off, he had taken her home. What else could a gentleman do? He certainly couldn't leave her to walk four miles in a soddenly transparent dress, when she was already shivering from the cold! What if she had met some oaf along the way, who thought to take advantage of her? *Like you wanted to,* said that insidious voice in his thoughts. She was schoolmistress at the parish school – the school that his family funded, had funded for fifty years now, for the good of their tenants and the villagers. A less suitable woman for him to find tempting he couldn't imagine.

The feel of her body against him, of her arms around him and her soft breasts pressed against his chest, rubbing against him with the movement of the horse, the feel of her rounded derriere, rubbing against his thighs, pressing against his manhood, had been enough to drive a saint wild.

The wet fabric of her gown was no barrier, and the water soon transferred to his breeches as well.

They might as well have been skin to skin, he could feel the detail of her body so clearly.

His cock had hardened in response, making the ride an exquisite agony. She must be an innocent, for she had appeared to genuinely not notice, even though Thaddeus' every stride had thrust the evidence of his arousal against her nether regions.

Which made his behaviour at the end of the ride all the more despicable.

Not only had he flirted with her, in a rather suggestively inappropriate way, but he had, at the end, kissed her…. Hard…. Full on the lips. He had not intended to, but, when she turned away, all stiff and unsure, after that ever so wobbly curtsey, and simply began to walk off, her ridiculously crushed and sodden bonnet perched on her equally sodden hair, he had not been able to stop himself.

He wanted a reaction, wanted more than just a departure.

He did not know why - he was, obviously, simply a fool. But he had gone after her, grabbed her and pulled her to him. In the middle of the damned village street, for pity's sake! And she had tasted divine. Her innocent response had been to press into the kiss, and the feel of her body fitting so perfectly against his had roused his passion like no woman had for years. Had the chiming of the town clock not interrupted, he might almost have taken her there, on the street. He was, most definitely, a fool.

And, he was no further ahead with solving the governess problem.

He was just as frustrated by that as before, but now, he was frustrated in an entirely different way, and sodden as well. He sighed, and steeled himself for Johnson's response to his maltreatment of his attire.

Continue reading

'The Earl's Unexpected Bride'

at

https://www.amazon.com/dp/B01FJEQPXM

AR
Arietta Richmond
Regency Historical Romance
Arietta Richmond's
Regency Romance

ARIETTA RICHMOND, GRACE AUSTEN, ISABELLA THORNE,
KATHERINE KEATS AND SOPHIA WILSON

Regency Romance

The Earl's Missing Christmas Heir

A Clean & Wholesome Regency Romance

Grace Austen

Dedication

This book is dedicated to you, my readers!

Many warm thanks for your encouragement, emails, and kind reviews! You are what makes my work so special.

ARIETTA RICHMOND, GRACE AUSTEN, ISABELLA THORNE,
KATHERINE KEATS AND SOPHIA WILSON

Chapter One

The end was coming for the Earl of Rosedale. He could feel himself growing weaker, and he knew that it could not be much longer now. Reflecting on his life, he mulled over the one regret that stood out above all the others. With a sigh, he pulled the thick blanket over his chest to ward off the growing cold. He hoped his solicitor would arrive soon.

As the Earl lay in the ornately carved oak bed, he prayed that the provisions in his will would somehow make up for a decision he now bitterly regretted. He felt the sting of remorse so deeply that it brought tears of sorrow to his eyes. At least now, he told himself, he had tried to rectify the situation.

The Earl felt that his efforts at compensation would permit him to depart this life, leaving *all* his descendants well provided for. He only wished his solicitor would make haste.

His time was running out.

Before he closed his eyes forever, he desperately desired the assurance that he had not overlooked some final detail that would nullify his request or put his plan in jeopardy.

The Earl was not prone to foolish ideas. He was well aware that his children, George, Augusta, and Marjorie, would be less than pleased with the distribution of his wealth. He had ensured that they were well provided for, but like any father faced with the prospect of his own looming mortality, he could now see his life story with previously ignored clarity.

His three children were suited to their station; they were well-mannered and well-behaved as proper members of society, yet he knew their vices included greed, vanity, and pride. He was aware, painfully so in this dark hour, that the wishes clearly defined in his will would be met with hostility. The solicitor would therefore be invaluable to him to ease his mind and bring comfort to his soul as he prepared to leave his earthly affairs behind.

From his bed, the Earl gazed upon the stern countenance of his son George, the eldest of the three, and upon the anxious faces of his daughters. They were seated at his bedside, dutifully maintaining a vigil until his death. He looked at his daughters, and he could see his departed wife's features and dark auburn hair, but not the kindness that had shone in her eyes.

He wished that his wife had lived long enough to impart her charity and good nature to the children, but sadly he had raised them to adulthood with the knowledge and skills they needed for their duties as a proper lord and ladies, but without the compassion he had treasured in his wife.

Again, he thought about his wife and hoped that he had led a life worthy of heaven, for surely, she resided there. She had passed away many years ago, and there was not a day that went by when he did not think of her.

His one consolation in death was that he stood a chance of reuniting with his lost love. He closed his eyes and remembered her — her smile and her lovely laugh. He was lost in his memories when a footman announced the arrival of the solicitor, Mr. Stephen Montgomery. The Earl greeted him with as hearty a welcome as he could muster with his waning strength.

"Mr. Montgomery, I am pleased that you were able to arrive before my demise."

"Yes, Lord Rosedale, I apologize for any delay in my arrival."

"George, Augusta, and Marjorie, would you be so kind as to give your father a few minutes of privacy with Mr. Montgomery?"

"Father, we have no wish to leave you, not even for a moment," stated Marjorie as she dabbed at her eyes with a lace-trimmed handkerchief.

Augusta bristled. "Truly, is it so important that we must leave? Mr. Montgomery can have nothing to say that we cannot hear."

"I appreciate your devotion, but do indulge me. This will be one of the last favors that I ever ask of any of you."

"Yes, Father," the daughters answered, albeit begrudgingly. They stood and joined their older brother at the door.

Much to the Earl's relief, they left him alone with the solicitor. The Earl of Rosedale raised his hand slightly. "Would you be so good as to close the door?" he asked Mr. Montgomery. "I do not want our conversation to be overheard by the staff or my children. I would like to enjoy the privilege of passing in peace and not at the center of a family crisis."

Mr. Montgomery closed the door and walked to the bedside of the Earl. He lowered his voice and said, "I understand your insistence that the amendments to your will remain confidential until after your funeral. It is for precisely this reason that I was delayed this afternoon. There were several details regarding your affairs that I wanted to oversee personally, to ensure that they were irrevocable."

"Are they irrevocable? Can they be overturned or appealed?" asked the Earl, concern edging his voice.

"No, Lord Rosedale, they cannot. Your wishes will be carried out, and you may rest assured that all will be as you have arranged. I will see to it. You have my solemn vow."

The Earl looked at the younger man sitting beside his bed. The solicitor resembled his father, the elder deceased Mr. Montgomery, a great deal. The Montgomery Firm had been entrusted with handling the Earl's affairs for many years. The Earl of Rosedale trusted the younger Mr. Montgomery, just as he had trusted the elder. "I am sure you are aware that your resemblance to your father in mannerisms and profile is remarkable."

"I have been told that I do bear a strong resemblance to him. I consider it an honor to have been his son, may God rest his soul."

"Your father was a worthy man. I have been most fortunate that you and your family's firm will be overseeing my matters, as they will require delicacy."

"I am grateful for your continued trust in me, and you have my word that your final wishes will be executed in the exact manner you have requested."

"Thank you. I know you will handle any difficulties that may arise judiciously, and with compassion."

"Yes. That is precisely what I intend to do."

Chapter Two

Justina worked as hard as she possibly could. Dinner was at eight, and she only had a few more minutes to finish repairing the tear in the seam of the silken gown. Keeping a watchful eye on the clock in the servants' hall, she searched in her sewing basket for thread that matched the emerald green of the gown.

It was hopeless. She did not have any thread that color. As she faced the unpleasant prospect of informing the mistress that her gown would not be ready, she remembered that she had one more hope, and that was the housekeeper, Mrs. Stratton.

All of this anguish could have been avoided if only her mistress had not changed her mind three times that day. Justina could not hope to understand how the emerald green gown was any better than the other three gowns that her mistress had decided against in the last five hours.

But that thought brought her little consolation as she rushed to have the gown ready for her mistress to wear that very night.

She dashed down the hallway to the housekeeper's office and was disappointed to find her not there. The dinner party promised to be a large and important affair, and so Justina was certain that Mrs. Stratton was busy making last minute preparations, but where could she be?

She was about to begin systematically searching through the house, when she heard the unmistakable high-pitched voice of the housekeeper arguing with the cook. Breathing a sigh of relief, she rushed to the kitchen.

"I told you we were going to be serving forty people. What do you mean you don't have enough for the main course?" asked Mrs. Stratton, turning red with rage.

"I wasn't expecting them all to be coming to dinner. That never happens," answered the cook.

"I don't see how that is going to get us out of this," Mrs. Stratton snapped.

"I will come up with something. We may have to change the menu a bit," the cook offered, as her fingers worked at the edges of her apron.

"Change the menu? And who will have to hear about it? Me, that's who. You know how the missus can be."

Justina did not want to ask Mrs. Stratton anything at the moment, but she was left with no other option. She walked into the kitchen, and at first, she was not noticed, but then both ladies must have realized they had an audience.

"Justina, what is the meaning of this? Do you always make a habit of lurking about listening in on people's private conversations?" asked Mrs. Stratton, turning her anger towards Justina.

Justina was astonished that Mrs. Stratton was under the impression that the conversation in the kitchen, as loud as it was, had ever been private, still she dealt with the accusation with grace.

"Mrs. Stratton I apologize for the intrusion. I simply must have your help."

"What can be so important that you would interrupt me?" demanded the housekeeper.

"It's for the missus. She will be unhappy if I do not finish the repair to her gown, and I find myself in need of emerald thread."

"Thread? That is what this is all about?"

"Yes, ma'am. I was hoping you would be able to help me."

"Are you useless? How can you expect to be a lady's maid if you have no hope of solving a simple matter of thread? Go look in my sewing box and leave me alone."

"Thank you, ma'am," mumbled Justina as she left the two ladies to continue their argument. She returned to the housekeeper's office and rummaged through the sewing kit.

She found a thread that was nearly the same color and hoped that if she made the stitches small enough, it would suffice. Time was running out, and the mismatched thread was her only hope.

A half hour later, she ran upstairs with the mended dress and rushed to her mistress's room, knocking gently on the door.

"Come in"

Justina ushered herself in and closed the door.

"It is about time. What took you so long?" asked Lady Harrington in a frustrated tone.

Justina wanted to remind her mistress that she had changed her mind repeatedly and then selected a gown that used to fit her when she was quite a bit slimmer. The seam in the gown was sure to rip again, and Justina could only hope that the repair would hold for the evening.

"I am sorry. I do offer my apologies. Here is the dress."

"I cannot begin to tell you how disappointed I am." The woman clucked her tongue with disgust. "I afraid that if you do not show improvement, I will be forced to make other arrangements for a lady's maid. Now do something with my hair and be quick about it."

Justina felt anxious whenever Lady Harrington threatened her with dismissal. She had tried to do everything she could to satisfy her employer's constant demands, but there simply was no pleasing the woman. Tonight was just another instance when her mistress would be disappointed and angry and would find a way to see that Justina bore the brunt of her unhappiness.

Reluctantly, Justina endured the constant barrage of verbal and mental abuse, which was part and parcel of her employment at the Harrington's.

She could not afford to lose her position. If she was no longer employed by the Harrington's and was forced to leave without a reference, her future would be uncertain. She could very well end up living on the streets or forced into a workhouse. She fought back the tears as she swept up Lady Harrington's hair.

Justina breathed a sigh of relief when at last her mistress was dressed for dinner. With a few moments free, she went down to the servants' hall. She sat by the fire with a novel and a bracing cup of tea.

∿∿∿∿∿

Later that evening, Lady Harrington rang for Justina. Justina sighed - her moments of peace were at an end. She climbed the narrow servants' stairway and answered her mistress's summons. Arriving at her mistress's chambers, she found Lady Harrington to be in a most unhappy mood.

"Justina! How can such an embarrassment occur?"

"I am sure that I do not know, my Lady. If I may be so bold, what occurred?"

"Dinner was nearly ruined, and my dress was *not* repaired properly, just look at it!" Lady Harrington nearly spat her disdain as she pointed to a rip in the seam of her dress.

Justina was preparing to point out to her mistress that the rip in the seam was on the opposite side of the dress from the repair, but she did not have the chance.

Her mistress walked up to her and grabbed her by the arm, "Justina, you have ruined dinner and this dress. What have you to say for yourself?"

Justina wriggled her arm free of Lady Harrington's grip, and her mistress slapped her across the face. "Don't be impertinent! You failed to tell the housekeeper how many guests were coming for dinner, and the cook had to change my menu, and it's your fault my dress ripped again."

Justina stood in stunned silence with her hand on her face. She had never felt so helpless in her life.

She could not believe that this woman was blaming her for dinner. She had nothing whatsoever to do with the preparations of dinner, nor was she to blame for the fact that Lady Harrington could no longer fit into a dress. She looked at the floor and considered her options.

As her mistress continued her angry tirade, Justina was forced to listen to her insults and her abuse. She thought about the prospect of a workhouse and decided that, as horrible as she found her current situation to be, it was still preferable to the grim conditions of life as a pauper.

"Get over here and undress me, you ungrateful wretch. I ought to have you tossed out of here on your ear."

Justina complied with her mistress's wishes and tried to avoid eye contact as she undressed the woman and prepared her for bed. She was relieved when her mistress asked for nothing else from her before retiring. Justina picked up the torn evening gown from the floor and left the bedroom, closing the door behind her.

Her face burned where her mistress had slapped it, but at least she was free of her odious presence until the following morning. She walked towards the servants' stairs and was momentarily consoled by the fact that her evening could get no worse - but she was wrong.

"Well, what have we here?"

She heard the voice of Sir Harrington in the hallway and turned to face him. It was obvious by his slurred speech that he had been drinking. Justina hoped that he would not prove to be as ill-tempered as his wife.

"Good evening, Sir," she muttered, trying to slip away as quickly as possible.

"Where are you going?" he asked as he stumbled closer to her.

"To the servants' hall, my Lord. I have to repair this dress."

"There... there is no need to hurry away."

Justina glanced into his bleary eyes and felt fear inch up her spine. He was standing close to her, and she could smell the brandy on his breath. Sir Harrington had never said very much to her, and she was unsure what his intentions were that evening; however, he soon made them abundantly clear by running his fingers slowly down her arm. She went stiff.

"Sir Harrington, if you will excuse me, I must finish this." She clasped the dress to her chest like a shield and took a step back. "For your wife."

"Now, is that any way to treat your master? You will stay as long as I choose."

"Yes, my Lord," she answered, dropping her gaze.

"That's better. You are rather handsome for a lady's maid. Rather handsome, indeed." He touched her face in the exact spot where his wife had slapped her. Justina winced involuntarily, both from the pain and from a growing sense of revulsion.

"Sir, please. I must work on this dress for her Ladyship."

"I do not care about the dress, and what's more, I am not overly fond of her Ladyship. I do not find her as pleasing as I find you." He moved closer until she had no place to go. He pressed her against a tapestry on the wall with his bulk.

Justina's eyes stretched wide and panic swept through her. How could she get out of this without losing her position? She considered burning him with the candle sitting on the side table, making it look like an accident. But if she did, her dismissal would be sure. Her mind whirled.

He was breathing heavily, loud gasps that rasped up his throat.

She screwed up her courage. "My Lord, I am afraid I am quite ill. Please let me pass."

He stumbled a bit, pressing her harder into the wall. "Ill? You look well enough to me," he growled.

"I do not mean to be indelicate, sir, but I am ill with a sickness only women are prone to."

"Oh, that is different. Why didn't you confess earlier?" He recoiled with what looked like disgust. He staggered away from her, but before he left her trembling in the hallway, he added, "Another time then."

She scampered to the other side of the hall. When she realized he was no longer in sight, she ran toward the stairs. She changed her mind about her destination and did not stop running until she reached her small quarters.

Throwing the green evening gown onto her bed, she slumped onto the chair by the small fireplace. She had no intention of repairing the dress that evening, not after what she had endured. Lighting the fire in the fireplace with a candle, she huddled by it for warmth.

All she could hope for was that her master was so drunk he would forget about his interest in her, and that her mistress would change her mind about throwing her out. It had been a horrible night, and she did not know how she would be able to remain employed by such a hateful woman and such a lecherous man. Bleak despair filled her as she cried herself to sleep that night.

Chapter Three

Stephen Montgomery arrived at the residence of Sir Arthur Harrington unannounced. Sir Harrington was a knight, and Stephen normally worked for Earls, Marquises and Dukes. He felt no need to kowtow to the man by arranging his appearance beforehand. Arthur Harrington's reputation went before him, and it was not pleasant. Besides, Stephen was not there to see him in any case.

The solicitor was aware that Sir Harrington outranked him, but his business relationship with the upper class had given him the impression that he, too, was of high standing, especially when he was charged with performing a duty for one of his wealthier clients, as was the case that day.

His carriage arrived after luncheon. A footman met him at the door and accepted his card, inviting him into the foyer.

"Mr. Montgomery, is Sir Harrington expecting you?"

"No, but I am afraid you are mistaken. I am not here to see your master. Is there a Miss Justina Stanley employed in this house?"

"Sir, if you will excuse me, you will want to speak with the mistress, Lady Harrington. Please wait in the drawing room." The footman showed Stephen into the modest but well-appointed room.

Stephen waited patiently and remained standing; he was in no mood to socialize with the woman. He had business with Justina. He was quietly appraising the net worth of the family by their modest décor, when the lady of the house arrived to greet him.

"I am Lady Harrington. What is the nature of this visit?" she asked in a haughty manner.

"I am Stephen Montgomery, Solicitor. I am here on behalf of the Earl of Rosedale."

"My footman tells me that you have made an inquiry regarding my maid. Is that correct?"

"It is. I need to see her at once. It is a matter of some importance."

"What has she done? Why would your employer have an interest in my maid?"

Stephen detested the smug sense of superiority of the woman standing across from him. She was the wife of a knight, and yet she acted as though she was a person of the highest standing.

Stephen gave her a very polite smile. "That does not concern you in the slightest. I desire to see her at once."

Flustered, Lady Montgomery turned to the footman and ordered him to bring Justina to the drawing room.

The silence between Stephen and this overbearing woman would have been uncomfortable if he cared about her opinion, but he did not. The clock ticked loudly on the mantle as he waited patiently for Justina.

The footman arrived minutes later, accompanied by a petite young woman. She was an ethereal beauty with dark auburn curls, a heart-shaped face and the most arresting green eyes he had ever seen. He had not expected her to be so beautiful, and he was riveted by her handsome countenance.

To the amazement of Lady Harington, he bowed to Justina and introduced himself. "Lady Justina Stanley, it is an honor to make your acquaintance. I am Stephen Montgomery, solicitor to the Earl of Rosedale. Please forgive my abrupt presence, but I feel that it is incumbent upon me to make haste."

"Sir, I beg your pardon. I do not know the Earl of Rosedale."

Stephen could tell from the sound of her voice that she was nervous. He would do everything he could to make her comfortable. "Lady Justina, may I suggest that you sit down and steel yourself for some rather important news."

"Justina, don't you dare sit on the furniture," Lady Harrington said to the girl. Then she turned her attention to the solicitor.

"You are asking *my* maid to sit down in *my* drawing room? Sir, are you forgetting who owns this house and whose hospitality you are intruding upon?"

"Lady Harrington, this young lady is only your maid due to an unfortunate set of circumstances. In a moment, you may wish that you had struck a decidedly different tone when addressing her. Now if you will excuse us, I have business to discuss with Lady Justina."

"I am not leaving." Lady Harrington stuck out her bosom in the most unfortunate of stances. "I insist that you put an immediate end to this masquerade at once. Justina has work to do if she would like to retain her position."

Stephen knew that he was going to enjoy this more than he should. He detested social snobbery, and he was well pleased that Lady Harrington chose to stay so he could watch her reaction to the incredible news he had to share.

Stephen cleared his throat and stated, "Very well. As you wish." He turned his attention to the servant girl.

"Lady Justina, I regret to inform you of the recent passing of the eighth Earl of Rosedale. You are his daughter and the half-sister to the heir to the title, George Merchant. Your rank in society is Lady, and you have been formally recognized in the Earl's will. The Earl made arrangements that you be endowed with a generous annuity and a dowry, at the time of his death. Your immediate presence is required at the home of your family at Helmsford Park."

Lady Harrington's gasp was audible. Justina looked ready to faint.

Despite her employer's admonition not to sit on the furniture, she plopped down on the upholstered settee with a look of shock.

"But sir, I am an orphan. I was raised by a Mrs. Waverly of Grangerton before my employment. As much as I would like this fairy tale to be true, I am afraid that I am not a lady."

"My dear, it was the Earl himself who made arrangements for Mrs. Waverly to oversee your upbringing. Now, gather up your belongings. I would like to be on our way within the half hour."

Lady Harrington stood frozen in shock, blinking her eyes stupidly at what to her must have been inconceivable news. "Mr. Montgomery, you are mistaken. My maid cannot possibly be the daughter of an Earl."

"Lady Harrington, it gives me great joy to inform you that from this moment on, you must address her as the Lady Justina. You are to show her all the respect and honor that one of her class requires."

"Th-this is an outrage!"

"Furthermore, Lady Harrington," said Stephen with his best elocution, "she outranks you considerably, and I dare say that with her annuity she could buy your entire property and still have money left over to spend on hats and gowns for her delight. Good day to you."

"Sir, so it is true? I am a Lady?" asked Justina, her eyes wide.

"Yes, it is true. Shall we be going?"

"Allow me five minutes, and I will meet you at the carriage."

"Very good, Lady Justina."

Justina stood up and with a smile that seemed to light up her whole face, she raced out of the drawing room and, rather than running up the cramped servants' steps, she took the main staircase — reserved for those of family rank. Of course, she had to switch to the servants' stairs from the second floor to continue up to the attic; however, she gloried in using the main stairs at all.

Chapter Four

Justina smiled with shocked disbelief at the news she had just been delivered. She took the final flight of steps two at a time as made her way to her attic quarters. She grabbed the small stack of books that belonged to her along with her clothes and belongings. With shaking hands, she shoved everything she owned into a threadbare carpet bag. A few minutes later, she rushed back downstairs, out the front door, and into the waiting carriage.

She was a maid no more.

Justina could scarcely imagine what was happening. She was a Lady — a *real Lady*. She could not have been happier if she had been told that she was suddenly a princess. She stared out of the window of the carriage, trying desperately to get a glimpse of Helmsford Park, but all she saw were rolling hills and farm houses.

"Lady Justina, I assure you that you are in no danger of missing Helmsford Park," Stephen said with a smile.

"Oh, I know. I simply cannot wait to see it with my own eyes. Then maybe I will believe that all of this is real."

"My Lady, it is quite real. You may rely on it." The solicitor was grinning now.

Justina blushed at his smile. He was so handsome and charming, and he treated her with deference, making her feel like a Lady despite her plain clothes and worn out shoes. And there she was sitting with him as his *equal. No,* she realized with a start. Her new standing ranked her even higher. It was a world gone mad.

"Mr. Montgomery, sir, I am not sure I understand how this happened. Please explain to me once more."

"It would be my pleasure," he answered in a calm, soothing tone. "Your father was married secretly to your mother many years ago. It was a… well… a frowned-upon relationship. To maintain his ranking in society, your father kept the alliance a secret. After your birth, your mother became frail and ill. Unfortunately, she passed away. Your father was heartbroken, but he continued to keep the entire affair secret. After your mother's death, he arranged for your care with Mrs. Waverly."

Justina didn't take her eyes from Stephen's face. Her mind whirled, trying to digest what he was telling her.

"So, no one knew of his marriage to my mother?" she asked, incredulous.

"No one knew." Stephen shook his head.

"A fact that your father came to regret. He ended up marrying again, a match that was condoned by his parents. He subsequently had three more children. Your half-siblings."

"I have siblings..." Justina shook her head with wonder.

"The Earl was beside himself with grief, but felt that since you were born in mystery he could not acknowledge you. He paid Mrs. Waverly to raise you. He came to regret that decision and upon his death, he wanted to ensure that you had every luxury and privilege that you had been denied because he had not claimed you publically. In his will, he has officially recognized you as a daughter and has seen to your future wealth."

"When shall I meet my brother and sisters?"

"Upon our arrival. Although, I must warn you that there may be some concerns."

"Why would there be concerns?"

"Your brother has inherited the land, the title, and the property. Your sisters have generous dowries set up in their names, but you have been granted an extravagant annuity and a large dowry. There may be some jealousy."

"They would be jealous of *me*?" Justina couldn't fathom the notion.

"Yes, I am afraid so. Your father was quite wealthy, and you are now one of the wealthiest young ladies in all of England. Your annuity is worth more than what your father left to your sisters."

Justina's eyes grew even wider. "I am wealthy?"

"Yes, my dear, you are wealthy," Stephen said as he patted her hand. "Forgive me for calling you dear. I feel honored to be able to assist you in any way that I can. I'm delighted to have been the messenger to bring you such good news. I had great respect for your father, and I am privileged to be the man he trusted with his last wishes."

"Thank you," she said. Her cheeks grew warm. Mr. Montgomery was so handsome and when he touched her hand, she felt an unaccustomed spark of excitement. He was the first man who had ever showed her any inclination of kindness.

"Lady Justina, there over the horizon, you will see your new home, Helmsford Park."

Justina bit her lip with excitement. She peered out the window just as the grand establishment came into view. It was enormous, much larger than she had dared to expect. The house was a gray stone mansion with many windows and corner towers, and it stood easily four stories tall.

"Mr. Montgomery, is that it? Can that really be Helmsford Park?"

"It is your new home."

"How many rooms does it have? It looks to be amazingly large."

"By my estimation, nearly one hundred, counting the servants' quarters."

"I am unable to believe this. This cannot be real."

"It will all be real soon enough. Once you have arrived and are settled, we must prepare you for your life as a Lady. We must order a wardrobe for you at once. I have been given the responsibility of overseeing these details. We do not have much time. Your brother will be hosting a hunting party in two weeks, and there will be dinners and a Ball. You must have the proper attire to look the part of a Lady of society."

Justina gripped the side of the carriage. "Sir, you have been so good to me. I'm sure I shall never be able to repay you."

"It is my pleasure to assist you in any way that I can. It is not every day that I am graced with a client as beautiful as you."

Justina felt heat creep up her neck. She averted her eyes, but it didn't matter. His finely chiseled face, his dark curls and his probing, mysterious eyes were imprinted on her mind. His easy smile and charm made her feel as though she actually *was* beautiful — a feeling that was indeed strange and unfamiliar to her.

"I don't know what to say," she murmured.

"Do not say a word. And do not worry about anything. Your joy is my reward. Your father would have wanted to see you happy, and I gave my word to make that happen."

Justina gazed at the handsome solicitor as the carriage turned into the tree-lined lane leading to the house. He smiled at her with warmth, and his eyes were kind.

She glanced out the window, overcome with nerves as they drew closer to the house.

She clasped and un-clasped her hands, feeling their dampness. How would her siblings receive her? She had always wanted brothers and sisters, and now her wish was about to come true. She prayed they would welcome her with kindness.

They arrived at the entrance of Helmsford Park and Stephen assisted her as she stepped out of the carriage. He walked with her to the door and past the staff as they curtsied and bowed. Justina giggled nervously. She was being treated exactly as she imagined royalty would be.

Just inside the door, they were met by a man who was dressed in an expensive tailored jacket and trousers. Justina had been a maid long enough to recognize the craftsmanship that went into his clothes and his boots. She realized to her astonishment that she must be in the presence of her half-brother, the ninth Earl of Rosedale.

"Justina, it is a pleasure to welcome you home," he said somewhat stiffly.

Justina curtsied, "My Lord, it is my pleasure."

He waved his hand through the air. "We are family. You have no need to curtsy or address me in such a manner. You may call me George. May I present your sisters, Augusta and Marjorie?"

Any warmth Justina may have felt at her brother's welcome was soon forgotten with the icy stares she received from her half-sisters. In the last hour, she had been looking forward to having sisters, but she soon learned that her sisters were not of the same mind. They definitely were not pleased to be related by blood to a lady's maid.

"Lady Augusta. Lady Marjorie. I am so happy to meet you," she said, swallowing hard.

Lady Augusta huffed out her breath. "You do not have to call us Lady, since you are no longer a servant. If you are to call Helmsford Park home, you better learn how to behave, or else I fear you will be an embarrassment."

Justina felt ashamed. "Yes, of course."

Lady Marjorie smirked. "And those clothes… I hope no-one important sees you in our house wearing such a dress. They will think you are a scullery maid."

"Augusta, Marjorie, be civil," George said.

Justina looked at Stephen and mouthed the words, "Don't leave me."

The solicitor reached for her hand and gave it a little squeeze. If Justina had been raised as a Lady, she would have known how forward his behavior was, but she did not recognize it as such. She felt much better and wished that he could stay at Helmsford Park.

She did not want to be left alone with these people who were her family.

Chapter Five

Justina looked at her reflection in the mirror. She was unable to believe that the upper-class Lady staring back at her was truly *her*. She was dressed in a cerulean gown with silver gossamer embroidery. Her maid, Patience, had twisted her hair and interlaced silver ribbon in the curls in an elaborate style that made her neck appear long and graceful.

The gown was made of a silk that was far more exquisite than any material she had ever worn before in her life. She looked as though she were a fairy princess — she only wished that she would be able to act the part. She was terrified that she would forget her manners. Tonight was to be the first dinner party she had ever attended, and she knew that all eyes would be on her. She took a deep breath and tried to remember everything she had been told.

"Oh Patience, I am so nervous."

"My Lady, just watch everyone else and do what they do. You will be fine. No one expects you to be perfect. Just enjoy yourself and don't drink too much wine as you aren't used to it."

"You have done such a good job making me look like a real Lady. What would I do without you? My sisters expect me to be perfect. They told me not to embarrass them."

"Nonsense, you go show them you are just as much a Lady as they are. They aren't so perfect themselves."

Justina could tell by Patience's tone that there was no love lost between her maid and her half-sisters.

Justina giggled. She was grateful for Patience. She knew that she was acting with more familiarity than was proper, but she couldn't care. Patience seemed to be her only friend in the house. Her maid was an older woman, and she doted on her young mistress, which Justina deeply appreciated.

"My Lady, forgive me for speaking so harshly about your Ladyship's sisters. I meant no disrespect."

"None taken. This is your last chance, Patience. Do you want to trade places?"

Patience threw up her hands with exaggerated horror. "No, I do not. What would I have to say to those hoity-toities downstairs?"

"The same as me, not a word. I will just smile and act interested."

"Seems to me your training as a Lady's maid will do you well."

"You are terrible, but you make a good point." Justina looked at her reflection again.

"Yes I do, my Lady."

"Thank you for this, Patience. For your kindness and friendship. Perhaps, I can see that you have an increase in wages. No promises, however. I have no idea how these things work. How do I look?" Justina twirled in front of Patience.

"You look like a Lady. But no twirling, I'm thinking. And no sliding down the banister."

Justina laughed again. "You should have been a court jester at the Prince Regent's palace."

"I will say a little prayer for you, my Lady. Just hold your head up and remember, you have just as much a right to be here as any of them."

"Thank you," said Justina quietly as she took a deep breath and walked out of her chambers toward the grand marble staircase.

This was to be the first event of the hunting party that was hosted at the estate every year. Tonight, Justina would be attending the dinner, and seated at the table, with members of the aristocracy. Her heart pounded, and she could scarcely contain her excitement or her fear. She knew that she looked the part. Now, she just had to act the part. She had never felt so anxious as she descended the stairs into the great hall.

~~~~~
~~~~~

Justina heard voices coming from the drawing room, and she knew that there were to be over thirty guests in attendance. All eyes would be on her as she walked into that room, and she was not sure she was ready to take the first step.

She thought she might take a few minutes by herself to collect her thoughts. She walked to the enormous stone fireplace in the great hall and stood in front of it, watching the fire dance as the logs burned.

The crest of the Earl of Rosedale was carved in the stone above the fireplace. She was the daughter of the Earl of Rosedale. She should be strong and proud that she was a member of this family, no matter what anyone thought of her.

She gathered her wits and tried to find the inner strength to face the room full of strangers. How she dreaded facing the disgusted glares of her half-sisters. She was so lost in her thoughts that she did not hear someone walk up behind her until it was too late.

"My Lady, are you quite well?" The masculine voice was deep and resonant.

Justina gasped in surprise and turned to face a tall man with blond hair and the features of an aristocrat. He looked like a prince, and she wondered if he was, as she curtsied before him. "Yes, my Lord, I am quite well."

"I am pleased to see that you are. I thought you may have caught a chill. Allow me to introduce myself. I am Charles Seton, Duke of Wockshire. It is my pleasure to make your acquaintance."

"Oh dear! I mean, Your Grace. I am Justina Stanley, daughter of the late Earl of Rosedale. Please forgive me, I have never stood in the presence of a Duke before."

Charles smiled at her, his eyes shining with clear admiration. Justina wondered how he really perceived her. She assumed, by his deference and cordial manner, that he was ready to accept her as part of the ton.

"The flames are reflected in your green eyes, Justina Stanley. I dare say you are not only stunning, but unaware of it."

Justina's lips parted. She had no idea how to respond.

"My dear, it is true that I am a Duke. But to you, I am to be only Charles Seton, since you are the half-sister of the present Earl, my good friend George."

"Yes, Your Grace. I am the newest member of the family."

"Your story is quite interesting, although I doubt I am privy to the whole of it. I am sure that all of these changes must be overwhelming."

"You speak about it as though you know everything."

"I do have you at a disadvantage. I know most of the facts of your story from your brother, and you know nothing of me. That hardly seems sporting, does it?"

"I'm embarrassed to admit that I was a Lady's maid before I suddenly became part of this family."

"Do not be embarrassed. It seems to me that you are living a novel. I would consider myself fortunate if I were you to have had such an adventure in life."

"Surely not, Your Grace," she said. "While I was working as a maid, I am not certain I would have described my situation as fortunate. It was taxing work."

"Not many people are ever granted the opportunity to be both a maid and a Lady. I dare say you have experiences and stories that would make for an interesting book, and I'm sure you could entertain almost anyone in conversation. I can honestly tell you, without fear of reproach, that not many Ladies would be as interesting to speak with as you."

"Your Grace, I... uh, thank you. That is most kind of you to say. My sisters have treated me as though I still belong downstairs in the servants' hall. I fully expect them to ask me to fetch them tea or prepare their bath. Yet, you tell me that I should embrace my past and wear it proudly. This seems most unusual."

"I would wager that your sisters' comments are motivated by jealousy. You are far more handsome than either of them, and, in case you have failed to notice, neither of them is married, despite their rank. As to the matter of your past, embrace it. You were not born into this life, why pretend that you were? I believe with your beauty and your title that soon, it won't matter who you were before this moment. A Lady might not be proud of such a past, but then you are quite extraordinary."

"Your Grace, your words are most reassuring, I will pay heed to your thoughts, but may I be so bold as to ask a question?"

"By all means, I look forward to your inquiry."

"Why are you in the great hall and not in the drawing room with the other members of society?"

"I am afraid you have caught me. I was making my escape to the library before dinner when I beheld you, a beautiful Lady, possibly in distress, languishing by the fireplace. In truth, I find small talk tedious, and the conversations at such events quite dull. You have held my attention for the better part of ten minutes. I wager that is record for me."

"Are Ladies in society so boring that you are unable to endure their conversation?" This was a completely new thought to Justina.

"Lady Justina, I believe that you will soon enjoy the pleasure of finding out for yourself the answer to that question. I was going to the library, but now that I have found you, would you do me the honor of allowing me to escort you to the drawing room?"

"Yes, Your Grace, I would like that very much."

"As would I. But you must promise me that you will not discuss fashion, hairstyles or gossip. Do I have your solemn promise?"

Justina laughed. "You have my word. I would not know where to begin to discuss fashion and hairstyles. And I am unaware of any gossip—except regarding myself."

"Then we will get along splendidly," said Charles as he held out his arm for her. She placed her hand atop his, and together they walked into the drawing room. All eyes turned to watch them as they joined her brother George.

George and Charles laughed as old friends do, and Justina stood in their presence trying not to feel self-conscious. She was entranced by Charles. She could not keep herself from gazing upon his face as his blue eyes sparkled when he laughed. She had always imagined Dukes to be stuffy and unapproachable, but he was different. He was cool in his demeanor and manners, yet his smile was warm. And he had treated her—a former Lady's maid—as though she were a Duchess. He had made her feel as though she belonged in the room full of upper class ladies and lords. In his presence, she believed that she could brave the icy stares from her sisters and the gossipy whispers from the guests.

In the presence of this Duke, she could forget to be nervous. She told herself that if a Duke found her company acceptable, there was no reason why she should be shunned by the Lords and Ladies of the ton. She was wealthy and had a title, whether they chose to accept it or not. She was by rank, one of them. She was a Lady, now.

She just hoped that she could remember which fork to use at dinner.

Chapter Six

The hunting party had gone more successfully than Justina had hoped. She had not made a complete fool of herself at dinner, and the Duke kept her from being lonely for much of the time surrounding the meal. She only felt out of place when she was alone in the drawing room after dinner with the Ladies. By their very bearing and their talk, they seemed to consider themselves the select group of society, or the privileged few within upper class society.

Justina quickly discovered that all the members of the ton were Ladies and Lords, but not all Lords and Ladies were members of the ton. She learned that the ton was a powerful clique that decided all manner of details of society, from fashion, to who could join a club or be invited to tea. She soon found out that the Ladies at the hunting party were all members of this elite clique. All of them, except one, of course — her.

Rather than stand awkwardly in the drawing room, waiting for the gentlemen to return after their brandy and discussion of manly subjects in the smoking room, she made her way to the library instead. She found the company of books to be far superior to the social snubbing she was receiving at the hands of her sisters and their friends.

As the weekend continued, Justina found herself escaping to the library with regularity. It was in the library that the Duke often found her during the evenings. She had always loved to read and now she had thousands of books to choose from. The Duke confessed to her that he was an avid reader, also, and he made recommendations of books she may enjoy.

Oftentimes in the library, it was just the two of them, and they would spend a few minutes of pleasant conversation before joining the guests in the drawing room. It was there that Justina noticed that the gentlemen were far more receptive to speaking with her, while the Ladies treated her as though she belonged back in the kitchen with the staff. She wondered if there might be some truth to what the Duke and the solicitor had said after all. Was it possible that the Ladies were jealous of her?

Justina had not seen Mr. Montgomery in a week, and she wondered if he was well. With a bit of consternation, she admitted to herself that she had become not only fond of Stephen Montgomery, but she rather depended on him in her new life.

Her affection for Mr. Montgomery had a more comfortable, easy rhythm that her growing fondness for the Duke. For even with his kindness, the Duke seemed less approachable and more formidable than the solicitor.

Justina felt confused when she considered her feelings for the two men. They were both undoubtedly handsome, and both treated her as a Lady. When her thoughts ran along these lines, she scolded herself soundly. She was quite certain that neither would ever consider her as more than an acquaintance or friend.

She needed to put her silly romantic notions aside.

But that was easier said than done. Justina could not account for her mixed feelings, and she did her best not to dwell on them. Finally, she decided that she would rather spend her time *as a friend* enjoying the company of Charles Seton while he was with her, and then in the future — should he come around — she would enjoy the company of Mr. Montgomery *as a friend*.

By the time the hunting party came to an end, the Duke and Justina had indeed become close after a fashion. He had been her friendly face amongst unfriendliness, and she hoped against hope that she would see him in the future. The last night as the ball ended, they spoke by the fire in the great hall.

Justina felt breathless with both gratitude and something far more intimate. A warmth of affection spread through her as she gazed into his face. "Thank you for all that you have done for me. A man of your rank did not need to go to such lengths to make a former Lady's maid feel so welcome."

His eyes were dark, and his voice was low. "Justina, it has been my pleasure. I mean that from the bottom of my heart. I have found your company to be enchanting, and I sincerely hope that you consider me to be a friend."

And there it was. Those two words. *A friend*.

"Y-yes, I do," she stammered. She should be pleased that he called her a friend. After all, wasn't that what she had been striving for? But something deep inside yearned for more. "I consider you to be one of my dearest friends. Are all Dukes as kind of heart as you?"

"That I cannot say, but I will look for you in London. The season will be beginning after the Christmas holiday, and I hope that you will be in attendance."

"I am sure that my sisters would prefer I stay home and not embarrass them, but I promise that I will be there," she said, suddenly decisive.

"Your sisters and their friends are the product of idle time and idle minds."

Justina smiled. "I try not to mind them so much. Although, I do hate feeling like they are laughing at everything I do or don't do."

"My dear," he said, taking her hand in his large one, "do not worry. I will personally take you under my wing, and together we will make them beg for your friendship and good opinion."

She grinned, enjoying the sensation of her hand in his. "I don't know about begging, but if they could find something else to occupy their time, I would be pleased."

"Have no worries." He let go of her hand. "In London, you will be certain to meet many more people than this small clique. I must confess that I have always detested their plotting and tedious ways. I will enjoy sparring with them, and you are to be the winner."

"That sounds delightful. I will miss you." As soon as she uttered the words, Justina looked away, embarrassed that she had admitted such sentiment aloud.

But the Duke looked pleased. "I have to admit that I shall miss you as well. These past few days have been most entertaining. I ask that you permit me a correspondence with you."

"Why, yes. If you so choose."

He leaned down and kissed her cheek as they stood by the fireplace. Justina's heart nearly bolted from her chest as she stared into his blue eyes. He wished her good evening, and with a charming smile, he turned away to take his leave.

~~~~~

In the following weeks, the Duke kept his word. He sent her letters and even an early Christmas present, a small golden locket that was inscribed in Latin and English, *To thine own self, be true*. It was such a thoughtful gift—the only gift she had received from a man, and from a Duke no less.

Near Christmas, the family gathered for dinner and to exchange presents. Justina thought it odd that they exchanged gifts so early in the season, but evidently their father, the Earl, had preferred it that way. Justina was not surprised that the only gift she received was from her brother. Her sisters were cruel and seemed to be revel in their poor treatment of her.

"We simply had no idea what you would like," Augusta purred from the settee.
~~~~~

"We assumed we wouldn't be able to match the type of gifts you are accustomed to," Marjorie added, with a sly smile.

It was then that Justina finally came to the conclusion that she would endure their underserved hostility no more.

She took a sip of wine and as her sisters spoke French in front of her and laughed, her good nature reached its limits. She addressed them in a tone of voice that was not the least bit convivial.

"Sisters, for weeks I have endured your rudeness and your efforts to make me feel as though I have no place in this house. What have I ever done to deserve your wrath?"

Augusta straightened her posture to that of a cement pillar.

She answered, "You do *not* have a place in our home. You do *not* belong here. Your suspicious birth makes you calling me your sister repulsive. I prefer that you leave and never come back."

Justina gaped at her. Even knowing her nastiness, Justina had never thought Augusta would speak her mind so boldly. "Are you angered because of my money and the annuity?"

"That money does *not* belong to you, and it never did. Father hid you away for a purpose. Just because he had a moment of guilt doesn't change anything. Your mother was *common*. Worthless to society." Augusta sniffed. "If it was not for you, we would have it as our right. Marjorie and I are the true daughters of the Earl of Rosedale. Instead, our inheritance is in the possession of the daughter of some *trollop*."

Justina's anger grew.

"How dare you call my mother a trollop! From what I have seen of your behavior, you are hardly better than one yourself. So, it is only the money? Take it then. I don't care!" At that point, Justina was so hurt and angry, she hardly knew what she was saying.

"We would *never* accept anything from you — except your farewell." Augusta bit out the words.

George cleared his throat. "Ladies, please. This is *not* how father would want us to act. He was very clear in his will. Justina is a part of this family and should be treated as such."

"That is easy for you to say," spit out Marjorie. "You have inherited property and a title, and what are we left with? We have only our dowries and your generosity."

"Maybe if you spiteful old cats were less cruel, you would be married by now!" Justina cried, beyond caring. "Surely, you are well past marriageable age."

"That is rich coming from you!" said Augusta.

"Fine," Justina said, the fight draining out of her. "If you insist that I leave, then I shall. George, I understand that we have a house in London. Is that correct?"

"Yes, but it won't be open for a month."

"Please. Can it be opened immediately?"

"But the season doesn't begin until January."

"*Please*, George. I don't care, I can't spend another week in a house where I am clearly unwanted. I will leave first thing in the morning."

"What about the staff?" he asked.

"I care not what you do. As long as the house is open. If there are any expenses, take them from my account. I find myself in a unique position to afford it."

George looked genuinely crestfallen by her decision. He let out his breath in a long sigh. "All right, Justina. I will have Mr. Montgomery handle it."

"Perfect. If necessary, my dear sisters, you may make other arrangements for your stay in London when you come. I am certain that my presence would be too odious for you to share the same residence again. George, I will see you in January." She stood up and stormed out of the drawing room.

It was Christmastime, the season of love and family, but Justina found herself leaving for London to escape her family and perhaps find a love and acceptance that she would never know at Helmsford Park.

Chapter Seven

The house in London was large. At first, Justina thought she would be lonely, wandering around as the only member of the family in residence. To the contrary, she loved every second of it. Her friendly maid Patience accompanied her to London, as did a member of the kitchen staff, a footman, and two housemaids. It was a small staff for the size of the house, but Justina only frequented the drawing room, the dining room, the library, and her bedchamber.

Much to her delight, the staff that accompanied her were relaxed without the housekeeper and butler to strictly enforce every rule. After her time spent working as a maid to the Harrington's and then her rough treatment at the hands of her sisters, Justina rather enjoyed the peace and relaxed atmosphere of the roomy London house during the holiday season.

It was magical.

The upper class remained in their country estates for the month of December, but the wealthy Londoners had much to keep them occupied. Snow covered the trees in the park, and chestnut vendors were found on the corners. There were choir performances at churches and shows in the theaters. Justina was certain that no member of her family ever spent Christmas week in London, and she swore to herself that she would never miss it again.

London was especially pleasant for Justina due to the presence of Mr. Montgomery. His firm had been the preferred legal establishment to the aristocracy for generations.

He therefore enjoyed privilege and popularity. He not only kept Justina company, but he took her out and about. She was well-received in the houses of his friends, and no one was overly concerned about anybody's status.

It was nearly Christmas day when she received a letter from the Duke. It was short and polite. When she had first arrived in London, she had sent him a letter. When a reply was not forthcoming, she assumed that he had forgotten about her, which she found curious.

As much as Justina enjoyed herself with Mr. Montgomery, she found herself thinking of the Duke from time to time. However, when he did not answer her correspondence, she supposed that he did not miss her nearly as much as he'd said he would.

Justina looked down at the gold locket he had sent to her as a present and wondered if she should take it off.

She read the inscription once again and decided that she would continue wearing it, if only to remind herself that, regardless of the Duke's feelings for her or anyone else, she should remain true to herself.

She turned to Stephen Montgomery for company instead. As the days passed, she grew more and more appreciative of his steady presence, his sense of humor, and his good spirits.

It was after dinner at a judge's house one evening that they had an interesting conversation. Their dinner companions were playing whist, and Stephen and Justina were enjoying tea by the fire.

Stephen gazed at her fondly. "I have enjoyed this Christmas season more than I ever have before. You have enriched the season for me."

A warm feeling spread through her.

"Thank you, Stephen. I have deeply enjoyed our time together also. And I cannot begin to express how much I have adored Christmastime here in London. I have decided that I will never again spend Christmas anywhere but here. My new family doesn't know what they are missing."

Stephen's eyes glowed, but then he grew somber.

"There is something I want to speak with you about regarding a sensitive subject. Justina, as a Lady, are you certain that you do not mind being seen with me at the theater or accompanying me to dinner at the homes of judges and merchants?"

Justina was quick to counter his concern. "No! You must never think that. Your generosity has touched me to my very heart. You have done everything in your power to personally see to my happiness this season. I am certain that you had plans before my sudden arrival here in London, and yet, you and your acquaintances have welcomed me and made me feel as though I was at home, more so than my own family."

"From the beginning, I was afraid you were going to encounter resistance with your new family. You might well remember that I tried to warn you of your sisters' spite."

"Yes, and you were right. I should have heeded your warning and left Helmsford Park at an earlier date. The hearts of those women are so hardened against me that they even refused to take my money. I offered them my annuity, and they were so stubborn that they would rather be unhappy without money rather than accept a gift from me."

"They are fools."

"I believe you are right. Although, now that I am thinking more calmly, I believe I was a fool to offer them my money in the first place." She gave a wry laugh. "But now I have come to a conclusion. I would like to purchase a house in London, so that I may never have to see them again. Can I do that?"

He gave her a look of admiration.

"As your solicitor, I would be honored to advise you in this matter."

"I can think of no one I would like to advise me more than you. I am counting on your help."

"We can start looking for a suitable house. I am certain that setting up your own residence is the best possible idea, but I would wait until spring to do so."

"Spring? But why should I wait? I want to buy a house now. I cannot endure the thought that my sisters could be joining me soon here in London."

"I can promise that it will be worth it if you wait. Spring is the best time to purchase property."

Justina was not happy with this proclamation. However, it was Stephen she was speaking to, and he always had her best interest at heart.

"You know that I trust you completely," she said.

"And I am honored by that trust. I want you to be happy." His look seemed deep with meaning, and Justina found herself blushing. Did he care for her beyond their friendship? Was he developing real feelings for her?

She gave a small nervous laugh, lightening the mood. Silently, she warned herself not to read anything into his words or gestures. Her imagination was sometimes too prone to take the vaguest evidence of something and enlarge it beyond recognition.

Of course, they had been spending a lot of time together, and she was unsure if it was the magic of the season or some kind of magic between them, but she found herself considering him as more than just her solicitor and friend. Despite her self-admonition, she thought of him often and always looked forward to their next meeting.

His dark eyes, devilish good looks and potent charm were a combination that was proving more difficult for her to resist, yet still, she was completely unsure of his feelings toward her. He never spoke a word that hinted at anything more than friendship.

~~~~~

Christmas Eve came, and the house was decorated with greenery. Justina made sure that the staff had a feast unlike any they had ever enjoyed before. It would be their little secret she told them, for she was in no mood to hear any censure of how she was treating her staff with too great a familiarity.

Naturally, they were perfectly willing to keep the secret if it meant a delicious feast suitable for the richest of Dukes.

That evening, Justina joined them in the servants' dining room, and they all had a marvelous time. They sang carols and drank punch and wassail. Being with the servants made Justina feel as though she was home. She had no one glaring at her and telling her that she was an embarrassment. Although, she was well aware that she was ignoring a rule regarding socializing with the servants, but she no longer cared about the rules, at least not on Christmas Eve.

The next day being Christmas, Justina woke early and attended Christmas services with Patience. They returned to the house and enjoyed a delectable lunch of roast goose and fig pudding. She had just sat down in the library with a glass of Christmas punch when the footman announced the arrival of a visitor.
~~~~~

Justina was shocked to see Charles Seton walk through the library door. She jumped from her chair, nearly spilling her drink.

"Happy Christmas! I brought you a gift," the Duke said warmly. He handed her a large present, wrapped in the strangest of ways with the paper suspended over what looked to be sticks at each corner of the gift. With her heart beating wildly, Justina opened it and discovered exotic blooms from the tropics. She breathed in their scent and was overwhelmed by his generosity.

Flowers such as these were ridiculously expensive and were grown only by the wealthiest in their hothouses.

"I have never seen flowers such as these before now, at least outside the pages of books cataloguing botanicals. Thank you, Charles."

"I thought they would brighten your day, here in the London winter."

"But Charles, London is perfectly wonderful during this season. I have had such a lovely time. "

"I came to wish you a merry Christmas," he said, gazing at her. "I could not bear you being alone here in this big house."

"I am not alone. I have a few members of staff."

"When I received your letter, I wrote to George. I hope you are not vexed with me." She wondered why in the world he would write to George about her, but she decided not to inquire. She was too pleased to see him to spoil it by thinking of her family.

"I was not expecting you. This is a grand surprise. I will ring for tea."

"George told me what your sisters said to cause you to leave during Christmas. I feel partially to blame for this."

"How in the world would you be to blame?" she asked, her eyes wide. "You have only been kind to me. I find you blameless in this matter."

"I am afraid that you should not find me so without knowing why I consider myself at fault."

"You are a gentleman and a Duke. I am certain that there is no conceivable way you could be accountable for the ill-tempered behavior of my sisters."

"Justina. You are wrong." He sat down beside her on the settee by the fire. His leg brushed against hers as he sat down, and she felt her pulse race. Had he brushed against her on purpose? She was so inexperienced with such things that she had no idea. She only knew that his touch confused her—made her self-conscious, unbalanced.

She was acutely aware that they were alone in the library. The servants were elsewhere in the house. At this realization, she became flustered and looked about nervously, but he did not appear to notice. He licked his full lips and leaned in closer. Her eyes went huge, and she could almost feel his mouth touching hers when the footman knocked to signal the arrival of tea.

Justina nearly jumped out of her skin. Guilt assailed her. What had they been about to do? She inhaled sharply and felt a sudden sense of disloyalty to Stephen.

The footman brought the tea, sandwiches and cakes, and withdrew. When they were alone once more, Charles finished his explanation. Much to Justina's relief, he ignored the entire matter of his attempted kiss as if it had never happened. "I am afraid that your sister Augusta has more reason to dislike you than just the money you have inherited. She may find our friendship to be even more reason to loathe you."

"*Our* friendship? Yours and mine? Why would she care about who I am friends with?"

"Ordinarily, I would tend to agree with you, but unfortunately you chose me as your companion at the hunting party. Augusta and I have a history, or rather she *wishes* that we had a history."

"What do you mean you have a history? What kind of history?" Justina felt dread edge into her heart.

"Your brother George and I have been friends for a number of years. It soon became apparent that his sister, Augusta, had feelings for me. As you might imagine, George thought it was a splendid idea that I might one day marry his sister. I remember we spoke about it."

"What happened?"

"There were many concerns. The greatest obstacle was my family and our traditions. But beyond that, I was unable to reciprocate her feelings. I knew that if I was allowed to marry her — and my family would have opposed it — I would never be happy. I found her to be petty, small-minded, and dull. I thought that I had managed to make it abundantly clear that we did not have a future."

He frowned a little as he spoke. "Seeing that she was George's sister, I tried to spare her any additional heartbreak by making my intentions known at the earliest moment - that I would not be marrying her. Obviously, she had already developed feelings for me, and I was too late."

"Do you believe she still cares for you?"

"Yes, unfortunately, I find that to be the case. After the death of your father, but before you arrived, George sent a letter to me listing the details of your father's will. He made the suggestion that Augusta cared a great deal for me and that her dowry was still generous. He wondered whether I would reconsider marrying her since I had not found a suitable woman to be the next Duchess."

Justina felt sick to her stomach. In spite of Augusta's horrid treatment of her, Justina couldn't help but feel a bit sorry for her half-sister. "Charles, if she still cares for you, then you are right to suspect that our friendship may be a thorn in her side. It is no wonder that she despises me — between your attention and the fact that I inherited the money she thought she stood to gain."

The Duke shook his head. "I would say that she considers you to be little more than a thief, and I must say that I understand how she came to such a conclusion."

Justina blanched, her face draining of color. "What do you mean by suggesting that I am a thief?"

He moved closer to her and answered in a whisper, "You have stolen my heart and my peace of mind." He was as near as her breath. "It is undoubtedly a sentimental notion, but one that I find to be the truth."

Her shoulders relaxed, and she regretted her quick words. The Duke really was so sweet. He leaned in again, and this time there was no interruption from a footman bringing tea.

From the moment the Duke's lips touched hers, Justina experienced a sensation unlike anything she had ever known. She felt herself slipping into a state of wonder. He kissed her kips, her cheeks, and her eyelids, and despite herself, she melted into his arms.

He gave her another kiss and then held her as the fire burned brightly in the fireplace, and the snow fell outside the window. Justina wanted to be content in his arms. She wanted to feel *right*, like she belonged. But she couldn't get Stephen out of her mind.

Yet, Stephen had never made any overture toward her. Not really. Justina was certain that he only considered her a friend.

And she liked the Duke. She *did.*

But there was something else bothering her, too. Something that had been niggling at her since she'd first met the Duke of Wockshire. She did not want to ruin the moment with such a question, but she felt that it was important.

"Charles?"

"Yes, Justina," he murmured.

"You didn't marry Augusta, but you still have not married anyone else. How can a Duke manage to avoid matrimony for so long?"

"I am afraid the answer to that question is not simple. We should discuss it at another time, not at Christmas."

Justina could not imagine why he wouldn't want to discuss the subject. And what had he meant when he'd said his family would not have permitted his marriage to Augusta? What secret was he keeping?

He had taken the liberty of kissing her, and he seemed to have feelings for her, yet he did not want to discuss his reasons for not marrying.

She thought of how her mother had married for love, but had been set aside as inferior and not worthy of being recognized in public. Justina refused to end up like her, a woman whose love and devotion went unappreciated.

A woman who ended up dying alone.

Perhaps Justina was being a bit melodramatic in her thinking, but she had to know. She faced him squarely.

"You have come to London to see me, and now here you are, by the fireside with me, holding me. I could be risking my reputation, such as it is, by entertaining you here without a proper chaperone. I feel that I must have an answer now. I do not mean to force your hand, but something inside—something in my heart—tells me that I must know why you are still not married."

He shifted with obvious discomfort and stood up. He walked to the fireplace and stared into the fire.

"Justina, I am afraid that you may not like what I must say. My answer will not bring you comfort. Can we find no means to avoid this? Can we not enjoy our moment together on this beautiful Christmas afternoon?"

"No, we cannot avoid this. My feelings for you could become deeper with every moment that passes. As I sit here with you, I feel I am no longer in control of my destiny. It is for that reason that I must insist on knowing why you have not married."

He did not look at her as he spoke.

"I care for you as I have never cared for another woman. There can be no doubt of my feelings for you, try as I might to keep them under control. I find you to be the woman of my dreams, yet to answer your question, you are forcing me to hurt you."

Justina could feel her heart racing. She heard his words, but why wouldn't he look at her when he spoke them? She wondered if she wanted to know his answer after all. But despite her rising anxiety, she knew that she needed to hear the truth. She could not remain in such a state of confusion and unknowing.

"Go on and tell me why you must hurt me."

"Of course, you know that I am a Duke. My family is in possession of one of the noblest lineages in the realm. My family has eternally made it clear that it is my responsibility to find a wife from my own class with a pure and untainted lineage. I have been unable to find a wife from among my own rank that I find even the slightest bit attractive, yet I am bound to marry to produce an heir."

Justina stared at him. "Charles, do you mean that you can only marry the daughter of a Duke?"

"That is the tradition of my family. It has always been that way for us. And that is what I did not want to say to you. I find myself losing the battle that rages deep within me. I have searched for a long time to find a woman who will be my wife and bear children of the highest noble blood. I have never found one that I could marry in all good conscience. Now, I am even more frustrated in my search."

The Duke returned to Justina and reached for her hand as he sat beside her. She allowed him to take it. Tears welled in her eyes. So now, she had the truth. Of all the Dukes in the land, she had to become fond of one whose family would never accept her. *Never.*

"Justina, I did not count on meeting you, and after I did meet you, I never imagined that I would feel toward you as I do. Can we not always be as close we are now, no matter whom I may have to marry? Can we not continue seeing each other?"

She jerked her hand away from his. What was *he saying?* Who did he think she was? "Absolutely not! How can you suggest such a thing?" She glared at him with disbelief. "My mother may have chosen to love a man who would not publicly claim her, but I will not."

He leaned close, his eyes intense. "I cannot live without you. You must understand, even if you were as Augusta and the known and accepted daughter of noble birth of an Earl, I still could not marry you. Don't you understand? I am bound by four centuries of tradition. It is my responsibility to protect the title and the blood line of the house of Wockshire."

"What is wrong with you? And what was wrong with my father? How can you justify taking advantage of a woman's heart? How can you sacrifice the love of a woman which she would freely give? For the sake of *your* reputation or so that *your* blood line remains pure? If this is love among the upper class, I want nothing to do with it."

Justina stood on trembling legs. Her heart wrenched inside her. How could she have been so wrong about this man? How could she have allowed herself to be swept under his spell?

"Justina," he cried, standing up. He grasped her arm. "Please reconsider. I care for you. I might even love you."

Her mouth dropped open.

"And this is how you show it? By asking me to become your woman on the side!"

She forced back her tears. Straightening her shoulders and raising her chin, she strode from the library. The tears began falling then, and she let them fall. He couldn't see them now. She did not even bother to ask him to leave. She just climbed the stairs to her bedchamber and threw herself on her bed.

She assumed that he must have left sometime after that because a knock at her door at dusk announced the unexpected arrival of Mr. Stephen Montgomery.

ARIETTA RICHMOND, GRACE AUSTEN, ISABELLA THORNE,
KATHERINE KEATS AND SOPHIA WILSON

Chapter Eight

Stephen was waiting in the drawing room when she came downstairs. She was both pleased and relieved to see him. She swallowed back the bitterness of her afternoon with the Duke. She needed some Christmas cheer, and seeing Stephen expectantly waiting for her, provided it.

"Lady Justina, how are you this fine Christmas day?" he asked with a warm smile.

"Better, now that you are here," she answered honestly.

"I am glad to hear you say so. I have brought you a present."

Justina smiled, touched.

"How lovely. Thank you, Stephen."

"It's nothing much. I just knew you would be spending Christmas alone, so I brought Christmas to you."

Stephen walked out of the drawing room and left her. She couldn't see what it was he was doing, and she wondered what his surprise could be. Just having him there, cheered her immensely, and she wished that the Duke hadn't come to visit earlier. She was better off without him. She closed her eyes. But if the Duke hadn't come, she might still be deluding herself into thinking that his intentions toward her were pure — that innocent friendship was all he wanted.

She opened her eyes and let out a long sigh. She had cared for the Duke. Somewhere inside, she probably still did. But her new knowledge of his character was quickly eroding any affection she'd held for him. She clasped her hands together.

She heard the front door open and then she heard voices, several all at one time, laughing and merry. Justina was amazed to see madrigal players, several barristers, a judge, and two merchants and their wives enter the drawing room to wish her a happy Christmas.

Everyone that Stephen had brought was someone she had met during her time there. Tears moistened her eyes. She had friends there in London, *real* friends. And most of them were thanks solely to Stephen. Her spirits improved with each song that the madrigal players performed. They chose delightfully cheerful songs that she could hear all through the house as she slipped out to confer with Patience and the staff. They did not have enough punch to go around, but there was the wine cellar. Justina gave orders to open the wine cellar.

Twenty minutes later, a long table was set up in the great hall. Wine and punch were set out with cuts of cold pork, thick slices of bread, and crackers and cheese.

Justina was so thankful that the staff came through on short notice. She told Patience to be sure that they opened a bottle of wine for themselves.

"But my Lady, you've already provided us with a Christmas feast. This isn't necessary."

Justina squeezed her hand. "But it is."

In the drawing room, Justina was treated to a joyful Christmas party. Carols were sung, charades and blind man's bluff were played, even a hand or two of whist. During the entire evening, Justina found her eyes drawn to Stephen. He was jovial and smiling and winked at her when he caught her eye.

Stephen had managed to bring her Christmas. It was the best Christmas present she had ever received.

After several bottles of wine, the guests decided that they would dance. Everyone was having such a marvelous time that no one cared if someone made a misstep or turned to face the wrong partner. The music was happy, and the company was good-humored. The party lasted well into the early hours of the morning.

Finally, everyone but Stephen had departed.

Justina faced him with a wide, if somewhat tired, smile. "Stephen, this has been so wonderful. I am truly grateful."

"I am glad you enjoyed it. I hope you don't mind that I invited guests to your house without your permission."

"Not at all. It was a wonderful surprise. Tonight, you are truly my knight in shining armor."

She felt such a kinship with him that she stood on her tiptoes and kissed him on the cheek.

She heard his small gasp at her touch.

He clasped her hand to his chest and cleared his throat. "There is to be a masked Ball at the Lord Mayor's house this New Year's Eve. I am wondering if you would like to accompany me."

"A Ball?" She stifled a yawn. "Yes, that sounds like fun. I would be happy to accompany you."

Stephen smiled and let go of her hand. He bid her good evening. She wished him good morning, and they laughed as he left. She climbed the stairs and could not help but smile. Stephen and his friends had restored her lagging spirits. She hummed a Christmas carol all the way to her bedchamber, where she collapsed on her bed in exhaustion.

~~~~

Justina did not hear from the Duke in the days that followed Christmas, for which she was grateful. The more she pondered the situation with him, the more disillusioned she became. She found her feelings toward him turning first to anger and then to pity.

The Duke wasn't likely to ever find true love. Not with the expectations of his forefathers. She felt sorry for him, but that was all. Her confusion was gone, replaced by a surety of emotion that made her heart sing. Ever since Christmas had passed, she knew where her true affection lay.
~~~~

Three days after Christmas, Stephen sent her a lovely bouquet of flowers and stopped by for tea. She was always delighted by his presence, for he never asked for anything in return. He simply came and enjoyed her company, just as she enjoyed his.

Justina wondered how she had ever found herself wavering between him and the Duke.

~~~~~

The night of the New Year's Ball, Justina dressed in a beaded ruby-red ball gown. She had a black lace mask over her eyes, and her hair was curled in round ringlets held by a black tiara. Patience had once again outdone herself. Justina looked in the mirror and saw that she still wore the necklace Charles had given her. She felt an odd sensation in her heart as she unlocked the clasp and pulled it from her neck. She held the locket and thought of the words inscribed within. She *was* being true to herself. She opened a drawer in her desk and dropped the locket in it.

Stephen was waiting downstairs in the great hall when she descended the staircase. He was dressed as a cavalier, complete with a feather hat and mask. Justina paused for the slightest moment, taking in his appearance. He was strikingly handsome.

"Justina," he said with a low whistle, "you are breathtaking."

She smiled and floated down the steps.
~~~~~

She placed her hand on top of his to be led outside. "So are you," she responded with a smile.

His carriage waited out front. As they rode to the Lord Mayor's residence, Justina teased him. "Stephen, you are a handsome man. In that costume, I am afraid that I will have to fight other women for even a scrap of your attention."

His cheeks colored. "Don't be silly. Only you can hold my attention. That red dress makes you look like the fairy queen herself."

Justina was delighted with his compliment, and she wanted to keep their pleasant banter going. "You should be dressed as a highway man because I am certain you will steal hearts."

"Justina…" he said, his voice growing serious.

She tensed. Was he upset about something? "Yes, Stephen."

"It's nothing." He gazed out the carriage window. "Look, we are here."

The Lord Mayor's house was lit by candles and several footmen were standing outside in full livery. Flags and banners hung from the columns of the gray stone mansion. Guests were arriving from all directions, dressed in colorful costumes.

"Stephen, you didn't tell me it was going to be so well-attended."

"It always is. I thought you would enjoy the festivity."

"I am so pleased that you invited me," she exclaimed as the carriage came to stop.

A footman opened the door, and Stephen and Justina stepped out of the carriage. She glanced at Stephen and thought of the first time they had arrived somewhere together. It was back at Helmsford Park. She shook her head and looked at the handsome man at her side and could not help but smile at how long ago it all seemed. So much had changed.

Her *entire life* had changed.

The Lord Mayor himself greeted them and invited them to partake of a glass of punch and make merry. Stephen led Justina to the ballroom, and they immediately took to the floor to dance an Irish jig. Justina laughed with delight and danced with Stephen three dances in a row.

It was indeed a heady night. As Justina had predicted, some ladies hinted for a dance with Stephen. He obliged them, while various gentlemen lined up to dance with her. More than once, she caught Stephen's eye during the evening, and every time, his gaze made her blush.

All evening, they danced and laughed with Stephens's friends and acquaintances. Justina felt like she had entered the fairy realm, wondering if she would have to return to her life as a maid when it was over. She gazed at Stephen and hoped that she would always be this happy.

At the close of the ball, they climbed back into the carriage. Justina's feet were sore from all the dancing, and she fretted that she would be hobbling by the next morning. On the drive back, Stephen sat beside her in the conveyance instead of across from her.

He put his arm around her, and she laid her head sleepily on his shoulder. It had been a wonderful evening.

"Stephen, thank you for this evening… for Christmas… for New Year's… for everything," she murmured. "I have never had so much fun."

His arm tightened around her shoulder. "I told you when I met you that I wanted to see you happy."

"Yes, and you meant it. "

"I gave my word to your father. But I must admit something."

Justina had nearly dozed off, but at his words, she roused. A confession? She prayed it would not spoil her impression of him. He was her friend and her companion, and she could not imagine living in London without him.

"What must you admit?" She held her breath.

"Justina, do you remember when I told you to wait to buy a house until spring?"

"Yes."

"I was not completely honest. You can purchase a house anytime you want to, and I will help you."

"Then why? Why did you lie to me?" She worked to quell the sense of disappointment in her heart.

"I wanted to have time to win you over."

"You what?" She sat up straight and looked at his shadowed face.

"I know it was silly of me, but I have loved you since that day I saw you at Lady Harrington's."

Justina stared at him. Could it be true? She blinked, and the only thing she could think of to say was, "Stephen, I looked so dowdy in my maid's uniform."

"I did not see your maid's uniform. I saw a beautiful woman instead. I was not expecting to fall in love with you."

"You *love* me?" The words were beginning to take hold, and her heart raced.

"Yes, I love you. And to prove my sincerity, if you were to allow me to court you and to marry you, I would see to it that your annuity remains yours. I would not want you to ever doubt my love for you as genuine."

"Stephen, you want to court me and *marry* me? In public, for all to see?"

He gave her a strange look. "Why, of course, in public." He grabbed her hands. "I hope that I have not spoken hastily."

She shook her head, and tears came to her eyes. "I can think of no man I would rather be courted by than you," she said. Joy filled her heart.

She watched his expression and could see his excitement at her words.

"You agree then? Our courtship would perhaps give you time to grow to love me." Raw hope filled his voice.

"If you asked me to marry you today, I would say yes."

His eyes widened. "Justina, dare I hope? Could you... could you care for me?"

"I *already* care for you, and I know in my heart that I will love you deeply. I can think of nowhere else I would rather be than here in London with you."

He grabbed her up and hugged her to his chest. "My darling, we can live anywhere you choose. Anywhere! You have made me so happy."

He pressed his lips to hers, kissing her over and over again. And it felt *good* and *right*. Justina laughed and wrapped her arms around him.

Stephen tenderly touched her cheek with the back of his hand. "Justina, your happiness is my only concern. So, you will marry me and be my wife? After an appropriate time of courting?"

Justina thought of the locket in the drawer in her desk and the words inscribed on it: *To thine own self, be true*. She looked into Stephen's dark eyes, and she said without hesitation, "Yes. I will marry you. You love me for *me,* as I truly am, and you do not wish to change me. Just as I have no wish to change you. You are perfect as you are. I gladly say yes, my dearest Stephen."

Stephen leaned close until she could feel his breath caress her face. Again, he touched his lips to hers, at first tentatively, and then with a deeper pressure and need. She returned his kiss with an ardor equal to his own. A flame was ignited within her that began to burn brightly. The passion and love she felt in Stephen's kiss was only the promise of more to come.

As he held her in his arms, Justina closed her eyes and thought of their future together. He wanted a courtship, but she hoped to convince him to be married by spring. She opened her eyes and looked up at him. He smiled at her and reached for her hand, pressing it to his lips.

Justina laughed with joy. Marrying him was most definitely being true to herself and to her heart. And she didn't need the locket to tell her so.

The End

Thank you for reading *The Earl's Missing Christmas Heir!*

Are you interested in more

Grace Austen Regency Romances?

After the 'About the Author' section, you'll find a

sample of 'The Duke's Unwilling Bride'.

About the Author

Grace Austen loves everything Regency. Sometimes, she feels she was born in the wrong century! When she fell in love with Greg Austen and took his last name in marriage, she was delighted and honored to be sharing the name of the most famous Regency author of all.

Immersing herself in the world of Regency Romance is Grace's favorite thing to do. In her "real" life, she loves to spend time with her husband and three children. They have a little Malti-poo puppy who enjoys a good cuddle on anyone's lap - she's not fussy!

When not writing and caring for her family, Grace loves to explore antique shops, garden, talk long walks by the sea, and read! She loves to watch movies and munch on popcorn with her husband, and she would never turn away a piece of dark chocolate! Visit her at: http://www.GraceAusten.com

Get the News First!

If you **love Regency Romance**, go to:
http://graceausten.weebly.com/lp.html
to hear about all **New Grace Austen Romance Releases!**
I will let you know as soon as they become available!

Thank you, Friends! I appreciate your kind support. You are my motivation.

Much love,

Grace Austen

Escaping the Vicar

Amelia's father was in trouble. To save him from ruin, she agrees to be courted by the odious vicar, Mister Prior. Dutifully, she shoves aside her love for Mister Halberd, sacrificing everything for her family. The vicar swoops in like a vulture to claim his prize, but he doesn't count on Mister Halberd's plan to rescue Amelia. But Mister Halberd's time is running out, and Amelia's engagement seems written in stone. And then, there is still the matter of her father's secret debts...

The Duke's Daughter's Portrait

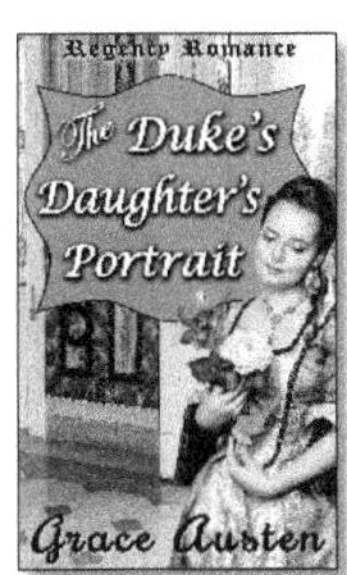

Amelia Gale has one purpose: Find a rich husband. She dons the finest gowns and makes herself available at every society ball. And she is miserable. Escaping into side rooms becomes normal. One evening, the Duke of Reinbrook is lurking near the fireplace with his own dark secret. The two spar. Fate takes over, and Amelia ends up painting his young daughter's portrait. Watching Amelia deal with his motherless daughter brings a salve to the Duke's heart. When Amelia's father makes a devastating arrangement for her future, she finds herself in need of the Duke to rescue her. But, will he?

Teaching the Earl's Daughter

After her father's devastating investment, Prudence feels compelled to take the position of music instructor to The Earl of Pembroke's daughter, Annabel. While Prudence grows to love her young charge, she has continual clashes with The Earl. He is insufferable, and Prudence decides she must leave. When Annabel grows deathly ill, she puts off her resignation. In the turmoil, she discovers the true reason for The Earl's harsh treatment. Will the truth free Prudence to see The Earl for who he is?

Lord Henry's Missing Fiancé

Lady Teresa's banishment to America has ended. On the ship back to Devonshire, she meets Lord Henry. Sparks fly, but unfortunately, he's engaged to Lady Eleanor. Teresa's father forces her into a courtship with the odious Colonel Wertford. When Lord Henry's fiancé goes missing, both Lord Henry and Lady Teresa find much more than either of them bargained for.

Rejecting the Earl

Margaret Cooper will stop at nothing to marry The Earl of Canark. His wealth and title will secure her family's future. However, she doesn't foresee the attentions of Mr. Fitzgerald, the lowly son of a knight. The man infuriates her with his bold and cunning wit. When The Earl disappears, Margaret risks everything to find him. Mr. Fitzgerald interferes. She finds out the shocking truth, and it's not what she thought it was...

Vexing the Earl

Dorothy Evans sails to England to claim her inheritance of the lavish estate of Moorway. She discovers a journal and reads of her aunt's doomed love affair with the Earl of Wainright. When Dorothy meets his son, she determines to seek revenge. But she doesn't count on the young Earl's dashing good looks and maddening charm. Will her revenge ruin every chance for happiness and love?

The Duke's Dangerous Love

In this clean and wholesome Regency Romance, Amy Chippering is plunged into the dark world of Kall Signon, the future Duke of Kent. Innocent of what his ominous secret really means, she allows herself to be swept away with his gorgeous good looks... Is there anyone to save her?

ARIETTA RICHMOND, GRACE AUSTEN, ISABELLA THORNE,
KATHERINE KEATS AND SOPHIA WILSON

Regency Romance

Here is Your Preview of
The Duke's Unwilling Bride

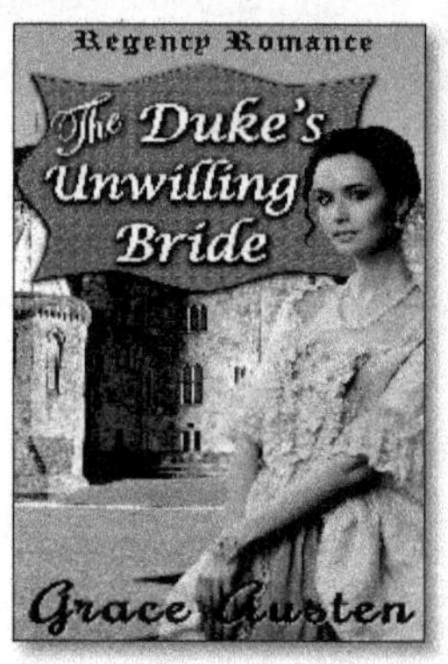

Stella Moorland is disenchanted with social privilege. Harboring noble, if misguided, notions, she falls in love with a servant. Oslo Riley, a young Duke, tries to warn her away, claiming he knows the servant's true character. But Stella will not be swayed. She is certain the Duke is simply flaunting his privilege...

Stella Moorland was one year shy of twenty years old when she found herself the last of her sisters as yet unwed. She was the fourth of four girls in the family, and her sisters were all happily married to titled men. Stella loved her sisters dearly and held them in the highest esteem, but she could never quite see eye-to-eye with them. She did not relish the idea of marrying a man simply because he was "suitable" as their mother would say.

"But Stella," her sister Beth said to her right after she became affianced. "A title is merely a product of birth. It does not mean you cannot love your husband. Robert means everything to me. You saw our courtship and how tender he was. The cold fact of his title does not take away from his genuine affection, or mine."

"What if I were to feel genuine affection for a servant boy or a boot black?"

Her sister gasped, obviously hoping very much that Stella was making a joke. "Stella, you don't mean...?"

"No, sister, there is no one special in mind. I only meant it as a hypothetical, but your horror is answer enough. Oh Beth, I do love you, but I'm afraid we are not of the same mind."

"At least, you can give the men that mother picks out for you a chance, Stella. Promise me that much. Swear to give them a chance into your heart. That is all I can ask of you."

"I will give them a chance," Stella said, but deep inside, she wasn't sure that she would.

In truth, Stella had walled-off her heart to any man who did not meet her exaggerated idea of worth.

She liked to think of herself as an open-minded woman, but she had an intense prejudice against her own kind. Stella spent a great deal of time reading novels, and in nearly all of them, she came upon hard truths about her class of people—they were often the villains. It was the servants and the schoolteachers who were kindly and good people.

Stella suspected she was taking this to heart in a way that was unhealthy, but she allowed her fantasy to continue. She liked to think she was a person who saw all of her fellow humans in an equal manner, but this was distinctly untrue. However, not in the way one would think.

Stella saw her societal lessers in a brighter, better light than those who were of the landed gentry. What Stella did not consider — what she refused to consider — was that she was not doing those "common" folks any favor.

In her assumption of their innocence and purity, Stella was attributing an identity to the working class that was not their own and was not a sweeping truth in any sense of the word.

In her own way, Stella was acting in the same manner as those of her own class who so infuriated her.

In her glossing over of the common humanity of servants and cooks, she was no better than those who looked down on them as subhuman. Stella dehumanized the working class by imagining them as some kind of celestially-perfect beings.

Of course, as a young lady of ten-and-nine years, Stella could perhaps be forgiven for her false notions of the world, but that did not prevent her from learning things the hard way.

"You will, of course, need to attend," Lady Moorland said to Stella calmly as she stirred milk into her tea.

"Mother?"

"The Ball. Have you not been listening to me?"

No, Stella had not been listening to her mother at all. Her mind was still fully within the pages of the Fielding novel she had been reading in her window nook behind her bedroom curtains.

"Must I?"

"Stella, do you want to live here with your father and me forever? We must find you a suitable match, and the way to do that is through social means. You are a beautiful young woman, but not so beautiful that you put off a beacon. You must be seen, dear. You must have the eyes of young men rest upon you for them to fall in love with you. It is simply the reality of the world."

"Can I not wait to fall in love myself?"

"Oh, daughter of mine. You have so much to learn. It is the men who fall in love first. That is how it is done. A man will fall desperately in love with you, offer for your hand, and then take you down the aisle. The woman's turn does not come until later. After you have married and spent some time under the same roof as your new husband, that is when the woman's love comes. A man's love is fast, but a woman's is more delicate. It takes more time to blossom. Women learn to love. Men are mired in it with their appetites and their basal nature."

Stella did not argue with her mother because there was nothing to be gained by it, but it sounded to her like her mother was suggesting that she settle — settle for much less than true love and to reconcile herself to whatever situation she found herself in.

That was what the Lady Moorland was suggesting to her youngest daughter, which made Stella enormously sad. Again, Stella's mind wandered to those noble under-classes, allowed to marry for love as they pleased, their marriage beds unsullied by the shame of unfulfilled yearnings and forced love.

Stella was so very young.

"I understand, Mother."

"Good. Good. The ball will be lovely, dear. Simply lovely. It is the very ball at which your sister Melinda met Lord Rucker two years past."

Lady Moorland took the final sip of her tea and stood to take her leave of her daughter. She moved around the small table and placed a soft kiss on Stella's forehead.

"Ah, Stella," Lady Moorland whispered. "You hold such a special place in my heart. I was once much like you, an idealistic, young woman. I only hope that you avoid the same mistakes I have made. Idealism is most unwise in an eligible young lady."

Stella looked up at her mother, surprised by such a revelation. What exactly was her mother admitting?

As Lady Moorland left the room, Stella thought she heard her utter, "It only leads to pain."

Continue Reading

'The Duke's Unwilling Bride'

at:

https://www.amazon.com/dp/B01M3UO064/

ARIETTA RICHMOND, GRACE AUSTEN, ISABELLA THORNE,
KATHERINE KEATS AND SOPHIA WILSON

Here is Your Preview of

Charming the Earl

Anna Quinlan is soundly snubbed by the man of her dreams. Shocked and frustrated, she increases her efforts to snag the Earl, having no comprehension of what really drives the man...

"You know, Edmund, it would be a boon to your public profile if you made a social appearance once in a while."

"I was in court this morning," Edmund said, looking up from his book with good-natured annoyance.

Marvin had been his father's best friend. When the man grew old and decrepit, he had come to live with Edmund at his estate. He had the most irritating habit of giving Edmund advice, most of it unsolicited.

"Beggar's Court hardly counts as a social appearance. I can't imagine it will help you find a suitable bride. Well, perhaps a bride... but a suitable one, I think not."

"Marvin, is it a personal goal of yours to see me married before you leave the mortal coil?"

"Your father made me promise I would at least *try* to get you married. He had the foresight to recognize it would be no easy task to get the idea of matrimony through that thick skull of yours. As he said, you are quite like a stubborn billy goat on the topic."

"My skull is thicker than a billy goat's, I would imagine," Edmund said, rapping the side of his head with two knuckles. "And I have no intention of getting married. My work is what matters to me. I've never met a society woman who cared a whit for another soul. Unfortunately, ladies of society care more about silks and table patterns."

"Your own patterns could use a change."

"Marvin, are you listening to me?"

"What?" the old man said, cupping his hand to his ear while he puffed on the pipe that hung jauntily out of the side of his mouth. "Hmm. Me pretending to be deaf used to make you laugh."

"When I was ten, I don't doubt it."

"You know, I'm not asking for much. One Ball. The season is long, and one Ball is only an evening of your time. It is your duty as an Earl to take a wife. And there are no court sessions in the evening as far as I'm aware."

"First of all, it is not my duty to take a wife. And you won't leave this alone until I agree, will you?"

"That or I die."

Edmund sighed deeply and looked at his novel, his eyes scanning the pages, but the meaning of the words not quite making it into his consciousness.

Finally, he put a thumb in the book and looked up at his elderly house-companion, who had a grin the size of Devonshire on his face along with a notable twinkle in his eye.

It was clear that the tussle of words had been won by the wily old man, and Edmund would have to acquiesce.

"Fine," Edmund relented. "Will you choose the least objectionable of these events for me?"

"It will be on your social calendar by morning. Shall I have Betsy send one of your coats out for brushing? The navy with the high collar and the gold buttons perhaps? I've heard some ladies remark kindly upon it."

"My valet can certainly take care of my coat." Edmund moaned. "I suppose you'll be wanting to come along with me to this social event to goad me into all sorts of miseries."

"I would not miss it, young Lord. I feel as if I shall be your father's eyes from beyond the grave."

"You will do him proud, I am sure. He was always carping on me about courting. May I be free to read my book now, or is there more you would like to pester me about? You do know that my solicitor's wisdom depends upon my books?" He gave a sly smile.

"That is a novel. I can see it from here, but I will take my leave nevertheless."

When Marvin finally exited Edmund's parlor, leaving the smells of sweet pipe tobacco and victory lingering behind him, Edmund found himself unable to continue reading. He was too thoroughly distracted. He stood up from his writing desk and absentmindedly stoked the fire that was burning low. It was not exactly cold yet, in mid-September, but it was sufficient for one to get a chill if not careful, and Edmund could not afford a chill. There were too many whose livelihoods depended on him.

Edmund was most definitely a member of the aristocracy, but he was not particularly popular among their kind, as he devoted most of his time, funds, and energy to helping those of the lower classes. He also spent a good deal of energy on campaigning for a drastic change in debtor's laws. Edmund was far from the only member of the aristocracy to know that the laws were deeply and morally wrong.

His father, for instance, had been keenly aware and even lamented it… but none of them did anything more about it than commiserate. Edmund's own neighbors thought him a total lunatic for his interest in the lives of the less fortunate. Edmund assumed Marvin was of the same opinion, but in a less good-natured way.

Typically, Edmund's fellow elites could not fathom one of their own being more interested in social justice than in the latest social gathering of their own class. Edmund rarely appeared at such events, but that did not mean he was not a frequent topic of discussion. He and his "little projects" were often talked about derisively.

Perhaps a wife would not be the worst thing for me, Edmund mused. Surely, it was possible that there was another creature who shared his passions. And possibly, one such young lady could see her way clear to share a passion for him as well.

Edmund ran his hand over his chin, and his thoughts continued. In truth, he had never believed that finding a kindred soul was completely impossible. However, he had never felt it to be particularly pressing either. His father and Marvin were both wise men, and there might be something to their thoughts that a man cannot live an entirely happy life alone. Still, Edmund did not feel as if his prospects were very hopeful on this front. He gave a rueful smile. Perhaps, he must resolve to open his mind.

With a lighter heart, Edmund returned to his novel and was able to have some laughs at the expense of the bumbling central character in the lively picaresque.

He stayed up long into the night, as was his custom, smoking several cigars down to their nubs and turning pages rapidly until the novel was finished. Dawn was near when Edmund finally found his own bed and fell to sleep. As the sun rose shortly thereafter and shone full in Edmund's slumbering face, the young Lord was blissfully unaware of the changes that were about to run rampant through his ordered life.

~~~~~

The Auctioneer's Ball. The three words echoed in Edmund's head in the most irritating fashion. They were the least pleasing words the young lord could imagine being shoved together. Why, the phrase existed as if entirely for his displeasure.

It was true that Edmund had granted Marvin freedom to schedule an event for him to attend, but Edmund could hardly fathom a more unpleasant choice. The Auctioneer's Ball, indeed. It was the annual gathering of London's finest, where there were silent auctions on pieces of unbearably hideous art, and to make things indelibly worse, it was a *masked Ball.*

Edmund's only advantage in social situations was the ability to avoid people he did not want to see or talk to. With the masks to hide their identities, all of Edmund's most dreaded acquaintances would be able to saunter right up to him and trap him into unending conversations about vagrancy laws and how they should be tightened — or some other privileged nonsense. It was a perfect nightmare, and it was all that Edmund could think about while he was on his morning ride.
~~~~~

His horse was taking the road at a slow gait, trotting around the outskirts of London, and the two of them had all the appearances of being at peace, despite Edmund's mental struggles. Due to his thoughts, Edmund did not register that he was being addressed until his horse was stopped by someone grabbing at his horse.

Edmund came out of his trance and looked down to find a stooped old man holding the bridle in one hand and the tiny hand of a dirty child in the other.

"I'm sorry, what did you say? Were you speaking to me?" Edmund asked, his full attention now on the present.

"…hoping you could help us, kind sir. Please forgive my forwardness. This is my grandson. My son passed years ago, but that's neither here nor there. You see, I can't feed him no more. I love young Richard, but his life may be better elsewhere."

"There is a place where I can set you up in a room and perhaps find you work," Edmund said without hesitation. "Here, I will walk."

Edmund dismounted, and despite protestations from the old man, he helped him and his grandson onto the horse. Edmund took the rein in his hand and began to walk toward the center of the city. He had a friend who ran an inn and allowed some of Edmund's clients to rent rooms at no cost while Edmund located suitable work for them.

Of course, the rooms weren't free at all, as Edmund always recompensed the owner.

Along their walk, Edmund found out that the man's name was Uriah, and he had no one in the world but his grandson.

His wife and son had passed away during the same month several years past. It was clear from the way the old man spoke that he would have given up his grandson in an instant if it was better for the boy, though it would indeed break the man's heart.

"I don't know how we will ever repay you," Uriah said more than once.

"If helping my fellow man requires repayment, then I should like to see the scoundrel who accepts. The honor is truly mine."

Edmund made sure that the old man and his grandson were set up properly in a room and informed them that he would be glad to check on them in a few days' time to see how they were faring.

These were not just empty words for Edmund. His greatest grievance with the other members of his social class was their often callous nonchalance with words and promises. When Edmund told someone he meant to do something, he did it. He bade farewell to Uriah, put his hat on his head, and retrieved his horse from the inn's stable boy, tossing him a coin as he did.

Just as Edmund was mounting his horse, a voice hallooed to him from across the street, and before Edmund could manage to leave, the source of the voice, a man in a startlingly green coat and a tall, black hat, was walking across the street.

Edmund watched his approach with genuine dismay, an unwelcome emotion to the young Lord, for he worked at maintaining an even temperament, particularly so early in the morning.

Lord Michael Riley, the man approaching him, was the very worst of his kind: an arrogant Lord with no regard for anyone but himself.

The man was known to brag about the quick rate with which he went through house servants. These days, he was forced to pay an exorbitant amount to secure anyone, and they all still left because he treated them so poorly.

"Good morning, Edmund," Michael said, tapping his gold-tipped cane on the cobblestones. "I trust I find you well, as you are outside of a seedy establishment, the likes of which you seem to prefer. You look grimy enough. Suits you, doesn't it?"

"A pleasure as always, Michael. Now if you don't mind, I'll just—"

Before Edmund was able to mount up, Michael Riley put his cane between Edmund and his horse.

"I heard a rumor this morning that you are on the guest list for the Auctioneer's Ball," he said. "Care to tell me if this is true?"

Edmund was astonished at the quickness with which Marvin had acted in securing his invitation, but he could not deny the truth of the matter, not that it was important to Edmund whether Michael wanted him to be in attendance or not.

"It is true," Edmund said. "I will be there to outshine you with my gallant nonchalance. I won't even have to feign it. I genuinely won't care about being there. For all *your* practiced boredom, it never quite sells."

Edmund was surprised to see that this barb seemed to hit home more than he would have expected.

Michael colored and turned his gaze away from Edmund for a brief moment. Edmund had unintentionally struck a nerve, and he could not deny taking a certain pleasure in it.

"I can assure you it will sell with Anna Quinlan."

"Is this a newly eligible young lady? Surely you don't expect me to know of her? What with my preoccupation with seedy establishments and such."

"The finest creature I've ever laid eyes upon," Michael said. "The truest form of her sex: graceful, demure, and intelligent."

"I am certain that since you believe these things about her, I would find her as attractive as a garden gnome. If you need to be put at ease, you have my assurance that I will leave you alone to fail at your own leisure. Is there anything else you need from me? I am famished and wish to take tea in my own home."

Lord Michael Riley had nothing to say in response to Edmund… no witty retort, and no more insults, his sparring talent fairly shallow at the best of times.

He managed only an additional grimace.

Edmund mentally dismissed the entire interchange as he rode away, his horse's hooves clapping against the cobblestone road.

Continue Reading

'Charming the Earl'

at:

https://www.amazon.com/dp/B01M4JFE25/

ARIETTA RICHMOND, GRACE AUSTEN, ISABELLA THORNE,
KATHERINE KEATS AND SOPHIA WILSON

Just One Christmas Kiss

Isabella Thorne

ARIETTA RICHMOND, GRACE AUSTEN, ISABELLA THORNE,
KATHERINE KEATS AND SOPHIA WILSON

All rights reserved

Copyright © 2016 by Isabella Thorne

Please visit Isabella's website at www.isabellathorne.com

Chapter One

One mistletoe: a kissing bough that was the only concession to the holidays her Aunt Alda would allow. Matilda had picked it herself two months prior, and now the green, leafy bough hung with a red ribbon above the doorway of the parlor, red berries waiting to be plucked.

Of course, they would not be plucked, for there was no one to kiss and there would be no holiday Ball. Matilda's aunt, Lady Claridge, her father's eldest sister, hated Christmas with a passion. The old widow had no patience for the frivolity of holiday festivities. In fact she had no patience for anything with the slightest resemblance to fun.

If it were not for Matilda's young brother, Clarence, she would not mind so much. He was only ten and he deserved a true Christmas, filled with parties and plum puddings and ice skating, but alas, that was not to be.

Even the weather was not cooperating. There was not a single snowflake and it was already the middle of December.

"She is looking at you, Mattie," whispered Clarence, from beside her. "And she looks cross about it."

Matilda stepped back from the window. She was being rude to the guests, and though she was not the hostess of this particular... party, she was still expected to entertain.

They were, after all, her potential suitors. Lord Gibbon and Lord Mullens were engaged in a fierce discussion over the finer points of politics, ignoring her completely, while Warwick was helping himself to the canapés. Warwick was the only one of them paying her any mind at all, but Lady Claridge and her clear-eyed gaze left no doubt of her opinions on Matilda's behavior.

It was Aunt Alda's fault for inviting three gentlemen over at once; whenever men gathered in a group they found each other the most diverting entertainment and Matilda was inclined to let them go their way and leave her alone.

"They are too old for you anyway," Clarence said, wrinkling up his nose and making a face like a dour old man while hobbling forward to his sister.

Matilda stifled a giggle. This was precisely the reason she had rescued Clarence from the school room. She needed his levity. Clarence was not wrong, either. All of the men had grey in their hair, and their bellies had gone to paunch. "Maybe Auntie should snag one for herself," he whispered.

"You devil," said Matilda, though privately she agreed.

At least they would be gone soon, before the sun set and the roads turned slick with ice.

At least since the private gatherings were not as formal as a Ball, Aunt Alda did not see the need to allow anyone to stay at the house, which suited Matilda just fine, but she would dearly love a Ball, with guests her own age instead of with one foot in the grave. She stepped into the center of the room and Lord Gibbon was at her side a moment later, offering her a flute of honeyed wine. Matilda took it, dodging his fingers as they tried to brush against hers.

"I was so sorry to hear about your parents, Miss Claridge. Dreadful business, and with the boy so young."

"The boy is my brother. His name is Clarence," she said a bit tartly. "And he is now the Marquis of Dartmount. He is not '*the boy*.'"

"I'm sorry. I meant no disrespect. A true pity," he repeated, trying again to touch her hand in a conciliatory gesture. But it was Lord Gibbon who had swooped in the moment the news had reached his ears, quick as a vulture over fresh carrion. Matilda's father had not allowed suitors; he had thought her too young. Matilda was inclined to agree with her father, at least, she was too young for Lord Gibbon.

The fire that had stolen her parents a year ago had forced her to leave her home as well. At first, it was just until the repairs were finished, and then, well she had to remain on with Aunt Alda as her chaperone. After all, her Aunt reminded her. There was no hurry to rebuild Dartmount. It would be a while before Clarence was old enough to live there on his own; she would never be Lady of Dartmount. Her home, even if it were rebuilt, was lost to her, as lost as her parents.

She would marry and be at home wherever her husband lived. She wanted more than anything to go home, but the truth was she no longer felt at home anywhere. Home was where her family was, and the only true family she had was Clarence. Of course, there was Aunt Alda, and her brother, who appeared occasionally when he could be bothered to escort them about town or get funds from Aunt Alda's account, but it was Clarence Matilda thought of, when she thought of family — Clarence and her parents — now dead.

She took a deep breath. "Thank you, Lord Gibbon." She looked past him. Aunt Alda gave her an approving nod. He must be the wealthiest of the trio, then. "It has been trying for my brother, but we will get through it together. It is so good to have family nearby; is it not?" She asked, casting a brittle smile at Lord Gibbon, who sputtered.

It was well known that his own sister was a veritable shrew who was destined to remain on the shelf, and Lord Gibbon spent most of his time at his club to avoid her. Matilda was tempted to see how shrewish she could be, just to drive the man off. Even if Lord Gibbon had been ten years younger and a stone or two lighter, she was disinclined to consider him for a husband. He was as boring as a lump of stone himself.

It was two hours later before she was rid of the lot of them. Matilda sank into a chair. There was nothing more exhausting than socializing with people you had nothing in common with. Clarence had been collected by his tutor and had long ago gone to bed, no longer required to wear the guise of a young Lord.

"I have never been so happy to see the back of a man," Aunt Alda said.

Matilda turned to her, surprised. "Truly? I thought you were hoping for a proposal this very evening, the way you kept throwing me at them."

"Oh, they all offered for you well before this evening, dear. But I thought you should at least have a chance to meet them before I accepted. I see now that none of them will do."

Shocked did not begin to cover it.

"I did not think that would matter."

Aunt's look could have stopped her heart.

"My dear child, while I did not agree with my brother's decision to cloister you away like a child, I would not thrust you into a marriage with a man whose company you do not at least enjoy."

Clarence and Matilda shared a look. Since they had moved in with Aunt Alda, the woman had done nothing but order new clothes for Matilda, and organize small social gatherings to show her off. She could wear a new dress every day and never run out, at this point. It had seemed as if she was in a great hurry to marry off her niece.

"I see," said Matilda, feeling as if she did not, at all, see. "Thank you, Aunt Alda."

Aunt Alda pursed her lips over her glass of sherry.

Chapter Two

The next morning, Matilda had her maid dress her in her thickest dress and walking coat. She pulled on her gloves, pulled a mink hat down over her hair and tucked her hands into a matching mink muff. Then, she dragged her maid out for a walk. Poor Emily was a London girl, and the country walks Matilda embarked on often had the woman gasping for breath. It wasn't like she was terribly old, only a few years older than Matilda herself. She just preferred her needlepoint.

Matilda knew she would much rather ride in a carriage than walk anywhere at all. Truly if a carriage could have taken her from the drawing room to the dining room she would have ridden. She insisted that any amount of fresh air would give her an ague. Matilda, however, found the out of doors invigorating and would rather walk than ride closed in a carriage, unless the weather was particularly unpleasant.

"May I come with you?" Clarence asked, meeting her at the bottom of the stairs. He looked as though he had escaped mid-dressing, his shirt was half tucked and his buttons were undone. Matilda grinned. Somewhere, his valet was cursing.

"You will have to dress first," said Matilda, quirking an eyebrow. "And you best be quick about it, if Auntie catches you she will make you stay home for your schooling."

"Too late." Auntie had not stayed late abed this morning, though she still wore her dressing robe. "Auntie has caught you, and you may not dodge your lessons, young man," Aunt Alda said. "It is important for a young gentleman to be well-educated."

Clarence rolled his eyes. Matilda patted him fondly on the top of his red curls and he went stomping up the stairs, dragging his feet.

"Do not stay out long, Matilda. The cold will dry out your skin and give you wrinkles. You do not want to look like a hag, do you?" Aunt's primary concern in all things was maintaining Matilda's youthful looks.

"Yes Aunt," said Matilda. She took Emily by the arm and tugged her along outside before her Aunt decided it was not worth the risk.

The cold was biting, with a strong wind that dug its nails beneath her clothes, finding a way in under the layers. Matilda nestled deeper into her furs. Emily was muttering something she could not make out, but it was probably not flattering toward her. Perhaps it was best she did not know.

She would have left Emily at the house if propriety would have allowed it. It was not her fault that Emily must come with her. They marched away from the house and across the flat lawn, where the grass had gone yellow and dry from the winter frost.

She took her favorite path, the one that followed a narrow, frozen stream and ran through the garden and through the thicket of trees beyond. Often she saw squirrels and rabbits, but not today. Perhaps they were all warm in their burrows. It was cold.

"We should turn back, Miss," Emily said for the fifth time.

Every time Emily suggested turning back all it meant to Matilda is that she wanted to go all that much further. She knew it was petty, but she couldn't seem to help herself. Plus she knew, once she turned around, she would be cloistered with her Aunt for the duration of the day. "In a while," Matilda said looking at the sky. All that was missing was snow. Grey skies promised it, but they had let her down thus far.

"Did you hear that?" Matilda stopped short and held out an arm for Emily to do the same. Something rustled in the underbrush off the side of the trail. Maybe it would be a rabbit. She didn't want to frighten it off before she had a look.

"Good Lord," said Emily, stepping in close to her. "It's some sort of animal."

"Oh do not panic, Emily, really, it is probably just a rabbit or a squirrel finding the last of its winter stores. You are as flighty as an untried horse sometimes." Emily harrumphed. Apparently Emily didn't like being compared to a horse, although Matilda thought the comparison was decidedly flattering. Matilda detached herself from Emily's grip and stepped toward the rustling sound, intending to investigate whatever it was in the bush so that they might continue their walk without her maid having a fainting spell.

She bent to pull back the concealing branches. The creature bounded out with a happy bark, thick tail wagging. Emily shrieked in fright.

"It is only a dog," said Matilda. "And a friendly one, by the looks of it." She frowned, wondering where it had come from. Had someone lost the animal and left it out in this freezing weather?

The dog in question was huffing softly and circling Matilda as if she might have a pocket full of tidbits. She patted its head and the creature sat down at her feet, looking up hopefully, with tongue lolling.

"It is filthy. Where did it come from?" Emily asked, looking about.

Matilda, who was scratching behind the dog's ears, had not noticed that the animal was quite dirty. She looked up at the sound of more rustling and a sharp whistle. This came from the path they had stepped off, and the source was immediately apparent.

A man she had never seen before came down it, holding a gun.

For just a moment Matilda startled. Perhaps her maid's timidity was wearing off. Half of the man's face was hidden in shadow by his hat, pulled down against the cold. His face was ruddy with the wind, but Matilda was immediately entranced by his eyes. He seemed like a raptor, his golden brown eyes were so sharp, peering from beneath the hat, watching her until she felt all adrift. She felt as if he missed nothing. He turned then, and spoke to the dog.

"Leto, you traitor, are you leaving me for the first pretty lass you see?" His deep rumble of a voice, barrelling out of his broad chest, was a pleasant sound to Matilda's ears, and his faint accent only added to the intrigue. It was certainly not a London accent; perhaps northern Matilda surmised, maybe as far as the lowlands. "Ah, Miss, did she jump on you? She is just a pup, still learning."

Matilda looked down. Her cloak had come out of the meeting a little worse for wear, but whether that was the dog or the brambles, she could not be sure.

"No, I am afraid the mess is mine," Matilda said, brushing at the dirt.

Emily scoffed, letting her mistress know just what she thought of that, and of the man. He was close enough for her to get the measure of him now. Rugged, that was the word for it. His eyes were a sharp, raptor brown and his nose thin and straight, but he smiled at her, showing even white teeth and a smile that went all the way to his eyes. They brightened with pure joy. He had an aristocratic look to him, although he was dressed as a huntsman or groom. His clothes were sturdy, well-made, if rather rumpled, and his boots looked of a good leather, but well-worn. Leto, the dog, trotted over to him and leaned against his legs. Instead of pushing the dog away, he patted her head.

"Did we interrupt your hunting, sir?" Matilda asked. "I hope we did not scare away the game."

"Oh, no, no. Leto d-did that long b-before you did." He laughed ruffling the dog's head and Matilda relaxed too.

She did not want him to leave just yet, until she knew more of him. "I have never met another soul in these woods. I confess; you gave us quite a start."

He pulled his hat from his head and ran his fingers through his hair. It was the color of bronze, and his eyes seemed to go one shade darker as he looked at her. She was surprised to see how young he looked, not much older than herself, with not a gray hair at all in that unruly mop of curls.

"Where are my m-manners? One forgets, after so long..." he shook his head as if to clear it. "I s-suppose, well, w-we have not b-been introduced." His stutter seemed to get worse when he looked at her. He looked down. "I wouldn't want to give offense."

"I would drop a glove," Matilda said, "But I am disinclined to take one off."

"No. No of c-course, not, in this cold."

I am your r-recent neighbor, L-lord Barrington, he said with a slight bow

"I am Lady Darcy, the niece of Lady Alda Claridge, recently come to Claridge Hall."

Emily gasped with the impropriety of it all.

"Emily, I cannot have a conversation with the gentleman if we are not introduced."

"Quite right," Emily said, askance.

"Pish posh," Matilda said.

And Lord Barrington laughed.

It was quite a deep musical sound that hit her somewhere deep in her belly.

She took a breath to settle herself.

I've r-recently inherited this m-monstrosity," he said gesturing past the copse where Leto had gotten herself stuck. "I live just beyond those trees there."

Squinting, Matilda could just make out three black spires between the barren trees. She had never noticed it before. She had not even realized Aunt had a neighbor on this side of the estate, and she had never heard of a Lord Barrington and, of course, Aunt Alda knew everyone who was anyone. Some of her confusion must have shown on her face.

"I am n-new to the area. I would not expect you to know of me," said Barrington. "I'm afraid your Aunt w-would not approve of me."

"Why ever not?"

He pulled himself up and looked quite deliberately over her shoulder as he spoke. "I am Lord Barrington now, but until quite recently I was Neville Kronel, esquire, a professional man."

Matilda was shocked that he said the whole sentence without a single stutter. She supposed an attorney might need to suppress the stutter, or he wouldn't have much business.

"Oh, how delightful," Matilda said. "A barrister. Have you ever represented a murderer?"

"Miss!" Emily shrieked.

"No, I have n-not," Lord Barrington said. "I am afraid my work was mostly dusty papers, rather than c-court speaking. Nothing so exciting or gruesome as m-murder."

"Still, this is the most excitement I've had in an age."

Emily was tugging not so discreetly on the elbow of her walking coat. The maid did not approve of meeting strange men in the forest, nor of spending an ounce of extra time in the out of doors, it seemed. Matilda brushed her off. "Miss, you will be ruined," she hissed with just a bit of malice.

Matilda ignored her warnings. "Lady Matilda," she said, with a dip of a curtsy she pulled her gloved hand from her muff and extended it to him. Even gloved, a jolt struck through her at his touch and she raised her eyes to those impossible golden eyes.

He took her hand and smiled brightly, but did not speak.

"No luck on your hunt, then?" she asked trying to recover herself.

Barrington reached down to ruffle the top of Leto's head. "Afraid not. She gets too far ahead and runs off all the pheasants before I catch up. Exuberant girl. But we will get there. Time and patience."

The wind gave a screeching renewal, more insistent than Emily's tugging. Leaves flew in twisters about them and trees swayed overhead. Emily whimpered.

"Is that… snow?" Matilda held out her kid-gloved hand. Snowflakes drifted down, lazy, not knowing how long she had waited for them. "Oh! It is!"

Matilda twirled about, laughing.

Leto hopped up and bounced beside her, barking. Emily and Barrington must have thought her mad, but it did not stop her; there was nothing like the first snow of the year.

"My Lady I really think we should be going. Your aunt will be expecting us home by now," said Emily, her voice sharp. *Really, whose maid was she?*

"This is turning into rather a storm now," said Barrington. "Come now, Leto, leave Lady Matilda be."

No sooner had Matilda noticed the snow than it began to pick up its pace. It blew about the three of them violently, whipping into Matilda's eyes. A tree gave a warning creak.

"You may be right, Emily, we should hurry home." Matilda did not want to leave, but at least she knew the intriguing man's name, and unorthodox though it was, they were introduced, after a fashion.

ARIETTA RICHMOND, GRACE AUSTEN, ISABELLA THORNE,
KATHERINE KEATS AND SOPHIA WILSON

Chapter Three

Matilda had barely taken a step when, with a tremendous tearing, the beleaguered tree came down. It took out the branches of its neighbors on its way, causing chaos and havoc and a commotion so loud she clapped her hands over her ears to muffle it, and dropped her muff. Barrington looped an arm around Matilda's waist and pulled her back, shielding her with his body as shards of tree splintered off. Dirt and snow rose in a cloud around the impact. Emily shot Barrington a look that could skin his hide and he stepped away from Matilda, looking alarmed. Really Emily, Matilda thought with annoyance, the man was only being kind.

"Now we will die out here, all for the foolish adventures you call walks," Emily groused. "When I accepted this job I did not expect it to involve daily peril," she muttered.

"I do not think it is safe for you to journey all the way home, especially with the tree downed," Lord Barrington said, retrieving her muff from the ground. It was covered with snow, and wet.

"Please, come to Brackenburrow until the storm passes. It is nearer. At the very least I can offer you the comfort of a sleigh ride home."

Though he offered it, Matilda was not certain if the man did not truly wish them to go or not. His nervousness was evident despite the impaired vision offered by the storm, but Emily did not give her a chance to politely decline.

"Thank you, my Lord, we would appreciate that very much," Emily said. "Come now, my Lady, your Aunt will understand the necessity of it. With the tree down we can hardly climb over the trunk of it." She looped her arm through Matilda's and they followed Barrington through the thicket. Leto whined, anxious, and hugged Barrington's side as they picked their way around the fallen tree.

Brackenburrow was only a five minute walk, but by the time they reached the front door they were crusted with snow and shivering from the cold. It piled up around their ankles out of the protection of the trees and soaked through Matilda's stockings. From the outside, she would have called the house intimidating, even menacing. The style was older and dark, with gothic arches and spires. Inside, however, was a different world. Here, Christmas had come. Every surface was covered in evergreen sprays, velvet ribbons, and branches of holly. Spiced, heady smells filled her nose, like cinnamon and pine.

The man turned around when Matilda did not immediately follow him through the hall and blushed when he took in her attention to the decorations. "It is excess-sive, is it not? It's j-just... I've always loved Christmas. MY grandmother d-decorated, and well... I guess I got her Christmas b-bug."

"Your grandmother? Is she here?" asked Matilda.

"No. no. She p-passed on two years ago on Christmas Eve. This s-seems a way to honor her." He looked down and spoke more carefully. There is a f-fire in the sitting room and we can dry off a bit there."

Reluctant to leave the holiday splendor though she was, the thought of a warm fire became a more immediate interest to her when Matilda's body gave a violent shiver. She tried to stifle her disappoint that he thought the cheer was excessive. It was just the right amount of festivity, if you asked her. It must have been the Lady of Brackenburrow that decorated it so. Another, more alarming bit of disappointment rushed through her at that thought. She cast about for a polite way to ask after her.

"Is there a woman responsible?" she asked, gesturing at the decor.

Barrington held the door for her, and she and Emily stepped into the warmth of the sitting room. They scurried over to the fire. Even here, the decorations persisted.

"Ah," said Barrington. "No. No there is not. I live alone, apart from the s-servants. And the d-dogs of course."

Matilda smiled, hiding her face from Emily by taking a sudden interest in the mantle. It was carved with bucks. "Dogs? More than dear Leto?" Matilda asked.

So he *was* a bachelor. Perhaps his earlier comment about the decorations being excessive spoke more to his self-consciousness than any dour spirit toward the holiday. It was most endearing.

"Quite a f-few more. I find them the b-best sort of company. My b-best hunting dog has just had a litter, so Leto had to step into her shoes." His eyes brightened as he spoke of his hounds and his stutter all but disappeared. "Not the same, though she tries, dear me." Barrington was tugging off his gloves and stepping out of his jacket. "I should call for the s-servants now, excuse me."

When he was gone, Emily rounded on her. "What sort of servants are not waiting about for their master's return? He is an odd sort, my Lady. Living alone in this dark place with naught but dogs for companions? Odd indeed."

"Emily!" Matilda rebuked the girl. "That is most rude. He was kind to take us in and if he prefers solitude, I can hardly fault him for that. He seems a nice enough man. His dogs are certainly beautiful."

"Only you would think those beasts beautiful!"

Chapter Four

Brackenburrow, though dated, was a fine place, and there was no doubt the man had wealth. His accent suggested Scotland, but then how had he ended up here? She was dying to find out. Barrington returned with a narrow man, made smaller by Barrington beside him, carrying a tray.

"I hope this suits for now. I ah… I am not sure what is proper but, the maid did offer to run a bath for you." He blushed furiously at that and clasped his hands behind his back. "She said there were also some things to change into, though they would not be up to your usual standard, and quite out of style. They belonged to the former Lady Barrington."

Emily's eyebrows were in danger of vanishing.

"A bath sounds lovely, thank you Lord Barrington," said Matilda. "My maid will assist me, so there will be no impropriety."

She had done it in part to see Emily burning to argue and partly because she was truly freezing in her sodden clothes and if she took a chill, Aunt would never let her outside again.

When the water had been run up, Barrington's maid came to fetch them. They followed her, a woman as old as Aunt, through the house and up the stairs, where a copper tub sat steaming.

"Do not say a word, Emily, just help me bathe and dress so we may hurry down. I know you do not approve, but here we are and you must deal with it. You must want to get out of your wet clothes as well."

Emily pursed her lips. She did as she was told, but her mutinous glare could have kept the water hot. Quick as she could, Matilda bathed and dressed with Emily's reluctant help.

When they went down again, Barrington was seated by the fire, surrounded by dogs. The dogs barked when they entered, as if they were not used to visitors.

Barrington stood up at their approach. He had dressed in dry clothes, neater than the ones he had worn in the woods, and had brushed back his damp hair. Matilda smiled at him, wading through the dogs to reach the fire's warmth.

"Thank you for your hospitality, Lord Barrington. I know we met under unusual circumstances, but I do hope you will not be a stranger now, when we live so near to each other," said Matilda.

Emily was still fighting her way through the dogs, who seemed determined to become friends with Emily simply because she didn't like them. She shrieked when one licked her hand, which made them all the more excited. Matilda hid her smile behind her hand.

"They do not see much of people, and so each encounter is like Christmas day to them," Barrington said. "And I never have the heart to scold them for it when it is my fault they are unused to people."

The house moaned as a strong gust of wind pushed against it and a draft found its way between the boards, but the old wood held firm. For now. Matilda wrapped her arms about herself and stepped closer to the fire, and Barrington.

"I suppose the storm has not let up at all, has it?" The faded velvet curtains had been pulled across the windows. "My aunt will be so worried, but there is naught to be done about it, I would not send a footman out in this to pass her a note."

"I am afraid I have already done so. I would not want your Aunt to worry. He has already returned."

"Oh," Matilda was surprised that the man who seemed so unassuming in words had taken charge in actions.

"I should have had dinner made..."

Matilda could not tell if he were speaking to her or to himself. He did not look up from the carpet except in darting glances.

"You need not go through all that bother for us. We had a filling breakfast and I have not even the smallest pang of hunger yet."

It was a lie. Her stomach was growling from the arduous walk and the taxing trudge through the snow.

Breakfast had been nothing more than tea and crumpets. Unfortunately, her stomach decided that was the moment to tell the truth and gave a piteous whine. The dogs turned in alarm, and even Barrington took notice. Matilda covered her midsection with her hands to keep any other traitorous sounds in.

"Yes... I c-can see that. Full as a t-tick, are you? Brackenburrow might not look like m-much, but the kitchen can whip up as fine a meal as any. No need to be frightened of the c-cobwebs and the rats; they will not make it into the supper."

He left, ostensibly to ask the kitchen to prepare a meal, and the dogs trailed after him.

Poor Emily, rumpled and cross, took his place beside Matilda at the fire.

"He is a bizarre man, my Lady. Cobwebs and rats? What was that?" Emily shivered.

Matilda smiled to herself. "A joke, I believe. You may have heard one before?"

"I do not think he is funny, and his dogs are out of control. I should have kicked them."

"You will not," said Matilda, eyes blazing. "Do you think Clarence would like one? He is a lonesome boy, out here in the country. A pup might be just the thing for him."

"A p-pup is a wonderful gift for a b-boy," said Barrington, startling both of the girls. How a man so large could walk so quietly, she did not know.

"My first d-dog was my best friend as a youth, and a truer one I have not found to this day. I would be happy to sh-show you the litter, Lady Matilda, since you will be trapped in my home until the storm releases you."

He gave Emily a hard look that made Matilda question how much of their conversation he had overheard. Perhaps it was best if they were separated.

"I would enjoy nothing more." Matilda held out her hand and Barrington, after a moment's hesitation, offered his bent arm. She laid her hand upon it. "Stay here, Emily, I know how you dislike dogs."

Emily opened her mouth to argue. Then she shut it and sat down on a chair. Matilda knew she would hear all about it later.

Barrington led her out of the room and down the long, cold hallway. The carpet was faded, the oriental designs washed out and scuffed by countless footsteps.

"Did you grow up here?" she asked. Portraits dotted the walls, but they lacked any lighting to make them more than shadowed figures. Though the front of the house had been lit with candles to showcase the holiday decorations, the farther they went from the front door the less there was of that.

Barrington shook his head. "No, I grew up far from here. You must be thinking it would be a gloomy place for a child to live. My home was not so different from this, truth be told, but filled with family it seemed a cheerier place."

"How did you end up here?"

He paused just outside one of the doors. Through the paneled wood, Matilda could hear quiet whimpering.

"My great-uncle passed and I was the closest living relative. It was rather a rude surprise, leaving home for this. I only met the man once, when I was a child. As you can see, he did not keep up to date with the furnishings or the staff, and so here I am."

Barrington twisted the doorknob and let her into the room. "But come now, these little beasts are far more interesting than the dusty history of Brackenburrow."

The pups had only just gotten used to walking about on their own legs and their bandy-legged progress around the room had Matilda giggling. She knelt down on the ground and invited them on to her lap.

"Oh be careful there. Give them an inch, as they say." Barrington made as if to help her back up, but she waved him away.

Three puppies clambered up her legs and snuffled her face with black, wet noses. This only made Matilda laugh harder.

"It tickles!" she cried.

"I did warn you," said Barrington.

"Clarence would love them all, though I am not sure how Aunt would feel about it."

"I can imagine how your maid would feel about it."

Matilda shrugged. "Even she could not resist these. They could hardly make much trouble - look at how small they are."

"If their mess should be proportionate to their size, someone should inform them of that. But I imagine you are far too busy for a dog, with all of the Christmas dinners and parties a woman like yourself must be attending?"

She looked up at him. He was looking at her from the corner of his eye, from beneath the lock of hair that had fallen forward in an unruly fashion as it dried.

"Sadly, no. Like yourself, I am new to the area and my Aunt has no use for Christmas gatherings, nor even decorations. However often I have pleaded, it has all fallen on deaf ears. Her only cause to open her doors at all is to see me safely married."

"S-so you have m-many s-suitors," the stutter was back, full force. "Of course you do, a beautiful woman like yourself," he answered before she could correct him.

Matilda had worked up a mess of loose fur in the vigorous attentions she had been giving the puppies. She pulled it into a pile. "Not any which count," she said looking up at him. "None who…" She shook her head. She was saying too much.

"I do so love Christmas," she said. "And Auntie hates it."

"Surely not?"

She gave him a look.

"That is a shame. You look most p-put-out by it."

"I do love Christmas, and it was always such a big to do at home before… I just am not used to having it pass by without any fanfare." She bit her lip to keep from going on.

A reserved man like Barrington would not appreciate a woman spilling her feelings out on first meeting.

"Though I did manage to hang a kissing bough above the parlor door. She did not deny me that, though she glares at it whenever she passes underneath, as if it personally insults her."

Now that had made her think of kissing *him* beneath the mistletoe! Would he duck his head, too shy to meet her eyes before bringing his lips to hers? Or would he surprise her and be suddenly bold, arresting her with his golden gaze and locking his mouth on hers? Oh, she would happily pluck a berry from the bough's branches to find out.

Barrington cleared his throat, and the hint of pink on his neck made her wonder if he was thinking the same sort of thoughts as she. Instead he reached out a hand and drew her up beside him.

"We should return before your m-maid tears out her hair fretting." He offered her his arm with confidence this time and she took it, rising to her feet with the aid of his strength.

"Why did you not decorate this part of the house? It looks so cheery out there, and then, well, rather bleak back here," she asked, as they walked back along the hallway.

"I plan to, but I have not had the t-time for it yet."

Matilda turned to him. "You decorated it yourself? No, but it is perfect!"

Barrington *was* blushing now, she was sure of it. "Just a hobby of mine. I do love Christmas, and it reminds me of home."

"I did not mean to embarrass you. It was charming and you must have an artistic side to manage it all so beautifully. I am impressed, Lord Barrington. Will you be hosting a Christmas party, or is this all for yourself?"

Barrington laughed. "Just for m-myself. Is that terribly p-pathetic? I am not one for parties, all the noise and the p-people you hardly know. You must think me a bore."

"Not at all," she was quick to say, for she did not want him to mistake her. She could not say more, however, for they had reached the room where Emily sat, looking as petulant as she had when they had left. Any hint of affection Matilda's part would net her more of an earful from Emily, and likely get back to Aunt.

"The storm has let up. We should hurry home before it starts again and leaves us stranded for the entire day." Emily rose as if she meant to storm off right then. When Matilda arched a disapproving brow, Emily tacked on, "If it suits you, my Lady."

Barrington walked over to the window and drew back the curtain. Emily was correct, the snow had stopped and the wind had died down to a gentle, desultory, breeze.

In its short life, the storm had managed to drop what looked to be a foot of snow on the ground, though some of it was blown into mounds much higher than that. It would not be an easy walk.

"You cannot intend for us to walk back in that, Emily. We would be out there an hour to travel the few miles to home, if we did not freeze to death on our way," Matilda said, turning round to frown at Emily.

"If we linger here much longer, it will be dark before we are on our way and then where will we be? Lost in the woods."

The girl could be so melodramatic.

"Please," Barrington broke in, holding up a hand to stop their bickering. "Allow me to take you back in the sleigh. It will be no trouble at all and will save you from wet boots."

Matilda frowned at Emily. She was not ready to go home, but she supposed Emily was right. "Again you are too kind, Lord Barrington. We are sorry to be a bother."

"Nonsense, it is no bother at all. There are few things as enjoyable as slicing through f-fresh-fresh-fallen snow in a sleigh, especially with... with..." He took a deep breath. "Excuse me."

Barrington returned a quarter of an hour later, during which time Emily and Matilda had sat in steaming silence, with rosy cheeks from the cold and evidence of snow on his boots. He did not seem to notice the slushy tracks he had left in his rugs.

"There we are, all ready to go," he said, gesturing for them to precede him out the door.

Matilda tugged on her almost dry fur stole and muff and stepped out through the front door. The sleigh was pulled by a beautiful proud horse. The stout black horse with furry legs, was standing patiently just down the front steps, a light dusting of snow accumulating on his thick coat.

There was no driver, and the horse stood on its own without even a stable boy at its head. Emily snorted in alarm.

"W-what is it?" Barrington asked. They had stopped at the top of the stairs. "Is s-something the matter?"

"Your horse must be well-mannered to stand so on its own," said Matilda.

"Are *you* driving us home?" Emily asked, at the same time.

"Emily!" Matilda said, aghast at the brazen rudeness.

"I meant nothing by it, my Lord, only I was surprised to see you do not have a driver." Emily had the brains to look ashamed at her outburst, at least.

"Ah, yes. That is strange? Well, I prefer it. Being outdoors, and really there is nothing like being up on the front seat with the wind in your face." Barrington flashed a brief, abashed smiled, and rubbed at the back of his head. "As to you, Lady Matilda, old Lux there is just like Brackenburrow, well-built, past his prime, and sure to outlast the rest of us."

Emily climbed into the low seat of the sleigh and pulled the fur blanket over her lap. Matilda hesitated, one hand poised on the rail.

"May I ride up front with you, Lord Barrington? You made it sound so exciting."

To Barrington's credit, his eyes widened for the barest of moments before he replied. "O-of course. We may weigh down the runners a tad— not that you are anything but light as a bird! — but it should not be any trouble for Lux."

He climbed onto the front seat and held out a hand to help Matilda up.

Seated beside him in the narrow front seat, she could not fight down the trill of nerves in the pit of her belly. She thought he would let her watch and perhaps speak on the technique, but he handed her the reins the moment they set off.

Even her father never let her hold the reins, thinking driving was not something a lady needed to learn.

"Steady now, Lux will do the work, you just need to give him an idea of where you hope to go. Bit to the left, there you are." Barrington's accent grew stronger when he was speaking to his dogs or his horse, Matilda noted, moments where he was distracted. "Do you r-ride, Lady Matilda?"

"I do," she said, "although it has been a while since I have had the opportunity to do so. He is very responsive, isn't he?" she said glancing at Lord Barrington with a bright smile.

In truth, she had little work to do. Lux was a pliant, gentle creature, who ploughed tirelessly through the snow, sending great white waves flying past them on both sides.

"What a joy, you were quite right!" Matilda exclaimed, as they swooped around a bend in the road.

"Give him a cluck and he will pick up the pace. He is not too old for that," said Barrington.

Matilda obliged, mimicking the sound she had heard her driver make, and Lux broke into a canter. The wind stung her eyes and her hair whipped around her face, but they were nothing compared to the rush.

Too soon, Grantchester Hall came into view.

"Easy now, pull him back a bit," Barrington said, the deep rumble of his voice cutting through the whipping wind. "Gentle on his mouth."

Matilda tugged backward on the reins, but Lux gave a spirited shake of his head and continued on. "He will not listen. He is having too much fun!"

"He n-needs a f-firm hand, give him a bit more arm than that."

She could hear Emily in the back, reciting the Lord's Prayer. Matilda leaned back against the reins, but the horse seemed to sense her hesitancy.

"May I?" Barrington reached for the reins, taking her hands beneath his and, together, they pulled back. In truth, she did hardly any of it herself, he had left her none of the burden. "There we are; and after I extolled your virtues, Lux!"

Lux came to a halt in front of Grantchester. He seemed pleased with himself. Emily hopped out the moment the sleigh stopped, grunting as she sunk knee deep into the piled up snow.

"Will you come in for a warm drink? I must have some way to thank you for going through all of this trouble for us." Matilda saw his face, joyful from the sleigh ride, shutter. He glanced up at Grantchester; then shook his head.

"Th-thank you, but I must refuse. I cannot leave the pups long."

It had the sound of an excuse, rather than a reason. Matilda's smile faltered, but she fixed it back on.

"Of course," she said.

He helped her as she stepped down from the sleigh. She was silently mortified.

"Good day, Lady Matilda." Barrington said as he delivered her to her door. He tipped his head toward her, and headed back to the sleigh. It was certainly not good manners to beat such a hasty retreat. What was the man afraid of?

Matilda watched the sleigh loop around and travel back toward Brackenwood, cutting over the tracks they had made. She tried to ignore the sinking feeling in her stomach that said she would not see Lord Barrington, nor Brackenwood, again.

"Will you come inside, Lady Matilda?" Emily asked, all politeness now that Barrington had gone. "You can have a proper bath and change out of those secondhand rags."

She had forgotten she was wearing those. Matilda let Emily lead her inside, where Clarence, Aunt, and two of the maids were waiting in the foyer.

"Who was that gentleman?" Aunt's shrewd gaze told Matilda not to bother making up a fib.

"Do not worry, Aunt," said Matilda. "Emily was with me every minute, and we made it through the storm safely."

Clarence snickered, earning him a bop on the back of the head.

"I was worried about you, thinking you were lost in the snow, but seeing you pulling up in a sleigh, alive, beside a strange man I have never seen in my life, I have entirely new concerns."

"His name is Lord Barrington, and he is our neighbor. He was kind enough to let us shelter in his home, and to drive us home when the storm relented. Have you ever heard of Brackenwood?"

"So that old codger finally gave up the ghost, did he?" Aunt pursed her lips. "That must be his nephew. Strange boy, I have heard it said. Go up to your toilet, girl, and stop frowning. I can see the wrinkles on your forehead."

Matilda smoothed her brow with her fingers.

"You do know him? Strange, in what manner? He seemed a perfect gentleman," said Matilda, ignoring Emily's sceptical sounds at her elbow.

Aunt's nose crinkled. Her eyes crossed. Then she sneezed. "Is that *dog* hair all over your dress? And what is that ratty thing you are wearing?"

Matilda looked down. The borrowed dress still sported a ring of black fur. It was not ratty, just not up to the exacting standards Aunt preferred to clothe Matilda in.

"Really Aunt, you can be such a snob sometimes. Lord Barrington was very kind to offer me a change of clothes. I was soaking wet."

"What!"

"I told you, Auntie. No one was there to gossip and Emily was with me the entire time. Nothing untoward happened. He was very kind."

"Yes, I am sure kindness was all that there was to it," her voice was strangled.

"Really, how can you be so naive, Matilda?"

"What do you mean?" Matilda asked.

"You are an exceptional beauty, my dear, foolish niece, and the man wanted to imagine you in a dress of his choosing, or perhaps undress you. Have you not a wit of sense?"

Matilda blushed crimson, and shot a look at Clarence who was watching the conversation with rapt attention.

"Good heavens Aunt, the things you say. He was a nice man."

"He is a man!"

She gave Clarence a kiss on the tip of his nose and ran up the stairs before her Aunt could add another word.

Chapter Five

Three days later, a note arrived. The footman delivered it to Aunt, who sniffed at it, but passed it on to Matilda over the breakfast table. She did not recognize the crest pressed into the wax seal, nor the handwriting when she unfolded it, but with each word she read, her heart gave an antsy throb.

"From the giddy expression on your face, I imagine Lord Barrington the younger is a mite more handsome than the senior," said Aunt, scrutinizing Matilda's face over her tea cup.

The letter rambled, whimsical and distracted like the man who had written in, but he had not stuttered in his penmanship. It informed her that the decorations at Brackenburrow had been completed, the pups were now taking walks outside, and asked, would she and her chaperone like to come to tea on the morrow to see both of those new developments? Matilda very much would.

"He has invited us for tea, Aunt," said Matilda, looking up from the note.

"I am having tea now," Aunt answered, blithely.

"Do not tease me, please," Matilda begged. "Please, can we go?"

"Oh dear, you are smitten. Losing your sense of humor is the first sign of it. Do not glare at me girl, I have not said no, have I?"

"You have not said yes, either."

By way of response, Aunt beckoned over the footman who had delivered the note and was waiting in the doorway.

"Please inform Lord Barrington we would be delighted to attend tea at Brackenburrow on the morrow."

Matilda beamed. "Thank you, Aunt. It means so much to me."

"Yes, that is what I am afraid of."

Aunt Alda grimaced as she caught her aunt's hands and then pulled her into an unexpected hug.

Chapter Six

It was barely light when Clarence burst into the morning room. He was bundled from head to toe in thick wool, mismatched as if he had picked out his clothes himself.

"Brenna said I had to eat breakfast before I could go outside and play," he said by way of explanation. He snatched two jam-filled pastries off the tray and shoved them into his mouth at once.

"She probably meant for you to chew it, not swallow it whole like a reptile," said Aunt Alda. "If you choke to death you cannot play, you know."

He swallowed the mouthful and washed it down with a cup of juice. "Will you come out and play with me, Mattie? I built a fort yesterday, and you can build one, and then we can have a snowball fight."

"Only if you are prepared to be horribly beaten by your sister," Matilda replied, leaning across the table to tickle his ribs, buried beneath the layers of fabric.

He squealed and ran out of the room. A moment later, the front door opened and closed and she saw him run by the windows.

"You encourage him," Aunt sniffed. "Do not stay out long. You know the cold air will make your hair brittle and dry. No one wants a wife with straw for hair."

Matilda did not know if that was true at all, nor did she have any immediate plans for becoming a wife, at least not to the stuffy bores Aunt Alda brought for her perusal. There was no talking Aunt out of her odd beliefs.

"Do not be long," Aunt Alda said, as Matilda exited the house. "You will need time to prepare for tea at Brackenburrow today. I will have an outfit laid out for you. You pick the most unflattering items, is it intentional? Never mind. Run along now, let me have breakfast in peace," Aunt said, flicking her fingers toward Matilda.

Before Aunt could launch into a lecture on the latest fashions and selecting the best fabrics for one's figure, Matilda fled. Those discussions could last hours and were not, in Aunt Alda's mind, optional.

Gloved, coated, and booted, Matilda met Clarence outside. He greeted her with a snowball that missed, arcing over her shoulder and striking a tree behind her.

"You devil," she cried. Matilda snatched up an armful of snow and began packing it into a ball. "Take this!"

He dodged behind his fort, and the fight was on. It did not end until Clarence, panting and sweating, begged for a ceasefire. She had gotten the better of him, as promised.

Younger siblings had to be reminded of their older sibling's superiority on a regular basis, or they became impossible to live with and Matilda had just upheld her side of older siblings everywhere.

"It is only because you are bigger," Clarence insisted, as he plopped down onto the front steps.

They had been brushed clean of snow and ice, but the cold stone went straight through her coat when Matilda sat down beside him.

"That must be it." She was only a few inches taller than him and they were likely of a similar weight. He would take after their father, and would shoot past her in the next few years. "Are you happy, Clarence?"

She wanted to ask how he was coping with their parents' death, but if it was not already in his mind, she did not want to be responsible for putting it there.

"I wish Aunt would do Christmas properly," he said, frowning down at his hands with a troubled face. "It is no fun at all, this way."

Privately, she agreed with him. "We do have the kissing bough, though. That is something, is it not? And plum pudding, she did promise us plum pudding."

Clarence stuck out his tongue. "A kissing bough is for *kissing*. Yuck. But the plum pudding is fine, I guess."

Matilda saw him inside and warmed up with a cup of hot chocolate before going upstairs to prepare for tea. As promised, Aunt had set an outfit aside for her.

It was overmuch for Brackenburrow, but there was no point in arguing. The wine-colored dress had a low cut bodice which hung off the shoulders, precariously low, and the short, tight sleeves had puffs of white lace at the cuff. There would be petticoats to fill out the skirt, which was trained, and the hem was ruffled. She let her hair down and sat, while Emily brushed the smooth black veil to sleekness. That was only the start of it, and it was an entire hour before her hair was complete, braided and piled into a weighty chignon at the nape of her neck.

She had been blessed with a fair, porcelain complexion, one that Aunt made certain she protected, and so little time was spent on powdering. There was a moment of fuss when the clasp of her pearl necklace refused to open, but it gave way to Emily's stubbornness and Matilda was at last allowed to leave after slipping on her gloves. Her slippers were fashionable, but she would be grateful for the warming coals at the foot of the sleigh. Aunt was waiting at the front door, dressed in an even more elaborate gown than Matilda's. One of the perks of being a widow was wearing ostentatious fashions the younger crowd would never wear, Aunt insisted.

Chapter Seven

It was a silent ride over to Brackenburrow, for Aunt hated having to shout and the method of travel allowed for nothing else. When they pulled down the drive, Matilda was delighted to see that the exterior had been adorned with sprays of evergreen.

"How beautiful it is!" Matilda clapped her hands in delight, ignoring Aunt's pursed lips.

Barrington was waiting at the door. "G-good afternoon, Lady Claridge, Lady Darcy."

"You answer the door yourself? How unusual. Is this a new trend amongst the younger set?" Aunt's tone danced the line between insulting and polite. Matilda knew which one she meant to lean toward.

Either Barrington did not notice, or he took no mind of it. "A p-personal quirk, I am afraid. I c-cannot speak to what my p-peers do." His stutter was back, full force.

A servant did come forward to take their coats, at least, for she was certain the lack of that would have put Aunt over the edge. Another laid out their tea. Barrington had not lied, the food made in Brackenburrow's kitchens was as fine a fare as she had ever enjoyed. Even Aunt had nothing to curl her lip at.

"Is it not lovely what he has done with the place, Aunt?" Matilda asked. "He decorated it all himself, you know. What a Christmas spirit you have, Lord Barrington."

He looked down into his tea cup, but she could see the elusive smile at the corners of his lips.

Aunt sniffed. "Yes, quite lovely. Will you be throwing a party to show it off? There seems little point in going so far to decorate without having anyone to show it to. And I find there is nothing better than a Ball at Christmas. It would be a chance for you to meet some of the locals."

Matilda gaped. After how long and hard she begged her aunt for a Christmas Ball, now, she was suggesting such to Lord Barrington? "Aunt..." Matilda cautioned. "I am not sure Lord Barrington is any hurry for that, he has hardly had time to settle in."

"What better way to get settled in than with a Ball? I cannot think of one."

"But," Matilda began again.

Aunt Alda continued sharply. "Do not interrupt, Matilda, I am only giving him an idea, not forcing him. Were you not asking just the other day to attend a Christmas Ball? You were, I do remember now."

Matilda had asked for no such thing. That was before…. and had nothing to do with Barrington. She wanted to crawl under the table to hide her mortification. Barrington's wide-eyed expression was one she had worn herself many times while being lambasted by Aunt. He looked at Matilda, who lifted her shoulders in an apologetic shrug. There was not much more she could do.

"I—I will c-consider that, L-lady Claridge," he said. "Though I have never organized a party before and it seems rather beyond my c-capabilities. Nor do I think Brackenburrow is up to the s-standards others are accustomed to. My uncle's tastes were outdated. I haven't r-renovated."

"Oh do not say that, Lord Barrington. I think it was just charming here. There is something sentimental about it," said Matilda.

Aunt arched one angular eyebrow. "Charming, quite."

"If you two believe it is a good idea, perhaps…"

"I do, Lord Barrington, I truly do," said Aunt Alda. "I would be happy to assist you in the arrangements."

This made Matilda very suspicious. Aunt, who had rejected the idea of a Christmas party, was now campaigning for one. What was she up to?

Barrington gulped. He looked from Matilda to Aunt, and back again. "Th-thank you, that is a generous offer."

It was neither a yes nor a no, and Matilda felt he had handled it as well as he could have. Few were able to handle Aunt Alda.

She decided now was the moment to save him, for Aunt to push him any more would cross the line into rudeness.

"Lord Barrington, may I visit the litter? Aunt, you will not want to accompany us, I know how the fur causes a sneezing fit for you," said Matilda, sliding her chair back.

He leapt to his feet. "It would be my pleasure."

"Please do not dally long, Matilda," said Aunt. "The dressmaker will arrive at Grantchester before dinner, and you cannot escape that."

"Yes, Aunt."

The moment they escaped the room, Matilda turned to Barrington. "I do apologize for her. She is as strong-headed as a bull and will run roughshod over anyone. Do not feel obliged to throw a party to please her. Grantchester is perfectly suited for it, but she had no interest there, so this is some scheme of hers."

Barrington was quiet for a time. "Was it true what she said? You wished for a Christmas party?"

"Oh, that," said Matilda, embarrassed. "I did. It was a family tradition, before my parents passed. So I did, but it was for nostalgia's sake, and you should not let that persuade you. She should never have mentioned it. I am mortified."

The puppies greeted them at the door, rambunctious and bouncing, steadier on their legs than they had been just days ago.

"How quickly they grow!" Matilda said. "Will it be long before they can leave their mother?"

"Not much, another week. I am not sure if she will miss them or if she will be happy enough to see them go," said Barrington.

Limited by the boning of the corset and the tight seams of her dress, Matilda could not kneel down and hug the pups to her as she wished to. She settled for petting them from above, and took pains to ensure each one of the identical dogs received some affection.

"We should return before Aunt Alda comes looking for me. She takes few things as seriously as fashion, and visits with the dressmaker, but she attends me with the diligence of an abbess attending church."

Lord Barrington chuckled.

They walked in silence back along the narrow hallway. It was lit by the stained glass window on the far end, which let in enough sunlight, this time, that she could make out some of the faces in the paintings. The family resemblance was apparent in the high cheekbones and the strong nose, which Barrington had inherited, and of course, those arresting eyes.

"May I steal another moment of your time, Lady Matilda?" Barrington stole a glance at Matilda. "I thought you may assist me with something. A small matter."

Curious, Matilda nodded. "I would be happy to."

He led her to another room, far larger than the one that housed the pups. There was a darkness to it, from the wood rail and the wallpaper, with leaves the shade of juniper set off by bronze flowers.

Their brassy color reminded her of Barrington's eyes, when she could see them beneath his spirited fringe. A fireplace took up almost the length of one wall and there were more of the stained glass windows here, bearing the family crest. In the center of the room, stood a fully decorated fir tree.

"It is not the most impressive tree," said Barrington, one hand rubbing at the back of his neck. "But I thought it might do."

"Did you chop it down yourself?" Matilda asked, looking at the tree with more respect. She reached out to run her fingers over the needled branches. "I think it is perfect."

It was decorated with tiny candles and ribbons, with all the intricate care she had come to recognize as Barrington's work.

"I did. One of the benefits of Leto's imperfect hunting methods — gives me plenty of time for sightseeing. She thought it was a lark when I began to drag it back toward home, as if I had made her a great big stick to carry around. She kept grabbing on to it and I had to stop and shoo her away."

"Did she not stop when she received the first mouthful of needles?" Matilda laughed, picturing the scene. "But how can I help you with this? It looks just right, to me."

The tree was well-decorated with flat lead stars and crosses, little nets filled with nuts and sweetmeats, golden apples hung on the tree as if they had grown there. Dozens of candles lit it with a soft light and tiny dolls grinned painted smiles.

"My grandmother made the dolls," he said. "She was quite talented. She fashioned them after all of our family. This is my grandfather, and my elder brother, and uncle, and these, the servants and their children."

"You miss her," Matilda breathed as she touched one of the delicate faces.

"I do."

Barrington went over to the window. Beneath the sill was a heavy chest with iron hinges, which creaked when he lifted the lid. He bent over it, shuffling things around, then stood and returned, holding something in his hands. "I thought…" he began. "It is tradition, in my family for the women to place the star on top."

He held out the tinsel star, slightly rumpled from its time in storage. Matilda took it with care. She looked up to the top of the tree, which seemed an impossible distance away, even on tiptoes.

"You will need a chair, of c-course, I did not think this th-through, did I?" said Barrington. He was flushed, as if the room were not drafty.

"There is no need for all that bother. If you can just give me a small lift, I should be able to reach it. My skirts are enormous, but they do not weigh as much as they look like they should."

Matilda realized, a little guiltily, that she rather enjoyed seeing him blush like that. Barrington looked up, catching her self-satisfied smile, and cocked a nervous, crooked grin.

"If you say," he said. With no more hesitation, he swept in and wrapped his hands about her waist. They were so large they almost encircled her, and he lifted her into the air as if she weighed no more than his grandmother's doll. She gasped in surprise, and it took her a moment to collect herself.

"A little higher, please," she said.

She set the star on the topmost branch, fiddling with it until it sat just so. Anything less than perfect would not do the tree, impeccably decorated as it was, justice.

"You may put me down now."

He did so, setting her lightly on her feet before him. She turned before stepping away, and found herself just inches from his chest. Matilda looked up, one button at a time, until she was looking into his eyes. They did not flinch away. There was a wildness to them, or perhaps their golden color was so like that of a wolf's it just put her in mind of them. Her gaze dropped to his lips. She thought he was going to kiss her, but he did not and the moment passed.

"Aunt will be I-looking for me," said Matilda, breathless.

If Barrington had not pulled away, Matilda could have stood there for hours more, counting the flecks of bronze in the gold of his eyes.

"Thank you, Lady Matilda," he said, offering his arm. He cleared his throat. "I have not put the star on the tree since my grandmother's death."

Matilda suddenly realized how significant the star was to him.

"Thank you," she said. "Thank you for allowing me to be a part of your tradition."

"I would indeed like for you to be a part of my tradition," he said looking at the tree. "The tree has never been trimmed with such care."

She wondered if he would ever be able to actually look at her and speak without stuttering, but now, she was the one blushing, and it served her right for teasing him. Matilda had met all of the suitors her Aunt Alda had insisted she meet, but none of them had filled her with these sensations, these awful, anxious, niggling feelings in her stomach. None of them had offered anything even close to love or even amusement. He silently held out his hand and they returned to the sitting room and broke apart with a new awkwardness between them.

"There you are," said Aunt. She was standing at the fireplace, traveling coat back on and a glass of sherry in her hand. Trust Aunt Alda to commandeer another house's servants to do her bidding. "I was beginning to worry. We must depart at once if we hope to arrive before the dressmaker."

Aunt's cool gaze rolled over Matilda and seemed to see far too much of interest there. A servant brought Matilda her coat.

"Thank you again, Lord Barrington," Aunt said, herding Matilda toward the door. "I will be in touch about the party."

Matilda would have argued that Lord Barrington didn't say he wanted a Christmas party, but the thought of dancing with the man made butterflies fill her. She did want a Christmas Ball, but only if Lord Barrington wanted it too.

On the sleigh ride home, Matilda learned that Aunt did not need to speak to make her opinions known.

Chapter Eight

True to her word, Aunt did get in touch with Barrington about the Christmas Ball. When Matilda attempted to pry any information about it from her, she received a tight-lipped smile and not a thing more. It was driving her mad. Two days before Christmas, she was informed that she would be attending a party on Christmas Eve at Brackenburrow, and that her dress had been completed and should arrive that day. Clarence was the only thing that kept her from going mad with curiosity. The boy was a never-ending fount of energy. No amount of snow or bitter cold would keep him inside.

~~~~~

It was Christmas Eve at last, and Matilda was impatient for evening to come, so when Clarence asked to play outside, she jumped at the chance. They laced up their skates and wound their way down the stream that edged the thicket.
~~~~~

It was frozen through and cloudy white, marred only by the cuts from their blades.

Though she spent hours there, she did not see Barrington again in the forest. She listened for the sounds of barking, or the breaking of iced-over branches, only to be drawn back to the present by Clarence. Was he lonesome there, in Brackenburrow?

"Come on, Mattie, I will race you back home!" The little brat took off before she had a chance to respond.

With the head start and his boyhood recklessness, he beat her to the bend in the stream where Grantchester sprawled.

"I won," Clarence informed her. He sat down in the snow to pull of his skates.

"You did cheat," she pointed out.

They walked back to the house, he in his woollen socks, which were soaked when they reached the house, and she wobbling on top of her skates. Both of them earned a disapproving look from Aunt.

"Good heavens. You will need to bathe before we go to Brackenburrow. You as well, Clarence. And throw those socks away, they are ruined now.

"Yes, Aunt," they said in unison.

Bathed, scrubbed with pumice and oils, and finished with the elaborate affair of dressing, Matilda stepped in front of the mirror. Her figure was hugged by the tight ivory bodice trimmed in gold; then drowned by the voluminous, tiered, cream-colored skirts.

Her maid slid the bejeweled comb into the curls mounded on top of her head, and called it complete.

"I will meet you out there in a moment," Matilda called, waving them on.

Once they were out the door, she pulled a chair from the dining table and clambered up on it like a child. She probably should have put Clarence up to these shenanigans.

She nearly fell, trying to balance with her skirts weighing her down. She pulled the kissing bough down from its hook, tucked it beneath her arm, as she clung to the chair to climb down, and hurried outside.

The two women rode to Brackenburrow in Aunt Alda's fashionable carriage. Clarence was quite put out that at ten, he was not permitted to join the festivities, but his sister promised to smuggle him a piece of fruitcake.

They arrived just at dusk. Candles lit the place, hundreds of them, so that it glowed in the night like a star-studded sky. Matilda gazed up in awe as they entered. There was a pleasant hum of voices inside, but not the din of a large crowd. Servants took their coats, and she could see more bustling about, coming up from the kitchen. That had her Aunt written all over it. She even recognized several of the servants loaned to Barrington for the event. She had to wonder who was home to look after young Clarence, so many of Aunt Alda's servants were here!

The party was gathered around the Christmas tree, and they seemed to be playing a rowdy game of charades.

She recognized most of them as her Aunt's friends, but Matilda hung back, scanning the room for Barrington. He was standing aside with a flute of wine in his hand. He looked nervous, but happy. His unruly hair had already escaped his attempts at taming it, but his clothes were so fine and perfectly cut Matilda knew her Aunt had selected them.

Matilda crossed the room to him, skirting the crowd.

"I have brought you a gift," she said, presenting the kissing bough. "I noticed you did not have one amongst all your other decorations. It seemed a terrible oversight, and I wished to save you the embarrassment."

"That was kind of you. I know just the place to hang it." Barrington said, taking it from her. She noticed that he did not stutter at all. Perhaps he was less nervous in a crowd than with her alone. The thought made her blush.

He stopped to greet Aunt Alda, who graciously accepted the mulled wine he brought her.

"A wonderful party you have put together, Lord Barrington," said Aunt, with a wink.

Barrington and Matilda stepped out into the corridor which joined the main hall with the section of the house that led down to the pups and the kennel. He stopped at the juncture.

"Here, I think. Do you agree?" He reached up to hang the kissing bough from the doorframe.

Matilda looked up. The berries were bright red, against the green of the leaves.

"Just right," said Matilda. "Perfect."

"Almost perfect," he said and she realized he didn't stutter at all.

"Oh?" she began, but then he bent toward her in the confines of the doorway and captured her lips beneath his. There was nothing hesitant nor shy about him any longer.

The heat lingered on her lips when he pulled back, leaving her cruelly breathless. With his grin as wolfish as his eyes, he reached up and plucked one crimson berry from the mistletoe.

"Merry Christmas, Lady Matilda."

"Merry Christmas, Lord Barrington."

The End

If you enjoyed this story, please leave a review on the site where you purchased it.

Want more from Isabella Thorne?

You'll find a preview of

'The Mad Heiress meets the Duke'

after the 'About the Author' section!

ARIETTA RICHMOND, GRACE AUSTEN, ISABELLA THORNE,
KATHERINE KEATS AND SOPHIA WILSON

About the Author

Isabella Thorne is an author of Regency and Georgian Romance. The first grown-up books she read were historical, authored by Georgette Heyer, Victoria Holt and Anna Seton. Unfortunately, for her own daughters, the beauty and hallmark of Regency Romance, witty dialogue and the manners of the time, have been over-shadowed by explicit books instead of true Regency Romance.

With a return to romance, Isabella Thorne hopes you will enjoy her light, fun books. You can share them with your daughters with the guarantee that, although there is romance aplenty, and a bit of sexual tension and a kiss, there is nothing explicit in her books.

They are clean and wholesome reads with lots of humor and upbeat "fun poking" at the English mannerisms of the time.

Because Isabella loves the pageantry of the period, she loves to include true events or set stories during a war -- the English were involved in so many of them at this time!

You will find bits of history scattered through the books and an occasional historical figure, but these books are FICTION and not intended to be a definitive history. None of the Peerage mentioned in them, of any land, actually existed.

Isabella hopes that all the British and the die-hard historical readers will please forgive this passionate American if she makes any mistakes, and, if you find one, send an email off to isabellathorne58@yahoo.com so that she can make corrections.

Stop by her website, www.isabellathorne.com for a free story and a notification of special sales.

If you love her books, PLEASE REVIEW and SHARE, so that others can come to love them too!

Other Books By Isabella Thorne

The Georgette Quinby Series

The Mad Heiress Meets the Duke

The Mad Heiress and the Search for a Spy

The Mad Heiress Visits Vauxhall

The Mad Heiress and the Rose Room Rout

The Mad Heiress' Cousin and the Hunt

The Duke's Wicked Wager Series

Promise Me a Handful of Horses

Promise Me Daring

Promise Me This Dance

Promise Me Your Heart

Mischief, Mayhem and Murder: A Marquis of Evermont Regency Romance

Other Books by Isabella Thorne

Colonial Cressida and the Secret Duke

To find more Regency Romance stories, please visit my website

www.isabellathorne.com

Please Like Isabella Thorne on Facebook

https://www.facebook.com/Isabella-Thorne-Author-1737782389810565/

Share or comment on an Isabella Thorne Facebook post for a chance to win an Amazon gift card

ARIETTA RICHMOND, GRACE AUSTEN, ISABELLA THORNE,
KATHERINE KEATS AND SOPHIA WILSON

Here is Your Preview of
The Mad Heiress Meets the Duke

Book 1: The Georgette Quinby Series

Georgette had escaped to the garden. Even in winter, the green and growing things gave her comfort. She breathed slowly through her nose. Her breath puffed out like a little cloud. No doubt the tongues would be wagging. The *ton* would think her even crazier than normal to come out here in the cold, but she needed a moment - just a moment - to herself, in the cold winter air. Some time to gather her wits about her, to take some deep breaths. To remember who she was and how it had once been; how she had once been so blindingly happy, and then to remember how it was now. Breathe, she told herself as she pressed her gloved hands together over her stomacher. In. Out. Well, in as far as her corset allowed and then out.

The ballroom had been stifling - an absolute crush, packed with bodies and warring perfumes. And all of them turning their catty faces to her - looking at her with distain. She couldn't bear it for one moment longer.

"Look, it's the Mad Heiress," one of the young ladies had said tittering like a ninny.

"Is it really? I thought she'd killed herself." Her friend fanned herself as she looked slyly over the accessory at Georgette.

"No, you were misinformed," another said, craning her bejeweled neck. "I heard she flung herself off a parapet, after Lord Falks threw her over for Lady Julia."

"I heard it was a cliff," the first one said.

"I'm certain it was a parapet. But no matter. The point is, she survived."

"Poor thing. I'd rather be dead," said the first woman fanning herself quite vigorously.

"It was stairs," Georgette had said to the open air, once she had fled to the garden. "Stairs. If one must gossip, at the very least one should get the facts straight. I flung myself down some stairs."

She should probably stop talking to herself, she thought. She was already known as the Mad Heiress, and she hadn't done anything exciting for almost ten years. Lud, if the *ton* heard her grumbling to herself about stairs she would never rest in peace.

But honestly - a cliff? If it had been a cliff, she might have had some success. Instead, she had woken up in her bed, a few days later, with a sore head and a broken hip, like an old woman. And a fiancé who did not love her. She must not forget that.

Oh, Sebastien. Why?

Ten years ago she had been slipping out of ballrooms to meet him in the garden, the stolen kisses sweet on her lips: Escaping the candlelight and the weak punch and her stifling mother, hoping for a stolen moment with her beloved.

Ten years, and no one forgot. No one ever forgot. She clenched her fists. She would forever be the Mad Heiress. No matter that she had been but seventeen when Sebastien had informed her that his heart belonged to another.

No matter that she was twenty-six-years old now, and a chaperone, a spinster, firmly on the shelf.

No matter that she could not conceive of the sensibility and passion that had driven her up those stairs. She could not remember, but everyone else still remembered.

Deep breaths, she reminded herself as she rubbed her gloved hands over her cooling arms. Breathe in, breathe out. Or, rather, breathe in as deeply as one's corset allows, and breathe out. In, and out, through the nose.

Georgette froze. She sniffed the air. Someone was smoking a cigar.

Oh, bother.

She swallowed. Perhaps the gentleman would not realize she'd entered the gardens. She could surreptitiously sneak back into the ballroom. She made to turn back into the house.

He stood right in front of her. Grey flecked through his hair. She knew his eyes were dark blue, but the darkness of the gardens made them almost black. He peered at her with them, over a royal, aquiline nose.

The Duke of Eversley.

"I beg your pardon," he said. "I did not realize there was a Lady in the garden. I will snuff my cigar."

"Please don't on my account, Your Grace," she said, giving a curtsey. "I was just about to re-enter the ballroom."

He blinked at her. "I know you," he said. He tilted his head and looked at her, no doubt attempting to place her.

Georgette opened her mouth and then closed it again. Did he truly not recognize her?

"Ah, yes, Your Grace," she said. "I do believe we crossed paths several years ago, when I was newly out."

He continued to look at her curiously.

"I was engaged to your dear friend, Lord Sebastien Falks."

"Sebastien? But you can't have been engaged to Sebastien, he married my..."

She knew the moment he pieced it together, the moment he remembered. He colored, though it was difficult to tell in the darkness, and gave a small cough.

"I beg your pardon," he said. "I forgot, you see. It was all so long ago."

She couldn't help herself: she laughed. He stared at her for a moment as if she was demented.

Continue Reading

'The Mad Heiress Meets the Duke'

at:

https://www.amazon.com/dp/B01ICEAT4W/

Regency Romance
Isabella Thorne

ARIETTA RICHMOND, GRACE AUSTEN, ISABELLA THORNE,
KATHERINE KEATS AND SOPHIA WILSON

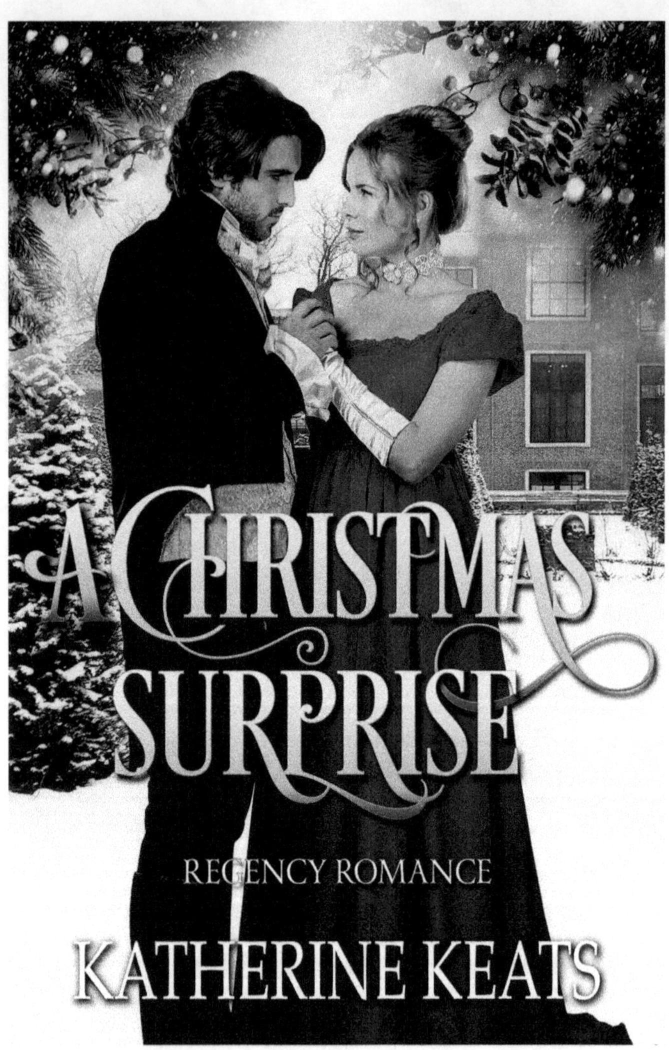

A Christmas Surprise
REGENCY ROMANCE
KATHERINE KEATS

A Christmas Surprise

Katherine Keats

Chapter One

He pulled on his horse's reins while lifting his gun to his shoulder and fired. In the next instant Major Silas Reeves was knocked to the ground. He lay there for a moment, stunned as the sound of bullets and men screaming echoed in his ears. Then a great rage came over him and he rose to his feet. He took hold of the reins and hoisted himself up into the saddle. Digging his feet into his horse's side, he spurred it onwards and skilfully wielded his sabre to great effect.

He knew not how long he fought or how many bullets he dodged. The soldiers he led looked to him for guidance, seeing him always in front of them, attacking the enemy fearlessly. They were encouraged to press on. The battle raged on for another hour and then suddenly Silas realized it was growing quieter. Looking around him through the gun smoke, he saw that the French had retreated and the battle field was theirs. Twenty British soldiers remained from his troop and the rest lay dead or dying.

"Lift up the injured and carry them back!" he shouted and the soldiers obeyed him.

Silas turned his horse around and rode back towards the camp. It was only as he dismounted that he became aware that he had been shot in the shoulder. He looked down at his blood-soaked clothes. Bewildered and exhausted he collapsed on the ground. For a few, blissful hours he was unaware of the horror and chaos that he had left behind at the scene of the battle.

Meanwhile miles away in the shire of Norholm, Louisa Fifett sat sewing a button onto her father's shirt. Her mind flooded with painful memories and feelings she would rather forget.

The desire for vengeance was like a fire in the pit of her stomach. Sometimes it burned blue and low as if it was about to go out. She would start to believe it might disappear at last but then it burst out in tremendous flames, threatening to overwhelm her. It was at those times that she felt she would never be able to sleep or laugh or even exist without pain again.

She moved the needle in and out of the fabric in a regular rhythm as she worked. A strand of her red hair came loose and curled on her forehead. Her delicate lips were pursed in concentration. She kept her hazel eyes lowered, not wanting her father to catch a glimpse of the blackness in their depths. She need not have worried. The doctor was fondly gazing at her, thinking how like her late mother she appeared at that moment. Then he sighed, thinking of Katherine, his elder daughter, and how he missed her.

"I wonder if we will see Katherine this Christmas or not." He wondered aloud.

At the sound of his words, Louisa's fingers slipped and the needle punctured the tip of her thumb. She stopped and lifted the thumb to her mouth to hide the little drop of blood that welled up there.

"I doubt it." She said calmly, "Charles will not allow it."

"You may be wrong there my dear - granted he may not be very fond of us. However, his constant thirst may drive him to agree to visit, for the chance to drink himself into a stupor at my expense!" chuckled the doctor.

"Papa you wouldn't!" Louisa looked up for the first time and the pallor of her face alarmed the doctor. He got up and walked to her side, taking the shirt from her hands.

"My love, you know I would never indulge him. However, his circumstances are such that he cannot afford to pay for his drink. Christmas is as good an opportunity as any to obtain free liquor from your relatives."

"I don't know how you can joke about the situation Papa!"

"You're right my dear, I should have been more careful." He replied soothingly, "It's just that I want to see Katherine and the little ones again. I can't do anything about her drunkard husband, but I think I can give Katherine something to ease her hardship."

"Nothing can ease her hardship!" exclaimed Louisa, "The Duke of Norholm saw to that!"

"Louisa it's been five years. The Duke died five years ago. How long are you going to blame that wretched man for your sister's situation?"

"I can't ever forget it." She said quietly

"You must forget it Louisa, if you wish to have a normal and fruitful existence." said the doctor.

"I know, Papa, and yet you must be aware that you are the only one I talk to about my thoughts. I would never be so unguarded as to express my malevolent desires in front of anyone else." Louisa said, half-jokingly.

"What malevolent desires? You wouldn't hurt a fly, my dear. You are your mother's image. She was so gentle and forgiving," the doctor said wistfully

"Drink your tea Papa, it's getting late and you have to make your morning rounds." said Louisa.

"What would I do without you dear? You always take care of everything for me.

After the doctor had taken his tea, Louisa cleared the breakfast dishes off the table and went to fetch her father's black bag.

He took it from her hand and, kissing her on the forehead, said "Shall we have a little fish for supper tonight Lou?"

"Yes Papa, I shall step out right now and get some from the market."

"No don't bother dear. You look tired. I think you haven't slept well last night. I'll give the neighbor's boy a penny to bring it for you."

He left, and Louisa closed the door after him, feeling a little ashamed.

He was such an indulgent father, and she knew he worried about her all the time. She felt she ought not to talk to him about her hate for the Norholm family. Nor would she have, had it not been that she had been sitting in front of the fire ready to burst and his innocent joke had made her boil over.

"I don't know what comes over me. Just yesterday I was happy thinking of the things I would stuff little Davy and Mary's stockings with on Christmas Eve and now I feel as if everything is an exercise in futility. While such evil people walk this Earth, how can the rest of mankind rejoice? Perhaps they will all fall sick and die like that cursed Duke of Norholm. Lord forgive me! I wish I could stop thinking about them."

She decided to go for a walk after all, thinking the fresh air would do her good.

Chapter Two

Silas struggled to remain seated upright on his horse. Two weeks had passed since the day he had been shot. His coat was torn and his breeches stained. He had not shaved for many days. He was cold and hungry. The bullet wound on his right shoulder gaped open and throbbed with every step his horse took. He had bound it up with rags torn from his shirt until he could tear no more. It had stopped bleeding but looked raw and unhealthy like rotting meat.

He had ridden many miles over the last few days, since he had been ordered to go on leave. He had not wanted to go home and at first had refused to accept that he could not lead the troops under his charge with a badly wounded shoulder. The army doctor had spoken with Colonel Harding and the Colonel told Silas he had been relieved. His replacement, Major Daniel Thornton, had been assigned to take his place in the Cavalry for a period of one month.

"I'm warning you Major Reeves, go home now before you compel me to make a note of your refusal to obey direct orders."

Silas stared at him in disbelief.

"As you are aware Major Reeves, there are a number of severely injured officers and soldiers that are in no condition to be moved at present. You will therefore have to ride home and seek further treatment there."

"Yes Sir. It seems I have no choice in the matter. I shall leave directly." said Silas.

He left that evening, without waiting for the doctor to change the dressing on his wound, which had become soaked with blood.

The journey home would normally have taken only a week, but Silas was compelled to travel slowly. He could not bear to allow his horse to pick up its pace past a gentle trot. Wherever he stopped to rest at night, he would lock himself up in his room and clean his wound himself, refusing all offers of help. He hated the fact that he had to return to Norholm Manor. The dark and dreary house was full of painful memories. There was no one there who he desired to see again. Only his aunt, the Baroness Rebecca Ware, lived there now.

"Easy there now Robin, gently does it. You know my bones ache with fever and I can't take your jolting." Silas murmured to his horse, who pricked his ears in response and slowed down to a gentle amble.

Not for the last time that night, Silas cursed his stubbornness, wishing that he had allowed the army doctor to dress his wound cleanly before he left the camp. He would have accepted offers of help at the roadside inns where he stopped, but they had annoyed him there.

He did not like the way the maids stared at him in awe, whispering amongst themselves about the handsome gentleman officer, wounded in battle, and how fine he would look, dressed up in his Major's uniform once they had cleaned him up. It reminded him of a time when he would have accepted their offer and invited the prettiest one to share his bed. He despised himself for the levity and lack of discipline he had shown as a younger man. It seemed that, no matter how hard he tried, he could not escape his past. Something or other would remind him of it, and now he had to return to the place where he had displayed the worst of his excesses.

At that moment, as he looked ahead through the mist that had hidden the road ahead of him, he saw something approaching him. He struggled to understand what it was and then he realized it was a man on foot. In his fevered and delirious condition, it appeared as if the man was familiar. Then it dawned on him who it was.

"Miles, Miles! Is it really you! Miles!" he shouted hoarsely and reached out towards the man. He saw his face and a hand stretched out to take his and then he fell from his horse and knew no more.

∿∿∿∿∿

Dr. Fifett wiped his hands on a towel and smiled at the elderly lady he had come to see.

"Mrs. Wrigley I've bandaged up your foot properly and now you must promise me you'll get out of bed tomorrow morning and try to walk a little."

"Doctor, you know I can't walk with a foot all tied up!" complained Mrs. Wrigley

"Well it may be a trifle inconvenient, but it is by no means impossible. Miss Elisa here will help you, and you can use your walking stick. It is important that you keep using your legs Mrs. Wrigley, or you may find that you have lost the capacity to do so."

"I'll try and do as you say doctor…"

"If you don't I shall have to come and get you up myself." laughed the doctor.

"Are you leaving then? It is very late. It was very kind of you to come see me but I'm afraid you'll have a hard time getting home at this time of night." fretted the old lady.

"No no, it's no problem at all. I'm used to walking about at all hours of the day. It'll take me just half an hour. I know all the lanes around here like the back of my hand. Goodnight Mrs. Wrigley and Miss Elisa."

Raising his hat to the two women, the doctor took his leave and walked out into the cold, November night. A thick, damp fog had settled on the trees outside. The doctor pulled his coat closer around himself and, gripping his bag tight in his hand, set off down the lane towards Norholm Manor. He knew Louisa would be getting worried waiting for him, so he walked briskly, keeping a sharp look out for the turning towards his own cottage.

He had been walking for about 20 minutes when he reached the place where he had to turn off the lane to Norholm Manor and towards his home. He stopped and listened. He thought he could hear the sound of a horse's hooves approaching him. This would not have been very strange; as late night travelers did sometimes appear there, but he felt sure he had heard the sound of a man groaning in pain.

He waited and soon he saw the outline of the horse coming towards him. It suddenly occurred to him that he was being rather foolhardy waiting for a stranger to approach him on a dark and lonely road in the night. Yet something told him that this was no robber or bandit and the sound of pain he had heard concerned him. He could see a figure slumped on the back of the horse. He watched as the horse ambled gently up to him. Suddenly the figure sat up straight and said something. He could not make out the words but he did not have time to wonder about it because the next moment the figure was lying in a heap at his feet. Dr. Fifett kneeled down and shook the man gently.

"Are you alright young man?" He asked loudly and hearing no answer he got up and with some difficulty hoisted the man up onto his shoulders. He noticed that he was wasted and weak. His weight was not as much of a burden as would be expected for a man of his height. He placed him over the horse's saddle and, taking the reins, led it on towards his home.

ARIETTA RICHMOND, GRACE AUSTEN, ISABELLA THORNE,
KATHERINE KEATS AND SOPHIA WILSON

Chapter Three

Louisa sat staring at the fire, biting her nails. Her imagination carried her to days gone by. It seemed as if she saw Katherine in front of her, laughing gaily as she rode on the rough swing her father had tied to the apple tree outside their cottage. Louisa sat crying a little distance away.

"Kathy, Kathy it's my turn now. Please let me up." She wailed.

"Just a moment Lou and then I'll give you a push." Said Kathy

She slowed the swing down dragging her feet in the dirt patch below. She got up and held her hand out to Louisa but the little girl was having none of it. She turned away and stuck her lower lip out, wrapping her arms around herself.

"What, are you sulking now? Shall I go away then?" asked Katherine.

"You took so long and now I'm hungry!" said Louisa

"Alright, here let's get some apples."

Katherine pulled Louisa up by the hand and then, placing a foot on the tree trunk, grabbed hold of the lowest branch to pull herself up. She managed to climb up into the fork of the tree and sidled forward on one of the branches. Louisa stood underneath looking up anxiously.

"Oh Kathy, Kathy, come down! You'll fall!"

Kathy leaned forward and, reaching out her hand, just managed to touch an apple with the tip of her fingers.

"Give me a stick Lou." She called

Louisa looked around and picking up a fallen branch held it up to Katherine. The older girl took the stick and swatted hard at the dangling apple. Down it fell but in knocking it with the stick, Katherine had lost her balance. She screamed as she slipped and fell, managing to catch at the branch on her way down. Louisa screamed now because Katherine was hanging from the branch with both hands about two feet above the ground. She ran up and held her little arms out.

"Jump, jump, Kathy. I'll catch you!" she called

Katherine giggled loudly.

"Will you really Lou? Will you catch me? What if I break a leg?"

"I shall catch you and I'll tie up your leg and make it all better."

Katherine let go of the branch and landed on her feet. Louisa wrapped her arms around her waist and cried

"Where does it hurt Kathy? Tell me."

"Hush I'm alright you silly goose. Here pick up your apple and sit on the swing." Said Kathy

Louisa sighed as she remembered how she wouldn't rest until she had informed her Papa and made sure that Katherine was really not hurt. She had always been very protective of Katherine, even though she was the younger sister.

Katherine was carefree and adventurous, easily getting into trouble, and Louisa would follow her around, warning her to be careful. Yet, she had been unable to save her from Miles, the late Duke of Norholm.

At that moment she heard the sound of someone stumbling on the doorstep outside. She got up and hurrying to the door threw it open. There stood her father, red-faced with exertion, holding up an unconscious stranger.

"Stand by Lou. Give me some space." He said and half carrying, half dragging the stranger, he brought him in through the door and laid him down on the floor in front of the fire.

"Leave him there a minute Lou, his horse is outside. Let me see to him first." The doctor rushed outside without giving Louisa a chance to say anything. Louisa clicked her tongue in exasperation.

"Oh Papa, have you started bringing your patients home now?" she said to herself.

Looking out through the open door she saw her father mounting the horse and riding it back down the lane. She sighed and closed the door, knowing he wouldn't be back for half an hour or more.

He would have to ride the horse down to their neighbor's farm, about half a mile away and leave it there in their stable.

She looked at the stranger lying unconscious on the floor.

"Wherever did he come from?" She wondered, and went to fill a kettle with water to boil.

Louisa rolled up her sleeves and went to work. She knew well what her father would want to be done, even though he had told her to leave the stranger alone. She placed a pillow under the stranger's head and unbuttoned his coat. She noticed the large patch of dried blood on his shoulder and, taking a knife, slit his coat sleeves from wrist to collar. The shirt underneath was already torn so she cut that off too. Then she took a clean blanket and covered him with it leaving only his right arm and shoulder exposed.

"Foolish man, whatever were you doing outside at this time of night, in your condition?" she muttered under her breath.

The stranger lay completely still only the gentle rise and fall of his chest indicating that he was still alive. The touch of his bare skin against her fingers had told her that he was burning with fever. She placed damp cloths on his forehead and in his armpits. Then, placing a tray under his shoulder, she washed his wound with warm water. After all the dried blood and dirt had been washed away, she poured a cup of spirits, that her father kept for cleaning wounds, over the stranger's shoulder. Finally, she dried and bandaged it up.

When Dr. Fifett came back he found the door unlocked. He opened it and, walking in, saw his daughter hard at work. She had folded the blanket back to the stranger's waist and was busy wiping his face and chest with clean sponge cloths.

"Louisa dear, I could hardly have done better myself." He said with pride.

"Now leave the rest to me and fetch some more blankets and sheets. We shall have to make his bed here tonight."

ARIETTA RICHMOND, GRACE AUSTEN, ISABELLA THORNE,
KATHERINE KEATS AND SOPHIA WILSON

Chapter Four

Baroness Rebecca Ware sat at one end of the dinner table at Norholm Manor and sipped her glass of Champaign. It did nothing to soothe her vexation and she glared at the steward standing beside her respectfully.

"Take away that fowl and tell the cook it is not properly done!" she snapped at him. She picked at the food on her plate after he had left. "It's been six months now and still no word from Silas. How does he expect me to pay for all my needs if he doesn't send me more money?" she said to herself.

"That boy has always been utterly heartless! I ought to have had at least three new dresses made by this time of year, and Marian will be visiting soon with her family. How will I endeavor to entertain her? If I know him at all he'll be playing at being a hero and will get himself killed at Waterloo. What will I do then? I'll be driven out of my brother's home and forced to live at the old house in London. How will I reside in a house with only six bedrooms, a cook and two housemaids? I shall be positively miserable!"

She dabbed at her mouth with a napkin and got up from the table, her appetite gone.

"Norholm Manor will be inherited by the Greys, according to the existing arrangements. There must be some way to alter those arrangements. What can I do to secure my future? I think I should wait for Marian and ask her advice."

Marian Holmes had been the Baroness' bosom friend since before their respective marriages. Marian had married Lord Holmes of Grimsworth and she had just one daughter whom she had thoroughly indulged in every way. Camilla Holmes was now a young lady of 16 years and very well aware of her status, having £20,000 settled upon her.

Rebecca, meanwhile, had been married by her father, Duke Edward Reeves of Norholm, to Baron Henry Ware. She had lived with him for 20 years and suffered under his tyranny so long that she had lost all sense of loyalty to her own family.

She blamed her brother, Alexander Reeves, for failing to warn her father about the character of Baron Henry Ware, whom he had attended school with at Eton. She suspected her father of placing the family name and honor above the happiness of his only daughter.

Twenty years after she married the Baron, Rebecca Ware was left a childless widow. Her husband had been killed in a hunting accident by being thrown from his horse.

His title and wealth had passed to his younger brother and Baroness Rebecca Ware had been forced to return to her father's house with the remainder of her fortune.

Her father had passed away two years later, leaving her to the mercy of her brother, Alexander Reeves, the new Duke of Norholm, and his young wife. They had been kind enough to her, but she resented the feeling that she was not the Lady of the house. She developed a violent jealousy of her sister in law, and did her best to poison her brother against his wife. Quiet by nature, Priscilla Reeves had done her best not to antagonize Rebecca. She gave birth to two sons, Miles and Silas and then, one night, died in her sleep when Silas was just 4 years old.

The cause of her death remained a mystery, and Alexander Reeves was devastated by her loss. He took to drinking more than was good for him and spent days locked up in his study, smoking cigars. His sons were largely neglected and the Baroness saw this as her opportunity to exert control over them.

One day at dinner she noticed that Miles was picking at his plate. She spoke sharply

"Miles finish your dinner child! It is ill mannered to leave food on your plate."

"But I'm not hungry Aunt…"

"Listen to your Aunt boy! Children should be seen and not heard." His father said.

"Yes Sir" Miles quietly bowed his head and the Baroness saw his eyes fill with tears. After dinner she placed a hand on his shoulder and stopped him as he was about to leave the room. She waited until her brother and Silas had left.

Then she sat down and still holding his hand asked "What is it child? Why are you so miserable?"

"Father wants to send me to Boarding School" he replied simply.

"I gather you do not wish to go?"

"No Aunt, I shall miss my home and Boarding School is a disagreeable place where the big boys bully the smaller ones."

"What if I asked your father not to send you?"

"Would you do that Aunt?" Miles asked eagerly.

"I might, but only if you promise me something." She answered.

"What is that Aunt?"

"You must vow to look after me as I grow older dear. Remember I have no one except you"

"I promise Aunt." said Miles, earnestly.

"Give me a kiss and run away now." She said.

The next day she met her brother walking on the lawn, after breakfast. She joined him and walked silently for a while. Then she gave a deep sigh, rousing him from his reverie.

"What is it Rebecca?" he asked, irritated, "I know when you have a bee in your bonnet, so tell me directly."

"Alex you are positively rude! After all I do for you and your boys, if you do not want me here tell me so and I shall leave..."

"Now don't start that, Rebecca, for the Love of Christ, out with it! Say what you want to say or leave me be."

"Alex I'm very worried about Miles. He grows more and more undisciplined every day. He is out playing at all hours and neglects his studies dreadfully. The tutors are unable to do anything with him. I fully support your idea of sending him away to School. In fact, I urge you not to delay and send him as soon as possible."

Alexander Reeves looked at her, surprised. "So you found out about my plan, eh, and you agree with it? Well that's a first! I thought you would be crying about how you'd be left all alone again with no one to chivvy around anymore. Alright, I know what I need to do." He stalked off without another word.

When the Duke informed his son, that night at dinner, that he would be leaving for school in a week's time, Miles looked at his Aunt for support. However, she sat silent, refusing to meet his eyes. Miles' heart was broken and Silas, who was 6 years old at the time, could not understand what had happened to his brother and what he had done to be sent away from home.

However, the Baroness was relieved, as the boys annoyed her with their incessant chattering, and got in her way when she wanted to host tea parties for her friends.

She would warn Silas that, if he was not a good, quiet little boy, his father would pack him off to school too. At first, he feared her and then, growing bolder with time, he decided it would be better to go to school with Miles rather than remain at home with the Baroness.

So it was that he was shipped off to school too. The two brothers came back only when their father, at last, succumbed to his unhealthy lifestyle and passed away.

Miles now became the Duke of Norholm, and a more dissipated rake was never seen. He drank even more than his father and would often spend months away from home in bad company. Whenever he came home he always had at least three young women as companions. The women were of ill-repute and slowly word of his bad habits spread around the neighboring villages.

The Baroness had lost her ability to manipulate him. Years later, when he died after falling ill with a mysterious illness that his doctors refused to reveal, she was relieved.

However, Silas turned out to be even less of a comfort to her. He bought himself a commission in the British Cavalry and went off to war. Before he left he warned her that she would receive only £5000 a month from his bank, to run Norholm Manor, and should her expenses exceed that amount, she would have to rely on her own resources.

That was why Baroness Rebecca Ware was so perturbed on this cold November evening. She had only a small amount of money left over from the monthly expenses and did not think it would be enough to host her friend Lady Marian Holmes, and her daughter Camilla, over Christmas.

"Yes my situation is indeed unenviable." she said thoughtfully to herself.

"Yet I feel Marian and I can put our heads together and plan some way of exerting pressure on Silas. After all, hasn't she seen me through many a bad time before? Yes, I shall wait for her advice."

Sighing contentedly, the Baroness went off to bed.

Chapter Five

Silas Reeves woke from an uneasy dream. He had been galloping down a never ending highway in the dead of night. Suddenly Robin, his horse, had stopped short, throwing him onto the road. Silas groaned in pain as he felt his shoulder give way. Someone was with him, but he couldn't tell who it was. His eyes felt heavy as if he couldn't open them. He tried to move and realized he couldn't.

Terror washed over him as he struggled to move his leaden limbs. When he opened his mouth to scream, no sound came out. Then he felt something or someone touch his arm and his fear subsided. He could feel the frantic beating of his heart slow down to a gentle, regular rhythm. He lay still and listened to the voices talking quietly beside him. Gradually he drifted into sleep again.

He did not know how long he slept, but this time when he woke, he was no longer afraid. He looked around him and saw that he was lying on a rough cot, set up on one side of a fireplace, in a kitchen.

A long, low table had been pulled to the opposite side of the room. Something was cooking in a pot on the stove. The scent made him feel hungry. He thought that the room was empty and no one else was there. Then he saw a girl seated at the table with her head laid down on her arms. She appeared to be asleep. His dazed eyes wandered over her red hair and settled on her face. He wished she would open her eyes. He wanted to know what color they were. As he watched, her lashes gently fluttered on her cheeks, and then she was looking at him.

It seemed to him as if he had been looking deep into her gaze for ages, when suddenly she sat up straight and her pale face glowed crimson.

"How long have you been awake?" she demanded sharply.

He turned his head away, annoyed. As he opened his mouth to speak he coughed instead and a sharp pain burst through his right arm. The next moment she was by his side gently lifting his head up and holding a cup of water to his lips. He drank gratefully and then frowned up at her.

"I hardly know whether I should thank you or curse you!" he said hoarsely. "Who are you and what have you done to me?"

The girl looked at him for a while, her face expressionless. Then she replied. "My name is Louisa Fifett. My father is Dr. Algernon Fifett and you are at present under his roof. You owe your life to him, for he found you near dead on the road to Norholm Manor and carried you here. At present that is enough for you to know. Don't tire yourself out thinking too much as you are still far from well."

"I should think so! What have you done to make me so weak that I can barely move my limbs? Injured as I was I have ridden thus far on my own…" he coughed again.

"You have been confined to bed for some days now. The combination of inactivity and the effects of Laudanum are responsible for your weakness. It was necessary to give you some for your pain. Your shoulder wound was badly infected."

"Louisa child, this is wonderful indeed! I see your care has succeeded in bringing our guest to his senses." At that moment Dr. Fifett entered the room and beamed at Silas.

"How are you feeling young man?"

"You are the doctor, I presume." said Silas drily. "Well I wish I could give you a more satisfactory answer, but as you can see from my condition, I am in a terrible state. I can hardly move and by the way…. What have you done with my horse and my uniform?" he demanded.

"Your horse is safe and sound in a stable nearby. Your uniform unfortunately was beyond repair. Still we have preserved it as much as possible for your satisfaction. Whatever belongings you had are all here in this bag I have hung up above the fireplace." said the doctor, gently.

"Rest, young man, and do not worry so much. You are amongst friends. We may not be rich, but we are honest and you need not be so anxious. If the Lord had willed, you would have died out there in the cold, but He brought you to us. There are many questions we would ask of you too, but for now, just tell us your name."

"Major Silas……" Silas was unable to complete his introduction for just then he was overcome by a fit of coughing.

"Alright Major, now just take a sip of this tea my daughter has brewed for you and lie back quietly." said the doctor, kindly. Exhausted, Silas did as he was told and soon fell asleep again.

Louisa impatiently picked up the cup from which Silas had drunk and placed it on the table. "I don't know what is to become of us Papa. You've carried home this injured army officer and a ruder man I've never seen. He never even expressed any gratitude towards you!" she said

"Louisa, it's almost Christmas time. Would you have me leave him alone in the street? It's alright dear, I know you're just tired and overwrought. After all, it is you who have nursed him back to health. I have had very little to do with it."

"Well I could hardly let you sit up with him all night could I? You are out all day visiting your patients and you need your sleep. Papa, that reminds me, it is getting late and you should be in bed."

"Yes dear and so should you. Don't fret about him anymore. His fever is gone and he will sleep like a baby all night. Hopefully the next few days will do much to improve his health as well as his mood. The injured and unwell are rather childish Lou, remember that, and don't take anything he says to heart."

Louisa smiled at her father's explanation and, bidding him goodnight, went to bed.

Chapter Six

The morning sunshine came through the windows and created a strange sensation of restlessness in Silas' mind. He had been under the care of Dr. Fifett and Louisa for more than two weeks. He could now get up and walk about a little, but he was still very weak. He missed his horse, Robin, and longed to go for a ride in the cold November mornings.

Earlier that day, with Louisa's help, he had washed with warm water and shaved his beard. He felt much better and was embarrassed when he recalled the rude way he had behaved when he first gained consciousness. He would have apologized to the doctor and Louisa but whenever he tried to do so they would interrupt him and talk about some other subject. It was as if his gratitude embarrassed them and they truly felt it was their duty to care for him.

"How long am I going to stay here?" he thought.

"Norholm Manor can't be very far. Aunt Rebecca will be waiting for me. Although I must admit she is unlikely to be distressed by my absence."

"Who is Aunt Rebecca? Does she work at Norholm Manor?" asked Louisa, coming into the room.

Silas had not realized that he had spoken aloud and he almost burst out laughing at Louisa's assumption concerning the identity of his Aunt. However, he controlled himself, having resolved not to reveal his complete identity to Louisa or Dr. Fifett. He did not want to startle them by declaring himself a Duke. He also wanted to delay any confrontation with his Aunt the Baroness. So he said

"Yes, my Aunt is one of the women employed at Norholm Manor."

"Why would she not be distressed by your absence? You ought to go back to Norholm Manor and let her know you are safe." said Louisa.

"That place is the last place in this world that I want to go to." replied Silas

"I can sympathize with you there. I thoroughly detest Norholm Manor too."

Now it was Silas' turn to be curious.

"What have you to do with Norholm Manor?" he asked.

"It, or rather its inhabitants, are responsible for destroying the happiness of my family." answered Louisa. "The late Duke of Norholm caused us much grief."

Silas was shocked at her words and for a while sat silent, watching her at her work. He thought how unlike she was to any other girl or woman he had known. The only women, other than the Baroness, that he had known were women of ill repute or the Baroness' maids.

He thought to himself of the way he would have behaved towards her just 6 years ago. He would have bought her a little present and then flirted with her until she was convinced that he was violently in love with her. He would then have invited her into his bed and had his way with her. When he grew tired, he would have paid her an excellent sum of money and married her off to a tradesman from town. He had done so many times and he knew that his older brother Miles had done the same. To his knowledge, none of the women he had so treated had any complaint. They all curtseyed and thanked him, telling him he was always welcome to come visit them whenever he felt like it. However, he had never looked at any of them twice.

He wondered what it was about her that made him feel he could not take his eyes off her. She was certainly very beautiful, but it was more than that. There was an innocence and selflessness about her. She seemed not to be aware of her own charms and never thought about her own needs. Her efforts to help her father were untiring and generous. Yet there was a darkness about her, as if a shadow had been cast over her heart, and Silas wanted to know what that shadow was.

Hearing her speak so bitterly about his dead brother filled him with dread and sorrow. He decided that he would find out what it was that Miles had done to so anger her and do his best to make amends. He was thankful that he had not revealed his true identity to her, knowing that she would probably have refused to have anything more to do with him had he done so.

Louisa looked at him curiously.

"Forgive me but your account of yourself does not appear to match your condition. You describe yourself as the nephew of a lady who is employed at Norholm Manor. However, your uniform is that of an officer."

"Yes, well, my aunt has fallen on hard times and is a companion to the Baroness who lives there. I was lucky enough to have a commission in the army purchased for me by my patron."

"I see." said Louisa, thoughtfully

"I can see that you have a thousand questions you would like to ask me, but are afraid of doing so for fear of appearing impertinent." smiled Silas

"Yes, well I would not wish to annoy you."

"On the contrary, you have every right to ask me questions having extended such great hospitality towards a complete stranger. I owe you my life and therefore do not find your curiosity at all impertinent." Silas paused and then said "If you will permit me, I would like to wait until your father returns in the evening, so that I can thank him myself, and tell him everything he deserves to know about the stranger he allowed into his home."

Louisa nodded and said "Yes, of course, you are welcome to do as you see fit."

"Then will you be so kind as to let me know where my horse is?"

"That I cannot tell you." Louisa shook her head as she continued.

"My father took your horse to shelter him in a stable nearby. I am not aware of the exact location of that place. In any case it is not advisable for you to go looking for your horse in your condition."

"Perhaps you are right, but I am not used to being an invalid and I must confess I am heartily tired of it."

"If the weather were more pleasant, perhaps we could have taken a walk down to the duck pond behind our cottage. However, at present I can suggest no diversion for you."

"Then I must go to work. If you would be so kind as to give me back the bag that contained my belongings, I have a journal that I have neglected for too long."

Louisa got up and, lifting the bag down from above the fireplace, held it out towards Silas.

"I gather you have not given in to curiosity and read the journal?" he asked, half smiling

"Had I been aware of its existence, perhaps the temptation would have been too much to bear. However, it was my father who placed your bag above the mantle on the night that you arrived. I had no reason to handle it."

For a while Silas wrote silently in his journal, while Louisa sat shelling peas for dinner. Suddenly there was a loud sound, as of a gunshot, outside and Louisa dropped the dish she had been holding. Silas struggled to his feet and moved towards the door.

"Wait, stop!" Louisa exclaimed but Silas had already opened the door and stood looking outside.

ARIETTA RICHMOND, GRACE AUSTEN, ISABELLA THORNE,
KATHERINE KEATS AND SOPHIA WILSON

Chapter Seven

It was almost dark outside and the sky was overcast. A cold wind blew into the room, carrying with it a few stray snowflakes. The ground outside was slowly turning white as the first snow of the season fell. Silas, looking out, at first could not see anything and then he saw the figure of a man struggling to get up from where he had fallen. The man rose with some difficulty and then stumbled towards the cottage. From his manner of walking it was obvious that he was drunk. He carried a gun in one hand and in the other a metal flask from which he stopped to take a drink. Finding it empty, he hurled it away and continued walking towards Silas.

"Merry Christmas! Merry Christmas Dr. Fifett!" he roared loudly

He reached the door and looked hard at Silas.

"Eh, you're not the good doctor! Who are you and what have you done with the doctor and his lovely daughter, my sister Louisa?"

Silas turned his head away in disgust as the smell of liquor on the man's breath assailed his nostrils. As he did so, he saw Louisa standing behind him.

"It's my brother-in-law, Charles Cooper." She said quietly, her face pale. "Let him in, it's all right."

Silas stood to one side and Charles stumbled in, still staring at him.

"Louisa my dear sister!" he exclaimed holding his arms open towards her as if he would kiss her. Louisa stepped backwards.

"What is the meaning of this Mr. Cooper?" she asked coolly. "Where are Katherine and the children? We were not expecting you this early. You usually arrive a week before Christmas."

"Yes well, hang it all! Is that any way to greet your older brother?" he demanded peeved.

"I've just walked 5 miles in the bitter cold and I'm very thirsty. Give me a bit of that wine your father keeps for Christmas."

"I'm afraid I cannot do that. Papa will not allow me to touch that bottle till Christmas Eve." She replied

"Well that is damned inconvenient...." he stopped, staring suspiciously at Silas again.

"My dear sister, who's this fine chap you have all nice and cosy next to the fire? Is he your beau?" he laughed loudly.

"Does the good doctor know who's visiting his precious daughter? Hey old man, if you need to get out quick when Papa gets home there's a window in the back room. Plenty of blokes have made use of that way out, let me tell you, when the elder girl Kathy lived here!" he winked and smirked nastily.

Silas looked at Louisa and the sight of her pale face and tear-filled eyes enraged him. "I know not who you are Sir, but it would behoove you to watch your language and refrain from smearing the character of those far above you in common decency!" Silas said coldly.

Charles glared at him angrily for a moment and then lifted his gun to his shoulder, pointing it at Silas. However, he could not hold it steady and before Louisa had a chance to react, Silas had caught hold of the gun's barrel and twisted it hard. Charles screamed, and fell to the floor, as his upper arm and shoulder were turned painfully together with the gun. He let go of it and cursed at Silas.

At that moment there was a knock at the door and Dr. Fifett came in, brushing snow off his shoulders. He looked at Charles lying on the floor and Silas standing over him, gun in hand. Then he calmly took the gun from Silas' hand and placed it outside the door. Next he shut the door and, taking hold of Silas by the arm, he gently guided him to a chair.

"Charles what are you doing here at this time of night and in this weather? Your wife and children are waiting for you."

"I came to tell you Papa, that your daughter and grandchildren are hungry." said Charles, sarcastically, pulling himself up into a seated position and glaring at the doctor.

"Give me £5 and I'll be off."

The doctor sighed and rubbed his face.

"Charles, I have already been to see Katherine this morning." he said. "I have given her more than £5 and she will spend it, as always, with far more discretion than you have ever shown."

"That is mighty generous of you. Will you give me a drop of something nice to drink before I leave? I'd like to talk to this fine fellow you have here courting Louisa. Does he know she's just like her sister Katherine the nasty...?"

The doctor interrupted him by placing a cup of hot tea in his hands. Louisa smiled, as she knew what would happen next. Within a minute of drinking from the cup Charles keeled over and had to be carried to bed.

"I apologize, Major Reeves, for my son-in-law's bad behavior.'" said the doctor, frowning. "If it hadn't been so late I would have packed him off home."

"That is your decision Sir, and you have every right to do as you see fit. You do not need to apologize for anything." said Silas

"Then let us have dinner for I am tired and hungry."

Louisa rapidly set the table and served dinner.

Afterwards, the doctor drew his chair back and looked at Silas." Major Reeves, let's have a look at that wound then." he said cheerfully.

Louisa undid the bandages and the doctor inspected the wound.

"Looks like it's healing nicely. Another week and it will close completely. You will have a nasty scar at first, but in time it'll disappear."

"An army officer does not fear scars, Sir." said Reeves politely.

"Yes and we need to talk about that too. You have been staying at my home for two weeks and more yet I know hardly anything about you."

"I shall answer all your questions tonight." Silas pulled his chair back from the table and began his story. Writing in his journal had enabled him to decide on a story that, while not completely true, was not so very far from the truth either.

"I was born Silas Reeves, the son of an army soldier. My father was killed in action. My mother, after his death, was compelled to take up employment to support herself and I. She took a place as companion to the Baroness Rebecca Ware at Norholm Manor. I grew up at Norholm Manor doing odd jobs for whoever required my help. When I was eighteen my Patron the Duke of Norholm bought a commission for me to be a captain in the cavalry. I have been fighting, off and on, since then. My hard work paid off and I was promoted to Major 6 months ago. I was injured while fighting at Waterloo. As a result of my injury, I was given leave for a period of two months. I was on my way back to my childhood home of Norholm Manor when you found me and carried me here. For that I am eternally grateful." Silas paused and said

"I feel as if it is time now to return to my home. I do not wish to take advantage of your kindness."

"I cannot permit you to do that. If you look outside, you will realize a snow storm has started. Neither your injury nor the weather will allow you to travel home. I realize that it is difficult for someone in your position to stay at home all day. Perhaps once the injury has healed, you will be able to visit town and find some temporary employment... the weather may have improved by then and you will be able to return to your home."

Silas was silent. "You are right doctor. I will take your advice."

He wondered how he could bring up the subject of Louisa and her obvious resentment concerning Norholm Manor. However, he was not allowed that opportunity.

"If you will excuse me then I think I shall go to bed as I am tired." said the doctor, bidding Silas and Louisa goodnight.

Louisa looked at him kindly

"You have had a hard life." She said

"Is your mother still waiting for you at Norholm Manor?"

"No my mother passed away when I was a young child."

Louisa sat thinking for a while and then a strange look came into her eyes.

"Major Reeves I thought you said your Aunt Rebecca was waiting for you at Norholm Manor and that she is employed there."

"Yes I did. The fact is, the Baroness Rebecca for whom my mother worked has seen me grow up before her eyes. As she is childless herself, she always regarded me as her nephew."

Silas hesitated a moment, before continuing, "I grew accustomed to calling her aunt privately, although I would never do so in front of anyone else. You overheard me talking to myself and calling her aunt. I was embarrassed and knew not how I could explain calling the Baroness aunt. I therefore went along with the explanation you provided about her being an employee."

Louisa stared at him silently and he grew uncomfortable.

"May I ask why you are questioning me so closely? Do you doubt what I have told you?" he asked.

"No I can think of no motive for you to lie about such a thing." She replied, a little doubtfully. "However, I was thinking how hard it must have been for you to live at Norholm Manor as a servant at such a tender age and that, too, without your parents."

"Yes well, as I have described, the Baroness was like a maternal figure and the late Duke of Norholm was my patron. He rewarded me for my service by making me an Officer in the army."

"So you know the family well and must have been intimately acquainted with the late Duke's sons, the eldest of which was Miles."

Silas shifted uncomfortably in his seat. "Yes I knew him."

Louisa got up and paced up and down, twisting her fingers.

"Then can you tell me why that man was such a monster? Was there no one to stop him from playing with the lives of innocent people? Did you, yourself, never remonstrate with him?"

Silas laughed humorlessly.

"Miss Fiffet I was a servant; I was hardly in a position to remonstrate with him."

"So you watched him destroy lives and said nothing!"

"Miss Fiffet I do not know what you are talking about. You mentioned once before that he wronged your family but I am not aware what crime he committed. He was kind enough to me…"

"Enough! I cannot talk any more about that man and hear you defend him. I am going to bed. Do you require any assistance?" Louisa's lips trembled and her face flushed with anger.

"I shall manage, but, Miss Fiffet…"

Louisa left the room without another word. Silas groaned with frustration.

"What is the matter with her? Why is she so angry? What did Miles do? Am I a fool for wanting to find out? Even if I manage to find out the truth, she will never forgive him or give me a chance."

He smiled ruefully to himself

"Silas Reeves, of all the women in the world you had to fall for the most unpredictable and morose one!" With some difficulty he prepared himself for bed and lay down to sleep.

Chapter Eight

Baroness Rebecca Ware was seated in her drawing room with her best friend, Lady Marian Holmes. They had just been served tea. Lady Marian's daughter, Camilla, had excused herself as she had a headache. Lord Holmes had not accompanied his wife and daughter on their visit, preferring to go to London instead. Lady Marian smiled affectionately at Baroness Rebecca and said

"Well Rebecca, what is that urgent matter you wished to ask my opinion about?"

"Marian you cannot imagine how anxious I have been. Silas completely disregards me and all that he owes me. I have brought him up as if he was my own son and he is so ungrateful. He has severely limited my monthly expenditure. You can see how I have had to limit the number of dishes I have served at dinner to just five."

"Yes Rebecca but how can I be of assistance to you."

"Well if he was home more often my problem would be solved. He would then be compelled to loosen the purse strings for his own comfort."

"There is no guarantee of that. What if he were to decide to live frugally himself? In any case you know he is a commissioned army officer and there is a war being fought. How can you expect him to stay home?"

"Perhaps if he were married, he could be persuaded to give up his army commission?"

"Ahhhh!" said Lady Marian. "I begin to understand you."

"Dear Marian, I would love to see more of you. I am so lonely here all by myself. If we could persuade Silas and Camilla to get married, all of our problems would be solved. He is sure to be a very attentive husband and son-in-law."

Lady Marian was silent.

"Just think, Camilla would be the Duchess of Norholm!" said the Baroness.

"Yes, well I do see the advantages of such a connection, but Rebecca, I do not understand how we are to undertake to persuade your nephew to take a wife when he is not here." said Lady Marian

"He is sure to come by Christmas. He did not come last year in this season so they are sure to give him leave now."

"Well it is certainly a match to consider, Rebecca dear, yet I am not entirely convinced we will be able to compel Silas to see reason."

"Leave that to me." said the Baroness. "I know well how to remind men of their duty and what is owed to me. However, you must prepare Camilla. I think we should have a Ball at Christmas and she shall have ample opportunity to charm Silas there."

"I shall endeavor to speak with her." said Lady Marian thoughtfully.

"Speak with me about what Mama?" asked Camilla, entering the room.

"All in good time my dear. Are you feeling better now?"

"No, my head still aches and I find being shut up in my room only makes it worse."

"Have some tea then dear." Baroness Rebecca said kindly.

Camilla looked at her suspiciously, having been used to being ignored by the Baroness on her previous visits.

"Yes thank you, I will have some tea, but Mama, you must tell me what you were talking about."

"Camilla. How would you like to be the mistress of Norholm Manor?" asked Baroness Rebecca. Camilla listened, intrigued, to the plot described by the older two ladies.

Chapter Nine

The snow continued to fall outside and piled up in drifts along the road to Norholm Manor. Silas woke up early the next morning and, getting up with some difficulty, washed and dressed himself.

He had determined to distance himself from Louisa and the only way to do that was to become more independent and not rely on her to do everything for him.

He gritted his teeth to overcome the occasional twinge of pain that shot through his arm and stoked the fire that had almost died down in the kitchen hearth. Then he set the kettle on the fire and placed the pot of oatmeal on the stove as he had seen Louisa do every morning, Soon, the scent of warm oatmeal filled the house.

Louisa entered the kitchen to find Silas seated beside the window looking out at the snow that refused to stop falling.

"You should sit closer to the fire." She observed quietly

Silas turned towards her.

"Miss Fiffet, I wanted to apologize to you for offending you last night. It is clear that I have overstayed my welcome here and indeed I have no business claiming your hospitality when I belong to a family that you detest."

"You are a servant for that family." observed Louisa

"Yes, but it is evident that is a crime in your eyes too. In any case I do not wish to cause you any more distress..."

"It is too late for that!" exclaimed Louisa. "It is all very well for you to act injured at my questioning and insist on running away, but where do you think you will go? The snow is piled up outside and even my Papa will not be able to go on his morning rounds today. I have been tormented by my hate for Norholm Manor for the last five years and your presence here makes no difference now."

"What is it you desire?" asked Silas frustrated. "If you hate the very sight of me, why do you not let me leave?"

"I want you to answer my questions!" answered Louisa

"I shall answer nothing till you tell me the source of your pain." Said Silas

Louisa was silent for a while and then she nodded

"Yes you are right. You need to know my story. My elder sister Katherine and I were brought up by my father since childhood. I do not have any memory of my mother, for she died in giving birth to me. My sister was four years old at the time. As long as I can remember, I have felt guilt for the death of my mother. I was very young when I resolved, in my childish mind, to become a replacement for my mother, by taking care of my father and sister."

"That is an insurmountable burden for a child." observed Silas.

"Perhaps, but it was my decision, and I stood by it to the best of my ability. As we grew up, my sister and I were best friends and had no secrets from each other. Then she began to grow distant from me. In desperation I confronted her one day and demanded to know what secret she was hiding from me. It was then that she told me she had fallen in love. My father would send her out every morning to walk to the neighboring farm and bring back milk for our breakfast. I would have gone but he insisted that she do it." Louisa's eyes took on a distant look as she remembered. Then she continued.

"On her way there she always saw a young man, loitering on the road with his horse. He would watch her and make her uncomfortable so that she hastened to pass him and get to the farm. Then one day he threw a basket of roses in her path. When she demanded to know the meaning of his strange behavior he dismounted from his horse and declared that he had fallen in love with her. All he wanted, he said was the pleasure of taking her for a ride every morning." Louisa fell silent and her eyes filled with tears.

"My sister was just 16 years old and completely unaware of the ways of men and the evil that they hide. She believed that he loved her truly and only wanted the pleasure of her company for a few minutes. She accepted his offer and allowed him to carry her part of the way to the neighbor's farm every morning. Gradually she grew closer to him and started confiding in him. That is when she grew distant from me."

"I can see how painful that must have been for you." responded Silas.

"Painful as it was, I was more concerned for her safety. I begged her to tell Papa, but she swore me to secrecy. She said she was desperately in love and could not bear it if she did not see him every morning. He brought a joy to her life that she felt she needed. Then one day she came home and all the light had gone from her face."

"What happened? Did he abandon her?"

"I wish he had. No, he told her he loved her and wanted to 'be' with her. They went for a ride longer than normal, into the woods, and there my sister lost her innocence." Louisa whispered, the tears spilling out onto her cheeks.

Silas sat with his head bowed. He wondered why he felt so upset. He knew well it was just what Miles would be expected to do and yet he had never thought of the impact such behavior would have on a girl or her family.

"She did not know what to do. I told her I would accompany her from that day on, but she refused. I wish I had told my father then, but she would not let me and I feared I would lose her trust. The next day she went and came back crying. He did not come to meet her. She would go every morning and he was never there. She knew only that his name was Miles and he was the Duke of Norholm. She dared not ask anyone about him. Then she grew sick and her belly started to grow."

Louisa wiped her eyes.

"We both knew what the cause of her illness was. She let out her dresses and stopped eating properly so that she wouldn't grow too obviously. One night she told me she was going to Norholm Manor to look for him. She found him waiting for her again the next morning. He told her he would marry her. All she had to do was run away with him. They would post the wedding banns and get married as soon as possible. She lied to me and said she had not met him. I found out only when she disappeared with her belongings."

"What happened then?" whispered Silas feeling sick at heart, for he knew the answer.

"My father searched high and low for her. I told him everything and he was so kind, he never once reproached me. Finally, one day a year later, he saw her in town. She was standing in line to receive charity at a church. She had a baby in her arms and was expecting another. She was married to a drunkard who slept all day and sent her to beg for food. My father pleaded with her to come home but she refused, saying she was responsible for her own situation."

"And so she was, my dear. It was a lucky day for me when the Duke threw her into my arms with a generous allowance in return for marrying her."

Silas and Louisa turned around to see Charles Cooper standing in the doorway.

Chapter Ten

Charles Cooper stumbled in to the kitchen and stood there shaking his head from side to side.

"I feel rather poorly this morning, for my head aches terribly. If you would pour me a drop of that brandy you keep for sore throats I'm sure I'd feel much better." he whined.

"Have some breakfast instead." said the doctor from behind him.

Charles turned to stare at him. "Look Papa is here!" he announced mockingly

"Do you know your lovely daughter is sharing the tale of her sister's misfortune with her beau?"

"What is it to you? You have not been particularly discreet yourself, spreading tales about your wife around town." said Dr. Fiffet. "Now, you can sit down quietly and have some oatmeal, or you can leave directly and make your way home through the snow."

"I can't eat that slop. Give me some money and I shall leave." demanded Charles.

Dr. Fiffet sighed and held out a small bag of coins. "Here take it and go home."

Charles grinned.

"That is most generous of you Sir. I shall return to my wife and inform her of your kindness. We shall surely come on Christmas and I hope you won't be stingy with the liquor then." So saying, Charles placed his hat on his head, pulled his coat tight around himself and walked out into the snow.

Dr. Fiffet bolted the door after him and turned to look at Silas.

"Have you had your breakfast?" he asked.

"I have indeed. Thank you" said Silas.

"Your wound will soon heal completely. I believe that you are now well enough to return home." said the doctor in a somber tone.

"But Papa, look at the snow! You have yet to bring back his horse!" exclaimed Louisa.

"It's alright dear, I will accompany him to the stable where his horse is sheltered, and set him on the way to Norholm Manor myself."

"Yes, thank you Dr. Fiffet, that is just what I desire." said Silas.

He got up and slung his bag over his shoulder turning to face Louisa.

"Thank you for all your care Miss Fiffet. I am grateful that you confided in me. I will write to you soon and endeavor to answer your questions regarding Miles, the late Duke of Norholm."

He walked out, followed closely by the doctor, and left Louisa feeling strangely upset. She should have been happy to see him leave. She had complained often enough about him to the doctor and yet she felt as if she had lost something.

Silas walked with Dr. Fiffet for about half an hour, until they reached the neighbouring farm. Dr. Fiffet knocked on the farm house door and they were invited in by Farmer James. However, Dr. Fiffet refused, saying that he had to get home soon.

The farmer led them to the stable and Silas was overjoyed to see Robin looking well and healthy. He thanked the farmer for all his care and offered to pay him. However, the farmer refused, saying it had been no trouble at all.

So it was that, a few minutes later, Silas found himself, having bid the doctor farewell and thanked him, mounted on his horse and on his way home to Norholm Manor.

On the way he kept thinking of Miles loitering somewhere on this very path, in wait for a young girl, all those years ago. He remembered Miles as a young child, crying because he didn't want to go to Boarding School and he remembered Louisa's tears as she described her sister's plight.

"Miles was no angel but then who could blame him?" he thought.

"Who was there to teach him compassion and kindness? Neglected by our father and deceived by our Aunt… was it any wonder he grew up to be selfish? Was I any different until I had the nonsense beaten out of me in the army?"

He saw, looming up in front of him, the building of Norholm Manor. He stopped for a while and looked at it, a feeling of dread coming over him.

"Who there will be glad to see me? Who will ask about my wound or offer to cook my favorite meal? There are plenty of servants who I have only to order once and they will run to do my bidding. How different that is from the care given by someone who anticipates one's needs and feels one's pain whether it is expressed or not. I wish…"

He stopped, for he could not express in words what he wished, but Louisa's face haunted him. He sighed and urged Robin onwards. As he neared the gates, the night watchman came running to open them.

"Welcome home, Sir!" he exclaimed. Silas nodded to him and rode through the gates. It seemed, as if by magic, that all of the servants became aware of their master's presence. The great front door swung open and the butler stood ready to meet him. Silas spoke kindly to him and then continued onwards into the parlour. He found it empty, with a great fire burning in the hearth.

"I am tired James, send for my boy Frank and tell the cook to serve dinner half an hour early."

"Yes Sir" said the butler. "Shall I inform Baroness Rebecca of your arrival?"

"Yes, I suppose you must", sighed Silas

"My dear Silas, is it really you?" his Aunt entered the room, having become aware of his presence without needing the butler to inform her.

"I was beginning to imagine that you were never going to come back home. Is this the way to arrive, unannounced and silent?"

"Good evening Aunt!" said Silas, drily. "I am glad to see you looking so well." He got up, with some difficulty, and kissed her proffered cheek.

"As well as can be expected considering the circumstance in which I find myself. You have thoughtlessly left me here in a difficult position. Why I am almost destitute."

"Yes, well, I sincerely doubt that Aunt." replied Silas wearily

The Baroness lifted her monocle to her eye and looked hard at him, unable to decide if he were mocking her or not.

"My dear Silas, what is the meaning of this? You have not enquired after my health even once. I have been extremely unwell in your absence. You may not be aware of this, but you have a duty towards me. I grow older every day and I will not be here forever. If you neglect your responsibilities what will become of your property?"

"I am not aware of that, and I am sure you will enhance my knowledge if I allow you to continue, but at present Aunt, I cannot."

"Why may I ask is that?"

"Well for one, I am weary and would like to rest. There are the minor issues of hunger and a healing wound. I have called for my steward and shall retire to my chamber with his help. Please enjoy your dinner and do not wait for me. I will dine alone in my room."

Silas, relieved of the need to speak with his aunt a moment longer, by Frank's arrival at the door, got to his feet and, placing his hand on Frank's shoulder, left the room.

The Baroness was annoyed but thought better of making a fuss.

"You can walk away from me now young man but I will make you listen to me tomorrow!" she said to herself.

Chapter Eleven

It snowed all night and the next day, when Louisa looked out through her window, she saw a thick white blanket covering everything from the grey horizon to their front door. She thought of her childhood and how she would have rushed outdoors with Katherine to play in the snow.

She found herself wondering what Silas was doing.

"He has probably been forced to go back to work at Norholm Manor." she thought.

"Perhaps the Baroness will excuse him, knowing he is injured and an army officer now. He is no longer just the son of her house maid."

"Louisa, why are you so quiet, child?" asked the doctor. "You used to chatter all day when our guest was here."

"I can't decide whether I did right in confiding in Major Reeves." Louisa answered.

"Do you think you did wrong?"

"The truth is, Papa, I cannot rest until I know why the late Duke of Norholm acted as he did. I cannot bear to think that he died with his reputation intact and is revered amongst his family and friends as an honest man. Katherine suffers every day of her life and there is no justice for her."

"Do you think Major Reeves, who is indebted to that family for all he has, will be able to provide any kind of justice?"

"Perhaps not, Papa. However, he seems to be a decent person and I could not hear him speak respectfully of the late Duke and stay quiet."

"Then it seems you had no choice, and had to tell him everything. In that case you should accept your decision and let the matter rest. Do not fret over it. There's nothing more you can do."

"Yes Papa. I better get to work now; Katherine will be arriving soon."

Dr. Fiffet watched as she left the room and wondered to himself if she would ever be able to find peace.

~~~~~

At Norholm Manor, Baroness Rebecca Ware was busy giving directions, to the servants, for the Christmas preparations. She had spoken with the cook already and was now choosing the decorations that were to be put up.
~~~~~

Breakfast was almost ready to be served and Lady Marian Holmes had joined her. Camilla had not yet appeared and Silas was still in his chamber. Half an hour later, the Baroness sent the steward to ask him if he wished to breakfast alone. However, before the man could carry out his orders, Silas came down himself.

"Good morning Aunt." he said, kissing her cheek

He then greeted Lady Marian, bowing formally to her.

"I was not aware that you had arrived." he said.

"Yes, I have been here for a week now." she smiled as she replied. After breakfast, the Baroness nodded significantly to Lady Marian, who took her leave, saying that she would check on Camilla, who appeared to be unwell.

Baroness Rebecca looked at Silas and said "She is not here just for Christmas you know."

"I'm afraid I do not know what you are talking about Aunt." said Silas.

"Have you given any thought at all to your future?" she continued. "You are the Duke of Norholm, and the sole heir to your father's estate. If you do not get married and produce an heir, the property and title will be lost to the Reeves family."

"I fail to see what that has to do with Lady Marian."

"She has a beautiful daughter with £20,000 settled upon her. I have spoken with Lady Marian and she is in agreement with me. A match between the daughter of Lord Holmes and the Duke of Norholm would be an excellent proposition."

"I see." said Silas coldly, "You seem to have settled everything amongst yourselves. So what is it that you wish to ask me?"

"My dear boy, I knew you would never oppose me. I have already directed the servants to make the arrangements for a grand Ball at Christmas. I shall also arrange for your engagement to be announced at the Ball..."

"Good Lord Aunt! Have you taken leave of your senses?" Silas stopped abruptly. "I apologize; I should not have spoken so hastily but how can you take such a decision without even consulting me?"

The Baroness sat up straight,, her mouth pinched and her eyes blazing. "Do you mean to say that you will not have Camilla Holmes for your wife?"

"No I will not! As if I should have to make myself any clearer!" exclaimed Silas.

"May I ask why not?"

"Well for one, I have never even seen her..."

"Well that is easily rectified!" the Baroness perked up.

"No Aunt, I don't care how beautiful she is, or how much money she has settled upon her, or what family she comes from. I cannot marry her."

"May I ask why not?"

"Let's talk about something else for a minute. I do not feel I have to justify myself at this moment. I wish to ask you something of importance." said Silas

"What could be more important than your marriage?"

"I wanted to ask you about Miles."

"What about Miles?" the Baroness asked, exasperated.

"He was in love before he died." stated Silas

The Baroness stared at him flabbergasted. "What are you talking about?"

"Don't deny it Aunt. I was away at war and he brought a girl to the house."

"How could you possibly know that?"

"I know it well and I also know that you turned her away. Do you deny it?"

"I do not! I was absolutely right to do so!" the Baroness exclaimed. Silas sat silently looking at her.

"She was the nameless, penniless daughter of a common doctor. She had aspirations and designs on the Duke of Norholm. I could not allow her to waltz in here and destroy this family's name!" she continued.

"So what did you do?"

"I don't remember the details..."

"What did you do Aunt?"

"She found a bracelet of mine lying on the breakfast table and, instead of returning it to me, she picked it up and hid it in her sleeve. When I found it missing, I had the servants search her. Of course she could not deny the theft and when Miles found out he raised no further resistance, and I had the servants throw her out."

"Admit it Aunt, you fabricated the entire incident. She was no thief; she was trapped by you!"

"If she was trapped, which I by no means admit to, she deserved it for being such a shameless opportunist!"

Silas lowered his head into his hands and groaned.

"Aunt, you know not what you did. Miles was in love with her and when you would not accept her, he became desperate!"

"That fool tried to sneak off at night and elope with her but I made sure he could not find her. I paid a servant to hide her away in a rented room in town, until she could be married to someone else. I paid a handsome amount of money to the first man who agreed to take her as his wife."

"So it was you who married her off to a drunkard and not my brother! That is how Miles died of a broken heart."

"Don't be a fool! You know well your brother drank too much. He drank himself in to an early grave."

"He drank to drown out the grief that you caused!"

"Silas, your brother was a weak fool! He was not fit to be the Duke of Norholm. The only person responsible for his downfall was Miles himself. I did all I could to save him from infamy and slander. He did not want to be saved, but you are different. You are a respectable gentleman and an Officer in the army. You have no foolish notions about love. Please do not ruin your future! Accept my advice and marry Camilla."

"What if I refuse? How will you plot and manipulate circumstances to influence me?"

"How dare you?" she demanded

"I will not marry Camilla Holmes, Aunt. That is my final decision."

Silas stood up and stalked out of the house. He called for Robin and when the groom's man brought him, saddled and ready, Silas mounted and galloped out of the grounds. He wanted to get as far away from Norholm Manor as possible. However, when he reached the lane that led towards the Fiffet home, he slowed down. He dismounted and walked off the lane into the woods nearby. The woods were dark and desolate. All the trees had shed their leaves. Their branches were laden with snow.

He knew that he had to tell Louisa the truth, but he didn't have the courage to face her. Her hate and anger made perfect sense now, but he could not bear to see the respect she had for him change into contempt, when she discovered that he was the brother of the man who had caused her sister's downfall. How could he explain to her that he had abused her hospitality and lied to her about his identity?

"The only thing I can do is to write her a letter." He thought. He climbed into his saddle again and turned Robin back towards Norholm Manor. He thought he would go back and write the letter, then deliver it to Louisa himself. However, he had barely travelled half a mile down the lane when he saw Louisa herself walking home.

"Major Reeves!" she exclaimed and her cheeks flushed. Her half smile filled his heart with a strange mixture of ecstasy and shame.

"Miss Fiffet, where are you coming from?"

"I was waiting for you!" She exclaimed artlessly, and then lowered her eyes, embarrassed.

"That is to say, it is customary for a doctor to check his patient's wound again after a few days and I had forgotten to remind you to come see my father in a week's time. Also..."

"Yes..." prompted Silas

"You promised you would answer my questions."

Silas' heart sank. It seemed he would have to tell her himself. He dismounted and, holding Robin's reins in one hand, said, "Come and walk with me. I will accompany you to your home. It is too cold for you to be walking outside. I will tell you everything on the way."

They walked together and Louisa listened as Silas spoke. He kept his sight fixed on the path ahead, not daring to look at her face. Half an hour later they stood in front of Dr. Fiffet's cottage. At last Silas raised his eyes. Once again he felt that he could not look away from her gaze. He was reminded of the first time he saw her hazel eyes and had lost himself in them. The difference was that then they had been soft, unfocused and half asleep and now her eyes were wide open and filled with tears of rage. For a long time, they stood and looked at each other. Then Louisa broke the silence.

"Thank you." She said, and her voice trembled.

"You have indeed answered all of my questions and now I have only one more request to make of you. Never darken my doorway with your presence again, Major Silas Reeves, Duke of Norholm!"

Silas let go of the breath he had been holding and felt it rush out of his lungs in a great sigh. He turned and swung onto his horse as the tears blinded him. Then he was gone, galloping home, and Louisa was left standing all alone in the snow, sobbing hard.

ARIETTA RICHMOND, GRACE AUSTEN, ISABELLA THORNE,
KATHERINE KEATS AND SOPHIA WILSON

Chapter Twelve

Dr. Fiffet whistled to himself as he walked briskly through the snow. He was returning home after making his morning rounds. He knew Louisa would have dinner prepared. She had told him she would have a ham roast ready when he got home. He was looking forward to sitting down to a nice cup of eggnog after dinner. As he neared his cottage he picked up his pace.

"Lord it gets colder every day! My toes are almost frozen." he grumbled to himself. Reaching the door, he lifted up his hand and knocked hard twice, then repeated the knocks more gently. It was the sign he had settled on with Louisa, so that she would know it was him and she could open the door. He listened for the sound of his daughter's feet hurrying towards the door but he heard nothing. He repeated the sign and waited. Still no one came. Foreboding filled his heart as he knocked a third time. He was just getting ready to set his shoulder to the door when it finally opened. He rushed in exclaiming

"How long you were Lou! Is everything alright?"

He stopped short and stared at her. Louisa refused to meet his gaze. She turned away and said, "I fell asleep Papa. I was tired. I shall have dinner on the table directly."

The doctor stayed quiet. Experience had taught him that, in some cases, quiet observation would provide more information than interrogation. So he sat down in front of the fire and removed his boots.

He waited patiently for his dinner and noted that Louisa barely touched anything. After eating dinner, he sipped his eggnog and waited, knowing that she would eventually break her silence. Louisa sat, staring at the fire, twisting her red curls around her finger.

Her face was pale and her eyes were swollen.

Finally, she burst out, "How could you father! You knew he was the Duke of Norholm from the day he told us his name! Why did you let him make up that ridiculous lie about being a servant at Norholm Manor?"

The doctor spoke soothingly, knowing that Louisa's use of the word Father, instead of Papa, indicated a dangerous rage.

"My love, you are right. When he identified himself as Silas Reeves I recognized him as the Duke of Norholm, as would have any man within a 50-mile radius of Norholm Manor. Therein lies your answer. All the men would have known him, but not the maids, and by choosing to disclose his actual name he informed me that he wished me to know who he was, but not you."

"Why?" she asked, the tears pouring down her cheeks.

"I am a Doctor my dear and it is my sworn duty to care for the injured and the ill, no matter what their identity. You, on the other hand, harbored a deep resentment against the Duke of Norholm. Is it any wonder he chose to conceal his title from you?"

"But how? How could you, Father, provide him shelter, knowing that he was the brother of the man who ruined your daughter?"

"He was the brother; he was not responsible for his brother's actions. Another thing I have learned, with time, is that you cannot judge a person until you know the entire story. We do not know the entire story. Only what your sister and her husband told us."

"It does not matter what the entire story was! He seduced her! He compelled her to run away from home!"

The doctor sighed and got up.

"Louisa dear, you are tired and you have had a great shock. I understand your anger and yet I cannot condone it. It is time you learned to control your rage and think more dispassionately. We are none of us absolute villains. We are all victims of circumstance."

At that moment there was a knock on the door and they heard the voice of a woman calling, "Papa, open the door! It is I Katherine!"

Dr. Fiffet opened the door and Katherine came in, holding one child in her arms and the other by the hand.

"Where is Charles?" asked her father.

"He left us outside. He said he had business in town." said Katherine.

"It was a good thing he did. Or he would have heard Louisa's words."

Louisa got up to embrace her sister. "I'm sorry Kathy!"

"Oh Lou…" sighed Katherine.

"Here put the little ones to bed, they are half asleep already and then we will talk."

Louisa did as she asked, kissing the children's cheeks as she laid them down in her own bed.

Then she returned to the kitchen, where Dr. Fiffet had poured out a cup of eggnog for his eldest daughter.

Katherine took Louisa's hand and made her sit with her.

"Louisa, you were a child when I got married, and I blamed myself for putting too much of a burden on you by telling you things that I should have kept to myself. Then, later, after I got married, I decided to forget about my past and accept what God had willed for me. So I never told you what happened after I went to Norholm Manor with Miles."

Katherine then repeated the story that Louisa had heard from Silas.

"So you see, it was all because of the Baroness. Miles was truly in love with me. We were both responsible for acting foolishly instead of confiding in Papa."

Louisa sat silently.

"Lou, forget about the past and ask yourself why you are so devastated. You are not responsible for my fate. There was nothing you could do to save me. I am happy now with my two precious children. I do not care what anyone thinks. I am at peace. That is all I want for you. Forgive the Norholm family. You will never be free until you do."

Louisa sighed. "I am so tired Kathy. Can I sleep with my head in your lap again, like we used to when we were little?"

Kathy agreed.

Chapter Thirteen

Silas Reeves paced up and down his chamber. He could not sleep. Louisa had declared that she never wanted to see him again. However, he could not forget what he had learned about Katherine. Was it possible that one of her children was rightfully the heir of Norholm Manor? How could he correct the deep injustice that she had suffered?

Christmas was fast approaching and he knew that his Aunt would not have given up her plan. Lady Marian Holmes and her daughter remained at Norholm Manor and it seemed he could not escape them. Whether he was walking in the garden or reading his correspondence in the parlor, they were always present, together with his Aunt, and trying to engage him in conversation. If their objective was to impress him with the beauty of Camilla, they failed, because whenever he looked at her all he could think about was that she was very young and childish. She seemed to regard the Duke as a mythical hero and her fawning admiration was a source of constant irritation for him.

"I must go to town tomorrow morning." he thought.

"I shall speak with that man Charles Cooper. Perhaps there is some way to remove him from Katherine's life. He is, in any case, more of a burden on her than anything else. I shall also speak with Dr. Fiffet and apologize to him for all that he and his family have suffered as a result of Miles and my Aunt."

The next morning, he left the breakfast table to call for his horse. The Baroness followed him outside.

"Where are you going Silas?" she asked.

"I have business in town, Aunt," he replied.

"I wanted to consult with you about the preparations for the Christmas Ball…"

"I trust you know all that needs to be done Aunt, I have no objection to anything."

"Yes I know dear boy. I knew you would come to see sense. You shall lead the dance with Camilla…"

However, Silas had already mounted his horse and galloped away without waiting to hear her plan. When he reached the doctor's cottage, he slowed down and wondered if the doctor was home. It would certainly be convenient to speak with him before going to search for Charles Cooper. However, he dared not go and knock at the door. He could not bear to see Louisa again. The pain of observing her contempt for him was too much.

"Perhaps if I wait a little while, someone will come out and I can determine whether the doctor is at home or not." He thought.

At that moment the door opened and Louisa came out with a little girl in her arms.

"Don't cry Mary. Your Grandfather will be home soon with pockets full of candy for you." she stopped as she saw Silas. Then her cheeks flushed and her eyes sparkled with anger. Turning she was about to go back inside when Silas spoke

"I beg your pardon Miss. I wanted to speak with the doctor."

"As you are aware, he has left for his morning rounds." she replied frostily

"Yes I had hoped to meet him in town but I thought I would check here first."

"Unfortunately you had no qualms about imposing your presence here, where you knew you would not be welcome!" Louisa's voice trembled.

"Miss Fiffet, whether I am welcome here or not is no concern of mine. I had business with the doctor and that is why I stopped here. I shall leave directly, as I have no desire to cause you pain. However, I would like to apologize for hiding my identity from you. At the time it seemed I had no choice. "

"There is always a choice between speaking the truth and lying! You would not know the difference." exclaimed Louisa.

Silas dismounted and approached her, his eyes intent on her face. She turned as if to leave but he caught her hand and held it firmly.

She trembled at his touch and felt her knees go weak.

"Then let me speak the truth now. I was devastated to learn from you about my brother's mistake. Whatever he was, he was all I had and I loved him. I decided then that I would do my best to repair the wrong that has been done to your family. Had Miles lived I am sure he would have done so himself."

"If that is all, will you be so kind as to let go of my hand!" Louisa tried her best to keep her voice steady.

"I may let go of your hand but I am not going anywhere. I am the Duke of Norholm and I will always be here to answer anyone that has a claim on me or my family. The day will come Louisa when you will admit that I have discharged all my debts. We will stand in front of each other as equals and I will ask for what is mine. That is my vow to you."

He let go of her and she swayed a moment as if she would fall. Then he was gone, leaving Louisa furious at her own reaction to him. What dismayed her most was that she was no longer angry.

That night she lay awake in bed for a long time.

"Perhaps I have been unjust." she thought.

"What would I have done had I been in his place?" As she thought about the answer to that question, she grew more and more uncomfortable.

"Lord help me! How could I have been so blind? Is it possible for me to accept that I was wrong and apologize? Will he accept it if I do?"

At last she fell asleep.

Chapter Fourteen

It was Christmas Eve. Norholm Manor was blazing with light. A huge Christmas tree stood in the centre of the ballroom, covered with delicate glass ornaments, ginger bread men and candy sticks. An intricately painted porcelain fairy was placed at the very top. Her hair was red and Silas sat in a corner staring up at her, oblivious to his guests. The Baroness laughed and chattered as she flitted from one group of people to the next, complimenting one and boasting to another. Soon it was time for dancing and the young couples took their places underneath the glowing ballroom chandeliers.

The Baroness appeared at Silas' shoulder

"Camilla is waiting Silas." She hissed, "You must ask her to dance. It is your duty to lead the way for the other couples."

Silas stared at her disdainfully.

"I am not going to dance Aunt Rebecca," he said, "You should ask someone else to lead the way."

He stood and walked out, through the house and into the grounds.

As he walked through the snow he saw a carriage draw up to the gates. He turned away, not wanting to meet more guests, but something stopped him. He saw two women and an elderly gentleman get out of the carriage. There were two children with them, a girl and a boy. However, what had caught his eye was a red curl, that had escaped from the bonnet of one of the ladies. He started forward to meet them.

"Dr. Fiffett!" he exclaimed

The doctor took his hand. "Thank you for the invitation Major Reeves." he said

"I wasn't sure you would accept it." Said Silas

"It's Christmas young man!" laughed the doctor. "The season of forgiveness, the Lord willed it to be so and that is why we are here."

"Indeed" said Silas, looking at Louisa.

She smiled and looked away, blushing. The others went on ahead and Silas took her hand to lead her in to the ballroom.

"Have you really forgiven me?" he asked

"It is you who need to forgive me." she said, "I was unreasonable and prejudiced…"

"Hush!" he said, "Say not a word more. From this night we will be the best of friends." He raised her fingers to his lips.

"The best of friends." she echoed.

He led her to the head of the line of dancers and opened the dance with her. The Baroness glared at him but could not say a word.

As they danced, Silas smiled at Louisa.

"Remember my vow to you?"

"I do." She whispered, "We stand before each other as equals. What is it you wish to ask of me?"

"My heart. It is in your possession. Return it to me please."

"You must pay for it first." she said mischievously, "However I fear not everyone here is happy with your choice of a dance partner."

Silas looked where she gestured. He noticed his Aunt staring daggers at him. He also caught a glimpse of Lady Holmes fussing around Camilla, who appeared to be in tears.

"Do not worry. I will handle everything," he said calmly.

After the dance was over, the Baroness took him by the elbow and led him to a corner. "What are you doing?"

"Just what you wanted Aunt Rebecca. I have found the woman who is to be my wife."

"That doctor's daughter? The sister of that girl Katherine? Did you think I would not recognize her? Why is she here? I threw that girl Katherine out once before and I will do it again!"

She made as if she was about to walk off but Silas stopped her.

"Aunt Rebecca, if you wish to remain in my home you must accept the girl who is to be my wife and her family. I shall propose to her, with her father's permission, and if she does not enter this house as my bride, you will not live here either."

He walked back to Louisa, leaving the Baroness wordless. For those two, the evening was magical and nothing could destroy it. Silas looked into Louisa's eyes and said "Louisa you have captured my heart. Ever since the day I met you, I felt there was something special about you. You have made me a better man and I want you to be by my side forever more"

Louisa answered "Your Grace, your words are music to my ears, but whatever do you mean? "

The Duke smiled broadly "Louisa I am asking for your hand in marriage. I want nothing more than for you to be my wife! And what's more, please call me Silas, just as you did when I was a guest at your house "

Louisa was almost speechless, but she managed to mutter a few words "Your Grace... I mean Silas, you have melted my heart and there is no possible way for me to refuse your proposal... Yes, YES! I will be your wife!"

Silas grabbed her by the hand and pulled her into a loving embrace "I've been dreaming about the moment I could hold you in my arms, and now it is real" He kissed her lips softly and sweetly, and for just that moment time seemed to stand still.

Epilogue

Three months later, Silas and the lovely Louisa were married in an elegant ceremony. They became more and more in love day by day. Silas arranged for Charles Cooper to be enlisted in the militia and invited Katherine and her children to live at Norholm Manor. However, Katherine chose to stay with her father, Dr. Fiffet, saying that the memories of Miles would be too painful. Dr. Fiffet was thrilled to have Katherine and the children at home with him, adding much life to the house.

Baroness Rebecca, from that day on, remained as mute as she had been on Christmas Eve and never interfered in her nephew's life again. She no longer had the power to manipulate Silas, nor anyone else.

About the Author

Katherine Keats writes sweet and clean Regency Romance. She's a hopeless romantic who loves music, dancing, and long walks on the beach. She enjoys writing stories of true love that defy all odds.

You can connect with Katherine on her Facebook page at:

https://www.facebook.com/KatherineKeatsAuthor/

Or follow her on her author page at:

https://www.amazon.com/Katherine-Keats/e/B01N3R8L65/

Get in touch at:

KatherineKeatsBooks@gmail.com

Other Books by Katherine Keats

Clean Regency Romance

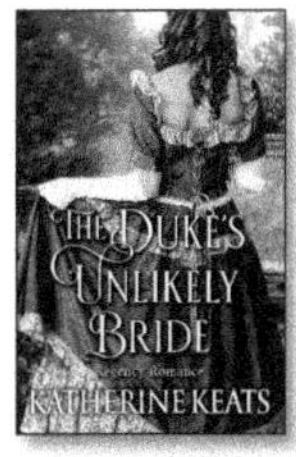

The Duke's Unlikely Bride

The Duke's Dangerous Dilemma

Rescuing the Earl

The Duke and the Dressmaker

ARIETTA RICHMOND, GRACE AUSTEN, ISABELLA THORNE,
KATHERINE KEATS AND SOPHIA WILSON

Here is Your Preview of

The Duke and the Dressmaker

Phoebe stared out of the window of the carriage, at the pleasant country scenes that passed her by as she was sped along bumpy and unkempt roads to Holly Field Hall, the estate of Duke Benjamin Harlow of Moorfield. She tried to still her nerves. It was to be her very first time visiting a stately home. Even though she was going as a trader rather than a guest, there was still a very real thrill to be felt at the thought of wandering through richly carpeted spacious halls. She tried to imagine the paintings in their gilt frames, the marble busts of old Lords of the property, and the many expensive and luxurious oddities she might encounter in the various rooms of that estate.

As she dwelt more and more on the grandeur that might await her behind the doors of Holly Field Hall, Phoebe found herself fussing over her dress. She convinced herself that she could see near invisible patches of dirt near the bottom of the pale blue gown. She caught sight of her face in the carriage window and tried to adjust her bonnet to sit a little straighter on her head. It was important to ensure that she looked perfect when meeting a Duke and his soon-to-be bride.

The carriage trundled right past the front doors of the grand mansion. They were large doors and could easily have admitted some kind of giant if one had somehow stepped out of a storybook to call. Phoebe looked to the many tall windows, seeing forms inside the house moving back and forth. It was impressive to think that nearly all of these shadowy figures must be The Duke of Moorfield's servants.

Judging from this cursory look alone, Phoebe felt certain that the man must employ something close to an army of staff. Were he so inclined, she felt he could probably arm each with a rifle and set out to conquer himself an empire easily the equal of Napoleon's. She smiled at the ridiculousness of the thought and tried to put herself in a more serious state of mind as she prepared for her day's work.

The carriage stopped around the rear side of the building. Here the house was shaded from the view of the general public and less effort was put into making this section of wall stand out. There were not nearly so many windows, and those which were here were far smaller in size. The stables were on this side of the house as well as the storage sheds used by the estate's gardeners. Above, grey clouds were darkening to an almost black pallor and Phoebe was sure it must rain very soon.

"Miss. Brooks?"

Phoebe turned from her inspection of the property's less glamourous side. Standing before her was an impeccably dressed manservant wearing red tailcoat, and white kid gloves. His whole ensemble looked like it had been freshly made for that day and Phoebe could believe that the moment a mark of dirt stained any part of it the whole outfit might be thrown into the fire.

"Yes, I am Miss. Brooks." The servant frowned, looking Phoebe up and down as if uncertain of her claim.

"You have brought the dress selections, yes?"

Phoebe put her hands to her mouth in a nervous laugh.

"Oh, yes, of course sorry. Just let me bring them out from the carriage; I got caught up admiring the grounds. You have a… I mean; His Grace has a lovely estate."

The servant said nothing, just watched impassively until Phoebe went back to the carriage and took up three packages, containing dresses, and her own bag of material, needles and other items necessary for making alterations to the gowns.

~~~~~

"Well it is about time," came a rather imperious voice from behind the door.

Phoebe felt her body bristle up at the words as she waited to be called in. Whoever the voice belonged to, though Phoebe felt she could hazard a guess, it was obviously impatient and not in good humour. This did not bode well. Invariably, clients brought their moods to the table when inspecting the dresses Phoebe and her family had created, and could always find a dozen more things to complain about when in darker spirits. Still, Phoebe had her job to do and she took one deep breath to calm her nerves before stepping into the room.

"I am sorry for the delay Lady Anna; I am afraid the post was not as reliable today as I had hoped."

Lady Anna, the Duke of Harlow's fiancé, was the epitome of high class. Her very shape was one that begged to be carved in marble to stand like some Grecian statue for all the ages to see.
~~~~~

Her hair was like a field of wheat basking in the sun and was placed into a fashionable up-do, with pretty ringlet curls cascading down the sides of her face. Her eyes were azure and the colour of her skin porcelain, save for a healthy red glow about her cheek and on her lips. It was a true pity to find such beauty marred by the irritated expression which glowered at Phoebe.

"I am sure it is not the young woman's fault," came the other voice in the room. "Miss Brooks can hardly be held to account for her driver's faults." Phoebe smiled and took a moment to study the other woman who sat by Lady Anna's side. She too was quite a beauty, but of a less refined aspect. Her long brown hair was pulled back into a chignon and tied up with green ribbon that matched her dress. Her face was round and extremely pleasant to look on when one studied her natural smile. There was nothing artificial about this woman's manner and she seemed singularly at ease in the world; a stark contrast to Lady Anna.

"Am I to presume that you are Lady Olivia, His Grace's sister?"

"I am indeed."

"I have two dresses for you try on for the Ball. Lady Anna, I have your dress made to the design you brought in to our shop and only have a few matters that might need alteration when you try it on."

Lady Anna stood immediately and looked to the servant who stood in the doorway. "You may leave us now; I'll call if you are needed again. Olivia, do you mind helping me out my dress. I may as well try mine first if it will take the least time."

Soon, Lady Anna was dressed in the frock she had commissioned Phoebe and her family to make for her. The dress consisted of a white satin petticoat, heavily ornamented about the feet and shoulder straps with dense frilled tulle creating beautiful ruffles to the gown that reminded one of lapping ocean waves. A short sash of the same material as the petticoat was drawn high on her, just below her bust and tied at the back in a full bow. The dress was cut in a V-neck but still served to show off Lady Anna's full cleavage in a manner that was tasteful while also alluring. Phoebe's mother had designed the cap for the gown: more white satin and gathered tulle. It was cleverly brought together to look like she was sporting a cap made of pure white roses and dove feathers. To Phoebe's mind, it was the kind of gown that could have been as much a wedding dress as full evening wear.

"Can it be gathered any closer about the waist?" Lady Anna said after a long and thoughtful look in the mirror. Phoebe smiled. As a long standing client of her father's business, she had come to know Lady Anna's mind somewhat. She was a woman given over to finding fault wherever she could, and she never gave praise for anything if it could be at all helped. That she could only complain about the waistline on the gown was a sure sign that the dress was to her liking.

"That can easily be achieved by my shortening the length of the sash just a little further so that it draws tighter about you."

"Could you not simply tie the sash tighter as it is?" Olivia asked. She had been watching Phoebe closely, and seemed to be taking mental notes on her craft.

"Absolutely not," Phoebe, said without hesitation.

"If we draw the bow tighter, it will not be so full in look and we'll have an ugly length of cloth dangling down the back... No, I will cut it maybe by half an inch to begin with and we will see how it looks then."

"Well, do be quick about it," Lady Anna ordered.

~~~~~

Almost as soon as Lady Anna was satisfied with her dress, she made excuses as to why she could not stay to help Lady Olivia with her gowns. It came as a relief to Phoebe and she found her body relaxing from the stiffness that had overcome it.

Lady Olivia was a pleasant and vibrant young woman, the complete opposite of her sister-in-law apparent. She did not shy away from conversation with Phoebe and even called for tea to be brought for them along with a selection of sandwiches, of which she encouraged Phoebe to enjoy as much as she pleased.

"I have always enjoyed embroidery and try my best to make my own gowns," Lady Olivia explained as they took a break from trying to alter the pale green dress that would be hers for the Ball. "I am nowhere near as proficient as you are though, Miss Brooks. Honestly, the dress you made for Lady Anna..."

She paused a moment, and her eyes seemed to glaze over from the mere memory of it.
~~~~~

Phoebe smiled and took a bite of her cucumber sandwich, careful to take the kind of dainty bite that ladies of class would take.

"I am sure your dresses are perfectly beautiful Lady Olivia. My proficiency comes only from having devoted my life to fabrics and designs. I am sure you could happily outclass me in almost every other field. I cannot play on the piano save for the most basic of pieces, and I cannot carry a tune with my voice either."

Lady Olivia sighed forlornly and looked out the window. The heavens had opened shortly after Lady Anna's exit, and had doused the land in a tremendous rain that hammered insistently on the window.

"It is absolutely ghastly out there. I am sure Lady Anna regrets leaving as quickly as she did."

Phoebe smiled, secretly enjoying the idea of her most difficult customer being drenched by this downpour. "I do hope she manages to stay dry," she said, keeping her conversation within societal boundaries.

"And how will you be returning to London?"

"With the evening Post coach." Phoebe answered.

Lady Olivia frowned as she looked at the sheer volume of water splattering in giant globules against the window. "I doubt that option will still be available to you the way it is coming down. The roads around here turn to slick mud, and can sometimes become flooded when the nearby river bursts its banks. You would be better served staying over here for the night and returning to London tomorrow."

Phoebe's mouth fell open at so kind an invitation from someone so far above her.

"Why, Lady Olivia, I couldn't possibly. You've already been so kind offering me lunch and your conversation."

Lady Olivia smiled and shrugged her shoulders.

"It's really no trouble at all. Besides, I might only be asking you to remain so that I might prevail on you to look through my own dress work and give me some instruction on how to improve my craft."

Phoebe tried to supress an embarrassed smile, but found she could not.

"I would be very happy to do that much in return for your hospitality Lady Olivia.

Continue Reading

'The Duke and the Dressmaker'

at:

https://www.amazon.com/dp/B01M8IPP15/

KATHERINE KEATS
The
DUKE
AND
The
Dressmaker

Here is Your Preview of
Rescuing the Earl

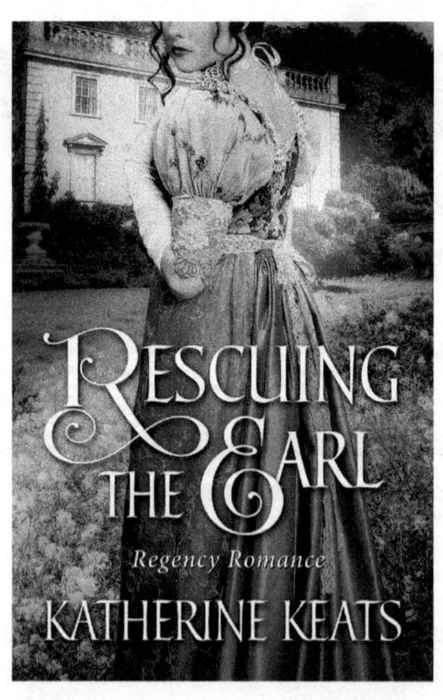

Chapter One

The rooster had yet to crow, the horse had yet to stir in the barn and it was likely that Maria and Johnathon were only now considering the unpleasant prospect of rising out of the comfort of their beds. Abigail had to guess the hour to be no later than four, but there was no staying in bed. She had the sort of mind which, once awake, could not be persuaded to lie about beneath the covers. The mornings were coming on earlier now and looking to the window, the ink black of night had already begun to recede to a dark, brooding blue speckled with the strongest of stars, and still waiting to receive the warmth of the sun, which promised to spill out above the horizon in less than an hour.

Moving out from the bed, Abigail wormed her feet into a pair of hardy and unbecoming boots. A shawl which lay carelessly discarded on top of her bed sheets was taken and she bundled herself tight within it like some hibernating mouse. In the dark she shuffled to her door and lit a lantern before venturing out into the house.

In the kitchen, Abigail set a fire going in the stove and put on the kettle for a cup of coffee. She pulled a chair close to the fire, enjoying its warmth and the extra light and tried to hold on to the few snatches of the night's dream. She was close to forgetting it already and would have let it go if it were not such a beautiful illusion. She remembered the warm sands of the beach and being in company with a man. Her father was there, somewhere in the background. He was walking barefoot in the sands: a sure sign of a dream. From time to time she had looked at him with nervous worry that he might fall. There was more to the dream, but try as she might, Abigail could not dredge forth any further memories.

By the time Maria wandered, bleary eyed, into the kitchen to begin work on breakfast, Abigail had already finished her coffee and was looking through the stores to see what supplies would be needed to be bought from the village in the next days. They were short of meat, but that was always a common theme. When the sound of footsteps caught her attention, Abigail rose up to her full height and smiled at the maid. "Good morning, Maria."

"Miss Carter, what are you doing up so early? You should have woken me and I would have made you your coffee."

"Oh, nonsense." Abigail waved her hand to dismiss her servant's worry. "You shouldn't have to suffer an earlier start just because I can't stay in bed for any length of time."

Maria smiled, fingers twirling a lock of her brown hair as she was want to do when embarrassed. "Well then Miss, I shall get started on preparing breakfast."

"Thank you, though maybe do not lay on quite so much toast and preserves today. You know my father is a glutton and will eat anything set before him. I am anxious to see us at least trying to live within our means."

The maid smiled, "Leave it to me, Miss. Johnathon is helping your father from his bed now, I believe."

Abigail nodded and began to move to the breakfast room to wait on him.

Mr. Carter was the kind of person who impressed you to see. To say he had been dealt a bad hand by life would be akin to saying a soul being led to the hangman's noose was having a bad day. Abigail had not yet turned five when a kick from a foul tempered cart horse had crippled her father so that he could never walk again.

Only two winters later, Mrs. Carter had been carried off by a sudden illness, and Mr. Carter was left to care for his daughter almost alone. Despite this, Abigail had found her father to be a man of continual good spirits and possessed of an ability to see the rainbows in every storm. Sitting in her favourite chair at the table, she found a smile spreading to her lips as her dear father was wheeled into the room by Johnathon.

"I saw your little light shining under my door frame at god knows what hour this morning," Mr. Carter said. "Were you trying to steal yourself a midnight feast from the larders?" He looked up at Johnathon, "What do you say Johnathon, do you think our cupboards are so bare because we have an opportunistic thief in our midst?"

The servant could not help but smile as he drew back from the table. "I am sure I would not like to speculate on that sir," he offered.

"I'm sure if Johnathon were bolder he would note that your waistline points easily to the real glutton in this house, father."

Mr. Carter grinned, not minding at all his child's admonishments. "Well, someone is sounding very serious this morning... let me guess, you've been going through the larder and worked yourself into a panic over how much we can afford this month?"

The two fell into rather usual conversation, with Mr. Carter making comment on the odd pieces of news he had heard from visitors who had called in over the last days. Many in the community took opportunity to visit the bright and affable cripple and often brought gifts of food, which helped Abigail stretch her budget for each month a little further. While she did not like to admit it, they would never get by as comfortably as they did without the kindness of their neighbours - and that kindness might not have been so cheerfully given if Mr. Carter was not an eternal ray of sunshine for those he met.

"There was one very interesting piece of news. I hear your old friend David has returned home."

"You mean Lord Gillingham?" Abigail queried, making sure her father used the proper term of address. "I do not know why that should concern me in any way. I have not seen him since we were about twelve years old, not long after he broke our bedroom window climbing the oak in our garden. I am sure he has quite forgotten about me." At once, she brought her tea to her lips and looked out toward the garden.

"Oh come now, Abigail, you were very sweet on the boy when you were younger. Honestly, I believed at times that there might be some invisible rope that kept you both tied together; it was so hard to part you."

"Well, that was quite some time ago and his father, old Lord Gillingham, was very good at seeing an end to that friendship." Abigail took a bite of toast, chewing for a long moment and giving occasional glances to her father. "I suppose I should ask how he is, though?"

Mr. Carter's grin broadened as though he had been told a most hilarious joke. "I do not know all the particulars, but he has been advised to spend a long turn at home to get away from the caprices of London."

"No doubt overworking himself." Abigail offered.

Mr. Carter shrugged his shoulders. "I know he was fighting for King and country in France until the death of his father last year. I do not know what occupies him now. I imagine he has much to tend to with managing his father's lands, though that could be done far more easily here than in London."

"London has a natural lure for those who can afford its luxuries," Abigail countered. "Perhaps he has some woman in London who he intends to propose to, or simply enjoys the Balls and parties."

Even as she said this, she felt the tang of something unpleasant on her tongue. Though it had been years since she had last seen the Earl, it seemed some part of her childhood fancy for the lad lingered within and the thought of him happily married to another woman displeased her.

"Whatever the reason, I am sure we shall find out more when he descends. All eyes are on Hartley Hall and I am sure the Lord himself will likely call on us in due course." Mr. Carter flicked a little splodge of butter off his cuffs before draining the last of his coffee.

Abigail took a deep breath and put down the last crust of her toast, her appetite having deserted her. "I think, father, I will begin the day's chores; we have at least a dozen clothes that need mending and I must go to the village for fresh food at some point."

Mr. Carter let out a sigh and grabbed the last two slices of toast from the rack for himself. "Suit yourself then. Don't go fussing about me today if you are busy; Johnathon is more than capable of looking after me."

Rather than going to the drawing room for her work, Abigail took a moment to step out into the garden and enjoy the fresh breeze. She was surprised how much the talk of her old friend had rattled her. She and Lord Gillingham had been as inseparable as her father had claimed, in their youth, and she still felt the wound of losing her friend. Though the old Lord Gillingham had never given a reason for separating his son from her, Abigail knew the truth of it. She and her family were beneath the Lord's notice and he feared his son being drawn to an imprudent match in later life. As she stood and considered the past, a strong scent of the sea wafted over on the wind and drew her back to her dream of the previous night. The other man in her vision had been David, she was certain of that. He had changed and was now a man, but she was certain it was David who she walked with in her dream.

Chapter Two

On one front, the Carters had always been clear: though they would accept the kindness and charity of others, they would never ask for it. Consequently, Mr. Carter was at the mercy of chance as to when he might be permitted to escape the confines of his home and travel the three miles down the roads into the local village.

A journey into the village was a rare treat for him, they having long ago sold the family carriage to help make ends meet, Consequently, Abigail could only bring her father out on long expeditions when neighbours and friends were kind enough to offer assistance.

Rattling noisily down the country road, Abigail smiled at her father as he looked out enthusiastically on the passing countryside. "It is such a treat to be out. I cannot say I even remember when I was last able to go to the village."

"It was in early January, father. Two months ago," Abigail said.

"We must remember to thank Mr. Stafford for his generosity in lending us his carriage. Will you be willing to stretch the purse strings to having a meal at the inn today, or are you going to have us home for dinner?" Mr. Carter's eyes were like a cat's begging for cream.

Abigail laughed at her father's antics. He was trying to manipulate her, gazing on her with those hopeful eyes at the prospect of a meal cooked at the local boarding house.

"I am sure Maria will be very much saddened to hear how little regard you have for her cooking."

Mr. Carter smirked. "Don't try to make me out to be the villain. Maria is a fine cook, but, every once in a while, the stomach craves different fare made by different hands. Just because we have to be cautious with our money does not mean we have to live like fasting monastics."

Abigail let out a defeated sigh and slouched back in her seat. She could not deny her father such a simple pleasure, especially when he had so few to begin with.

"I've already brought enough coin for a meal, just as long as you do not try to drink the inn dry."

"Hardly likely," Mr. Carter laughed. "I would be more concerned with my eating all of the meat pie the inn has to offer."

The inn was filled with villagers, fishers from the local harbour and the farm workers from the fields nearer by. As Abigail wheeled her father into the establishment, aided by the courteous landlord, she noticed a large group of men engaged in a game of cards.

By their loud boisterous voices, most of them were quite drunk, and the pile of money on their table suggested that they had all put quite a lot of their worldly wealth behind their hands. On seeing the crowd, Abigail frowned. She did not like the look of the lot and made sure to find herself and her father a table as far away from the group as she could manage.

"Look there," Mr. Carter said as they waited on their drinks to arrive, "I do think that is Lord Gillingham on that table."

Abigail had sat with her back to the gamblers and had to turn full about to look for the man. Sure, enough, there was a gentleman, whose clothes betrayed him as being of some means, but she could not imagine the loud rakish looking gentleman to be David. "I am sure you must be mistaken father, Lord Gillingham would not be caught dining in a small inn such as this, let alone gambling away with the fishers and farm workers."

Mr. Carter kept his eyes on the group and shook his head. "I am telling you, that is David. It may have been years since I last saw the lad, and you may have been both children then, but I would recognise him as surely as I'd recognise you."

The loud slam of a fist into a table made Abigail jump and she did not turn about again to give the wealthy looking gentleman another look. She kept her eyes on her father and let out a disgruntled sigh. "Well whoever that man is, I wish he'd take his gambling elsewhere. The fisher folk always seem more heated when they gamble for high stakes."

Mr. Carter studied his daughter's face for a moment then looked to the innkeeper, who had not yet begun to get them their drinks.

"If they are making you uneasy my dear we could just leave."

Abigail shook her head vehemently.

"No. You so rarely get a chance to get out, I am not going to spoil it by begging to return home on account of a few loud men."

Despite her best efforts to put on a smile for her father, Abigail's mood did not improve once their drinks and food arrived. As she and her father ate their ample meal, the din of the gamblers was becoming ever louder in proportion to the growing stakes on the table. The wealthy gentleman, who her father still eyed from time to time, was losing money like someone had cut open his coin purse and showed no sign of letting up.

"In just a few more hands I dare say that man will be gambling away the shirt on his back. Some folk really must learn when it is not their night." Mr. Carter shook his head.

Abigail watched as her father looked past her at the table, barely taking his eyes off of the wealthy stranger as he popped another boiled potato into his mouth.

"Well, if he can afford such losses..." she didn't finish the sentence as another cheer erupted from the table, signifying another hand lost to the rich fellow. Abigail took a deep breath to ebb her frustration. "I think I might ask for another drink father, would you care for more beer?"

Mr. Carter nodded and Abigail grabbed his tankard, stalking over to the innkeeper. The man seemed as troubled as she was by the gamblers, and kept a weather eye on them.

Abigail looked to the table and noticed that Anna, the innkeeper's daughter, stood very near to the wealthy gentleman. No doubt the girl was impressed by the rich man's ability to shrug off such great losses of capital for she had her hand placed very inconspicuously on his shoulder, her finger appearing to caress near to his neck.

Abigail looked to the Innkeeper, unsure if he had noticed his daughter's less than proper attentions.

"I am sorry for the ruckus Miss. Carter," the man offered as he took her father's tankard and poured out another round. "Never seen the fisher folk so hungry for a game. That young Lord Gillingham is getting a right good fleecing. If he doesn't call it a night soon he might well find himself stripped to the bone by those scavengers before the night is out."

Abigail did not like hearing her old friend's name mentioned a second time and turned back to the gamblers to attempt a better look at the rich young man. He had short dark hair, much as she remembered David to have, but with his back toward her there was not an awful lot she could make out. Still, just the way he sat there: drinking, gambling and accepting the unchecked attentions of the landlord's daughter... she just could not accept it was the same man.

There was another shout. Evidently, the man had squarely lost another hand to the fisher-folk, and now got up from his chair, body swaying slightly as if in a stupor. Abigail frowned but kept her eyes on the man as he meandered over to the innkeeper, his balance maintained by Anna. The innkeeper's lips pursed thin as he looked to his daughter who hung onto the Lord's arm like some limpet to a boat.

"Perhaps, Anna, you might look to cleaning a few tables, I can see at least a dozen tankards need clearing." Abigail could see the annoyance in the young girl's face as she silently removed herself from the Lord's side and obeyed her father. "Lord Gillingham, I'm sorry to hear your game is going as poorly as it sounds."

"It is no matter, plenty more gold to replace it at home... and who knows, I might still recoup my losses before the night is out." In his drunken haze the man regarded Abigail and gave a smile that she mistook at first for recognition.

Unprompted she felt her heart suddenly beat a little faster and she offered a cautious smile in response.

"My Lord, it is good to see you again,"

"I do hope Miss that my friends and I aren't spoiling your evening with our noise... perhaps you'd like to join us?"

Abigail was stunned. It really was David, though his body seemed to have been usurped by a creature wholly different to the sweet good natured boy she remembered. She opened her mouth to reply, but the air seemed to disappear from her lungs and no words formed as she watched the man sidle closer to her. He had not recognised her. His politeness and attention to her was nothing more than the smooth talking of an inebriated rake and it hurt Abigail to realise it. Disappointment etched her face as she drew back from his advance.

"You remember Miss. Abigail Carter, I am sure, my Lord, she is out with her Father." The Innkeeper's words were well timed to prevent the Lord from making a move he might regret.

The mention of Abigail's name seemed to act well as a bucket of cold water thrown over his face and Lord Gillingham immediately seemed to regain a measure of sobriety.

"Miss... Miss Carter... I didn't... I didn't recognise you." The man's voice was quiet and apologetic.

Abigail fancied she detected the tinge of embarrassment on his already rosy, drunken cheeks.

"I cannot say I recognised you either my Lord... you've... you've changed so much." That was politest way thing she could say at that moment, but, even then, it was obvious to any listener that she did not mean her words as a compliment.

The Lord shuffled his feet and ran a hand nervously through his raven black hair. Abigail studied him closely, relieved to find a spectre of the person she knew, beneath the hazy veil of drunkenness that clung to him. He still held a trim figure, unmolested by the glutton's frame that so often clung to the rich. His sharp patrician features had not been dulled down the years, and his square cut jaw and arched cheek bones still leant him a degree of nobility. It was his eyes which were the most changed. Abigail remembered them being cerulean blue, like two clear rock pools on a beach. Now, addled by alcohol, they were blood shot and watery. It was a shame.

"It is... It is very good to see you. Might I pay my respects to your father?" The Earl asked.

Abigail took a sharp breath, disliking the smell of alcohol that permeated the air about the Lord. "Father has had quite a long day," she said with a stilted tone. "Perhaps you could call on us another time?"

Not wishing to endure this changed creature, who was once her best friend, any longer, Abigail took her father's drink from the innkeeper and gave a curt nod to the Lord before leaving.

At their table, Abigail tried to reconcile the thoughts that seemed to rush through her head. She was trying to convince herself that she was disgusted by Lord Gillingham. She wanted to be righteously offended by his drunkenness and the way he let the innkeeper's daughter hang off him. Still, there was still the kernel of pleasure at seeing him again, and the hint of his true self hidden within. He had seemed visibly embarrassed to have been found by her in the state he was in, as if he too knew he was not presenting his true self to the world.

Uncomfortable though their meeting had been, Abigail had to accept that her speaking with Lord Gillingham might well have been for his ultimate good. He became a lot quieter at the gambling table and it was not long before he took his leave of the group. He had failed, it seemed, to recoup any of his losses, but at least he had made a break before he had to give up anything beyond coin.

From time to time, Abigail's attention moved across the inn to the Lord who sat alone in a corner. Anna was still finding excuses to hang about him as she did her work, but any interest the Lord had for her before now seemed spent. Seeing him rebuff Anna's attentions pleased Abigail more than she cared to admit. He sat in morose solitude as he finished the bottle of wine he had before him, and finally stalked over the innkeeper to settle up his bill.

"I'm surprised the young lord has anything left to pay up with," Mr. Carter whispered.

He too had been watching Lord Gillingham with intense interest and did not seem to like what he saw as the Lord tried to pay off the innkeeper with a golden pocket watch, the very same she suspected had been his father's favourite timepiece.

Abigail hated what she was seeing, hated what had become of her friend. It had been eight years since she had last seen him, but she still could not accept that the Lord had undergone such a radical change of basic nature. She had determined to say nothing more to him, nor to pay him undue attention, but as he lurched away from the innkeeper and to the door she could not help rising and going to the innkeeper's side.

"Sir, do you mind giving me that watch, I will pay for Lord Gillingham's outstanding debt."

The innkeeper looked at the delicate timepiece in his hand. It was worth more than a few drinks and he was loathe to give it up, but his moral compass succumbed to Abigail's request and he handed over the watch as she doled out the appropriate coin for the Lord's bill. A moment later, she was chasing the man out into the night.

Lord Gillingham stood bent over and heaving. The rush of fresh evening air had not suited him and he seemed to struggle to keep his breathing regular. Abigail felt uncomfortable as she watched him, worried that at any moment he might begin to vomit.

"My Lord, is your carriage nearby? Can I call your servant to look after you?" she asked, keeping a cautious distance.

The Lord turned and looked at Abigail for a moment, his face unreadable in the dark. Abigail could hear him taking several deep lungfuls of air as he began to straighten up.

"I did not bring any servant with me or my carriage. I will walk back to Hartley Hall."

"David, Hartley Hall is miles away, I can't let you walk back there alone in the dark, not in the state you are in!" Her words were harsh and she crossed her arms as she spoke. "Stay right where you are and I'll collect my father."

"Please... Miss. Carter, I am quite alright. Do not trouble..."

"Do not object please," Abigail interrupted. A note of anger permeated her words and brought the Lord to silence. "Stay right there and do not dare move. I do not need to be chasing you down the roads in the dark."

Continue Reading

'Rescuing the Earl'

at:

https://www.amazon.com/dp/B01MSR0QUL/

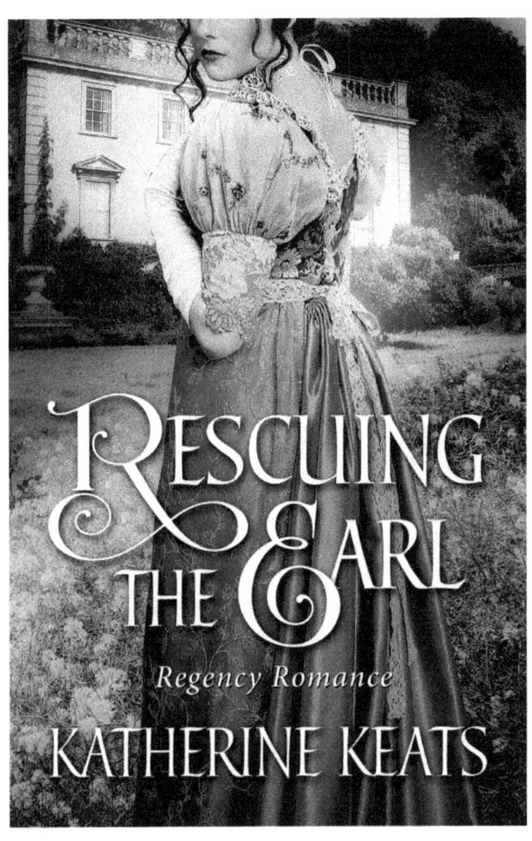

RESCUING THE EARL
Regency Romance
KATHERINE KEATS

ARIETTA RICHMOND, GRACE AUSTEN, ISABELLA THORNE,
KATHERINE KEATS AND SOPHIA WILSON

The Duke's Christmas Blessing

Sophia Wilson

Chapter One

Finding love is not the same as finding someone to love… people often fail to understand that you can love someone without them ever being yours to begin with, but what a beauty it is when you find both.

Patrick Hann, the esteemed Duke of Cumberland, smiled, thinking of the woman who had made him the happiest man alive, as he put his quill down and folded his letter neatly to fit into the envelope which lay empty on his writing table. To my love.

Their meeting was not very unusual; a classic tale of how two lovers were destined to meet, it was as though it had been excerpted from the very first page of a popular romance novel. However, popularity alone has little value, for something that is popular may not always be for the reason of good. The scriptwriter was fate itself and no one could ever know what it foretold.

It was 'love at first sight' for Patrick and from thereon, the almost predictable love story unraveled itself faster than most.

She was beautiful and no man could resist looking at her, tempted by both her grace and striking features. If there was one woman who could be both the prey and the predator, it was her.

Patrick, on the other hand, was handsome, tall, with the musculature of a man ready for a fight, although his kind nature would never allow him to do so; many would still find his looks and attractiveness rather debatable but that did not mean women did not openly desire him. They had fallen in love quickly, without regret or hesitation, inevitably Patrick had then been thinking of a greater commitment.

The thought was not new and had been circling in the mind of the Duke of Cumberland for weeks now. His nerves, and minute insecurities that would find such pressuring moments the ideal time to amplify, had gotten the better of him on all the occasions and multiple opportunities that had presented themselves.

He was unsure if it was courage he lacked, or if he was simply afraid that she would respond with an answer he was not going to like, let alone be afraid to hear. Nevertheless, he knew he must ask her and that he had to do it soon, for reasons obvious to him - he was afraid he would lose her to another man and the thought alone haunted him, as persistent as a ghost still not in peace with its death.

"I have been doing some serious thinking, Armagh," Patrick said, calmly looking over to the man sitting beside him; the best friend of many years, whom he trusted with all his heart and its contents.

"Lord have mercy on us! Cumberland has been doing some thinking all by himself! To what good deed do we owe this miracle?" Andrew Curtis, the Earl of Armagh, said, mockingly, teasing Cumberland as he laughed at his own joke. Patrick laughed along with him.

"How dare you mock me and make me sound as though I am incompetent of using the genius mind with which I have been gifted," Patrick snapped back at him in great humor.

"Oh yes, but of course! I apologize for the misunderstanding – you are so well known to me, I clearly failed to see the obvious," Lord Armagh answered back wittily. Patrick smirked, knowing he would not win this verbal feud, but nonetheless always amused by his quick responses and his wit.

"Jokes aside, Cumberland. What is on your mind?" Lord Armagh asked, sincerely concerned with what it was that Patrick had wanted to say earlier.

"Well, I have given this great thought, and my heart agrees with the decision I have made... I am going to ask her to marry me!" he finally blurted out, finding the sensation odd and strange as his thoughts formed into words which he spoke out loud.

"Marry?! What?! When?" Lord Armagh asked, sitting on the edge of his seat, now eager to know more - but not due to excitement, instead in grave worry.

"Since she is the romantic type I thought she would love a romantic gesture on what would be the most important day of our lives, apart from the wedding of course! I plan to propose to her on Christmas Eve, so that is a week's time from now. After all it is a day of blessings; why not add another one to the beloved holiday?" Patrick said, casually, to his old friend while slouching on his seat outside in the garden, overlooking the greenery in front of him.

"Do you not think you are rushing this matter, Cumberland? It has been barely two months and you are already head over heels for her! Is that not odd or strange to you? I think you should be careful with such decisions, and take your time in getting to know the person entirely, before you make a lifelong commitment vowing yourself to them," Lord Armagh advised, trying to indirectly hint that he did not approve of their union, without wanting to come across as sounding jealous or petty.

"Love should not have to wait, Armagh! Not when the woman that you know will keep you happy is right in front of you! Would you turn down an offer to be happy, or avail yourself of it when the opportunity presented itself?!" Patrick said, amused by what he thought was the Earl's silly suggestion.

"Are you certain about this, Cumberland? I would not want you to get hurt, simply because you did not think the matter over well enough," Lord Armagh asked him, with genuine care.

"I have never been more sure about anything in my life, Armagh. I love her and I want to marry her, it is as simple as that," Patrick said calmly.

He looked straight at his worried friend, who had been more a brother to him throughout their years of friendship.

Lord Armagh felt his heart sink a bit, he could now see from Cumberland's face that he had completely fallen for her and it was no longer a matter of discussion. *How do I tell him it is not as simple as he thinks it is?*

Chapter Two

The rest of their afternoon meeting had passed by mostly in large voids of silence, for Lord Armagh could find little to contribute to Cumberland's entire wedding plan, which he was narrating to him in great excitement. Feeling guilty of more than one thing, Lord Armagh shortened his visit and asked to be excused, saying that he had important matters to deal with.

Patrick did not think twice of it, as it was not uncommon for Lord Armagh to have other commitments since he was a particularly busy man owning multiple factories and businesses across the county.

As he got up to leave, Lord Armagh tried to hide his uneasiness as best as possible, for he could not begin to imagine how he was supposed to tell Cumberland of the scandal he knew about, regarding his great love. Debating whether he should even tell him or not, Lord Armagh left, still mid-decision, finding the responsibility much too great to bear at that very moment.

I should have told him the moment I knew, but am I really to blame, when I did not think it was my place to tell him to begin with? It is so typical of him to rush things that require even greater thought and care!

Knowing his friend, Lord Armagh was well aware of how Cumberland was fond of romance and love, and thought he had found it in many women before Lady Diana, ones he had never courted, but secretly had always wished to. But now, for the first time, it was as though gold had struck Cumberland, ever since he had met Lady Diana at a Ball two months ago, and she had shown clear signs of interest in him. Lord Armagh had never thought of it too seriously, keeping Cumberland's previous history of falling for women he had never married in mind - little had he known that this time it was going to be different, and his friendship was going to be put to the test.

It was not that Lord Armagh thought it ill for them to be together, but being his watchful and caring friend, he took it upon himself to analyze the women that could be possible wives for Cumberland, given that he was too gullible to ponder over the essential details about them on his own. He had not told Cumberland yet about the incident he had, himself, witnessed a few days earlier, and now, hearing of his wish to propose, the secret was eating him alive.

You have to tell him, Armagh... you must. This would change his decision entirely! She is not the woman she claims to be and your first feeling about her was indeed not wrong... but he is so blinded by love, would he even believe me? What if he actually forgives her instead? Would it change anything? What if it would not? Who knows?

But you must tell him, Armagh! It is your duty to. You know the truth and hiding it from him is as though you are lying to him, how will you live with yourself? How do I tell him though? What if it means nothing? Would this be betraying him if I kept quiet about this? Will it do any good telling him and breaking his heart? How do you tell a man that the woman he loves was kissing another man just a few days ago?

After thinking through it thoroughly, Lord Armagh decided not to tell him; not yet.

ARIETTA RICHMOND, GRACE AUSTEN, ISABELLA THORNE,
KATHERINE KEATS AND SOPHIA WILSON

Chapter Three

Despite convincing himself that he had made the right decision, the guilt was strong and overbearing, and Lord Armagh began to keep his distance from Cumberland to avoid showing his awkwardness around him.

Patrick, completely consumed by wanting to propose to Lady Diana, paid little heed to his friend's absence, thinking that he may have been busy with the festivities of Christmastide, even though every year it was almost a tradition for them to celebrate together.

A few days before Christmas Eve, by coincidence, the two of them met at a dinner even, though there was little coincidence between them as they had almost the same social gatherings and friends, neither of them had thought to run into each other there.

"Ah! Armagh! Nice to see you here! Nice to see you at all!" Cumberland greeted him joyfully as though he had not seen him for months.

"Cumberland. Nice to see you too, my friend," Lord Armagh replied, stuttering, not having realized before that the Duke of Cumberland, too, would be at the event or maybe he would have opted not to come. Cumberland embraced him warmly.

"Where have you been? I hope it is a lady that occupies your time and not work! Mind you I do not like being replaced or neglected, but for a special lady I am willing to forgive you and your distance," Cumberland joked with him, laughing heartily.

Lord Armagh laughed softly, trying to act as natural as possible.

"I may be joking, but I am also serious Armagh, it is time you settled and found yourself a wife, too! Court one fine lady and make sure to slither your way next to her under the kissing bough on Christmas Day, and before you know it you will be falling for each other! That is how love stories begin, my friend. Little do you know!" Cumberland patted him on his back smiling ear to ear and giving a soft chuckle.

"Not all love stories begin the same way, you should know that Cumberland. Every book, every story is not the same and I beg to differ, but kissing a woman once under the bough will prove nothing to me, nor establish anything between us. I, unlike you, will make sure I do this very slowly," Lord Armagh replied with a hint of frustration in his voice.

Cumberland noticed that he was not happy to talk about the topic and said nothing more. Lord Armagh was not quick to anger, or be irritated, and so Cumberland found this behavior rather odd. Instead of questioning it, he let it be, thinking that maybe he had had a tiresome day, or week for that matter.

"All I meant was, you should let yourself loose a little bit! Unwind yourself and allow yourself to flow with the wind, as I am doing with Diana. I just want you to be as happy as I am," Cumberland said, with the utmost sincerity, looking at his friend's apathetic face.

The last sentence echoed in Lord Armagh's ear, *He wants me to be happy, but how do I tell a friend who is like a brother to me that I do not think the woman he wants to marry is right for him?*

Still debating whether he should say something or not, Lord Armagh went into deep thought, pursing his lips shut so that he would not say anything out loud while he was doing so. *I should tell him. I will tell him now. I can't let him marry her without knowing the truth,* Lord Armagh finally concluded, convinced that it was all in Cumberland's best interests and that it was better it come from him, rather than anybody else. Just as he opened his mouth to speak, a woman not too far from them called out for Patrick. Lord Armagh looked up to see who it was... *not now.*

Lady Diana walked over to the two gentlemen, looking as stunning as she usually did, dressed in a silk dress and pearls, smiling as she approached Patrick and Lord Armagh.

"Good evening, gentlemen," she said, in her sultry voice, as she grew near enough for a greeting.

"Good evening," Lord Armagh replied shortly.

"Good evening, my beautiful Diana," Patrick said, loud enough for the people around them to hear, as he took her hand in his and gave it a soft kiss.

"You spoil me, Your Grace," Lady Diana said playfully, as she showed her pearly white well-aligned teeth and gave him an attractive smile.

"I hope I am not interrupting anything," she said, realizing that the two of them had been in conversation before she had joined them.

"No not at all, we were just catching up. It has been a few days since we have seen each other," Patrick replied instantly, not wanting her to feel as though she was unwanted, or that she should leave.

"Have you now? I thought the two of you were inseparable! If I marry you, I suppose Lord Armagh will come along, too!" Lady Diana joked, while Patrick laughed along with her. Lord Armagh forced himself to smile, trying to be as polite as he could, although all he wanted to do was be as far as physically possible from either her, or both of them.

How can she be so casual, while having been intimate with another man, carrying herself with so much dignity while she plays out a boisterous affair and then talks about marrying another one, at a public party such as this one? Surely, she does not know of his plans to propose! And who was the man I saw her kissing? I only saw them for a mere second but he looked so familiar! If he ever spoke out about her infidelity after Patrick and she were married, it would be purely chaotic! He would be devastated... crushed.

"Are you alright, Lord Armagh? You look a little pale. I hope that you are not sick, but instead in good health," Lady Diana said to him cunningly, always trying to show Patrick that she, too, cared about the people that he did.

"Yes… Yes I am fine. Thank you for asking. I just feel a little light-headed, I will go and get myself some water, thank you. You two enjoy your evening, I don't think I will be here for long anyway," Lord Armagh said, excusing himself in a hurry, yet again. This time, however, Patrick had noticed, and he began wondering what had gotten into him.

I must go and find the man she kissed, if I can't tell him right now I should at least know who it was. Cumberland would demand to know, too, if I told him. With his decision set in mind, he walked straight out the mansion doors and called for his coach; he was set out on a mission. *Expose Lady Diana.*

ARIETTA RICHMOND, GRACE AUSTEN, ISABELLA THORNE,
KATHERINE KEATS AND SOPHIA WILSON

Chapter Four

It was nearly dark but Lord Armagh knew he had little time, there were two days to Christmas Eve and if he did not find out, and prove Lady Diana's deception, Patrick may end up marrying a woman who had never loved him to begin with; something he would never be able to recover from.

He directed his coach towards Patrick's estate, his heart palpitating with uncertainty of what exactly it was he was doing. The coachman, although confused, did not question the Earl's orders and followed the instructions he was given. At the complete cloaking of darkness in the sky, the Earl reached the estate.

The footman opened the door for him and he gave a quick greeting before he hurried inside to see if any of the maids or housekeepers had seen the man he had seen that day. Lord Armagh made his way through the hallways, unable to recognize any of them, as he did not know their faces nor their names.

Wanting to change his strategy and limit his search, Lord Armagh decided he would speak to Miller, the steward of the estate, directly, instead of questioning the numerous household staff and wasting time; Patrick could be home any minute and every second was precious.

"Excuse me; do you know where I can find Miller please? It is rather urgent," Lord Armagh asked one of the housemaids who was busy wiping dust off a shelf.

"Yes, your Lordship. You will find him in the library making sure the books are all in alphabetical order," the housemaid told him.

"Thank you very much," Lord Armagh said sincerely, as he headed towards the library Patrick had specifically made for himself.

"Miller?" Lord Armagh said, knocking on the half open door before opening it wider and looking inside, hoping to find him there.

Miller was reading the spine of a book in his hand before he turned to look at who it was calling his name.

"Yes?" he responded as he turned.

"I was looking for you," Lord Armagh said, relieved that he had found him.

"Oh your Lordship, I am deeply sorry, I did not recognize your voice," Miller said nervously, seeing that the Earl stood before him and believing it was almost a sin that he had disrespected him by not addressing him properly.

"That is alright, Miller, there are greater matters that require our attention," Lord Armagh said, knowing that he was a good man who would never disrespect anyone.

"Yes your Lordship, what brings you to the estate? Is there anything I can help you with?" Miller asked, concerned. He knew Lord Armagh well and it was unlike him to visit at this hour, in Patrick's absence.

"As a matter of fact there is. I need you to tell me whose duty it is to tend to the plants out near the old willow tree," Lord Armagh asked, recalling he had seen the two of them kissing beneath the tree.

Lady Diana leaning back on the tall tree's trunk and the unknown man facing his back towards Lord Armagh, making him unrecognizable.

"That would have to be Henry, the gardener," Miller answered, confused and wondering why the Earl of Armagh would come all this way to ask about the gardener.

"Thank you so much, do you know when I could speak to him maybe?" Lord Armagh asked.

"Yes your Lordship, I am afraid the only time you could speak to him is after he returns from the holidays since he has taken a few days off. Excuse me if I am overstepping the bounds your Lordship, but perhaps you could tell me why you need to see him so urgently? Maybe I could arrange something for you?"

Miller spoke sincerely, still baffled by the entire series of events.

Lord Armagh went blank the moment he heard that the gardener, the only person who could have known about it or seen them getting intimate, was not to come back until after Patrick would most likely have proposed. There was nothing he could do, not now; he had to let fate take its own course.

"I, uh… no thank you, Miller, there is not anything else I need. I just saw my hedges and I thought they needed a little more trimming, mine too has taken his days off of work and I thought Patrick has a very good gardener. I thought I would ask if he could come by maybe, but that's alright, I suppose the hedges will do just fine as they are. Thank you anyway, Miller. I shall be on my way now," Lord Armagh quickly crafted a story to back up his mysterious and strange behavior, hoping that it sounded convincing enough.

Bidding him goodbye, Lord Armagh rushed to the coach and headed straight home. *I tried, I really did. Maybe Lady Diana will decline the proposal because she is in love with another man? Let us hope she will. I am sorry, Cumberland, but sometimes getting your heart broken saves you from something far worse later on.*

The coach drove into the dark, while the Earl constantly convinced himself that he had done the best he could.

Chapter Five

Christmas Eve had come and the irony of its arrival was such that some woke in the morning with pure joy and excitement about the festivities that were set for the day and the plans they had, while others worried if this day, and all the others that followed it, would bring with it change that they would not be able to recover from, or if anything in their lives would change at all. Nevertheless, everyone got out of their beds, all the same, but so very different in their fates.

Knowing the Duke of Cumberland, Lord Armagh had predicted that he would propose to Lady Diana somewhere during the afternoon, when she was most likely to visit before the Christmas Eve dinner. It was a known tradition that Lord Armagh and Patrick would have Christmas Eve dinner together regardless of any situation that could possibly separate them on the occasion. They always found a way to be together on this day, as it was a day that they respected as one on which to be surrounded by only friends and family.

They took turns every year to host the dinner, going back and forth between each other's estates, once at Patrick's estate and the next year at Lord Armagh's; this year again it was Patrick's estate where the dinner was agreed to be held.

Wanting to avoid being there too close to the time of the proposal, Lord Armagh deliberately chose to leave his home later than usual. As the coach went its way in the direction of Patrick's estate, Lord Armagh felt himself hoping for the best; hoping that Lady Diana would have declined marrying Patrick by now, and that he was simply on his way there to somehow mend Patrick's broken heart if she had.

Stepping through the front doors upon his arrival at Patrick's estate, and entering the parlour, Lord Armagh felt a sinking feeling in his chest for the second time; except that this time, it did not feel as if he was slowly drowning, it was as though his heart was being plunged to the depths of a vast ocean.

"Ah look who finally made it!" Cumberland exclaimed at first sight of Lord Armagh.

"Yes, hello Cumberland... I see congratulations are in order," Lord Armagh greeted him, while suspiciously looking at the woman he had his arm curled around. *She did not say no?*

"Yes, they are! Lady Diana here has agreed to be my wife and I could not be a happier man, this is the best present anyone could ask for at Christmas," Patrick said, gleaming with pride and joy as he tightened his arm around his new fiancé. Lady Diana smiled, showing no signs of shyness; not even in the slightest amount.

"That... that is great news. Congratulations... I hope you two are happy," Lord Armagh struggled to say out loud, whilst also indirectly wishing, in his own mind, that they would be happy either with this union or without it.

There was an awkwardness in the room as Lord Armagh looked around, trying to comprehend why everyone was looking at him blankly - perhaps he had accidentally said out loud what he was actually thinking? *Oh right!*

He walked over to Patrick and embraced him warmly after realizing simply wishing congratulations was not enough. Patrick embraced him back and the awkwardness was gone.

"I hope you two always remain such great friends," Lady Diana said, smiling at seeing them embracing each other.

"I will have to correct you on that Diana. Armagh is not only a great friend, he is my brother and the only one I have. If I am any happier than I already was, due to our engagement, it is due to seeing him here with me. Thank you brother," Patrick confessed emotionally, patting Lord Armagh on the back after he finished his sentence.

Lord Armagh felt a sudden surge of the guilt he had been trying to bury inside him for days; the gates were open and his shame flooded him.

"Well I will let you two have your time together. I am afraid I have a little business that needs to be taken care of and it requires my personal appearance. I assure you I will return in time for dinner, I hope you don't mind, Cumberland? I won't be long," Lady Diana said empathetically.

"No not at all. I will request this, however, that you return as quickly as you can," Patrick said raising her hand in his to place a kiss upon it.

"I will do my best. There is nowhere else I would rather be," Lady Diana responded, smiling at him as she did.

"That is all I needed to hear," Patrick said, as she excused herself and left the room.

Armagh, tell him now. You waited too long trying to make this situation comfortable for you... but this is not about you! This is about a man who considers you a brother, as you do him. If you wait any longer and then they have issues with their marriage or anything alike, somewhere... somehow... it will be your fault, too. It is never too late to tell the truth... you still have time.

"Are you inclined to a game of cards?" Patrick asked grinning, knowing that he would never decline. Their history playing cards was one that left it debatable as to who was the better player. The competition between them was tough and they had been tallying their wins for years.

"Of course I am, after all I find so much joy in reminding you that you struggle to win against me," Lord Armagh said, teasing him as he laughed.

"We will see about that!" Patrick said laughing, accepting the challenge.

This is excellent. A few rounds of playing cards and a little liquor in my blood... I will then be able to finally tell him and this heavy burden will be off my shoulders for good!

After an hour or so of both wins and losses, as they both reconnected and made up for those days they had not been together, Lord Armagh mustered the courage to say what he had wanted to tell him for such a long time.

I will let him win this round... and then... then I will say it.

As they continued playing, Patrick noticed that Lord Armagh was making amateur mistakes, costing him the game.

"Armagh, are you going easy on me now? I may be an engaged man with a soft side now, but do not insult me by allowing me to win!" Patrick said, catching on to what Lord Armagh was doing.

Lord Armagh smiled at him uneasily, *it was time.* As he constructed the proper sentence to say to Patrick, a footman rushed in the room without either permission or announcement.

"I beg your pardon, Your Grace but I am afraid there has been an accident," the footman said frantically, seeming on the edge of panic.

"What? What do you mean? Who had an accident?" Patrick asked, baffled, his eyes wide and consumed with fear, already hoping it was not the person he thought it was.

"It is Lady Diana, Your Grace. She has been hurt and rushed to the eminent doctor's residence for immediate medical attention," the footman said, looking to the ground as a sign of both respect and condolence.

"What?! Diana?! I must go! I must go now!" Patrick said in terror, as he got up and asked for his coat immediately.

"Do you want me to come with you, Cumberland?" Lord Armagh asked, rising to stand with him, ignoring what he had wanted to say a few minutes ago, before the horrible news.

"No, it's alright, Armagh. I will be fine on my own," Patrick said, looking at his friend with a more confident look, reassuring him that he was no longer panicking and thinking reasonably.

Lord Armagh nodded and Patrick left.

Oh Lady Diana, how is it that you can break his heart in more ways than one?

Chapter Six

Patrick sat in his coach as it rushed him to the doctor's residence as fast as possible, his vision blurring and the heart in his chest pounding as loud as the hooves of the horses that drew the coach. He did not know what to think or what to imagine. If she were hurt at all, he would not be able to bear it, whether it was a scratch or worse; he knew full well that he could not stand to see her injured in any way.

Knowing that it was times like these that truly put love and its vows to the test, he began trying to prepare himself for whatever ordeal he was about to face. *That is what love means; putting yourself aside for someone else.*

The doctor's butler answered the door, and asked, rather stiffly, what the Duke required. He replied, rather proudly at the word, that the Lady Diana, who had recently been brought here, was his 'fiancé'. The Butler showed him into a parlour, and requested that he wait, whilst he spoke with the doctor, who was with the lady now. Patrick paced the floor, unable to rest as he waited.

Within a short time the Butler returned, and requested that Patrick follow him. On the floor above, the Butler ushered him through a door, into a large bedchamber.

Immediately, his eyes went to the bed, and he saw her lying there; eyes closed. Walking to her, his eyes welled up with tears, for her arm was bandaged, her leg appeared splinted and bound, and bandage was wrapped around her head.

"Diana…" he softly whispered when he approached her and lightly touched her arm.

"She is alright, just getting some rest," a voice from behind him said. He turned to see who it was and saw that it was an older man, wearing glasses and dressed elegantly.

Before he could ask who he was, he introduced himself.

"I am her physician and Lady Diana is in good hands here with me. She hit her head when the carriage hit a rock and tumbled down a nasty hill. Thank the Lord it was not too steep, otherwise it could have been much more dangerous than it was. At first I believed her leg to be fractured, but it may simply be badly twisted – nonetheless, I have splinted and strapped it in place to make certain that it heals. She also has a cut on her arm and forehead. . The wounds will heal faster than her leg, but she will heal just fine. It will not be too long before she is walking and well," the doctor comforted him, smiling a reassuring smile.

Whilst Patrick knew that this physician was well renowned for his skill, he had, until hearing the reassurance, still been terrified.

"Thank you! Thank you so much! I was so worried. I have never seen her like this, so fragile, so weak. I cannot thank you enough for taking such good care of her," Patrick said, putting his hand on his chest as he spoke sincerely.

"It is my calling, you need not thank me. It is nice to know that she has someone who loves her so much. She will heal much faster with that kind of love and care," the doctor said, smiling at Patrick.

"Now if you will excuse me, I have been called to another noble patient. Please, feel free to stay with her – ring for my staff should you need anything, Your Grace. She should wake soon enough - it would be best not to wake her yourself." the doctor advised Patrick.

"Yes, of course, thank you for opening your home to her." Patrick nodded his agreement to the doctor's instructions, smiling as he did.

After the doctor left, he pulled up a chair beside Lady Diana's bed, and sat, holding her hand, looking at the engagement ring she was wearing, that he had given to her not more than a few hours ago. He kissed her hand as he always did, and a tear finally surrendered, falling down his cheek.

After an hour of waiting beside her faithfully, Patrick thought he would have a little walk in the hallway to stretch his legs and rest his back that was now beginning to ache from sitting so still in the chair for so long. He stepped outside and looked left and right unsure where it would be polite to go, in the doctor's residence. A passing footman showed him to a small parlour, only a few rooms away, and assured him that he would have tea sent up.

Moments later a woman was also ushered into the parlour, and promised the delivery of tea. She sat across from him and, both unsure of what to do, they made eye contact.

A little while later, she looked Patrick's way. It was rather improper for them to be here, alone, yet these were unusual circumstances. They had not been introduced, and he wondered who she was.

Their silence was interrupted by the arrival of tea and cakes. The footman placed the tray on the low table between them, bowed, and left.

Apparently deciding that being polite, and conversing, was more important than being proper, she spoke into the embarrassed silence that had surrounded them, even as she took up the teapot and poured.

"I do not mean to be invasive of your privacy, but I was wondering who you are here for?" the woman asked.

Patrick looked up from the cup that he had just been handed, and then saw, truly looking at her for the first time, that the woman who was talking to him was breathtakingly beautiful.

"I... um... I am here for my fiancé," Patrick said, uneasily.

"I am so sorry. I hope she is alright," the woman sounded so sincere.

"She will be..." he replied, without wanting to look at her, as her beauty was quite distracting.

There was silence again.

Patrick looked up and saw that now she was staring into her cup and that maybe she was feeling as lonely as he was; maybe she, too, had a loved one in one of the beds, here in the doctor's house.

"Who are you here for?" Patrick asked her.

"My father. He was in an accident and I don't think he's going to get well anytime soon," the woman smiled sadly, with humility, as though she did not know how beautiful she actually was.

"I am sorry but no, you must not think like that. You must be strong and positive for yourself and for him. Everything will be alright," Patrick said, smiling at her, knowing that all that he said was crafted from thin air; it would not stand on its own.

"Is that why you were crying moments ago?" she asked, softly smiling.

Patrick looked at her, surprised that she had noticed.

"Thank you, I don't mean to be rude or impolite. I do appreciate the kind words, but my father has been unconscious for months now. I know what it is like waking up in the morning thinking that today is the day he's going to open his eyes and then going back to sleep because he didn't... and then you repeat this cycle for days, hoping, wishing that one day will come with change. It is like being stuck; you can neither go forward nor backward," she said to him, explaining why his statement did not comfort her.

Patrick nodded, knowing that there was nothing he could say; sometimes it was best to be quiet about something you do not know or ever could.

"Well I must go to check on him, it is hard being far from his side, whether he knows it or not, the doctor has been most kind, allowing him to stay here, and me to spend so much time here – I cannot imagine what would have happened, otherwise."

The woman shuddered at her thoughts, then rose from her seat.

"I can only imagine," Patrick said nodding.

"It was nice to meet you..." she said as she was leaving.

"Nice to meet you, too," Patrick said smiling at her. It was only then that he realised they had not exchanged names – he had no idea who he had just been speaking with.

He got up himself and walked back to the room where Lady Diana lay.

"Patrick?" said a feeble voice as he walked through the door.

Lady Diana was awake.

Chapter Seven

"Diana!" Patrick exclaimed, rushing to her side and taking her hand in his.

"Patrick," she said, smiling, weakly touching his face and looking into his eyes.

"I thought something terrible had happened... you frightened me. For this one moment, one small second, I thought I had lost you... I...", Lady Diana put her finger on his lips, "shh, don't say it. I am alright, that is all that matters," she said, trying to comfort him. He nodded teary eyed and leaned in to kiss her.

There was a knock at the door, and they broke from their kiss to see who it was.

"Sorry, if I am interrupting," the handsome, well-dressed man said, standing at the door.

"No... not at all," Patrick said, wiping away a tear and straightening up, trying to regain his composure and make it appear that he was not, in fact, almost crying.

"Nice to see that you are awake, Lady Diana," the man said, approaching her and smiling as he did so.

"Thank you," Lady Diana said, her words drifting off as she was mesmerized by the good looking man who was concerned with her health.

Patrick noticed that there was something not quite right.

"I am sorry, who are you again?" Patrick asked in an investigative manner.

"Pardon me for not introducing myself, Your Grace. I am Dr. Drake, Dr Entwhistle's assisting physician. As I believe he mentioned to you earlier, he has another patient that needed immediate attention. I will be looking after Lady Diana whilst he is absent. I trust that is acceptable?" Dr. Drake said, looking once at Patrick and then again at Lady Diana, smiling.

"Certainly," Lady Diana replied, smiling at him eagerly.

Patrick could not understand what it was that was bothering him, clearly the two of them had never met before, and he was simply her doctor and she, his patient. *Why do I feel a hint of jealousy when there is no need for it? She only agreed to be my wife earlier today. Cumberland, you really just need to get some rest. Diana would never hurt you like that.*

Almost fully convinced, he watched protectively as Dr. Drake examined her, checking her injuries and asking if she was in any pain.

Once he left, Patrick pulled his chair back up beside her and sat with her.

"Patrick, you really ought to get some rest," Lady Diana said stroking his hand.

"I am alright," Patrick said, fighting to keep his eyes open and his back straight.

"Patrick, listen to me carefully, I am fine. I am no longer in so much pain and I am healing. I am stuck in a bed and not going anywhere. You have done more than enough today and it has been exhausting. Please, don't be so hard on yourself. Go home and get some rest and I will see you in the morning, I know that the doctor's staff will take good care of me." Lady Diana spoke in a loving tone but perhaps it hid ulterior motives for why she wanted him to leave.

Patrick looked at her, staring at her face that he loved so much.

"First thing in the morning then," Patrick said, accepting her permission to leave.

"First thing in the morning," she said smiling.

"If you need anything let me know, take care my love. Get better soon for me," Patrick said, getting up and kissing her on her forehead. She nodded. Patrick left.

After an hour or so, Dr. Drake knocked on the door again. Lady Diana was excited to see him; she had been waiting for the moment when he would come again.

"Hello, Lady Diana. How are you feeling now?" Dr. Drake asked, with a smirk on his face, as he walked towards the bed.

"Much better now," she said, in a playful tone.

"I am pleased to hear that," Dr. Drake said, still smirking.

"I have good news," he continued.

"Of course you do," Lady Diana said, smiling.

"What does that mean?" Dr. Drake asked, noticing her interest in him.

"A handsome face like that could only bring me good news I hope," she flirted with him.

"That may be true but this handsome face has found himself a new beautiful face that he is beginning to enjoy the sight of," Dr. Drake flirted back. Lady Diana smiled with her eyebrow arched.

"What is it, doctor? What is the good news?" she asked.

"The good news is that your leg seems to be much better and it turns out that it is not broken, but simply sprained. That means you will be able to go home in a few days," Dr. Drake said.

"That is not good news at all," Lady Diana said with her sultry eyes looking straight at him.

"Oh really? What part?" he asked, enjoying her company.

"I think you know what part, doctor," she said, highly amused.

Dr. Drake looked at her, admiring her boldness and quite caught in her eyes.

"I think I will rest now, doctor. Thank you for stopping by," she said, being playful.

"Don't worry, I will come again," he said, smiling as he ran a finger down her arm as he left.

Over the next few days, he visited her again... and again, and each time they got closer and closer together.

Chapter Eight

Patrick visited Lady Diana at the doctor's residence as often as he could, sometimes twice in a day if his schedule allowed him. He noticed that Lady Diana's behavior was strange and he could not quite understand why. It was as though she was now being distant from him, but Patrick tried to be understanding of her situation. He knew she had gone through an accident and it had barely been two days since they had been engaged, it was a lot to absorb and it would need time to settle in, for both of them; but more for her.

He noticed that, when he greeted her or kissed her hello, she never returned it with the same enthusiasm. Her greetings were dull and her kisses were formal. Worried that she was still in pain, he did not speak of it, although it bothered him.

"Did Dr. Drake see you today?" Patrick asked casually, simply wanting to know.

"What? Why do you ask?" Lady Diana asked defensively.

"Well, because he is your doctor. What good is he if he does not come to check up on you?" Patrick explained himself, trying to hide his frustration with the invisible barrier between them.

"Yes... yes he does," Lady Diana tried to say with a straight face, hiding her true emotions when she heard his name.

"Good," Patrick replied shortly, not wanting to say anything else that could lead them to argue or bicker.

They sat in silence, Lady Diana did not start a conversation and Patrick, frankly, did not want to talk about anything when she seemed so uninterested and jumpy.

"I suppose I should be going, I have business I must attend to," Patrick said, getting up to leave, hoping that Lady Diana would tell him to stay or something alike.

"Alright, take care," she simply replied, without a second thought.

Patrick looked at her, appalled at how she did not seem to care, and put on his coat, leaving, feeling a little hurt. He actually did business to attend to, that he had been postponing because of Lady Diana - because he wanted to spend time with her.

After Patrick left, brief moments later, Dr. Drake came into her room, without knocking and closed the door after him.

"I was wondering when I would get to see you," Lady Diana said, a gleam sparking in her eyes.

Dr. Drake walked straight to her and held her face, kissing her on the lips passionately before he said anything or allowed her to.

They kissed for a few seconds until he pulled himself away and let her go.

"Hello to you, too," Dr. Drake said, sitting on the bed beside her.

Lady Diana smirked, loving how unpredictable he was and how he sent tingles down her spine.

"I was going to come earlier but then I saw your fiancé sitting there with you and I left. He took an awfully long time to leave," he said, kissing her on the hand after he finished his sentence.

"I tried to get him to leave earlier, I was barely talking to him but still he insisted on sitting with me, in silence. Can you imagine?" Lady Diana said, laughing cruelly.

"I can, who would not want to sit here all day and look at such a beautiful face?" Dr. Drake said, romantically.

"You spoil me! I have only been here two days and you have already fallen for me?" she asked running her finger sensually on his arm.

"I have not simply fallen for you, I am a gone man now," Dr. Drake said, touching her leg.

Lady Diana looked up at him to see what he was indicating and if it was the same thing she wanted from him. In his eyes, she found the answer. Dr. Drake got up and locked the door, returning to her. She did not stop and she did not think twice about the one she was betrothed too.

It was too late.

ARIETTA RICHMOND, GRACE AUSTEN, ISABELLA THORNE,
KATHERINE KEATS AND SOPHIA WILSON

Chapter Nine

Everything continued as it did, Patrick visited, Lady Diana paid little heed to him, Dr. Drake would visit soon after and they would be intimate yet again. Not the tiniest shred of guilt welled up in Lady Diana; she did not care for Patrick. She had never loved him.

Two days later, whilst Patrick was sitting on his usual chair reading the newspaper, Dr. Drake came in, knocking.

"Today is the day," he said, walking in.

"The day for what?" Patrick asked puzzled.

"Lady Diana has healed wonderfully and may leave. She need not stay here any longer. She may return to her home," Dr. Drake said with a straight face, trying not to grit his teeth as he did.

"Oh thank you! Thank you so much," Patrick said, shaking his hand. This was the day Patrick had been waiting for, his patience had grown thin and he only held on to the fact that they loved each other and would be married soon.

He was sure that, once she was home, things would change and she would go back to being herself again. He looked over to the woman he had sat loyally beside and saw that she was not happy to leave.

"You get to go home now," Patrick said, trying to see if she was as happy to hear the news as he was. She nodded without smiling.

Patrick felt embarrassed and humiliated by her response, how Dr. Drake had seen that she was unwilling to go with him, but he ignored this for the sake of their relationship.

He called for a maid to assist her to dress and prepare, assuring her that his carriage was outside, and that he would convey her to her home. Once she was dressed, he returned to the room, and reached to help her stand, but she refused, saying that she did not need help. He felt hurt, but said nothing of it, as they left.

Within a few minutes they were on the way home.

Upon reaching Lady Diana's home, a footman helped Lady Diana step down from the coach and Patrick walked over to help her, offering his hand; she declined.

Inside, her Lady's maid helped her to her chambers to change into fresh clothes, leaving Patrick to wait in the drawing room. Lady Diana joined him some time later, and they were served tea and biscuits as the evening approached.

"It is so good to see you sit here with me. Kind though the doctor was, as he should be, for the fees that we pay him, his house was rather depressing, I am glad you have come home," Patrick said smiling at her, sipping his tea.

She vaguely nodded. Patrick watched her carefully for a minute and saw that she still seemed to have no interest in his presence whatsoever. He had finally had enough. He carefully put his tea cup and saucer down on the table and went to sit next to her on the chaise.

"Diana…," he began, taking her hand in his, "… I know it has been difficult for you the past few days and I cannot imagine what it was to go through what you did, but it was not easy for me either. Seeing you hurt broke me and every second I thought of you and how you must be feeling. I am sorry that I could not be there with you all of the time, but let's not forget the promise we made to each other before all of this happened. We loved each other and we still do, and to help you remember…" Patrick knelt down before her, still holding her hand.

"What are you doing?" Lady Diana asked, confused but annoyed.

"I am reminding us again of our commitment. Diana, I love you and I cannot be without you, if there is anything these few days taught me it was that I need you, so please answer this for me again, like you did before… will you be my wife?" he said kissing her hand as he finished his question.

"No!" Lady Diana said, snatching her hand back from him.

"What?" Patrick asked, as if he may have misheard her.

"I am sorry Patrick, but no, I cannot be your wife," she said coldly, repeating herself.

"I… I don't understand… we were engaged…" Patrick stuttered completely in shock.

"That was then and this is now and right now, I do not want to marry you. Go home," Lady Diana ordered.

"No... not until you tell me why it is that you have changed your mind? I thought you loved me?" Patrick asked regaining his senses a little.

"I never did. I was forcing myself to marry you! I only wanted to marry you for your wealth! But now I love someone and everything has changed. Are you satisfied now, knowing the truth? Now please, go home. I cannot bear having you here a moment longer," Lady Diana said rudely.

"Who is he? Who do you love?" Patrick asked now furious with her confession.

"It is none of your business who I love, because I am no longer yours," she replied, taking the ring off her finger and placing it in his palms. Patrick looked at the ring he had so lovingly given her, the ring that had been his mother's, that he had hoped would be cherished by his wife in turn, and closed his fist around it.

"It's that doctor isn't it? I trusted you! I stayed for you! You could at least have had the decency to tell me when you did not want me!" Patrick said, controlling his tone but enraged.

"I am telling you now!" Lady Diana almost yelled, fed up with spending a second longer with him.

"Very well. If that is how you feel, I will leave c," Patrick said rising to his feet and turning to the door. Lady Diana grabbed her things and marched out of the room, calling for her maid. *What a stupid thing love is,* he thought as he looked at the ring in his hand. *How stupid, indeed.*

Chapter Ten

Somehow, Patrick kept control until he reached his home. Then, alone in his chambers at last, he fell to the floor on his knees, his hands clasped in despair around his face. *What just happened? How did this happen? Why did I not see it coming?*

After some time had passed, with him feeling that he was losing his mind and feeling his lowest, Patrick knew that there was only one thing to do. He called for his valet, dressed in the first coat to hand, and instructed that his coach be prepared. In minutes he was heading straight to the only man he trusted, and the only one who could help him - Lord Armagh.

~~~~~

The knock on the door was wild and frantic.

"Armagh? Please?!" a familiar voice desperately asked from the other side.
~~~~~

"Yes, Yes, come in!" Lord Armagh replied getting up to open the door to the library himself, after recognizing whose voice it was.

Before Lord Armagh could open the door, Patrick already had. Lord Armagh stared at the state of his friend; Patrick was pale and his eyes bloodshot red. Tears welled up in his eyes that could neither decide to trickle down his cheek or stay where they were. His hair was ruffled and his voice weakly cracking when he tried to explain why he was here.

"Cumberland?! What happened?!" Lord Armagh asked, leading his friend inside and closing the door after him, so that no one else would hear what was going on.

"It... she... her..." Patrick struggled to say. Lord Armagh understood immediately and reached for his long term friend, embracing him.

"Okay, don't say another word. Just calm down and take a deep breath. Everything is going to be alright," Lord Armagh said holding him tightly, while Patrick fought back his tears. Lord Armagh felt a lump in his throat. *I should have told him myself.*

After an hour of calming Patrick down and forcing him to drink tea, with a little brandy for good measure, and water, Patrick was stable enough to sit without crying or panicking. They still had not spoken about what had happened but Lord Armagh did not want to push him either.

"She left me for another man," Patrick finally said, not looking up from the full cup of tea he held in his hands.

Lord Armagh stared at him blank and shocked.

"What?" he asked him, although he had heard clearly what Patrick had just said.

"Yes, she left me for the man who was her physician at the doctor's residence – his assistant. Can you believe it? It seems she cares nothing for her reputation or mine, and that she never loved me to start with." Patrick spoke apathetically.

"No... No I can't believe it," Lord Armagh lied.

"I was there beside her as much I could be. I worried about her every second and she leaves me for the man who was taking care of her because he was paid to do so. Taking advantage of his position," Patrick said, his hand trembling as he picked his teacup and brought it to his lips.

"I am so sorry, Cumberland. I really am, you deserve better," Lord Armagh said without thinking.

"I deserve better? She was everything! How could I not see it coming, that she was too good for me? I did not deserve her," Patrick said, still unable to meet Lord Armagh's eyes.

"Cumberland... there is something I need to tell you and I do not know how you are going to feel about this," Lord Armagh began saying.

Patrick looked up from his cup, waiting for Lord Armagh to speak, watching him with his confused eyes.

"A few days before you had the idea to propose... I was strolling outside your estate as I usually do and..." Lord Armagh watched as Patrick's expression changed to one of concern, "I will skip right to it... I saw Lady Diana kissing another man. I did not see his face but I did see hers," Lord Armagh said in a rush, feeling the instant relief as he did.

"What?! You saw her kissing another man and you never thought to tell me?!" Patrick got up angrily.

"Listen, I can explain…" Lord Armagh tried explaining before Patrick interrupted "No! You lied to me! All of you lied to me! I trusted you, Armagh! You were a brother to me! How could you not tell me!" Patrick said, caught in the toxic concoction of sadness and anger.

"Listen…" Lord Armagh tried to speak again, but Patrick over rode his words.

"I don't want to hear another word from you! I am leaving this instant!" Patrick said almost yelling as he tried to walk towards the door.

"Listen!" Lord Armagh yelled loudly, grabbing onto Patrick's arm and forcing him to turn around and face him.

"If you think you cannot trust me, then fine! Be that way! But if you believed we were brothers for even a second in your life, then you have to listen to me! It is my right to be heard!" Lord Armagh said sternly, looking Patrick straight in the eye. Patrick stared at him, frowned, then he pulled his arm away, sitting back down where he was. Lord Armagh sat back in his seat.

"I wanted to tell you the moment I found out, but you were not there. The next time we met, you told me you were going to propose. You were so happy and so I had to think about how it was I was going to tell you. Every time I tried to tell you, I could not. Before I could, you were engaged. I thought she would say no, because she was kissing another man, but that shameless woman did not. I even tried telling you after your engagement, when we were playing cards…"

Patrick cut in to Lord Armagh's explanation "- when you began purposely losing.... and the footman came in?" Patrick said softly, realizing that his friend was telling the truth.

"Yes," Lord Armagh nodded.

"I am sorry Armagh, this is my fault. I know you would never betray me..." Patrick said as he pulled the ring he had given Lady Diana out of his pocket, "... she hurt me, Armagh... and this is a constant reminder of it. I want you to get rid of it... throw it into the river," Patrick said holding it out on his palm.

"Cumberland, you need not apologize to me, your believing in me is more than enough," Lord Armagh said, taking the ring from his hand.

He studied it closely.

"Cumberland... is this not the ring that belonged to your mother? The one you vowed to give to your wife?" Lord Armagh asked, in shock at how he had simply handed it over to him to get rid of.

"Yes," Patrick replied, avoiding looking at it.

"Then I cannot throw it in the river for you," Lord Armagh said, still holding the ring in his hand.

"Why not?" Patrick asked.

"Because once I do, it will be gone forever and this is not a forever thing. Yes, you are in pain now and you will miss her but one day, you will want this ring back and until then I will keep it safe for you... then you can have it back," Lord Armagh said, slipping the ring in his pocket.

"Are you saying I will love again?" Patrick asked, confused.

"Yes, that is exactly what I am saying. This is not the end," Lord Armagh said smiling at his friend.

Chapter Eleven

Two weeks later, when the broken hearted had yet to heal their invisible wounds completely and the ones that had broken other's hearts were nowhere to be seen, another tragedy had come upon Cumberland's loved ones.

Lord Armagh had been in an awful accident.

Rushing through the same doctor's door, with the scenario of praying that another loved one was alright, Patrick helped Lord Armagh to a chair in the doctor's receiving room, then left at the doctor's request to pace back and forth in the parlour, waiting to know if Armagh was going to be alright, asking, again and again for the footman or Butler to bring him news.

A half hour later, the Doctor Entwhistle walked out and beckoned him into the room. Armagh was bandaged and pale, but otherwise appeared himself.

"Armagh!" Patrick said, both happy and sad to see him this way.

"Your friend is alright, Your Grace. Just a few bruises and scratches, luckily nothing serious," the Doctor said, smiling.

"Thank you so much," Patrick said, shaking the doctor's hand.

"I would, however, prefer that he stayed here tonight, so that I can check him again in the morning, and make certain all is well. The footman will help him to a room, if you would be so good as to keep him company." The doctor smiled again, and beckoned his footmen forward.

Once he was settled into bed to rest, Lord Armagh almost immediately fell asleep as the laudanum he had been given to numb his pain also made him drowsy.

Being the loyal friend he was, Patrick wanted to wait until he was certain that Lord Armagh was completely alright. Patrick settled into the same small parlour, and rang for tea. Sitting where he had the last time he was there, he thought how different things were, yet the room was just the same. Then, just like the last time, the same woman he had met before came into the room, and sank into a chair with a deep sigh. She looked up and saw Patrick, and smiled.

"Good afternoon my Lord," she said smiling widely.

Patrick smiled back at her.

"Good afternoon my Lady," he said politely.

"You never asked my name, but it is Amy," she said boldly.

"And you never asked mine, but it is Patrick Hann, Duke of Cumberland," he said, nodding his head and smiling.

"I am so sorry! I did not know you were a Duke, Your Grace," Amy said embarrassed at having addressed a Duke so casually.

"That is alright, you need not be sorry. I may be a Duke but I am no different than anybody else," he said humbly. Amy knew what she felt was strong and real, but she ignored it. *She liked him.*

"I saw you sitting here and I wanted to ask how your fiancé is?" she asked uneasily.

"She's alright now, but has, sadly, decided that she wishes to marry another man," Patrick said, laughing at himself as he said it. Amongst society it was a scandalous situation, but he had best get used to acknowledging it.

"I'm sorry I asked," Amy said not very sad to hear that.

"That is alright. How is your father?" Patrick asked, changing the topic.

"He woke up a few days ago, doctors are calling it a near miracle. You can't imagine how happy I am!" she said, her joy obvious in her face.

"That is wonderful news! I am so glad to hear that!" Patrick said, genuinely pleased, and it was apparent in his face. Amy noticed that for some reason, he actually cared; she loved it. Amy looked at him admiringly, there was something about him that made her feel good. Patrick was looking at her, too, he had noticed it when they had first met and noticed it again.

She was breathtakingly beautiful.

"Amy?" a man's voice called out, interrupting their odd but wonderful moment.

"Yes, I am here," she said turning around as the man who had called her name approached them.

"I have brought the coach, get your father so that we can go home," the man said coldly. Amy nodded obediently. He walked away without another word.

Patrick watched the man, wondering who he was and why he had spoken to her in that rude manner, but before he could ask, Amy told him herself.

"I am engaged and you just met him. I am sorry but I have to go," Amy said, sadly smiling as she rushed off before Patrick could say anything.

Patrick sat where he was, feeling both jealous and ignited with fury over how the man had mistreated her. Feeling both of these things intensely, he began wondering why he felt those things to begin with. *I barely know her, so why do I care for her so much?* The answer was simple, but he told himself an easy lie; he denied it.

Chapter Twelve

Amy and Samuel Dunn were far from the ideal couple but alas, their wedding plans had already begun now that her father, William, was home and regaining his health.

All day, as Amy tended to wedding details and planning, her heart refused to be involved in any of it.

For some reason unknown to her, she kept thinking about Patrick (he might be a Duke, but she could not think of him as anything other than Patrick...).

"Is everything going as planned?" Samuel asked as he joined her in the drawing room, where he had seen she was in deep thought.

"Yes, but... I wanted to... I wanted to ask you something," Amy asked him hesitantly.

"What is it?" he replied in an uninterested tone.

"Since Father just got back home and since I am tired from those sleepless nights watching over him, I was thinking we could postpone the wedding, at least until we both are no longer tired from what we had to go through," Amy asked, not knowing how he would respond.

"Amy, are you suggesting that we should postpone our event according to your wishes? What about my wishes?" he asked her, impolitely.

"It would be so much easier for me," Amy lied, making up an excuse to push the wedding as far as she could. She did not feel right about it.

"The answer is no, Amy. I have put a lot of work into this and watching it go undone, is not what I want," he said, nodding his head as he walked away. Amy felt the rush of sadness as the terrible feeling borne of the thought of marrying him grew bigger inside her. *If I do this, I do this only for you Father,* she said to herself, wiping a tear off her face. She would do anything for her father; even marry a man she did not love.

Two days before the wedding, an unexpected knock at the door was about to change everything. The footman walked into the drawing room where Amy sat, reading a boo,k meaning to calm her nerves. The footman announced that it was the Duke of Cumberland, and she smiled in both delight and confusion as he walked in behind him.

"Hello Your Grace, to what do I owe the pleasure of your visit?" Amy asked, shocked and clearly happy to see him.

"Hello Amy," he replied stunned while looking at her.

"I came to visit you before your wedding. I hope you don't mind," Patrick said, trying to sound convincing and to conceal how he had only come to see her again, one more time.

"That is awfully nice of you. Please sit down. Shall I call for tea?" Amy offered an empty seat close to her.

There was that instant spark again.

Before long, with tea delivered, the somewhat awkward conversation had relaxed, and they found themselves deep in conversation. They spoke of their interests and their lives, and found themselves enjoying each other's company very much. Suddenly, Samuel walked through the front doors and heard Amy's laughter and another man's voice coming from the drawing room. Samuel marched in, fury on his face.

"What are you doing with my fiancé?" Samuel asked, grabbing Patrick roughly by his clothes.

"Nothing!" Patrick said, keeping his hands still even though he felt like fighting back.

Samuel looked over at a frightened Amy and, releasing his grip on Patrick, walked over to her angrily, roughly grabbing her by the arm.

"This woman here, she belongs to me! Mine! Do you understand that?" Samuel yelled at Patrick.

"Let go of me, Samuel! Samuel, you're hurting me!" Amy cried as she tried to loosen his grip on her.

"Let go of her! That is no way to treat a gently reared Lady!" Patrick warned Samuel.

"Why? What are you going to do about it? Let me tell you, nothing! She is my betrothed and I will treat her however I want to!" Samuel said, laughing evilly.

Patrick walked over to Samuel, taking hold of his lapels and, driven by a startling fury, pinning him against the wall. Samuel dropped Amy's arm in shock. Patrick drew on all of his boxing training, using the gentleman's sport in a most ungentlemanly way, and punched Samuel in the face without wasting a single second. He had wanted to do that to him ever since he had heard the way he had spoken to Amy before, now he finally had the opportunity to. Samuel fell to the floor, looking at him with fear and shock as he wiped the blood off his lip.

"Get out. I will do worse with you if you ever come anywhere near Amy again. You do not deserve her." Patrick warned him as he took a handkerchief from his pocket and wiped the blood from his knuckles. Samuel got up, still holding his lip whilst walking out the door.

Is it not strange how one thing leads to another, how one encounter with one person can lead to saving the life of someone else?

Chapter Thirteen

What once had seemed like a dark world full of cruel people to Patrick had now become the exact opposite. He had found the silver lining in a dark cloud and it was Amy. When Samuel had left, she had explained how she had felt forced to marry him, how she did not love him the tiniest amount to begin with, but how he had won her father's heart and, for her father, she had agreed. She had learnt later on in their engagement that he only wanted to marry her for the wealth she would inherit from her father and how she had thought of ending her relationship with him once she had discovered that. Fate had it such that her father met with an accident before she could do anything and so she let Samuel's treachery go.

Both Patrick and Amy had already felt before that there was undeniably a strong attraction between them. Patrick soon sought permission to court her and neither of them could have been happier.

They had fallen in love quickly, following their instinct and pure intentions for a loyal love that they had found perfectly in each other.

It had been three months and Patrick had decided to ask Amy, the following week, to marry him. This time however, Lord Armagh had urged him on to do so, instead of being hesitant about it. Lord Armagh had met Amy and he had liked her for Patrick instantly.

Everything was finally going well and everyone was briefly happy; briefly because one day Patrick had an unexpected visitor show up at his doorstep.

The footman had allowed her inside, not knowing that Patrick would have objected. The visitor sat stiffly in the drawing room waiting for Patrick.

Patrick entered the drawing room not knowing who the visitor was. When he caught sight of the woman before him, he felt the immediate anger rising through his body, he clenched his fists. *How does she have the audacity to come here!*

"Leave, Diana! Leave right now!" Patrick said loudly and angrily.

"Wait, Patrick! Listen to me! I have something to tell you! Something you have to hear from me," Lady Diana said, crying loudly and with real tears.

"You have one minute Diana, that is all I can give you," Patrick said impatiently, only agreeing in the hope of making her leave all the sooner.

"I am sorry I left you like that, Patrick. I have seen now how wrong I was. I love you Patrick, I should have never left!" Lady Diana wailed loudly.

Patrick looked at her surprised as she apologized.

"Why now? Why would you choose to tell me now? What has changed?!" Patrick demanded to know.

Lady Diana looked at the floor before she said the next six words that were about to shake his world and turn it upside down again.

"I am expecting your child," she said without making eye contact.

"What?" Patrick asked again, feeling weak at the knees as he looked for a chair close by and sat down.

"You are going to become a father," she repeated, looking at him with glistening eyes.

Patrick felt as if he were about to cast his accounts.

Chapter Fourteen

The next morning, even though Patrick was still struggling to make peace with the revelation that had come from Lady Diana the night before, he knew what was the right thing to do, and he intended to do it.

Waiting in her drawing room for Amy, Patrick paced around as though all hell had come upon him.

"Patrick! I was expecting to see you last night, where were you?" Amy asked, walking in delighted to see him.

When Patrick turned around and Amy saw his face, she knew in the instant that something was wrong. He looked ill, but clearly there was bad news he had to tell her.

"Amy... I don't even know how to tell you. I have been feeling sick since last night. I know what I have to do but I don't want to do it," Patrick said vaguely.

"What are you talking about? Everything is going to be alright," Amy said, coming to him and placing a caring hand on his arm, trying to console him.

"No Amy, it is not!" Patrick said still in shock.

"What is it Patrick? Tell me please! You are frightening me!" Amy said still holding onto his arm.

"Last night.... Lady Diana, my ex-fiancé - came to my estate... she... she was crying... saying that she had made a mistake," Patrick began telling her.

"Well she did, but it's too late to go back," Amy said, relieved that the problem was not so great.

"Amy, she says she is expecting my child," Patrick said, looking at Amy as though he was about to cry.

Amy let go of him and took a step back.

"I am sorry Amy, but I have to take care of my unborn child. Surely we have made mistakes but that child does not deserve to live fatherless because of the differences between Lady Diana and me. There was only one time, one time when, I am ashamed to say, our passions overcame us, and I did not resist. But once was, apparently, enough. I cannot simply leave her to tend to this herself. I need to be the child's father. I am sorry, Amy. I love you still but I cannot break your heart any more than I was forced to. Goodbye Amy,"

Patrick spoke with tears in his eyes, not looking at Amy as he could not bear to see what he had done to her. The pain would be too great. He rushed out of her home without looking back.

After that, the two of them did not see each other, forced to go their separate ways.

Why is my life comprised of such great tests, ones that I will never pass and always fail; tests that are much too difficult for a weak man to survive through? Why is love the biggest blessing but also the greatest enemy and why am I cursed with never being with whom I love?

Just like that, his nights had become sleepless once again, his appetite had diminished into only having breakfast, and he barely smiled. He thought about Lady Diana, increasing with his child, all of his waking moments, and it was eating him alive.

He could not abandon the child; it had nothing to do with Lady Diana. Although many would have been delighted to know they were to be parents, the nature of this was entirely different; the parents barely spoke to each other and were not able to be alone in the same room together. Yet, he must marry her – no matter what he did, the scandal would be great – marriage would at least minimize it. Patrick was sure now that he was destined to live a miserable life with the woman he despised the most. There was no happy ending here, maybe for other people, but not for him.

ARIETTA RICHMOND, GRACE AUSTEN, ISABELLA THORNE,
KATHERINE KEATS AND SOPHIA WILSON

Chapter Fifteen

Hours passing had turned into days, long days into weeks, tiring weeks into a month and yet it felt like forever. Every day was a struggle. Lady Diana and Patrick agreed on nothing and having her visit his house again and again, after the bad history between them had proved more difficult to deal with; even the tiniest of situations regarding them or the baby to come turned into heated arguments.

One day, before the marriage he dreaded could come about, Lady Diana was strolling in the garden at Patrick's estate when someone saw her scream in pain, and almost fall to the ground in agony. Lady Diana was carried to a bedchamber, and a coach was sent to fetch the doctor to her. Patrick fretted, wanting to know if everything was alright with his unborn child.

Lady Diana screamed in pain as water trickled down her legs and the maids and housekeeper barred Patrick from the room.

Never having been remotely close to a situation like this before, Patrick did what he would usually do when he was stressed and anxious and when matters where no longer in his control, he paced, praying every prayer he knew, for the baby to be alright and for Lady Diana to at least survive. Pacing the hallway, Patrick bumped into a man he thought he would never see again; but alas it seemed that, as Doctor Entwhistle's assistant physician, he was here. Perhaps it was inevitable for them to meet again.

"Get out of my way." Dr. Drake told Patrick in an antagonizing tone.

"Why should I?. I don't have the time or energy to waste with the likes of you," Patrick replied, controlling his anger and emotions at this difficult time as best as he could.

"I am not here to pick a fight or bicker with you. She left me, too. But as a doctor, I have no choice – if Doctor Entwhistle is not available, I must attend a patient." Dr. Drake said, admitting that things had a way of coming back to the person who did them, whether it was a good deed or a bad one.

"She's here," Patrick replied, thinking that he should know since he may care, as Patrick did not care in the slightest amount.

"She is?! What for?! Is she alright?" Dr. Drake asked, surprisingly worried about her health and condition.

"I don't know if she's alright, which is why I am pacing. I hope she is alright, her and the baby. She is the patient you have been called here for!" Patrick said, still saying his prayers under his breath.

"Her what?" Dr. Drake asked, again confused wondering if he may have misheard Patrick.

"She is pregnant with my child and she is due to give birth," Patrick said, not very proud of the fact that she was.

"Wait, when did this happen?" Dr. Drake asked, knowing that, according to his knowledge of both her and medicine that could not be possible.

"When we were together... before you two met. She came to my estate a month ago saying she was pregnant. I did not know how far along she was, but I suppose she is in labor now," Patrick said, his anxiety slowly getting the better of him.

Dr. Drake thought to himself, calculating the events and the details Patrick had told him.

"Will you excuse me? If she is in labor, I must go to her – it's what I have come for – you summoned a doctor."

He rushed into the bedchamber, just as another wail of pain drifted out. Fifteen nerve-wracking minutes later, Dr. Drake came back out into the hallway, his face pale and numb, full of despair as he approached Patrick.

"What happened?!" Patrick asked, judging from the expression on Dr. Drake's face, that something had happened to the innocent baby.

"There is bad news and worse news, I am afraid I have to tell you, and, believe me when I say this is very difficult for me to tell you," Dr. Drake said, but not in his usual casual tone - this time it was obvious that he was very disturbed.

"Just tell me, please," Patrick almost pleaded, knowing his heart could only take so much.

"The baby is weak, it was born too early and it will need to be watched over and taken care of constantly. The chances of the baby surviving are not certain, but we hope that it will," Dr. Drake spoke with great difficulty, stressing every word so that it came out right and understandable.

"What!? How can it be that it is born early?! This is about the right time is it not? I may not know much, but I do know of the duration!" Patrick asked, frustrated, thinking that maybe Dr. Drake was using this as a ploy to distract him or manipulate him.

"There is other news and, once you know it, it will all make sense," Dr. Drake said with a heavy weight in his stomach and a lump in his throat.

"What is it?!" Patrick asked, panicking.

"The child is not yours. It is mine," Dr. Drake said, feeling sick at what Lady Diana had done to him.

"What?" Patrick whispered softly. He did not know whether to believe Dr. Drake or not, but it did make sense. It made sense of how the baby could be early, even though the calculation of months did not align. Somewhere in his heart he knew it was the truth, but he could not easily accept it.

"But... but..." Patrick said softly staring into the blankness as he focused on the wall.

"There is no 'but'. When Diana left you for me, she told me she was increasing after a little while of being together. She had found out when it was only maybe two months and I knew it was the truth because I am a Doctor, but she lied to me.... ."

Dr Drake looked grim as he spoke.

"She told me she did not love me and that she had lost the child and instead... she went to you, claiming that it was yours. Well now you are free of this unneeded responsibility she was forcing upon you. The child is mine and it is weak, so I suggest you leave me now to see the child that needs me. I hope that you will allow us to stay here, until it is clear whether the child will survive or not?" Dr. Drake said with a softer tone than he usually used. His voice was pleading, and, while Patrick wanted nothing more than to throw them from his house, he was not so heartless as to do so.

Patrick nodded curtly, knowing that the battle for the child's survival was not his, but Dr. Drake's instead and that he was right about it all. He turned away with his dignity and pride still intact and prayed sincerely that they all would manage to live together and find happiness. He went to inform his staff of the need to take care of them, until such time as they could leave.

~~~~~

One week later, the baby passed away and Lady Diana, stricken with grief, and rejected by society for the scandal, chose to retire to a country estate of her family, far away from everybody, choosing a different life altogether. Dr. Drake continued to work with Dr Entwhistle, determined to save other lives, as he had not saved his child's, and none of them ever met or wrote to each other again.
~~~~~

ARIETTA RICHMOND, GRACE AUSTEN, ISABELLA THORNE,
KATHERINE KEATS AND SOPHIA WILSON

Chapter Sixteen

The moment Patrick recovered from the shock of discovering that the child was not his, he made his way straight over to Amy's home, praying that he could mend things with Amy, now that he knew the truth. He had left Amy broken-hearted without ever imagining he could do that to her, and he did not want to spend any more time keeping her in that pain.

Patrick asked the footman to not announce him, so that there was a greater chance of him actually being able to speak to Amy and explain everything to her.

She walked into the drawing room looking radiant as ever, showing clear signs of the strong and intelligent woman he always knew she was.

"Patrick? What are you doing here?" Amy asked at the first sight of him.

"I... I came here for you," Patrick said, realizing how much he had missed her voice and his name on her lips.

"What do you mean you have come for me?" Amy asked, a little insulted, considering how they had parted.

"I should never have left you and I wish I never had," he said to her before she interrupted him.

"I am sorry Patrick, but if this is some great apology to have me come back to you, let me tell you now that it will not work. I am not some ornament you decide when to keep and when to get rid of. You made the right decision and we both are aware of it. I had great respect for your decision, it was that of a man of ethics and care and that is what I loved about you... but you being here right now is the exact opposite of that. You cannot play with people's hearts Patrick, I will not allow it," she said sternly, stating her points and opinion as clear as day.

Patrick walked over to her and held both her hands in his.

"Amy, I love you, but that is not why I am here. The child was not mine. Lady Diana lied about it and fabricated the entire story when she realized that the man she had left me for was not good enough for her. She told him that she did not love him any more and she came to me, saying that baby was mine when it was the other man's all along," Patrick explained to her calmly and carefully.

"How do you know for certain?" Amy asked him, completely baffled.

"The man she was having an affair with was her doctor; she had met him while he treated her. There was no baby at the time. Right after she was ready to leave the hospital she left me for him and they both knew the baby was his. She used it to trick me and I fell for it because she knew I would. And now the child has arrived, too early, and died, despite the doctor's best efforts to save it." He looked sad, saying it, and Amy softened a little.

He sighed, and continued "She played me like a puppet on strings. The truth is, I care little about what she did to me and how she hurt me, but in all of this mess, you were caught in our web and you had to suffer. I never wanted to cause you any pain and, because of me, you suffered. I hope you will find it in your heart to forgive me," Patrick said, still holding onto her hands, never wanting to let go.

"I will not lie and tell you that I forgive you at this very moment, but I can tell you this, that I love you, too, and that I am willing to forgive you one day," she responded, placing her hand gently on his face, smiling at him. Patrick felt so overjoyed that he leaned in to kiss her, not really expecting her to permit it, yet to his delight, she kissed him back.

"Does that mean you forgive me?" Patrick asked after kissing her, mesmerized by her entire being.

"No, it does not. Ask me again like this tomorrow," Amy said playfully smiling.

<center>~~~~~</center>

The two of them worked on their issues and resolved them together with great understanding and love.

They had courted for a month when Amy finally declared out loud to him that she had entirely forgiven him for that incident and that they could now finally move on and begin their lives together for the future.

Two months later, a wedding had been planned, for Christmas Day. Patrick, thankful to God for being given a second chance at love, could not imagine marrying Amy on any other day. Last Christmas had set in motion a horrifying sequence of events, events that Patrick had believed he would never heal from.

Yet this Christmas would be the happiest day of his life, and this time, Lord Armagh was as excited as Patrick was.

Epilogue

This time, it had actually happened for both of them.

Surrounded by friends and families, both the Duke of Cumberland and Amy Smith declared their love for each other at the altar and were pronounced husband and wife. It was a lovely ceremony and everyone wished the new couple well, knowing what each of them had gone through to find true love. The tests and trials were great but they had managed to find a way for their love to win, for true love is much too strong to be overcome by anything at all.

Soon enough, Lord Armagh, too, found himself a wife and they all celebrated together, becoming like one family together that had stuck together through thick and thin.

Love was never the problem, people are and, although I would hate to admit, maybe I, too, was the problem at one point. I was too naive to know what real love demanded and too gullible to know when love was not real, but with life comes its lessons, its ups and downs and I will always live for the ups.

No amount of wealth can make up for what I have with the woman I love now, her being beside me with the vow of being together till death do us part is stronger than any force on Earth. I will protect this, I will honor it, and I will live up to it to the best of my ability. I love Amy, and I will always love her. She has shown me what nobody else could, that love alone is meaningless, it must exist with forgiveness, humility, sacrifice, selflessness, respect and all the things you would want your partner to do for you.

I am lucky enough to have found such a woman in my life and I pray that we all are gifted with such great a happiness as the one Amy has given me. I thought I knew what happiness was, but now I know what it is and how valuable it is.

Amy read the letter and tears welled up in her eyes yet again, they always did when she read the letter Patrick had read out loud on their wedding day. Patrick kissed her, embracing her tightly. **This** was love.

The End

Subscribe to Sophia's email list at:

http://eepurl.com/bUHS6v

to be notified of new releases and to receive special offers.

Visit and Like Sophia's Facebook page at :

http://www.facebook.com/SophiaWilsonAuthor

You also will enjoy the next Regency Romance book from Sophia,

'The Duke's Second Chance at Love'.

You can read the first chapter after the 'About the Author' section.

About the Author

Miss Sophia Wilson lives in Stoke-on-Trent in England with her cat, William. She loves to write by the water.

Sophia has been a fiction writer for eight years and is a fan of Jane Austen and everything historical.

Sophia loves to write with memorable characters, surprising plots twists and of course, the dynamics of love that capture readers' imaginations.

Visit her Facebook page at :

https://www.facebook.com/SophiaWilsonAuthor

Other Books by Sophia Wilson

The Duke's Deception

The Duke's Indiscretion

The Duke's Deadly Secret

The Duke's Dark Desire

The Disappearing Duke

The Duke's Redemption

The Duke's Unveiling

The Duke's Destiny

The Duke's Temptation

Captivating the Duke

Betraying the Duke

<u>Capturing the Duke's Heart</u>

<u>Melting the Duke's Heart</u>

<u>Rescued from the Duke</u>

<u>Capturing the Earl's Heart</u>

<u>The Governess and the Dispassionate Duke</u>

<u>The Earl's Lost Love</u>

<u>The Duke's Second Chance at Love</u>

<u>The Duke and the Earl's Daughter</u>

Boxed Sets

<u>Dashing Dukes</u> – includes The Duke's Deception, The Duke's Indiscretion, The Duke's Deadly Secret, The Duke's Dark Desire, The Disappearing Duke

ARIETTA RICHMOND, GRACE AUSTEN, ISABELLA THORNE,
KATHERINE KEATS AND SOPHIA WILSON

Here is Your Preview of
The Duke's Second
Chance at Love

Chapter One

Two kings… two kings ought to have let me win. The Duke scratched his head. The confidence and surety becoming less and less as he closely studied the circumstance before him. This was not the first time he had been in such a predicament; still the beads of sweat from the heat in the room formed on his forehead, glistening in the little light the room they were in had to offer.

"What is the matter, Oxfordshire? Have you begun regretting your carefully calculated decisions?" his friend from across the table teased him, enjoying watching the Duke in the state of uneasiness and so lost.

"What would possibly give you that idea? Must I remind you that it is I who taught you the strings to this?" the Duke replied, doing his best to hide the uncertainty that was visible as anything in the broad sunlight.

"Well then, play! Let us see your move!" Lord Barrymore urged him, his face that of a young man and his laugh whole-hearted.

You do not have any other options, you might as well play with boldness and courage, the Duke said to himself, now fully believing that he did not, in fact, have the upper hand after all. He placed the two remaining cards that were in his hand on the table face up. Lord Barrymore looked at them for a second and smirked, then he slowly placed his own two cards on the table. The Duke hesitatingly looked over at what cards he had played, knowing, somewhere in the back of his mind, that he may well have lost already. Two aces!

"I win dear friend, not to gloat in my victory but I did predict this was to happen, did I not?" Lord Barrymore laughed, dwelling on his easy win.

"Did you forget the countless times you have lost to me in this very game? Or the fact that you would not have even known how to play if it were not for me?" the Duke reminded his friend of over ten years, half serious.

"True, but in this case the student has clearly outdone the teacher, and mastered the game for himself!" Lord Barrymore laughed again; his laugh irritating the Duke now as it reminded him of his defeat.

"Well then Oxfordshire, I hope you have the money you owe me ready," Lord Barrymore said as he sipped on a new glass of liquor. It was not the fact that he had lost to Lord Barrymore in a cards game that was bothering the Duke, it was the fact that they had been playing all evening and the bets had increased to a large amount of money. The Duke casually pressed his pulsating temple trying to think of how to narrowly escape this situation, all the while regretting that he had had too many drinks and let the bets get out of hand.

I have put too much time and effort into the new factory up north to let a silly card game take a chunk of it. If I pay him this money now, the whole factory will take months longer to open and be functional and I cannot afford such great a loss.

So much of my investment is caught up in the factory. Father always did say to never drink and bet!

"Have you worked out the numbers and decided how it is you are paying me?"

Lord Barrymore teased him, casually sitting in his chair with both feet now resting on the table.

Think Robert, think! What can you do now?

"I would like to propose a deal," the Duke said to his friend.

"A deal on a bet? Interesting. What kind of deal are we talking about?" Lord Barrymore asked, intrigued. This was all highly amusing to him.

"The kind of deal that would interest you and be to your benefit, as well as mine," the Duke convinced him, having come up with a plan instantly.

"I am eager to learn more, do tell me what exchange could be so great that it surpasses the amount of money you owe me, dear friend," Lord Barrymore said with a spark in his eyes.

Between the two of them he was always the one more daring and more willing to try new ideas - when they were young they had called it stupidity and carelessness, but now that he had grown up to become a handsome young man, it was rewarded and called courage and bravery.

"Instead of paying you the amount that will come off so heavy on my financials, I am willing to wed Nora," the Duke said, mildly inebriated; his judgment clouded by alcohol as he took another sip of his drink to wash down what he had just offered.

"Nora? You mean my cousin Nora?" Lord Barrymore asked, his voice showing confusion and shock combined.

"Yes precisely, I shall wed her and you shall pardon my debt," the Duke said, knowing that he had played the right cards ultimately, as he smiled to himself, proud of his ingenious plan and how it was working as he liked.

"Why would you marry Nora? We both know she is not a Lady to your taste," Lord Barrymore asked, still trying to grasp why it was that the Duke was willing to marry her.

"See, I know that she is orphaned for three years and her life now revolves around a more, let's say... common lifestyle. Her grandmother is old and simply cannot provide her with the luxuries that a woman her age would want to afford. I also know that you have been aiding her; she is now a responsibility you never asked for, an invisible rope tied around your neck. You can't set yourself free and it is harder because simply no-one wants to marry her, if they had, she would be married by now. Even your money could not buy her a husband. I owe you money, but I am sure you marrying Nora off to me is something worth more to you than a few pounds from a measly card game. Now tell me... where am I wrong?" the Duke said, challenging him as he leaned back in his chair, pleased with himself after having played his final card. *The ace.*

He lit a cigar and placed it in the corner of his mouth, casually taking a puff before exhaling the smoke out.

Lord Barrymore watched him in awe, he was frustrated inside that he had pulled all the right strings and that even at the end of a game he finally thought he had won, it was the Duke that still had the upper hand; but the man did always impress him.

That was the difference between them - growing up, the Duke was a brilliant student without studying, he was casual and laid back and he did not take defeat or failure as an answer, the word could simply not exist with his name in the same sentence. His reputation, among the many that knew him, was that of an intelligent prosperous man; every day he proved it.

"Fair play, Oxfordshire. Who knew the details I share with you about my life would come to be thrown in my direction?" Lord Barrymore laughed at the irony, enjoying the challenge.

"Ah but Barrymore, I suppose that is something I forgot to teach you," the Duke mocked him, laughing.

Lord Barrymore looked at him and laughed at the devil that would show inside him from time to time.

"So what do you say, old friend? Do we have ourselves a deal?" the Duke asked, already knowing his answer.

"Sometimes I simply despise you, I really do. Yes, we have a deal, Oxfordshire," Lord Barrymore said grinning.

"To Nora then?" Lord Barrymore said raising his glass.

"To Nora and my continuous streak of beating you at your best," the Duke raised his glass. The glasses clanked and they laughed.

Losing money is far worse than keeping the fantasy of love alive. I now have a woman and I have not lost a dime. Bravo Robert, bravo!

Continue Reading

'The Duke's Second Chance at Love'

at:

https://www.amazon.com/dp/B01MFAKAUZ

Regency Romance
The Duke's Second
Chance at Love
Sophia Wilson

Here is Your Preview of

The Duke and the Earl's Daughter

Chapter 1

Lady Molly Richards was celebrating her nineteenth birthday with her closest family and friends in Dorchester. It was the year 1815 and Nathan Richards and his wife Grace, the Earl and Countess of Dorchester, had been in uplifting spirits during the celebrations. Their daughter Molly; smart, talented, and beautiful, had been drawing the eye of nearly every man she had come into contact with since she had been presented to society.

Being a Wednesday evening that their beloved child's birthday had fallen upon, the Earl and Countess had to contain their more elaborate plans of celebration for the following Saturday. The Ball was well underway in planning and the Earl had spared no expense as his sweet daughter was quickly approaching the in-between age; the age where more often than not a man would select a wife a few years younger than she and those who were older than her would not get a passing glance.

"Mama!" Molly cried from the dining room where she sat prettily with her bosom friend Anne.

"Yes my love," the Countess replied.

"Could you please fetch Charlotte and have her make a tonic for dear Anne's little sister?" she asked, "it appears she has had a little too much to drink this evening."

"Of course, my dear," she answered, smiling at her daughter.

Molly turned back to her friend, her long blonde curls swinging from side to side as she did so. Her blue eyes sparkled in the light of the candles overhead and the Countess could not help but sit and stare at her daughter in admiration for a moment.

A few moments later, Molly found herself utterly beside herself in laughter as Anne's little sister had toppled sideways out of her chair. She assisted her to the best of her abilities to the sofa at the end of the room.

"Dear Mary," she began, "you really must be more considerate of your health poor thing," she commented through her stifled giggles.

Anne could hardly hold herself up from laughing and handed her sister an extra handkerchief to wipe her eyes and nose.

"Really Mary, I am surprised Mama lets you out of the house at all these days!" she shouted.

Lord Dorchester entered the room in a state of surprise at seeing the event unfold as it had.

"Mary," he said, "please allow me to fetch my coach to take you home, shall I?"

Mary nodded sheepishly. The drink had clearly gotten to her on a deeper level than was expected. Lord Dorchester assisted her to her feet and stabilized her on his arm as he led her from the hall, handing her the tonic Charlotte had prepared for her as they went. By this point, nearly everyone had gone and the hour was growing late.

"Perhaps we should get ourselves ready for bed Molly dear," Anne suggested with a slight yawn.

"I think perhaps you are right Anne, I could not drink or eat another bite if I wanted to," she laughed as the two ladies went upstairs to change.

"Good night Mama!" she called from the stairs, still arm in arm with Anne.

"Good night sweetheart, and happy birthday," her mother replied, waving them on.

Dressed and ready for bed, Molly pulled back the covers on the bed and fluffed up the pillows while Anne finished dressing and washing.

"It was a lovely time was it not?" Anne asked her from behind the partition.

"It was indeed Anne, and I am so fortunate that I should not have had to endure my family all on my own. I am glad you could be there," she said, climbing into bed. Anne came out from behind the partition, brushing her hair gingerly and joined her on the other side of the bed.

"I would never abandon you to your own devices silly girl. We both know how unwell you handle such things," she said laughing.

Anne settled herself under the sheets with Molly and turned to face her.

"How many invitations have gone out for your Ball, dear?" she asked excitedly.

"Too many," Molly groaned, they've invited most of the world I think!" she exclaimed.

This made Anne laugh.

"You know I think I saw a letter from the Duke on the table when I arrived this evening. Do you think it was his sending word that he should be able to attend?" she rambled.

"Oh pish!" Molly exclaimed, covering her face in embarrassment.

"Do you remember when you first laid eyes on him, Molly?" Anne asked eagerly. "I do for one; it was the most adorable thing I had ever witnessed. You could hardly speak!" she cried and threw her head back in hysteria.

"Oh hush," Molly waved at her.

"It was nothing but a girlhood crush, you know that," she went on.

"I most certainly do not know that," Anne snapped. "You have been in love with the man ever since I can remember from that day on."

Molly was silenced, recalling memories of the night she had first met the Duke. He was charming and handsome, dark brown curls that never fell out of place and green eyes that shone in even the dullest light.

"You're thinking about him again," Anne pointed out.

"Only because you made me," Molly retorted hotly back at her.

"Whatever you say dearest, I only want for you to be happy in life and if you were married to the Duke!" she began, getting all worked up again.

"Hush," Molly ordered as she rolled over and blew out the candle.

She closed her eyes and tried to steady her heart rate, but Anne was right. She was thinking heavily about the Duke now, and she had noticed the letter sitting on the table earlier that day which her parents had stashed with the others. And now, here she was thinking about him in a long-tailed coat, gliding up and down the dance hall with her in her favorite dress, his eyes sparkling emeralds in the candle light.

Continue Reading

'The Duke and the Earl's Daughter'

at:

https://www.amazon.com/dp/B01N8R9FAS

ARIETTA RICHMOND, GRACE AUSTEN, ISABELLA THORNE,
KATHERINE KEATS AND SOPHIA WILSON

Other Books from Dreamstone Publishing

Dreamstone publishes books in a wide variety of categories, ranging from Romance to Kids Books, Books on Writing, Business Books, Photography, Cook Books, Diaries, Coloring books and much more. New books are released each month.

Be the first to know when our next books are coming out

Be first to get all the news – sign up for our newsletter at

http://www.dreamstonepublishing.com